The Stars of Ember

A Night lore Book
Genesis Batista

First Edition: 2024

ISBN: 979-8-9884421-7-2
Paperback

Hardback Edition 2025

ISBN: 979-8-9884421-8-9

Published by Genesis Batista

First Cover Design by Genesis Batista

This book was written entirely by human hands and mind, without the use of artificial intelligence or AI-powered writing tools. I do not endorse or support the use of AI-generated content in the creation of this work. Every word, idea, and creative element within these pages is the product of natural human creativity and effort. This statement serves to affirm my commitment to authentic, human-created literature.

Edited using Beta readers

Hardback design by Artscandare
Interior design and map by Genesis Batista

Printed in the United States of America

REALMS

FAULKNER'S DEATH

HIGH ISLES

THE CANYON OF SILVER

RO

FOREGROUND

MIRO

UHN

DYASERA'S END

TERRA GULF

ICE WIND DESERT

ZAY'NATH

USHOR

BOWMAN PORT

RYSLAN GULF

ORIT

SINWYN

SEA

ILYEVES

JD

HELLS GATE

MORADAI

MORADI CITY

ASS

FAELYS

Contents

Warning

Please be advised that this book contains material that may be distressing for some readers. While this story celebrates LGBTQ+ love and relationships, it tackles challenging themes including mental illness, violence, and trauma. The narrative includes scenes depicting panic attacks, physical and emotional abuse, sexual situations, and other intense scenarios. At its core, this book explores the complex journey of surviving narcissistic abuse, and falling in love again.

These themes are handled with care and purpose, woven into a story of healing and self-discovery. However, the content may evoke strong emotional responses or discomfort. If you are sensitive to such topics, please prioritize your mental well-being before proceeding.

This book contains:
• LGBTQ+ themes and relationships
• Mental health struggles and panic attacks
• Physical and emotional abuse
• Sexual content (consensual and non-consensual mentions)
• Violence and trauma
• Narcissistic abuse themes
Reader discretion is advised.

Love is love.

To those who dream of monsters in the dark—careful what you wish for, because some creatures don't just taste your desires... they make them real. I'm talking to you.

Slut. ♥

CHAPTER 1

Ronan

Fucking hell, I was humming again.

The old habit crawled up my throat like a disease I couldn't shake, a remnant from a life I should've forgotten centuries ago. But here I was, watching the rise and fall of Atreya's chest as she lay passed out beside me, and my traitorous mouth was forming melodies like I was some kind of undead songbird.

The wards were down, and I'd done what they said couldn't be done—snatched the queen right out from under Ramses' nose. The look on that bastard's face when the shadows swallowed us whole? Worth every risk.

Sweet chaos, what a show it had been. The arena erupting into mayhem, Servat's screams still echoing off the walls, panic spreading like wildfire through the crowd. And there I was, playing my part perfectly, while Eldra's rebel crew thought they were the ones pulling all the strings.

Idiots.

The memory of how I'd gotten roped into this clusterfuck was crystal clear—probably because it started with me getting cockblocked in the seediest tavern this side of Tor.

I'd been riding high on willing barmaid blood, the iron-rich taste still coating my tongue, when I first laid eyes on Gaelinantis Otear. Gael, the pretty-faced bastard who'd end up dragging me into this mess. The tavern was exactly what you'd expect—damp wood, dim lights, and the kind of clientele that made thieves look respectable.

Xaneth, the arrogant prick I called master, was putting on his usual show. "The King of Ember has extended his hospitality to us," he'd boasted, fangs out like some fresh-turned fledgling who couldn't control himself. "We are honored guests within his realm."

My master was always stupid that way. Couldn't keep his fucking mouth shut if his life depended on it.

Most of the patrons were either too enthralled or too drunk to care about the fanged asshole bragging in the corner. But not Gael. No, that crafty son of a bitch knew exactly what he was doing.

"Welcome, traveler," he greeted, smooth as aged whiskey. "What brings you to this corner of depravity? Besides the—well—depravity."

I should've known right then that my night was about to go sideways. But the blood high had me stupid, and when he pulled out that flask from the Old Country, I watched Xaneth fall for the bait like the greedy bastard he was.

I rolled my eyes and languidly turned my head to look at Gael. A frock of blonde hair hung down around his shoulders, and his blue eyes glittered the way mine would when I found easy prey.

Intrigued, I dropped the barmaid from my lap. The corner of Gael's mouth twitched in what might have been amusement. "And you. Would you care to join me upstairs? The night is long, and the company here grows tiresome."

I flexed my fingers and smirked. "I do love the hospitality of this country," I said, letting my fangs show just enough to make the threat clear.

Xaneth grunted and turned away, eyes glazed with blood-drunk stupor. "Whore," he muttered.

The word rolled off me like water. Xaneth would let me have my fun tonight because he was riding his own high, too caught up in his delusions of grandeur to care what his "spawn" did.

We climbed those creaking stairs to a loft room that smelled of mold and desperation. Cobwebs decorated the corners like pary drapes at a funeral, and moonlight leaked through a grimy window, painting everything in shades of grey.

"I've fucked in worse places," I said, yanking off my shirt and kicking my boots across the warped floorboards. The cheap wood groaned under my feet like it was considering giving up altogether.

Gael watched me with those too-bright eyes, a wolfish grin playing at his lips. "I've no doubt," he replied, "but tonight, you won't be sharing a bed with me."

I froze mid-strip, muscles coiling tight. "Oh?" My eyebrow arched high as a gallows. "And what game are we playing then, pretty boy?"

The bastard didn't answer. Instead, he reached into his satchel and pulled out something that made the air *wrong*. With a flick of his wrist, he tossed it onto the hay bed. The object hit the straw with a soft thud that seemed to echo in my bones, and then reality started to tear itself apart.

Before I could move, Gael closed the distance between us. His hand slammed into my chest, and I stumbled backward through the portal's maw. The world dissolved into a kaleidoscope of color and pain, every cell in my body screaming as I was ripped from one place and spat out in another.

When my vision cleared, I found myself sprawled on a carpet worth more than everything I'd stolen in the past century. The Solaris crest sneered down at me from every tapestry, and three figures stood around me like executioners at a hanging.

I folded my hands behind my head and stretched out like I was lounging on a beach instead of potentially moments from death.

"Well," I drawled, "this is definitely the most creative way someone's ever tried to kill me."

A woman with dark blue hair narrowed her eyes and glared at me. Another man stood next to her, whose eyes were white and void of pupils.

Eldra was the kind of beautiful that made you want to bleed.

Dark hair like spilled ink framed a face that belonged in the kind of paintings rich assholes hung in their mansions to make themselves feel important. But it was his eyes that made my fangs itch—blue-grey and burning with their own inner fire, like he'd swallowed starlight and couldn't quite contain it. The bastard knew exactly how pretty he was, too. Used it like a weapon, all that devastating beauty honed to a killing edge.

I propped myself up on my elbow, tasting the tension in the air.

"Well, isn't this cozy?" My finger jabbed accusingly at Gael's perfect face. "If you wanted an audience, pretty boy, you could've just asked. Though I have to say—" I let my gaze drift deliberately over our newfound company, "—this is taking foreplay to new heights. I call top bunk."

"Still running that smart mouth, Ronan." Gael's smile was all teeth, no warmth.

He rattled off introductions like he was reading a shopping list. Madsen—the woman with murder in her eyes. Hisen—the creepy fuck with white eyes that reminded me of maggots. He didn't bother with Eldra. Didn't need to. Power rolled off him in waves that made my skin prickle. If he was anything like his father, I was in some serious trouble.

I got to my feet with exaggerated care, brushing nonexistent dirt from my clothes like this was all perfectly normal. Like I hadn't just been magically kidnapped mid-hookup. "Points for dramatic flair," I drawled, meeting Eldra's burning gaze head-on. "Though I usually prefer dinner before being whisked away to strange rooms."

"Your master talks too much," Gael cut in. "Word is, you've got an invitation to Ember."

I rolled my eyes so hard it hurt. "No shit. What gave it away? The endless bragging or the part where Xaneth practically shouted it from the rooftops?"

"You've been around a while," Hisen's corpse-eyes fixed on me. The words slithered out like he was tasting them.

"Fascinating observation. Got any other brilliant insights?" My tone could've stripped paint.

Eldra moved then, all liquid grace and lethal intent. Each step brought him closer, and my body tensed like a bowstring about to snap. "Ember's walls are warded," he whispered, soft as silk over steel. "No one crosses without the king's blessing. It's supposed to be impossible."

A smirk tugged at my lips. "Let me guess—" I leaned forward, close enough to catch his scent (smoke and lightning and something ancient that made my head spin), "—you need the impossible done?"

"Precisely." His smile was sin incarnate. "And Xaneth can't know."

I crossed my arms, feigning boredom while my mind raced. "And who's the lucky soul I'm supposed to spirit away from the most heavily guarded city in the realm?"

"The Furian Slayer, Atreya."

The laugh burst out of me before I could stop it, echoing off the walls like broken glass. "The Queen?" I wheezed, clutching my sides. "You want me to kidnap the fucking Queen of Ember?" I straightened, wiping tears from my eyes. "Either you're all insane, or I'm still drunk on barmaid blood and this is some wild hallucination."

Nobody laughed with me. Their faces remained carved from stone, and my amusement dried up like water in desert heat.

"Oh," I said softly, the smile dying on my lips. "You're serious. You actually want me to snatch the queen from under the king's nose. From a city that's locked up tighter than a Preistess's—"

Eldra nodded, "Yes. And we believe you are one of the few who can do it."

Madsen snorted.

I leaned forward, resting my elbows on my knees, and regarded them with renewed interest. "Do you now?" I mused, intrigued despite my survival instincts screaming at me this was a terrible idea.

But if I listened to that all the time, my life would be incredibly boring. "And why, pray tell, would you think I could—or would—do such a thing?"

With a subtle gesture from Eldra, the room emptied until it was just the two of us, the tension between us palpable in the silence that followed. Eldra's piercing blue-grey eyes never wavered from mine.

"You've been a vampire a long time," Eldra began, repeating what the white-eyed freak said before. "But unlike Xaneth, you don't possess the gift of walking in sunlight. You're just a spawn."

I narrowed my eyes at the thinly veiled insult, my pride stung by his blunt words. "Careful, Eldra," I warned, my tone low and even. "You wouldn't want to insult someone you're trying to recruit, would you?"

He ignored my warning, continuing as if I hadn't spoken. "However, I just so happen to be in possession of a Daylight ring."

I scoffed at that. "A Daylight ring? You're a liar. Everyone knows they were all destroyed after the Dead War that sank Maradi City."

Eldra's expression remained unfazed. "Not all," he corrected. "There was one that survived. An old heirloom saved from the ruin. My father had a penchant for collecting rare artifacts. He always believed they'd serve a greater purpose one day. He was one of the Kings during that war."

With a flick of his wrist, a small object materialized in his hand, seemingly conjured from thin air. The ring he held between his fingers was a thing of beauty and power, its band forged from an unknown, lustrous metal that seemed to absorb the light around it. At its center sat a stone that was the color of the midday sky, a deep and vibrant blue that pulsed with an inner light. Intricate runes were etched along the circumference of the band, runes that spoke of ancient magic, of binding oaths and promises made in blood.

"This," Eldra said, holding the ring out to me, "is your key to walking in the sun. With it, you can move freely during daylight hours, undeterred by the fatal touch of the sun's rays."

I reached out tentatively, half expecting the ring to vanish like a mirage, but the cool metal was solid against my skin. The weight of it was reassuring, a tangible symbol of possibility, of a world that had just expanded its borders for me.

"Let's say I believe you," I said slowly, turning the ring over in my hand, admiring the way it seemed to sing with latent power. "What's the catch? These sorts of gifts don't come without strings attached."

Eldra's lips curved. "The catch," he said, "is that you succeed in your mission. You bring us the Furian Slayer, Atreya. Do that, and the ring is yours to keep."

He nonchalantly waved his hand toward the chamber's window. The curtains, heavy and dark, were pulled back by an invisible force, and sunlight—pure, unfiltered, deadly sunlight—poured into the room.

I recoiled instinctively, a half-scream tearing from my throat as centuries of ingrained fear of the sun's wrath took hold. Every fiber of my being braced for the agony of being burned, the searing pain that I had been taught would be the end of my kind.

But the pain didn't come.

My breath hitched, caught between relief and disbelief, as I slowly extended a hand into the beam of sunlight. The rays kissed my skin, and I felt... nothing. No burn, no blistering heat, just the gentle caress of a sun I had not felt since my human days.

Tears, unexpected and unbidden, welled in my eyes.

How long had I wanted this?

Eldra watched me with an unreadable expression, but I could see the satisfaction in his eyes. He had proven his point, demonstrated the ring's power, and in doing so, had secured my cooperation more effectively than any threat or promise of wealth could have.

The curtains closed, the warmth of the sun ray, and the ring vanished. I held back a strangled whine.

"Get the Queen, and you get the ring."

"How am I supposed to get her beyond the wall with that shield?"

Eldra met my gaze then. "We have that taken care of."

"How do I know you won't just kill me after?"

"A blood vow," Eldra stated, as though he had read my mind. "It will guarantee that neither of us can betray the other without suffering grave consequences."

He stepped forward and extended his hand, palm up, in a silent request for my cooperation. I hesitated for a moment, knowing the gravity of what a blood vow entailed. It was an ancient ritual, a covenant as old as time itself, binding two parties in a pact of blood and magic.

With a slow, deliberate motion, Eldra drew a small, ornate dagger from within his cloak. The blade was slender and sharp, its surface etched with runes that glowed faintly with an otherworldly light. He pressed the edge to his palm, and with a swift, sure cut, opened a shallow wound. Crimson blood welled up and I fought the urge to taste him.

I watched, transfixed, as he closed his eyes and began to chant in a language that seemed to twist the air, making the fine hairs on the back of my neck stand on end. The blood from his palm rose, defying gravity, and formed into a small orb that hovered above his hand. It pulsed with each word he spoke, growing brighter, its core ablaze with a fierce, inner light.

Then, Eldra opened his eyes, and they were no longer the clear blue-grey I had become accustomed to. They were pools of liquid fire, reflecting the intensity of the vow being forged. He reached across the space between us, the glowing orb of his blood following the command of his outstretched hand, and hovered before me, waiting.

"It is your turn," Eldra said, resonating with the power of the vow. "Your blood must join mine."

I took the dagger from him, the metal warm from his touch, and with a steadying breath, I replicated his action, slicing my own palm. My vampiric blood, darker and thicker than Eldra's, merged with the glowing orb. The moment our bloods touched, a shockwave of energy coursed through the room, and the orb exploded into a cascade of light that enveloped us both.

The light seared into my flesh, branding the vow into my very being, and I felt an unbreakable bond snap into place. A bond of trust, of necessity that linked my fate to Eldra's until the terms of our agreement were met.

As the light receded, the cuts on our palms healed over, leaving no trace of the wound—only the lingering sensation of the vow that now connected us.

And that led me here, with the wretched woman unconscious on the forest floor.

The moon, a silent witness in the sky, bathed us in a pale glow, outlining her formidable form in silver. I tapped a finger on my chin in thought, considering the woman who lay before me, the so-called Furian Slayer. Atreya. Her reputation preceded her, a whirlwind of tales painting her as a savage warrior, a force of nature in battle. Yet, here she was, unconscious and vulnerable, her soft breaths and peaceful visage betraying none of the ferocity for which she was renowned.

I couldn't help but let a smirk play across my lips. The Furian Slayer? More like a slumbering kitten, I mused. The rumors whispered of a creature so violent and fearsome that even the bravest souls would cower in her presence. But as I watched her now, those tales seemed as fanciful as the bedtime stories told to frighten children.

I recalled the few times our paths had crossed previously; each encounter was a game of cat and mouse that left me more amused than intimidated.

Her threats were like sweet nothings to my ears, a delightful attempt at being menacing. I had simply laughed.

"Sleeping beauty lost in the woods," I said aloud.

CHAPTER 2

Atreya

T he arena's screams ripped through my skull as consciousness slammed into me. No sand beneath my fingers, no scorched metal stinging my nostrils. Just soft moss and the thick scent of earth and decay. Moonlight filtered through the canopy above, casting silver shadows that danced across my skin.

A figure sat nearby, the rhythmic scrape of knife against wood filling the silence while flames licked at the darkness.

Ronan.

"Servat." His name tore from my throat like broken glass. "Where is he? What happened?" The sob that followed burned, memories of his lifeless body searing through my mind like acid. I could still feel the warmth of his skin, the perfect fit of his hand in mine, the way his eyes had begged me to run.

Ronan's gaze flickered up from his whittling, amusement dancing in those predator eyes. "Welcome back to the land of the living, sweetheart.

Head still intact?" That smile of his could cut diamond, but it never touched those cold eyes.

"Servat!" I needed answers, and this bastard's games made my blood boil.

He set his wood aside with deliberate slowness, unfolding his long frame like a jungle cat stretching before the hunt. "Since you're so desperately out of the loop," he purred, twirling his blade with lethal grace, "your precious Servat's gone. Vanished in a rather spectacular display of light, if I do say so myself."

"You heartless bastard."

His laughter died, sharp and sudden as a blade to the throat. "Heartless?" The word dripped from his lips like poison honey. "Sweetheart, I'm being fucking kind. The wards are ash, Ember's bleeding out, and Servat—" His knife tapped a rhythm against that perfect jaw, metal catching moonlight. "Let's just say his grand finale set the night on fire. Your handiwork, if we're keeping score."

He invaded my space, close enough that his breath ghosted across my lips. Pine and metal. Death and desire. "That lightning show of yours? Pure fucking poetry. Though the ending?" A cruel slash of white carved across his face. "Explosive. Thank the Gods—I was dying of boredom."

I jerked back, his words slicing deeper than any blade. That feline grin of his mocked me, promised pain wrapped in pleasure. "It was an accident." The confession tasted like ash on my tongue, guilt a lead weight in my gut. The memories played on repeat—a horror show I couldn't escape. If I'd controlled it better, moved faster... Servat would be breathing. Living. *Here.*

"Of course it was." Ronan's eyes glittered like shards of obsidian in the dark. "But dead men don't give a fuck about intentions, do they?" The knife danced between his fingers as he watched me, predator-patient. A shiver clawed down my spine, ice following fire.

My legs trembled as I fought to stand, everything spinning. Ronan tracked my movements with that detached fascination reserved for dying things. Despair circled like a vulture, talons sinking deep. Servat was gone—the one soul who'd seen past my thorns, who'd loved the monster beneath. And now?

Now I was alone.

Servat is dead.

My heart splintered, tears burning. I could still feel him—the phantom press of his body against mine, the echo of his laugh in my ears. Any second now, he'd appear. Flash that crooked smile. Tell me this nightmare wasn't real.

"He said two paces behind him. Two paces." The words hung in the air, bloody and raw. What had he meant? Had he known? Had he chosen this end, chosen to leave me?

Ronan's expression shifted, indifference warring with something darker. "Ah, the classic 'two paces' play," he mused, "Yet he waltzed right into that storm. Makes you wonder if it was really an accident—or if dear Servat finally got tired of dancing."

I bristled at his implication, "You dare suggest he wanted this?"

Ronan's expression didn't shift—a marble statue carved from pure arrogance.

"I dare suggest nothing, sweetheart. Just calling it like I see it. People do crazy shit when death comes knocking—some fight like rabid dogs, some roll over and show their belly." His eyes glittered with cruel amusement. "And some? Some dance right into the reaper's arms. Maybe dear Servat wanted you free as badly as you wanted out."

My nails carved crescents into my palms, blood welling beneath the surface. "He wouldn't have—" I swallowed, "He couldn't have. He loved me."

Loved.

Past tense. Because he was dead and I'd put him there.

Something flickered across Ronan's face—disgust, pity, or maybe just indigestion. His lip curled as he watched my hands shake. "Love?" He spat the word like poison. "That most toxic of infections. Turning warriors to puppets and kings to corpses." His voice dropped to a silken purr. "It makes fools and martyrs of us all, doesn't it, little queen?"

Grief sat in my gut like lead, while rage burned through my veins like fire. Every word from his mouth was oil on the flames. "You know *nothing* of our love," I snarled.

What the hells would this ice-cold bastard know about real connection? About the kind of love that burns so hot it leaves scars?

He raised those deadly hands in mock surrender, but that knife-edge sneer never wavered. "Oh, my sincerest apologies." The theatrical bow he gave could've graced any royal court. "Love is sacred, isn't it? Pure as freshly fallen snow." His eyes glittered with malice. "Though I do wonder what thoughts dance through a man's head in those final moments. Shame we'll never know."

A thoughtful hum vibrated in his throat as he cocked his head. "He was the King's brother, wasn't he? Keeping it all nice and cozy in the family, were you?"

I shook my head, exhaustion weighing on every limb. "Can we not do this now? This isn't the time for your—"

"Charm? Wit? Dazzling personality?" Ronan interjected, his smirk widening.

"—*games*," I finished, the word barely more than a whisper. I couldn't handle his twisted version of entertainment, not with Servat's blood still metaphorically dripping from my hands.

"Speaking of family matters—" His fingers made an obscene gesture that set my cheeks burning. "If you and the King's brother were playing hide the scepter, does that make the kid his? Or—" The bastard had a talent for finding raw nerves and dancing on them with steel-toed boots.

Then one thought slammed into me, choking me.

Vryseris.

My son.

"Where is Vrys?" My eyes raked the darkness—nothing but shadows and silence and the suffocating press of forest. Panic surged through my veins, hot and electric, choking off my breath. Servat dead. My son gone.

"You left him?" I half-shrieked.

Ronan's shrug was pure insolence. "The little Prince isn't exactly bleeding out in a ditch. I agreed to extract *you*. Didn't say shit about playing nursemaid to royal offspring. Do I look like a mother hen to you?"

"I didn't exactly plan on getting dragged into the night like a sacrificial fucking lamb! I didn't have time to pack a bag and leave a note. I was trying not to *die*." My voice cracked on the last word. *And now my son's paying for my desperation.*

"I'm not marching back into that shitstorm to get my head mounted on Ember's walls!" Ronan snapped. "You're out. You're breathing. Now I need to get you to Eldra."

"Eldra? The hell are you talking about?" *King Eldra Solaris?* "I didn't agree to that!" I couldn't go to Eldra, couldn't trust him. He was a stranger, an enemy, and I would never put my son in his hands.

The playful malice in Ronan's eyes hardened into something deadly serious. "Eldra Solaris, yes. Your consent wasn't exactly high on my priority list, sweetheart. But when Ember's wards are dust and her throat's exposed? It's the only play left. That city will fall faster than a virgin's virtue once word gets out."

"Safest for *who*? You want me to walk right into the enemy's arms? Eldra and I aren't exactly sharing any love for one another! And my *son*—"

"And who exactly crowned Eldra the villain in this little drama?"

"I didn't take you for a rebel sympathizer."

I should kill him right fucking now. Walk back through the blood and ashes to find my boy. I couldn't waste another breath on Ronan's games, couldn't let him toy with me while Vrys—

A sardonic smirk curved Ronan's lips, one eyebrow arching with lethal grace. "Sympathizer? Please. The realm's politics bore me to tears. But survival?" His eyes glittered like fresh-spilled blood in the darkness. "Now that's a game worth playing."

"I need to go back," I said, trying to push past the veil of despair. "I need to find my son." I couldn't waste any more time on Ronan, couldn't afford to indulge in his games and jabs. I had to find Vrys, had to save my son.

"I think the hell not." Ronan crossed his arms, looking for all the world like a spoiled brat denied his favorite toy. The pout on those perfect lips made me want to punch him. Repeatedly. "Do you have any fucking idea what it took to get your royal ass out of there?"

"How did we—" Memory slammed into me like a fist. Darkness. Complete and absolute. And those *eyes*—Ronan's eyes blazing red as hellfire as he dragged me through shadows that felt alive. "How did you...?"

His knife disappeared with lethal grace, but those predator eyes never left mine. "Let's just say I've got a few party tricks that would make your court magicians shit themselves." That damned smirk again. "When the wards went down, chaos made a lovely smokescreen. You're fucking welcome, by the way."

My patience snapped like a bowstring. "Eldra's forces have been trying to gut Ember for *years*. I quite literally decapitated his friend, or did that slip your mind? His *help*—" I spat the word, "—comes with a price that'll drown us all in blood."

"With Ember's throat exposed?" Ronan leaned forward. "How long before Ramses's head decorates a spike? Before the four corners descend like vultures to pick the city's bones clean? You know how big the All Realms are? Don't answer that. Pretty little bird born in a cage."

"And you think Eldra will play savior without wanting his pound of flesh?"

"I never claimed he was a saint."

"So the King Beyond the Wall, the fucking *rebel*, is going to save Ember from itself? He'll gut Ramses—" *maybe the only mercy in this mess* "—and then he'll murder my son." Horror clawed up my throat.

Ronan went still—that deadly stillness of an apex predator about to strike. "Listen carefully, because I won't repeat myself. Eldra Solaris might be called rebel, monster—but the man has honor. Your boy's safe. In fact," his lip curled, "keeping the prince breathing is probably top of his priority list."

Something in his tone made me pause. "You sound awfully sure about that."

"I am."

"Why?"

"Not your concern."

"Like hell it isn't! You know his secrets, speak of his *honor*—when his men turned Hyperion's Market into a fucking slaughterhouse? You don't know *shit*!"

His mouth thinned to a razor line, like he was biting back words that could start wars.

The tension between us crackled, each of us poised on the edge of an argument neither wished to have. Ronan's eyes held a glimmer of defiance, yet beneath it, I sensed a calculated calm.

I was tired. Exhausted. *Broken*.

A sob ripped through my chest before I could strangle it.

"Oh hell no." Ronan recoiled like I'd pulled a knife. "I don't do the crying thing. Cut that shit out."

Ronan stood awkwardly as if the sight of tears was as foreign to him as warmth is to ice. He cleared his throat, obviously out of his element.

"Look," he managed, "I get this is all kinds of messed up. But we're in crisis mode, and I can't handle you falling apart right now."

I sniffled pathetically. "I changed my mind about leaving—without Servat."

"Fantastic timing. Really," he said acidly.

Something in me hardened, crystallizing like steel in fire. "Your empathy is *staggering*." My fists clenched tight enough to draw blood. "What's it like, thinking you're superior because you're dead inside?"

He invaded my space, all predator grace and cruel beauty. "I think because I can think past my fucking feelings, we might actually survive this shitshow."

"Right. Trading one tyrant for another. Brilliant plan."

Ronan's laugh was sharp enough to cut. "Our little chats are so... stimulating."

"If by stimulating you mean makes me want to stab you, then yes."

"For someone who just escaped death, you're awfully picky about your savior."

"I just murdered the only person who gave a damn about me," I snarled.

He waved it off like swatting a fly. "Yeah, I was there. Don't need the replay."

His dismissal hit like a knife between the ribs. "Saw? You stand there on your fucking pedestal, acting like you've never lost a goddamn thing in your life—"

Something dark flickered across Ronan's face, there and gone. "Oh, I've lost *plenty*. But I learned to bury the dead and keep walking. Otherwise?" He showed his teeth. "You end up in the ground right next to them."

"How practical." My lip curled. "Tell me, does anything crack that ice-cold exterior? Or is everything just one big joke to you?"

For a heartbeat, something raw and painful flashed in his eyes. "Careful, Your Grace. Don't mistake my restraint for weakness."

"Restraint?" I barked out a laugh. "You don't restrain shit. You just refuse to feel anything at all."

"And you," he snapped, closing the distance until I could taste the mint on his breath, "are drowning in your precious feelings. How's that working out for you?"

"Vrys should be here. Servat should be here. All that pain, and they're both just... gone."

Ronan dissected me with his stare. "Pain's the only currency that matters in our world, sweetheart. Spend it smart or watch it bankrupt you. The tragic tale of the weeping queen and her dead lovers. Tell me, does wallowing in self-pity typically save kingdoms? Because if so, Ember's about to enter a golden fucking age."

"You think this is funny? My heart isn't your personal playground!"

He pressed close, lips brushing my ear. "Everything's funny if you're watching from the right angle. Life's just one big cosmic joke, and we're all dancing to someone else's tune. You, my queen? You just happen to be center stage."

"It's not fair—"

His hand slashed through the air. "Fair? Fair is a bedtime story mothers tell their brats. The sooner you wake up from that particular fantasy, the longer you'll survive."

Thunder cracked overhead like breaking bones. Heat built behind my eyes, electricity dancing beneath my skin.

"Oh, for fuck's sake. Another temper tantrum."

I snarled, and lightning split the sky, striking mere inches from his boots. The bastard didn't even blink.

"Well, well. Look who's finally showing her teeth."

Power thrummed through my veins like liquid lightning, drowning out everything but the need to destroy. My fingers sparked and crackled as raw energy begged for release. With a feral snarl, I unleashed hell—lightning exploding from my hands in a deadly arc. The bolt hit a massive oak with a thunderous crack, showering the forest floor with burning splinters. Animals scattered into the darkness, their terrified screams echoing through the trees.

Before I could summon another strike, Ronan slammed into me. His hands locked around my arms like steel shackles as he dragged my thrashing body toward the pond. Lightning danced over our skin.

He hurled me into the water like a ragdoll. The cold hit like a thousand knives as I sank beneath the surface. I kicked upward, but Ronan was already there, pinning my arms as I fought like a wild thing. My knee found his ribs with a satisfying crunch. He didn't even loosen his grip.

"That the best you've got, little queen?"

I wrenched one arm free, calling lightning to my fingertips. The water lit up like daylight as electricity turned the pond into a boiling cauldron of death. Ronan yanked me against his chest, using my own momentum to trap me.

"Parlor tricks won't cut it, sweetheart."

I slammed my head back into his face, feeling bone crunch. The victory was short-lived as he spun me around, fingers digging into my shoulders hard enough to bruise. The water churned around us, illuminating his bones in a grotesque dance of light and shadow. But those eyes—those fucking eyes never wavered as power crackled between us.

"Said you'd have to do better." Blood trickled from his split lip. "I don't die easy."

Raw magic surged through me in a tsunami of rage. The pond boiled and steamed as lightning split the water in every direction. Ronan's grip was iron, unmovable as a mountain while chaos erupted around us. His eyes blazed crimson in the darkness, reflecting my storm.

My elbow found his solar plexus. His breath left in a rush but those fingers might as well have been forged from steel. The bastard was stronger than he looked. *Much* stronger.

It dawned on me—he wasn't letting go. He'd hold me under these dark waters until my storm burned itself out.

Something inside me fractured. The wild magic faded like smoke, lightning dissolving into nothing. My body went limp with bone-deep exhaustion. Only then did Ronan's death grip ease. I broke the surface gasping as he hauled us both onto the grass, collapsing beside me with a grunt.

We lay there in the aftermath, nothing but ragged breathing and rustling leaves. Ronan rolled to face me, lips curving into that infuriating smirk.

"Well. That was fun. Lovely evening for a swim, wouldn't you say?"

Tears slid down my cheeks in silent rivers, and for once, Ronan kept his smart mouth shut. The silence pressed in like a physical weight, thick with all the things we weren't saying. Grief crushed against my ribs, threatening to cave my chest in completely. Servat was gone. My son was lost. And I was stuck with this beautiful bastard who treated my pain like his personal entertainment.

Ronan broke first. "We need to move. Staying still makes us dead." He pushed to his feet with a grunt of pain, those lean muscles rippling beneath his soaked clothes. When he offered his hand, I took it—fingers closing around his like a vise. Not because I needed the help. Not because his skin felt like fire against mine.

The forest closed in around us like a tomb, ancient trees standing guard over fresh graves. Every crack of a branch had me jumping out of my skin, heart slamming against my ribs. I kept looking back, half-expecting—*hoping*—to see Servat's familiar stride, that crooked smile that made my world make sense.

But he never came.

My legs gave out like broken puppet strings. Ronan caught me before I hit dirt, his hands surprisingly gentle on my elbows.

"Easy there, little storm." His voice was softer than I'd ever heard it, almost caring. "You're running on empty."

I managed a nod, not trusting myself to speak. Running on fumes and fury and fuck-all else. How much longer until I crashed completely?

Eldra waited at the end of this path—maybe to kill me, maybe worse. But Joslynn had known where he was all along. That connection was the only thread I had left to pull.

"Fine," I surrendered. "But we do this as equals. I'm not some helpless princess for you to mock between rescue attempts."

Ronan's snort could've stripped paint. "Equals? Sweetheart, you'd need years of practice to match my particular brand of asshole."

"And modesty," I shot back.

He swept into an elaborate bow, all deadly grace and dark promise. "I'm a man of *many* talents, Your Grace."

CHAPTER 3

Atreya

"How long have we been trudging through this hellscape?"

Ronan's eyes flashed crimson over his shoulder. "An hour. Getting tired already, princess?"

I scanned the forest, everything bleeding into one dark mass of shadows and secrets. The trees were just fucking trees, rocks just rocks, but that stream? The one gurgling past us like a throat being slit? Pretty sure we'd passed it twice already.

"We're lost, aren't we?"

He answered with a sharp shake of his head.

"Then how much longer?"

"Gods, do you ever stop bitching?" The question ripped from his throat as he picked up his pace, boots crushing fallen leaves beneath them.

Without thinking—because thinking would've been the smart thing to do—I snatched up a rock and hurled it at his head. The bastard didn't even flinch. So I threw another one, harder this time. That got his attention.

"Stop. It." Each word dripped with barely contained violence.

I went for rock number three, but his hand shot out, wrapping around my wrist like a steel trap. His lips pulled back, revealing those deadly fangs that extended past Fae length. My pulse jumped beneath his fingers.

"I don't hit women," he purred, dark as sin. "But I do *bite*. Choose wisely, little storm."

This was the man who'd "rescued" me from Ramses. Maybe I should be grateful. But then again, Servat and I could've made it. Vrys could be here, safe in my arms instead of lost in the dark.

The moment he released my arm, I threw the rock.

It connected with a satisfying thud between his shoulder blades.

"How much longer?" I asked, sugar-sweet poison.

He spun around, those blood-red eyes blazing with fury. For a heartbeat, I thought he might actually tear my throat out. But then his face softened into something more dangerous—amusement.

"Aren't you just full of surprises?" A low laugh rumbled in his chest. "Not like the others at all."

I arched an eyebrow. "Was that supposed to be a compliment?"

He shrugged. "Take it however you want, sweetheart. Now move that pretty ass—we're almost there."

I followed, curiosity warring with survival instinct. Both were probably going to get me killed.

After a few more minutes of walking, I saw a light up ahead. As we got closer, I realized it was a house—a small, rustic cabin nestled among the trees. Smoke was rising from the chimney, and I could hear the sound of a stream burbling nearby.

"Welcome home," Ronan said, gesturing to the cabin.

I stared at him, incredulous. "Home? I thought you lived with Xaneth?"

As we stepped inside, warmth from the hearth wrapped around me. A pot of stew hung over crackling flames, the rich smell making my stomach growl despite myself. The cabin was simple enough—one room with a fur-covered bed in the corner and a wooden table with chairs at its center.

But then I saw it. Rising through the middle of the cabin like some ancient guardian was a massive tree trunk, its bark scarred and twisted with age. They'd built the cabin around it, as if the tree had demanded its space and the builders had no choice but to comply. Its branches pierced through the roof in several places, and despite being trapped indoors, leaves sprouted from them, casting strange shadows that danced with the firelight.

The longer I stared, the more unsettling it became. The trunk had been carved into, creating shelves that held dozens of glass jars. Their contents—herbs, liquids, things I couldn't name—seemed to glow faintly in the dim light. Crystals and wooden charms hung from the lower branches, clicking together like whispered secrets when the draft caught them. The old man's bed nestled between massive roots that had been worn smooth, and even the table was made from the tree itself, its surface rippling with rings that seemed to move when I wasn't looking directly at them. There was magic here—old magic, different from the electricity that coursed through my veins. It felt alive, watching, waiting. I couldn't shake the feeling that the tree knew exactly who—and what—I was.

Ronan gestured for me to sit at the table, then ladled me a bowl of stew.

But when did he have time to make dinner?

"Who lives here?" I asked.

He rolled his eyes.

I frowned. "Are we invading someone's home?"

"No. I was invited."

"Invited by who?"

"Don't you ever shut up?"

Just then, the door creaked open and an old man hobbled in. He was stooped with age, his back curved and his face lined with wrinkles. He leaned heavily on a gnarled wooden cane, his knuckles white with the effort of supporting his own weight.

"Ah, welcome back, Ronan!" he exclaimed, quavering slightly. "I see you've brought a guest."

He peered at me with rheumy eyes, his gaze lingering on my face. There was something unnerving about the way he looked at me, something that made my skin crawl.

"Who's this, then?" he asked curiously, pointing the cane at me.

Ronan grinned, showing his fangs. "Just a little something I picked up on my travels. Her name is Atreya."

My eyes snapped to him. Should he be telling anyone my name? Gods only knows how many soldiers are sweeping Ferenz right now looking for me.

The old man's eyes lit up with interest. "Well, isn't that just lovely?" he croaked, hobbling closer to me. "I haven't had company in ages. It gets so lonely out here in the woods."

There was something off about the way he was acting, something that didn't sit right with me. He seemed...different, somehow. Too eager, too friendly. Then again, I wasn't familiar with outside customs. Maybe they were all like this out here.

No. From my understanding, it's a Hellscape out here. Humans and Fae at each other's necks. Ramses always raided the human and lowborn Fae villages for slaves to bring back.

I felt the rise of my magic just under my skin. The electricity briefly bouncing between my fingers. I didn't trust Ronan, and sure wouldn't trust this old man.

"How do you do, miss?" he asked, his bony hand extending to take mine.

I took it, feeling a jolt of unease. His hand was cold and clammy, his grip like a bird's claw.

"I do well, thank you," I replied, trying to pull my hand back.

But he held fast, his grip tightening. "No need to be shy, dearie," he said, "You're safe here. Ronan wouldn't bring no harm into my home."

There was something in the way he spoke, something that made my hackles rise. He sounded...compelled, somehow. Like he was saying the words, but didn't really mean them.

I glanced over at Ronan, feeling a jolt of suspicion.

But Ronan just smiled, showing his fangs. "Of course not, old man," he said, "I promised you, didn't I? You're safe with me."

The old man nodded, his eyes glazing over. "Yes, you did," he said, dully. "I'm safe with you, Ronan. You'd never hurt me."

I felt a chill run down my spine. It was true, then. Ronan had compelled him, used his powers to bend the old man to his will.

And if he'd do it to this old man...what was to stop him from doing it to me?

Ronan peeled his muddy boots off by the door, leaving them in a heap on the mat. He padded over to the table in his stockinged feet, his movements silent on the wooden floor. He pushed the bowl of stew toward me, his eyes glinting in the firelight.

"Eat."

I crossed my arms over my chest, glaring at him. "I'm not eating until you tell me what you did to him," I said, jerking my chin toward the old man.

"And what makes you think I've done anything to him?" he asked feigning innocence.

I snorted. "Don't play dumb with me. I saw it. He's compelled or *something*."

He shrugged, unperturbed. "Maybe a bit. It will be daylight soon."

My eyes narrowed. "You used your powers on him. You made him trust you, made him think he's safe with you."

Has he done that to me? Would I remember?

He leaned back in his chair, steepling his fingers together. "And if I did?" he challenged.

I felt a surge of anger. "That's not right. You can't just go around controlling people like that." What the hell was it with the men in my life and control? I was sick of it.

He chuckled, a low rumble in his chest. "You'd be surprised what I can do, Little Light. Now, are you going to eat or not?"

I scowled at him, at his new nickname for me, my stomach growling at the delicious smell of the stew. I was hungry, but I didn't want to give in to him. Still, I didn't see what starving myself would accomplish. With a huff, I picked up the spoon and took a bite.

The stew was amazing, rich and flavorful with chunks of tender meat and vegetables. I ate in silence, shooting Ronan the occasional glare. He just beamed and watched me, seeming to enjoy my annoyance.

The old man hobbled over and sat in the third chair, his eyes fixed on me with an unnerving intensity. I tried to ignore him, focusing on my meal. But I could feel his gaze on me, could feel his attention like a weight.

Finally, I couldn't take it anymore. "Stop staring at me," I snapped, turning to face him.

He blinked, his eyes going vacant. "Oh, sorry miss. I didn't mean to make you uncomfortable."

I sighed, feeling a pang of guilt. "It's fine. I'm just...tired, I guess."

He nodded, his gaze dropping back to his lap. "Of course, miss. You must be exhausted after your journey. Why don't you go lie down? The bed is clean, I promise."

I hesitated, unsure of what to do. But the bed did look inviting, piled high with soft-looking furs. And I was tired, my eyelids drooping with exhaustion.

With a nod, I pushed my chair back and stood. "Thank you," I said, trying to sound polite. "I will."

It's all a single room, and I'm acutely aware that Ronan is watching me. So is the man. I sit down experimentally on the cot of furs and pull off my boots. My feet are cold, and I shiver, pulling the furs closer around me. I don't take off my fight leathers.

The old man goes past me, covering two windows, one on each side of the door, with thick curtains.

Right. Because the sun is coming up. And Ronan can't be in the sun.

The thought crosses my mind that I should rip those curtains off.

The Temple of Elrathilion materialized around me like a half-remembered nightmare. My mind was a fog of memories—Ronan dragging me to some hermit's forest hideaway, but everything after that was static and shadows. The prayer candles were dying, drowning in pools of their own wax, filling the air with the scent of smoke and dying flame.

A sound sliced through the silence—leather wings cutting air. I spun, my heart jackhammering against my ribs. There, hovering like death itself, was a creature torn straight from hell's sketchbook. Triangle head, teeth like broken glass, and a tail of scales that whispered against the air. Before I could scream, it vanished into smoke, leaving nothing but the bitter taste of fear in my mouth.

"Hello?" My voice echoed back to me, mocking.

The darkness answered with silence. Then—green light birthed itself from the shadows, pulsing like some otherworldly heart. I reached for it, drawn like a moth to killing flame, but it danced away from my fingers, teasing, taunting.

The orb played its game of chase, leading me deeper into the temple's belly. My feet moved without permission, each step echoing against stone like a countdown. The gods watched from their perches, their stone faces twisted with judgment. Wrong, everything screamed wrong. The air itself pressed against my skin like a warning.

The grand prayer hall spread before me as the orb slipped through massive doors. Candlelight made the room dance, throwing shadows that writhed on the walls like tortured souls. And there, in the heart of it all, stood Servat.

My breath caught. He was beautiful in his arena armor, dark skin gleaming with sweat, that smile I would have died a thousand deaths for lighting up his face. Joy and relief washed over me.

"Servat!" His name tore from my throat. I crashed into him, buried myself in his chest, desperate to breathe in the scent that was purely him. His arms locked around me, solid, real, alive. His heart thundered against my cheek, a drum beat of life.

"I love you." It rumbled through his chest. "I'll always be with you, Atreya. No matter what happens, I'll always be yours."

Tears burned my eyes. "You told me to hit you two steps behind you! Why did you go into the strike?"

His smile was gentle poison. "You will be okay, love."

I clung harder, as if I could keep him here through sheer force of will. But his body changed under my hands, muscles coiling like steel cables. His skin blazed hotter, hotter, until touching him was like embracing the sun.

I tried to pull away. His grip turned to iron. His face contorted, mouth stretched in a silent scream. His beautiful skin blackened, charred, those pristine white braids withering to ash. Blue-white lightning danced through his bones like death's own light show.

My screams shredded my throat raw. Lightning poured from my hands, striking him again and again, a storm of destruction I couldn't control. I was killing him. Again. Just like the arena. Just like before.

Stop.
Stop!
STOP!

"Wake up, Atreya."

Ronan's voice cut through the nightmare like a blade. Reality slammed back—hard, fast, brutal. My body was a live wire, electricity crackling beneath my skin, ready to explode. The taste of ash coated my tongue. Servat's screams still echoed in my skull.

Ronan's hands branded my shoulders, his grip iron-strong. Red eyes pierced the darkness, two burning coals in a face carved from marble. The shadows played across his features like death's own fingerprints.

"It was just a dream."

Fuck him. Fuck his calm. Fuck everything.

My heart was a war drum in my chest. Lightning danced through my veins, begging for release. I could still smell it—Servat's flesh cooking, his bones turning to char. The memory was a knife twisting in my gut.

Dream. Just a dream.

But Servat was still dead. And his killer's hands were on my skin.

I jammed my knuckles between my teeth, biting down until copper flooded my mouth. Tears burned hot tracks down my face. Ronan didn't move, didn't speak. Just watched. Always fucking watching.

Maybe Ramses was right. Maybe I was—

The thought died in my throat.

Sunlight had snaked through the curtains, a golden blade slicing across Ronan's hands where they gripped my shoulders. Smoke curled up from his flesh like spirits rising from a grave.

Memory of Servat.

Lightning.

Burning.

Screaming.

"No!" The word ripped from my throat. I slammed my palms against his chest, scrambling backward until my spine hit wood. The headboard creaked a warning.

Ronan's eyes widened—the first real emotion I'd seen crack that mask. "Atreya—"

"Your hands. The sun—it's burning you alive."

His flesh was a nightmare made real. Blisters erupted like volcanic peaks, skin blackening, charring. The stench of burning meat filled my lungs.

He glanced down, understanding darkening his face. A curse hissed through clenched teeth as he yanked his hands to his chest.

"Didn't you feel it?"

His jaw tightened, muscles rippling beneath pale skin. "I'm fine." Two words, flat as a blade.

Liar.

His hands were destruction given form. Flesh bubbled and wept, clear fluid running like tears. But even as bile rose in my throat, the impossible happened. Skin knit together like time running backward. Blisters burst and drained. Char flaked away, revealing raw meat beneath.

But the healing stopped short. His palms remained angry pink, white scars etched like ancient runes into his flesh.

The old man moved faster than his years should allow, materializing at Ronan's side like a ghost. "Blood," he rasped, eyes fixed on ruined flesh. "You need blood to heal proper, boy."

Ronan's fangs flashed like twin daggers in the dim light. The old man offered his wrist like a sacrifice to a dark god.

The sound of punctured flesh. The wet rhythm of swallowing.

I turned away, bile burning my throat. Wrong. This was wrong. Too intimate. Too raw.

Furs over my head. Darkness. Safe.

But I couldn't block out the sounds—couldn't unhear the feeding, couldn't unfeel the tension crackling through the air like lightning before a storm.

"Wake me when it's night," I choked out.

When the light couldn't hurt.

When I couldn't watch another person burn because of me.

CHAPTER 4

Atreya

I woke to the sound of rustling, my eyes snapping open. I was disorient-ed for a moment, my mind foggy with sleep. But as I sat up, memory came flooding back. The old man's cabin, Ronan's burned hands, the blood drinking...it had all been real.

I looked around, taking in the scene. The old man was up and moving, his stooped back bent as he rummaged through a chest in the corner. Ronan was sitting at the table, his back to me. He was dressed in a clean white tunic, his silver hair damp and dripping down his back. The old man had a large bowl of water and a towel beside him. Slowly the old man motioned with his hands and the water began to ripple, swirling into a huge sphere. It weaved itself through Ronan's silver strands, before sloshing back into the bowl.

"You're a water Fae?" I asked.

The old man's laugh was bitter. "Who knows? My mother was a fast one. Throw a rock down in Ratten, pick any bastard for a father. That's the joke." His shoulders lifted, fell. "Just good with water, is all."

Ronan chuckled and I looked him over. His hands were still pink and tender-looking, but the blisters and charring were gone.

The old man hobbled over, a bundle of cloth in his arms. "Here, miss," he said, holding out the bundle. "Take these. You'll be needing them on your travels."

I took the bundle, unfolding it to find three clean tunics and a pair of leather breeches. They looked like they would fit well enough. I glanced up at the old man, feeling a pang of gratitude. "Thank you," I said, trying to sound sincere. "This is very kind of you."

He smiled, his rheumy eyes twinkling. "It's nothing, miss. I'm just glad to help. You and Ronan seem like good kids. You deserve a hand up."

How sweet his words were, only they weren't real. This man couldn't help himself.

The old man was already hobbling over to Ronan, a look of vacant obedience on his face. "You will forget we were ever here," Ronan told him, low and husky. "You will remember nothing."

The old man nodded, his eyes going glassy. "I will forget you were ever here," he parroted. "I will remember nothing."

The old man didn't even glance at me, just kept staring at Ronan with that vacant expression. I felt a surge of disgust, but pushed it aside. I could deal with this later.

I dressed quickly in one of the tunics and the breeches, feeling a sense of relief at the clean clothes. If Ronan looked, I didn't notice. I used the water from the jug to wash my face, then sat down to lace up my boots.

I reached for the bundle of clothes on the cot, but Ronan got to it first, adding a loaf of bread and a handful of fruits into it before slinging it over his shoulder.

The old man didn't even say goodbye, just kept sitting at the table with that vacant expression. I felt a pang of unease as we left him there.

I could see the hearth's fire flickering in the window as we left, soon the night took that away too.

"Is he going to be alright?"

"He will be fine." Steel and ice.

"How can you be sure?"

"You love asking questions, don't you?"

"Do you do that to people often?"

"Sometimes."

"Have you done that to me?"

"No."

"How can I be sure of that?"

He stopped dead. My face slammed into his back—granite wall of muscle. He spun, predator-quick. "Would you like me to?" One step forward as I stumbled back.

"No," I snapped, my fingers already sparking with power.

Ronan's eyes narrowed, but he didn't press the issue. He just turned and started walking again. I followed behind him, my heart pounding in my chest. I didn't like being at his mercy like this.

We walked in silence for a while, the only sound being the rustling of leaves and snapping of twigs under our feet. I kept looking over my shoulder, but I didn't see anything. No one was following us.

"Where are we going now?" I finally asked, breaking the silence.

He let out an exasperated sigh.

"Somewhere safe," Ronan replied, not looking back at me.

"Where's safe?" I pressed, but he just kept walking.

"The next place."

"Where—" he slapped a hand over my mouth.

"Shhhhhhhhhh,"

I slammed my teeth into his palm, tasting salt and winter. Ronan's eyes rolled skyward, bored as ever.

"Listen up, princess," he hissed, low and dangerous. "I'm not the scariest thing stalking these woods. Plenty of nasties would love to tear into that pretty flesh of yours. Beast or man."

The rustling hit then. Heavy. Wrong. Getting closer. Ronan's head snapped toward the sound, muscles coiling tight. His eyes went hard as steel.

"Run."

One word. That's all it took.

My boots pounded earth, heart hammering against ribs. The thing behind us—fuck, it was gaining. Branches snapped like explosives. Hot breath and something else. Something worse.

I risked a look back.

Holy. Gods.

The beast was massive—bear-sized with a boar's body gone wrong. Spikes rose from its back like a fortress of bone. Two sets of eyes blazed red as hellfire, fixed on us with predator focus.

I wasn't going to let it catch me. Power surged through my veins, electric and eager. My fingers tingled, sparks dancing between them. One thought, that's all it took. Lightning exploded from my palm, striking the creature dead center.

Its screech split the night. The beast went down hard, thrashing against dirt and leaves.

But we didn't stop. Couldn't stop.

More rustling. More panting. More monsters.

"Ronan!" Fear made my words crack. "There's more."

"Keep running." His own breath came ragged. "Don't use your magic."

"But—"

"It'll draw more attention." Sharp. Final. "Just. Keep. Running."

The trees thinned out ahead. Starlight spilled through branches, painting everything midnight blue. Moon hung like a blade. But as we broke through the trees, my stomach dropped.

It was a cliff, the ground falling away in a steep drop. Below us, a giant river churned and foamed, its surface broken up by jagged rocks that poked up like teeth. It was beautiful and deadly, a sight that made my breath catch.

I turned to Ronan, my eyes wide. "Where are we supposed to go?"

He didn't answer, just kept staring out at the river. His face was pale, his eyes fixed on something in the distance.

"I hate swimming."

"You can't be serious—"

His hand locked around my wrist. One yank.

Then we were falling.

Sky and earth traded places. Wind screamed past my ears.

I barely had time to scream before we hit the water. It was a shock, the cold enveloping me like a vice. I felt myself going under, the pressure building in my ears.

I struggled upward, breaking the surface with a gasp. I treaded water, looking around frantically. Ronan was next to me, his own head bobbing up, silver hair plastered to his face.

"I hate water," he panted. "I really hate water."

The water was churning and foamy, the white rapids pulling us this way and that. I kicked and paddled, but it was no use. The river had us in its grip, tossing us about like dolls.

I was thrown forward, my head spinning. I felt a blinding pain, then everything went dark.

Consciousness slammed back like a fist to the jaw. Water everywhere—in my lungs, my nose, my mouth. Someone was hauling me up, up, up through the endless cold. I broke surface with a gasp that felt like swallowing glass.

Ronan's arm locked around me like steel, his other cutting through the water with brutal efficiency. My head spun, vision blurring at the edges.

"The hell happened?"

"Rock wanted to kiss your skull. Had to fish you out."

I tried to speak, but it came out a croak. I must have swallowed half the river.

Then—movement. A fin knifed through the surface, gray as death and bigger than any fish had a right to be.

"SWIM!" Ronan hurled me forward like a rag doll.

I didn't need to be told twice. I kicked off from him, propelling myself through the water. I didn't dare look back, just kept swimming.

But I could hear it behind me. The thrashing of its tail, the churning of the water. It was gaining on me.

Curiosity won. I twisted around.

Nope.

Nope.

The creature was massive, its body long and serpentine. It had a giant lantern attached to its forehead, the light glowing with an eerie blue light. Its mouth was open, revealing rows of razor-sharp teeth.

Then Ronan appeared, materializing between me and death. His eyes blazed molten silver, power crackling off him in waves. He raised one hand, and the river itself answered.

Water exploded into chaos. Waves rose like walls, crashing and churning into a vortex of pure fury. The creature's screech split the air as it thrashed, caught in Ronan's deadly dance.

"MOVE YOUR ASS!" he roared.

I didn't waste the chance he was giving me. I kicked harder, propelling myself through the water. I could feel the pull of the current, but I fought against it, my arms and legs burning with exhaustion.

Finally, I saw a glimmer of light up ahead. I kicked harder, my head breaking against frothing waves. I gasped in air, coughing up water, looking around frantically. We were in a small inlet, the water calm and peaceful. The river was just a few feet away, I could see where the river opened up to the sea.

I looked around, trying to get my bearings. The inlet was small, surrounded by steep cliffs that rose up on all sides. The only way out was a small opening that led back to the river, or up the sides of the cliff. I could see the creature thrashing about through the opening, its body coiling and uncoiling.

I turned to Ronan, relief washing over me. He was swimming next to me, his breathing even. His eyes were still blazing with that fierce silver light, his face pale and drawn.

Do all vampires have magic like that? Or was that just a Ronan thing?

"Thank you," I panted, trying to catch my breath.

His eyes returned to their normal color, the light fading away. "I hate water."

"You've said that. Any particular reason why?"

"No."

"Right."

Water dripped from my clothes, each piece feeling like it weighed a thousand pounds. The bundle strapped to Ronan's back hadn't fared any better—looked like it had been dragged through hell itself.

As if having the same thought, Ronan untied the bundle from his body and opened it right on the sandy shore.

The breads were mushed, completely wet. The only thing salvageable were a few pieces of fruit and a root vegetable. Ronan cursed under his breath, shaking out the wet tunics.

"I'll need to start a fire."

I looked down at the pitiful offering, feeling a pang of hunger. The few pieces of fruit and the root vegetable were better than nothing.

I watched him work, all efficient movement and fluid grace. He even made digging a hole look graceful. Wood went in, piece by piece, until the pit was full. Then he leaned close, his back to me. No flint strike, no warning—just *whoosh,* and fire erupted.

I scooted closer, hands outstretched toward blessed warmth. My clothes clung like a second skin, sending shivers down my spine. Then—something else. An itch. Not your normal, scratch-and-done kind of itch.

It only got worse, the itching spreading across my chest and stomach. I felt something wriggling against my skin, like worms or snakes.

Something moved under my tunic...

Something moved under my tunic.

Gods above please.

"Something's on me!" I shrieked. Ronan jumped up. I lifted up my tunic, pulling it over my head. And that was when I saw them. Massive leeches were attached to my skin, their bodies fat and bloated. They were a disgusting, slimy, brown color, their mouths attached to my flesh.

I let out a scream of horror, frantically pulling at the leeches. But they only seemed to cling tighter, their mouths sucking at my skin. I could feel them drinking my blood, pulling life from my body.

"Get them off of me!" I shouted, struggling to pull the leeches off.

"They'll fall off when they get enough blood!"

"Ronan! Get them the fuck off of me!"

"I'm not touching the damned things!"

"Ronan!"

"Light them up! Use your magic, damn you!"

I focused on the leeches, visualizing them erupting across my skin. Lightning flickered across my vision, across my flesh, and one by one they sizzled and plopped off with a high-pitched squeal. Where they had been attached, crimson rings of blood stained my skin.

"Disgusting," Ronan said, looking at my chest.

Instinctively I crossed my arms over myself, blushing. "Thanks for nothing!" I snapped.

"You're welcome."

"Bastard."

"Likewise."

"Why didn't I feel them?" I demanded, "I didn't even know they were there!"

"They must have attached themselves when we were in the river," Ronan said. "Leeches are attracted to blood and warmth. They would have sensed you and attached themselves."

"Why aren't you covered in them then?"

He looked at me incredulously, then raised a silver brow. "Seriously?"

"Oh, right," I said sheepishly. You'd need to have blood and warmth. Things Vampires didn't have.

He sat himself in the sand, peeling off his boots and socks and stretched his toes. He moved the boots close to the fire and then moved to pull off his shirt and breeches. I glanced at his body, his skin pale and smooth, his muscles rippling as he moved.

He stopped his motions and looked at me. I averted my gaze quickly.

"Take off your clothes," he said.

"Excuse me?" I squeaked.

"Don't be a pervert. Your clothes need to dry."

"I have nothing else to wear!"

"I'm not going to look at you if that's what you're worried about."

He had that way about him. The way he spoke that felt like knives licking across my skin. I ripped my shirt and leathers off and threw it at his face. True to his word, he didn't look up once.

Sand bit into my bare skin as I huddled there, knees pulled tight against my chest. Shivers wracked my body, but I wasn't about to let him see me weak. "What was that thing back there?"

"Which one?" Dry amusement colored his smile.

Right. Our little adventure had been a monster parade.

"Start with the giant pigs."

"Boarux," he said, like that explained everything. "Born in the rebellion, before the War of Fallen Skies."

My mind came up blank. Not a single mention in any of the dusty tomes I'd been forced to study. "Why?"

"Humans wanted better livestock. Brought wild boars to the Fae, begged them to enhance the beasts. Make them bigger, tougher." His lips twisted. "And the Fae, being the spectacular fuck-ups they are, delivered."

My eye twitched. Fae blood ran in my veins, after all.

"They're nearly immortal now. Strong as hell, smart as whips. When humans couldn't control them anymore, they just... let them loose. Now they roam wild, destroying everything in their path. Hunt in packs, the females guarding young like demons while the males tear anything that moves to shreds."

"I've never seen the like," I said.

"You have eaten it. I know the smell of the meat. It smelled like boarux when I was in your kitchens."

"What were you doing in the kitchens?" Vampires didn't exactly need three squares a day. Right?

"Fucking your cook," he deadpanned. Matter-of-factly.

I snorted. "Which one?" My mind flicked through our female cooks—all three of them.

"The one with the red hair," he answered, checking the status of the tunics drying on a stick.

I furrowed my brows. "We don't have any female cooks with red hair."

"I never said female."

I inhaled sharply and turned to face him.

Ronan just rolled his eyes, not even bothering to look up at me. "You're very sheltered," he said. "When you've lived as long as I have, you'll want to try new things."

I gaped at Ronan, my mind reeling. I hadn't expected that.

Because Ronan... fuck. He was beautiful in a way that hurt to look at, all deadly grace and predatory power. And he'd been with my cook. A *male*.

I'd always assumed he'd want the traditional path—marriage, children (if vampires could even have them). It was just... the way things worked. Right?

"So...men? You have relations with men?" I know some males do that. I've heard stories. "Does it...how does it...?"

One silver brow arched. "Would you like me to draw you a picture?"

I pushed the thoughts aside, feeling a flush rise to my cheeks. "I just thought... I don't know... Have you always known you didn't like women?"

"I didn't say that."

My frown deepened.

"For fuck's sake. Did Ramses keep you locked in a tower? Why limit yourself to one or the other?"

"You don't have to be so crass about it!" I snapped.

"You've never thought to kiss a female?" He blinked at me.

"No!"

His grin turned wicked. Those silver eyes danced. "Your face is going red. Oh gods, you are thinking about it! Is it the Blackwater girl? What's her name—Cynthia? No... Corinthia?"

"Corina?" The name came out strangled. He snapped his fingers together and pointed at me.

"Yes! You have a thing for the Blackwater family. She is a beauty. "

"Stop it."

"Oh, come now. Do tell me. I love a good scandal and I'm bored!"

"I've never done anything with Corina, or any other female," I hissed.

"But the brother. That's a different matter?"

I can tell by the way his eyes glittered that he knew. This stranger who hadn't known me for more than a few days could tell that Servat and I had been having an affair.

A stinging came in the back of my eyes, and I bit the inside of my cheek until I tasted copper.

"What was that thing in the river?" I asked, changing the subject.

Ronan raised a brow at the change in subject but didn't press the issue. "It was a Kolqua," he said, his voice neutral. "A type of giant fish. They're common in these waters. Highly territorial. I'm guessing the big one ran all the others out."

I shuddered at the thought. "Well, let's hope we don't run into any more of those."

He nodded, his eyes fixed on the flames. "Yes, let's hope not." He adjusted the tunics and shook them out. "Dry enough. Put this on." He tossed me the hooded tunic. It was still slightly damp but not enough to make me uncomfortable.

Ronan was scooping sand over the flames to put them out, throwing on his boots and refastening the bundle to him. "Time to climb."

I eyed the sheer cliffs rising on either side. "Climb what exactly?"

He looked me up and down, clicking his tongue. "Didn't sign up to be your personal carriage service."

"I'm not asking you to carry me, you bas—"

The world tilted as he scooped me up like I weighed nothing, claws digging into my ass. "Hold still, wench."

"Put me down!"

But we were already moving, his inhuman speed carrying us forward. He hit the cliff face with bone-jarring force, rock and dirt showering down.

The ground spun sickeningly below. "Ronan. Get me up. Get me up now."

"Gods, you're heavy."

I'm going to fucking murder him.

His claws dug into the side of the cliff and he was climbing. Every now and again, I was sure he was going to kill us both. As soon as we got to the top he dumped me on the ground.

I grabbed his hand and with all the strength I could muster, sent a jolt of lightning through him on his still pinkish hands. He yelped in pain and bared his fangs at me.

"Awe. Did that hurt?" I asked sweetly.

He straightened and cocked his head to the side, a small smile on his lips that angered me further.

"What's so funny?'

He blinked slowly at me, then pointed his finger at me and hissed, "It looks like you landed in Boarux shit."

CHAPTER 5

Atreya

The Boarux dung wasn't just a smell—it was a fucking assault. It crawled into my nostrils and made itself at home, laughing at the wind's pathetic attempts to disperse it. I lost it, screaming until my throat burned raw, until Ronan's hand clamped over my mouth, his fingers rough against my lips.

An hour of trudging through this godforsaken forest, and what did we have to show for it? A sky that couldn't decide if it wanted to be star-studded or cloud-covered, and the mocking chorus of crickets punctuated by some asshole owl. The silence between those sounds was worse—a void my mind couldn't help but fill with memories I'd rather tear out of my skull.

Charred flesh. Arena sands. The wet sound of—

No. Focus on the now. Focus on how every twig snap under my boots felt like stepping on broken glass, how each crack echoed like a beacon to the monster hunting us. If Ramses caught me... fuck. I didn't have to imagine what he'd do. I knew. The bastard had given me enough demonstrations to fuel a lifetime of nightmares.

Like that time, fresh into our marriage, when I was still playing the role of the wide-eyed, eager-to-please little queen. I skipped one dinner—one fucking dinner—thinking the worst he'd do was starve me for a day or two.

I wish that had been his response. Gods, I wish.

Instead, he brought a basin into my chambers, filled with what looked like white grain. He spoke with honey-sweet poison as he set it down, those rings on his fingers catching the candlelight like predator eyes in the dark. "Do you know how they prepare pheasant delicacies on Ilyeves, my love?"

"They find the youngest ones. The tenderest." His fingers traced the rim of the basin.

He forced my chin up, made me look at the writhing mass of white grain. "They force-feed them. Tubes down their throats, pumping and pumping until their stomachs are ready to burst. The pain makes the meat sweeter, they say. The fear makes it tender."

I tried to turn away, but his grip was iron. "Three weeks of this, and their organs swell to ten times their natural size. But that's not the delicacy." His laugh was a whisper against my ear. "It's what happens when they finally burst."

The white mush moved, and I realized with horror it wasn't grain at all. Maggots. Thousands of maggots.

Ramses retrieved a brass tube and spoon from the waiting servant, his movements unhurried, methodical. Like a healer preparing medicine, except his eyes gleamed with something far darker than healing.

His guards knew their roles without being told, their hands pinning me down like I was nothing more than one of those pheasants. Their fingers were everywhere—on my shoulders, my jaw, my head wrenched back at an angle that made my neck scream.

"Open," he commanded, but I kept my teeth clenched so hard I thought they might shatter. It didn't matter. His guards knew what to do, fingers digging into the pressure points of my jaw until my mouth was forced wide, my screams echoing off the chamber walls.

The tube was brass, cold and unyielding as he fed it down my throat. I gagged, choking on metal and terror as it scraped its way down, down, down. My body bucked, trying to escape, but there was nowhere to go. The first spoonful of writhing white made my vision go dark at the edges, and I could feel every single one of them moving—

"Where the hell are we going?" The question ripped from my throat before I could stop it. Anything to drown out the memory of squirming brass tubes and maggots.

Ronan's response was a grunt that would've made a cave troll proud.

"Oh, that's real fucking helpful," I snapped. "First word I've said in hours, by the way."

"And I was enjoying every blessed second of silence." His words cut like ice.

Bastard.

As if I'd chosen this little adventure. As if either of us had a choice in this damned situation.

"News flash, asshole—you aren't the only one who didn't want me here!" What is it about this man that made me forget all of the carefully constructed manners that had been drilled into me for years?

He was quiet for a moment, then: "Tor."

"What?"

"I fucking hate repeating myself, Atreya." My name on his lips was a curse.

"Tor? Are you out of your goddamn mind?" The laugh that burst from me was borderline hysterical. "That place is Ramses' personal hunting ground. His scavengers treat it like their own private buffet." One thing being the king's unwilling bedwarmer had taught me—the sick man loved to hover over his war maps, marking each town he'd bled dry. Especially Tor.

"I'm aware," he drawled.

"Then why—"

"Take a good look around, princess." He gestured at our surroundings with a sweep of his arm. "We're on the wrong fucking side of the river. Unless you fancy a midnight swim or a scenic detour downstream?"

I scowled, but the bastard had a point. Tor might've been hell on earth, but it beat freezing our asses off in the river. Or worse—running into the Kolqua again. My skin crawled at the memory. That thing belonged on a spit over the hottest fire we could build.

But there was another reason my stomach was trying to climb up my throat at the thought of Tor.

Aislinn Furian. The last ruler of that cursed place. She'd died without an heir, without hope—and I'd been the one to make it happen. My hands, my light, my guilt. Sure, Ramses had done the heavy lifting, turning Tor into a graveyard long before I was even born. But I'd been the one to snuff out their final spark of hope.

The trees parted like curtains at a funeral, and there it was.

Castle Furian. Holy Gods.

It wasn't a castle anymore—it was a corpse. A massive, stone corpse with its ribs cracked open to the sky, its walls scarred by claw marks deep enough to hide bodies in. The windows were empty eye sockets, glass long since shattered or melted into twisted tears. The gates hung like broken jaw bones, charred and splintered, barely clinging to rusted hinges that screamed with every breath of wind.

Nature was trying to claim it back, weeds pushing through stone like desperate fingers clawing from a grave. Vines spilled from every crack and wound, nature's funeral shroud for a dead kingdom.

The towers—my gods, the towers. They still reached for the sky like accusing fingers, their tops snapped off into jagged points. Once, they'd flown the Furian banners proud—silver on blue, hope on high. Now? Nothing but tattered ghosts whipping in the wind, each snap of fabric like the crack of a whip against my conscience.

My lungs forgot how to work as I took it all in.

Beyond the castle, the town of Tor stretched out in a tangled web of crumbling buildings and narrow, winding streets. What were once sturdy homes and bustling shops stood as hollow shells, their wooden frames weathered to a dull grey that matched the ashen sky. Shattered windows stared out like the empty sockets of skulls, their panes long since broken. Doors hung from rusted hinges, creaking mournfully in the gentle breeze.

The only signs of life were a few scrawny chickens pecking listlessly at the dusty earth, their feathers dull and ruffled. A mangy dog slinked past, its eyes gleaming with a feral intensity, foaming at the mouth.

Disease. That's what this place was.

Plague.

Blight.

Famine.

A faint wail echoed through the stillness, the cry of a baby somewhere in the distance. I knew a hungry cry when I heard it, though Vrys never wailed as sharply as this.

My heart pounded in my chest, each beat echoing in my ears. My breath came in short gasps, my vision blurring at the edges. I felt a familiar tightening in my chest, a crushing weight that made it hard to breathe.

These people didn't get the courtesy of a quick death.

Through the maze of broken streets, hollow-eyed figures shuffled like ghosts. The Fae were easiest to spot—their once-luminous skin now ashen and dull, pointed ears drooping, wings tattered where they hadn't already fallen off in papery shreds.

Some still wore the remnants of their court finery, silk rags hanging from skeletal frames.

The humans weren't much better. Children with distended bellies and stick-thin limbs huddled in doorways, their eyes too large in gaunt faces. Adults moved like ancient creatures, backs bent under the weight of survival, fingers twisted into claws from scrabbling in the dirt for roots and grubs. A woman passed by, her cheekbones sharp enough to cut glass, clutching a bundle to her chest that might have been a baby or might have been rags—it was too still to tell.

Both Fae and human alike shared the same haunted look, the same yellowed skin stretched tight over bones, the same festering sores that wouldn't heal in a place where magic had turned toxic and food was nothing but a distant memory.

Ramses should have put them all out of their misery if he wasn't going to help them.

I tried to speak, to warn Ronan, but it came out barely a whisper. "Ronan...I...I don't know if I can do this."

Dust swirled around me, a faint haze that obscured my vision.

But he didn't seem to hear me. "Come on," he muttered, already striding towards the castle. "We'll cut through Tor, see if there's anything of use, then head South to Paladin."

I stumbled after him, my legs trembling beneath me. My mind raced, memories flooding my vision. The smell of smoke and blood, the feel of ripping flesh and fur, Aislinn's accusing eyes as she lay dying at my feet.

And now her ghost was screaming '*Look. Look what you gave my people.*' *Clang Clang Clang.*

My boots echoed off the remaining castle walls as we made our way through the courtyard. The air was heavy with the stench of decay and rot. Bodies lay everywhere, some peeling apart. A dog was picking at bones.

I could feel Aislinn's ghostly eyes upon me, her spectral self whispering accusations in my ear.

"You should not have come here," it hissed. *"This is a place of death, of memory. You will only bring more suffering."* I ignore it and keep going. *"He will find you here."*

The wail grew louder, more insistent, until I could feel it vibrating through my very bones. My heart clenched, a pang of something like longing mixed with guilt stabbing through my chest.

Suddenly, a figure emerged from the shadows of a crumbling building. A woman, gaunt and hollow-eyed, clutching a tiny bundle to her chest. The baby's cries grew louder still, its small face scrunched up in distress.

I froze, my feet rooted to the spot. Ronan didn't seem to notice, kept striding forward with his usual single-minded determination. But I couldn't move, couldn't tear my gaze away from the mother and child.

Vrys.

I could practically smell his newborn baby scent, feel his tiny fingers wrapped around my finger. He was chubby. Well-fed. Happy.

All the things this child was not.

"Ronan, wait," I called out.

He spun around, scowling. "What now, Atreya? We don't have all night. This is time-sensitive. You know. The big ball of light that comes in the sky and gives me the ick?" He pointed upward. "Yeah. That. It's coming."

I didn't answer. Instead, I cautiously walked over to the woman. The mother looked up, her eyes widening as I approached. For a moment, we just stared at each other, two women linked by motherhood.

I thought I had it bad. Her freedom still came at a price. She would probably claw my eyes out for a bite of food.

Then, in a move that surprised even myself, I reached out and snatched the bundle from Ronan's arms. He protested, grabbing for it, but I was too quick. I thrust the bundle into the mother's arms, ignoring Ronan's outraged spluttering.

"That is meant for you!" he exclaimed, "I am looking for supplies, not trying to give them away!"

I just shook my head, feeling a strange lightness in my chest. It was a small act of mercy, of kindness, in a world that seemed to have forgotten both. And as I met the mother's tear-filled eyes, I knew it was the right thing to do.

"We have enough," I said quietly, turning away from Ronan's protests. "Let's just find what we need and go."

He huffed, crossing his arms over his chest. "Fine. But make it quick, Atreya. I haven't all night to stand around while you play at being charitable."

He led the way, his long strides eating up the distance as he navigated the winding streets of Tor. I followed, my gaze darting from one ruined building to the next. Everywhere I looked, I saw signs of the destruction Ramses had wrought. The shattered windows, the charred timbers, the very air thick with the scent of smoke and ash even still.

The sky was already starting to change color, and Ronan cursed as he stumbled over a pile of rubble.

He halted abruptly, jerking me from my thoughts. I followed his gaze to a small, weathered cottage. It looked little different from the others, its wooden walls grey and peeling, its roof missing tiles. But where the other houses seemed to loom over us, empty and menacing, this one looked... abandoned.

"It's been raided," Ronan muttered, his brow furrowed. "But it's better than sleeping on the street. Let's see what we can scrounge up."

I nodded, falling into step behind him. He approached the cottage cautiously sniffing the air, making an odd clicking noise in the back of his throat.

I mirrored his movements, my senses on high alert. But as we entered, it was clear that we were alone.

The cottage was tiny, a single room with a hearth at its center. What had once been a table and chairs were now splintered ruins, scattered across the floor. The cupboards were hanging open, their shelves bare. It looked like looters had already been through, taking what little of value this place had once held.

Ronan cursed, kicking at a shattered chair. "There's nothing here. Absolutely nothing."

I didn't answer, my gaze scanning the room. He was right, there was little enough to see.

I moved to the cupboards, pulling them open to peer inside. They were dusty, cobwebbed, but as I ran my hand along the shelves, my fingers brushed against something. A small sack, tucked away at the back and forgotten.

I pulled it out, the weight of it heavy in my hands. It was canvas, the top tied with a length of twine. I worked at the knot, my fingers fumbling with the knot.

Finally, it came loose, spilling its contents across the floor. Not food, as I had hoped, but something almost as good. A handful of silver coins, glinting in the fading light. A water skin, without holes by the feel of it. And a small pouch, the leather soft and supple.

I picked it up, feeling a familiar shape inside. My heart leapt as I worked open the ties, spilling the contents into my palm. A dozen or so of healing potions, each one a small vial of glowing liquid. They were what we need-ed.

I looked up, meeting Ronan's gaze. He had moved to stand behind me, his eyes fixed on the scatter of goods.

"Well," he said finally, "Looks like this dive wasn't a complete waste of time."

"Question is, who left them here?"

"We don't have time to look elsewhere for shelter." He looked up at the broken roof and sighed.

Above us, the roof was a patchwork of missing brick and gaping holes, the night sky visible through the breaks. Clouds drifted across the stars, and I could see the faint lightening of the horizon—the sun would be rising soon. We needed to find something to cover the open areas fast.

Ronan seemed to think the same. "Anything useable?" he muttered to himself, "Something to block the light, at least."

My gaze fell on the remains of the bed, tucked away in the corner of the room. It was little more than a pile of rags, the mattress stained and torn. I moved closer and saw that the blankets were still intact, if a little worse for wear. They stunk to high hell.

I stooped to grab one, pulling it free of the bedframe. It was thick and heavy, the wool scratchy against my skin. I shook it out, sending dust flying, and examined it. There were a few holes, but it would do.

"Ronan," I called, holding up the blanket. "Over here."

"That'll do," he muttered, already reaching for the blanket. "Help me get it up there."

I nodded, following him to the center of the room. The holes in the roof were large, but with the blanket, we could cover at least part of it. Ronan jumped, his fingers closing around the edge of a beam. He pulled himself up in one smooth motion, the muscles in his back flexing with the movement.

I handed him the blanket, watching as he spread it out across the beam. It hung down in a heavy fold, blocking some of the light. It wasn't perfect, but it was better than nothing.

He dropped down beside me, his gaze going to the sky. The lightening was more pronounced now, the stars fading as the sun rose. We didn't have much time.

"Good enough," he grunted, already turning away. "Let's get some rest. We can hardly do anything more now."

My stomach chose that moment to growl.

He raised a brow at me. "Perfect. How long until you die of starvation?"

"I had stew last night," I reminded him.

"And you would have at least had some fruit had you not given it away."

"I'm fine," I said. My stomach growled again.

"Try to sleep. I'll be up when the sun sets," he said.

I nodded, feeling a wave of exhaustion wash over me. It had been a long night, and we still had a long way to go. I followed him to the corner of the room, my gaze going to the remains of the bed.

The other blankets were still there, a tangle of wool and linen.

"Can you do without a fire?" he asked.

I nodded.

He sat down and leaned against the wall beside the cot. "Go to sleep."

Easier said than done. I still smelled like Boarux shit.

The floor was hard as frozen hell beneath me, but at least it was dry. I curled up on my side, using my arm as a pillow, trying to ignore how every bone in my body screamed for a real bed. For clean clothes. For anything that wasn't soaked in Boarux stench and memories of death.

"You're thinking too loud," Ronan muttered from his corner.

"Fuck *off.*"

"Such language from a queen."

I rolled over to face him, finding his silhouette in the growing darkness. "I stopped being a queen the moment I left Ember."

"No. You stopped being a queen the moment that bastard put that crown on your head."

The truth in his words hit harder than any physical blow. I squeezed my eyes shut, but the memories came anyway. The weight of that cursed crown. The way it had felt like a noose tightening around my neck. The cold metal against my skin, as cold as Ramses' smile when he'd named me his queen. That Gods awful dress they put me in to walk down the aisle.

My stomach growled again, louder this time.

"For fuck's sake." Ronan's irritation crackled through the darkness. I heard him shifting, then something small and hard hit my shoulder. "Eat it before I change my mind."

I fumbled in the dark until my fingers closed around what felt like dried meat. The smell hit me—spiced venison. My mouth watered instantly.

"Where did you—"

"Don't ask questions you don't want answers to." There was a warning in his tone that made me think twice about pressing further.

The meat was tough as leather and salty enough to make my eyes water, but it was food. I forced myself to eat slowly, to savor each bite instead of wolfing it down like the starving animal I felt like.

"Thank you," I whispered when I'd finished.

His grunt was barely audible. "Go to sleep, Little Light. Tomorrow's going to be worse than today."

"Worse than Boarux shit and dead cities?"

"Much worse." The way he said it made my skin crawl. "We're heading South. The perimeter around Ember may be safe from the creepy things in the woods. We are not anywhere near Ember."

Well, damn.

Sleep, when it finally came, was filled with nightmares of brass tubes and maggots, of Ramses' laugh and Aislinn's dying curse. And through it all, a baby's cry echoed, growing louder and louder until I couldn't tell if it was Vrys or that starving child from Tor.

In my dreams, they were the same thing—another life I couldn't save, another soul I'd failed.

Another reason why Ramses needed to die.

CHAPTER 6

Atreya

Servat's boots kicked up dust as he ran, the knife gleaming like death in his hand. Metal sang through air. My power surged—hot, electric, alive—and the blade exploded into glittering shards. The crowd's roar hit me, their bloodlust a tangible thing.

One more time. Just one more.

But then—god, then—that familiar ice-cold dread slithered down my spine. I'd lived this moment before. This exact fucking moment.

"SERVAT!" The scream ripped my throat raw. My legs wouldn't move fast enough—never fast enough. Lightning split the air, white-hot and merciless. Again. Again. Again.

The final blast lit him up like a star, and then... nothing. Servat—my warrior, my lover, my everything—crumpled like a broken doll.

Dead. Just... dead.

My mind fractured. Reality splintered. The scream that tore out of me wasn't human nor Fae—it was primal, feral, the sound of a heart being ripped in two. My knees hit stone, hands scrambling over his chest, searching for that familiar thundering heartbeat. Nothing. No warmth. No life. Just cooling flesh under trembling fingers.

"Servat! Servat, wake up!" I shook him hard enough to rattle teeth. "Please—please—" The words dissolved into desperate, animal sounds.

Those steel eyes—eyes that had burned with such fire, such passion—stared emptily at nothing. The arena fell silent, a thousand breaths held. Like they were watching some tragic play unfold. Let them watch. Let the whole damn world see.

I collapsed over him, salt tears falling on blood-streaked skin. My arms locked around him like iron bands, like I could anchor his soul to his body through sheer fucking will.

"No, no, no—" I stammered. "Not again. I can't—I won't survive this."

My body rocked, a ship lost in a storm of grief.

A shadow fell over us. Combat boots, scuffed and battle-worn. I looked up through tear-blurred eyes into Vrys's face—my son's face. His hair shifted like quicksilver, black bleeding to white. Just like his father's. Just like the dead man at his feet.

Those golden eyes—Ramses's eyes—narrowed to burning slits.

"When were you going to tell me?" Poison dripped from every word. "That I'm nothing but a bastard? That King Ramses isn't my father—he's my uncle?"

"Vrys," I whispered, his name a broken sob. "Vrys, I..."

But he just stared at me, his expression unreadable. He was Ramses through and through. That same cold, hard mask. That same biting anger.

I'd let Ramses shape him. Mold him. Servat might have given him life, but Ramses—that cruel, brilliant bastard—had given him everything else.

"I had the right to know."

"I know," I whispered, "I'm sorry, Vrys. I'm so sorry."

Those golden eyes burned into me, scorching away lies, leaving nothing but bitter truth. Then he turned—one sharp, violent movement—and stalked away, leaving me clutching the corpse of the man I loved.

Red hair suddenly surrounded me—a sea of flame. Chansie. Veren. Faces I knew from kitchens and fields and streets. Dozens of them. Hundreds. Each one armed with gleaming steel. Their eyes narrowed to predatory slits, knuckles white on knife hilts. A growl rippled through them—wolves closing in for the kill.

Darkness swallowed me whole, and all I could see were those red eyes, burning like hell itself.

"Treya, baby. What are ya doin'?" Joslynn's question drifted to me, a melodic whisper that cut through the haze of sleep. My eyes snapped open, and I bolted upright in bed.

My bed. My sanctuary.

Joslynn sat in the corner of the room, her deft fingers moving in a familiar rhythm over her needlework. Her dark, curly hair was pulled back into a neat braid, and a flowing burgundy nightgown cascaded down her form like a waterfall of crimson. Her eyes met mine, filled with warmth and a hint of amusement.

"Jos... Joslynn?"

An elegant eyebrow arched. "Ya. Dat be my name, girl. Why you sleepin' da day away?"

I launched myself out of bed, my movements so swift that I stumbled. I flung myself into her waiting arms, burying my face in the softness of her stomach. My arms wrapped around her, holding on for dear life.

"Joslynn!" Her name ripped from my throat, a raw sob. It felt so real. So achingly real. The world spun around me, and yet, in this moment, nothing else existed. I knew I was dreaming, that Joslynn was long gone, lost to the cruel hand of fate.

Yet, here she was. In all the endless years since her passing, I had never once dreamed of her. Never dared to hope.

"What on earth has gotten into ya, girl? You cryin' all da time?" Just a gentle chiding, her fingers beginning a soothing rhythm against my hair.

"I've missed you so much," I wept, "I-I miss you so much."

Joslynn's hands stilled, her touch a comforting weight. "Treya, I—"

"I know," I choked out, "I know. I just...miss you, Jos."

Silence fell over the room, a heavy blanket that smothered all else. The only sound was my ragged breathing, the quiet thump of my heart pounding in my ears. Logic screamed at me to pull away, to not indulge in this fantasy. But my heart, my treacherous heart, could not bring itself to let go.

After an eternity, Joslynn's fingers resumed their gentle stroking. "I missed ya too, baby girl," she whispered.

I sobbed harder, my fingers clutching at the delicate material of her nightgown. It held the scent of smoke and herbs, a familiar perfume that tugged at long buried memories. I burrowed deeper into her lap, desperate to be as close as humanly possible.

"Oh child. What's happened? Tell me. What happened to you?" she prodded gently, a call to lay bare my soul.

"I wish you were here," I whispered.

"I am here. I am here." I felt her arms wrap around me, a comforting band of steel and silk. A haven and a prison, all at once.

I don't know how long we sat there for. Long enough that my tears slowed to a stop, then dried on my cheeks. Long enough that my ragged breathing leveled out, and my clutching hands relaxed their desperate grip.

Finally, I sat up, wiping my ravaged face on my sleeve. Joslynn looked down at me, her eyes soft and filled with a deep, abiding love.

"Feelin' bedda, girl?"

I nodded, my lower lip trembling. "Yeah. Yeah, I'm good."

A warm smile spread across her face, her white teeth glinting. "Good. I ain't never wanna see ya cry, 'Treya.'"

"I-I did terrible things. Joslynn. I did such awful things," the tears threatened to return, hot and bitter in the back of my throat.

"Tell me what ya did, child."

I looked her in the eye, fully prepared to tell Joslynn all the things I had done. To see the disappointment wash over her face, to watch as the love in her eyes withered and died.

"I killed so many people. That night. I killed the Solaris Soldiers and our men. I didn't stop. And then Ramses put up the wall—"

"What wall?" Confusion knit her brows.

Of course. Dream Joslynn wouldn't know about the wall. Joslynn had died before the barrier had been erected, before our world had been shattered and remade.

"Ramses. He used Servat's gift. Servat created this shield around Ember, and Ramses perverted it. No one could get in or out. People started rebelling on the inside. Ramses sent some people for me to kill. I didn't want to. Not after all that had happened. I gave them coin. I told them to run. To hide. Ramses tracked them down. I had no choice. He would have-he would have tortured them. I had to kill them Jos. I had to do it."

"Shh. You are okay now. Everything is okay. Everything will be all right." A lullaby of forgiveness.

I collapsed against her, letting out a ragged sob. She held me close, her hands stroking my hair, her touch a comforting weight. I felt a sense of peace wash over me, a sense of forgiveness that I did not deserve.

"I'm so sorry, Joslynn," I whispered, muffled against her nightgown. "I'm so sorry for everything."

"Shh, child," she murmured, her breath tickling my ear. "You are forgiven. You have always been forgiven."

I pulled back, looking up at her in shock. "But...but how can you forgive me? After everything I've done?"

Joslynn's eyes were soft, filled with a deep love that I missed and craved. "Because I love you, 'Treya. And love forgives all."

CHAPTER 7

Ronan

The woman dropped like a stone into sleep, but peace didn't last for fucking long.

A moan slipped from her lips—and not the kind that would've made this hideout interesting. No, this was the start of another goddamn nightmare. When Servat's name whispered past her lips, I had to bite back a curse.

My muscles protested as I dragged myself away from the wall, eyes scanning our pathetic excuse for shelter. Sunlight pierced through the ratty blanket above like enemy arrows, but the makeshift roof was holding. For now.

Her face twisted, features contorting like she was being tortured. Fucking fantastic.

Last thing I needed was her screaming the place down again. These woods crawled with do-gooder humans and nosy Fae who'd come running to play hero. They'd burst in here with the sun at their backs, and then we'd all find out exactly how fast vampire flesh could burn.

Hard pass on that.

I pressed my fingers to her skin—cold, damp, like touching a corpse. Ironic, considering I was the dead one here.

"Wake up."

She flinched but stayed under, muttering "sorry" over and over like a broken prayer. Then the thrashing started, her body jerking like she was being electrocuted. My fangs dropped on instinct—a predator's response to wounded prey.

No. Fucking. Way.

When she finally settled, her stomach let out a growl that could wake the dead. I sneered, my own hunger clawing at my insides like a rabid beast.

Night needed to hurry up. I had to feed before I lost my mind. Every tiny sound she made—every sigh, every breath—had my predator instincts howling. One bite. Just one fucking bite. My fangs throbbed so bad I could barely think straight.

But I couldn't risk it. Not with her this close. The thought of sinking my teeth into that soft throat had venom flooding my mouth, the urge to rip and tear almost overwhelming.

That Daylight ring was the only thing standing between her and a messy death.

Just get her to Eldra. A few more weeks of this torture, then I could dump her off and forget she ever existed.

CHAPTER 8

Atreya

I surfaced from sleep like a drowning woman breaking water, hours before sunset. Just perfect. Stuck in this cottage with Ronan, who was doing his best impression of a pissed-off statue. His mood was darker than the shadows he was hiding in.

My stomach let loose another embarrassing growl. Ronan's head snapped toward me, those gold earrings catching what little light leaked through the shutters like tiny warning signals. At least he wasn't sporting any fresh burns.

"If I have to hear that monstrosity all night, I'll fucking gut myself," he hissed.

I rolled my eyes and turned my back to him.

I'd give anything to go back to sleep. Be with Joslynn again. I woke up with a sense of peace I hadn't felt in a long time. But, of course, it was short-lived. I still had the backdrop of my nightmare with Servat and Vrys.

Was Vrys okay? Was he safe?

Was Ramses keeping him safe? Or was he out scouting for me?

I sighed heavily, trying to push the thoughts from my mind. There was nothing I could do about it now. I had to focus on getting through the night with Ronan.

"What is your history with Eldra?" I asked carefully.

He looked at me with a blank expression. "None."

"You understand that Eldra and I have tried to kill each other? I get that you think he will be amendable to some sort of peace treaty. But I have seen what his soldiers can do."

Those Gold cloaks killed Joslynn.

"Well, you two just need to kiss and make up," he snarked.

"Isn't your master going to be looking for you?"

His eye twitched at the mention of Xaneth.

"Ramses would have hopefully taken care of that problem by now. I left enough evidence that this was all Xaneth's plan," he said.

"So you've been scheming this whole time?"

Ronan snorted. "Scheming implies a level of complexity. This was barely a plan. More like...improvising." He waved his hand dismissively, his pointed nose in the air.

I shook my head. "You know, you're not very good at this whole deception thing." I'm lying of course. This man was very good.

He shrugged. "I never claimed to be good at it. Just good enough. And I was right, wasn't I? You're here. Xaneth is most likely dead. Ramses is exposed."

"Yeah, well, let's not get ahead of ourselves. We still have to get through the night. And then there's Eldra." I still couldn't wrap my head around how Ronan thought this was a good idea.

But my thoughts go back to Joslynn's journal. Somehow she and Eldra were connected.

"What do you get out of this?" I asked.

He didn't move, didn't blink as he said, "Nothing."

I figured out his tell quickly. When he lies, he does his damnedest to be emotionless.

"Liar," I said.

He scoffed.

"You expect me to believe you would risk your neck by both my husband and Xaneth for the sake of a stranger you happened upon in a courtyard?"

His lips curled up at that. "I don't have a heart, nor none of the emotions that the Fae or even the humans have. If you are suggesting *guilt*, or *sympathy*... You'd be disappointed to know that I have neither."

I bit my bottom lip. "You said for me not to run from the truth."

"What?"

"In the courtyard when we met that night. You said for me to make you a promise. That I wouldn't run away from the truth. What is it?"

"You're skipping a few chapters ahead," he snorted.

"Tell me. Tell me what price my freedom has cost me."

"It cost you Servat," he snapped at me.

That did it. I jumped from the bed and slammed a bolt from my palm to the flimsy blanket hanging from the ceiling.

Ronan's eyes snapped to the bolt, his gaze fixed on the point where it had pierced the blanket. For a moment, we just stared at it.

The blanket billowed outwards, the dusty smell of it filling the air. Ronan cursed, leaping to his feet as the sunlight spilled in, bright and blinding. He lunged for the blanket, his fingers closing around the edge still in the shadows just as I reached for it.

We tugged on the blanket, our faces inches apart. For a moment, we just stared at each other, the only sound our heavy breathing and the rustle of the wool.

Then, in a move that surprised me, Ronan let go. My body flew backward, head snapping against the wall as I fell to the ground.

With a snort of disgust, he turned away. "You're impossible," he muttered, stalking across the room, using the darkest corners and shadows to avoid the setting sun. He wouldn't have to wait long for the sun to go down. He flung himself down on the remains of the bed, his back to me.

"Me?" I asked in disbelief. "Bring up Servat like that again, and I'll rip your intestines out," I seethed.

He didn't respond. Just lay there, his back a rigid line. I could see the tension in his shoulders, the tightness in his jaw. But he didn't turn around, didn't meet my gaze.

"What is the truth?" I whispered.

"The truth of the consequence of your freedom. Don't run from it. Don't run from Eldra. He will be your last hope."

I could feel my anger rising, a hot tide of frustration and fear. I wanted answers, not riddles. I wanted to know what I had really bargained for, what other price I would have to pay.

I've read where the wives of previous kings had been conquered and married to the new king.

Is that what I was walking into?

Ronan grunted. "I'll handle Eldra. You just worry about not getting yourself killed out here."

"Oh? You'll handle him?"

"You know what I mean," he says.

For a moment I heard Joslynn's clipped tone. *You know what I say.*

I couldn't help myself. I laughed. Ronan turned and narrowed his red eyes at me, and I laughed harder.

"What's so funny?" he snapped, flipping his silver hair over his shoulder with a scowl.

"Nothing," I chuckled. "You just reminded me of someone."

His scowl deepened. "Well, I'm glad I could amuse you."

I wiped tears from my eyes. "I'm sorry. It's just...you sounded like Joslynn. Her tone, the way she worded things."

"Who's Joslynn?"

My smile faltered. I hesitated. Was I really going to confide in Ronan? He was the last person I should be trusting. But there was something about the quiet way he asked that reached through me.

"Is she dead?"

"Yes," I admitted, "She died in the battle at the Hyperion Market years ago."

Ronan's expression softened ever so slightly. "I'm sorry," he said gruffly—like the words caused him physical pain to say.

I shrugged, trying to brush it off. "It's been a while. It still hurts, but...it's different now."

He looked so uncomfortable it was almost comical. His arms crossed over his chest, brows furrowed, mouth set in a thin line.

Bells tolled in the distance and both of us became still.

A roar of a dragon broke the silence.

CHAPTER 9

Ronan

My head snapped towards the sound, my dead heart pounding in my chest. The bells of Tor, tolling out a warning. It was a sound I hadn't heard in *years*, not since the War of the Fallen Skies. A sound that meant only one thing.

Dragons.

I leapt to my feet, my gaze going to the window that had been shuttered. The sun still hung in the sky, its light blinding. But even with the risk of burning, I had to see. I dashed to the window, my fingers closing around the sill as I hauled myself up and peered through the cracked shutters.

Pain lanced through my eye socket the instant I peeked through. Worth it. Because there, swooping over the broken bones of what used to be Tor, was a massive red dragon. Its scales caught the light like fresh-spilled blood, wings creating hurricanes as it descended.

Tor was nothing but a shadow of its former self. It had nothing worth taking. No Glory, no treasure—nothing that warranted a dragon raid.

Unless...

I whipped around to face Atreya. She'd gone ghost-white, those silver eyes of hers wide enough to swallow worlds. My hand slapped over my burning eye.

"What color?" The words barely made it past her lips.

"Red."

"Ramses." His name fell from her mouth like a death sentence. "Siorsen. Oh Gods—"

Siorsen roared again, the sound shaking the dust from the remainder of the ceiling.

I moved before thought kicked in, crossing the space between us in one stride. My hands locked around her arms, hauling her up like she weighed nothing. She didn't fight me—worse, she barely seemed to register I was touching her.

"What's happening?" Her voice came out hollow, eyes glazed like she'd already given up.

The scent of defeat rolled off her in waves, bitter as poison on my tongue. It made me want to shake her until her teeth rattled.

"Dragon's going to clean up the place," I snapped, not breaking stride. "We have to go, now."

She didn't respond, didn't even seem to hear me. But she didn't fight as I pulled her out of the cottage, into the fading light of day.

Immediately my skin ignited. The sun was just dipping below the tree-line. A few more moments and it would be safe for me.

But time wasn't on our side. The dragon was already torching buildings, and while I could survive a lot of things, dragon fire wasn't something I was eager to test.

Those damn bells wouldn't shut up, echoing off stone like a funeral dirge. The beast wheeled overhead, its shadow painting us in darkness. I forced myself to track it, even as my eye felt like it was being stabbed with molten iron.

Atreya whimpered as another roar sounded.

I gritted my teeth hard enough to crack them, keeping my gaze locked upward. The dragon banked around, and now I could see the rider—a dark silhouette of pure danger.

Ramses.

Damn him.

Where the fuck was Eldra with an army when you needed him?

The dragon wheeled around, its shadow stretching, and then dove down on the people of Tor. People screamed, running in all directions like startled ants. My skin sizzled, burning as the last light faded beyond the tree line.

I grabbed Atreya and bolted for the forest, putting as much distance between us and that fire-breathing bastard as possible. My flesh was literally falling off in chunks.

"Run faster," I demanded, my voice hoarse from the smoke.

"Ronan," she gasped. "I can't—"

"We're getting out of here if I have to carry your ass." My vision was going dark at the edges.

Needed blood. Now. I threw her over my shoulder like a sack of grain and launched us into the trees.

The trees swallowed us whole, branches weaving a dark canopy overhead that finally—*finally*—blocked out damned sun. My skin was knitting itself back together, but too damn slow. Every step felt like walking on broken glass, but I kept going, Atreya's weight nothing in my arms as I charged deeper into the shadows.

The screams from Tor faded behind us. Different sounds now—crashing, cursing, the thunder of boots through underbrush. Ember's soldiers, hot on our trail like the good little dogs they were.

Shit.

I caught the scent before I saw him—earth and green things, that particular Fae smell that always made my teeth itch. He moved like a ghost between the trees, silver armor catching what little light filtered down. My fangs dropped, throat burning with a need that had nothing to do with thirst and everything to do with survival.

I set Atreya down without a sound. She swayed like a drunk, eyes unfocused. No time to play nurse. I stalked forward, every muscle coiled tight.

The Fae never saw me coming.

My fangs punched through his throat like it was butter. Hot blood flooded my mouth, earthy and rich with magic. I drank deep, feeling his life force drain away while his power surged into me. Woodland Fae—connected to the green things. Perfect.

I reached out with his stolen magic, and the forest answered. Vines erupted from the ground, weaving around us. Leaves exploded from bare branches, creating a living fortress. The soldier crumbled to dust at my feet, and I grabbed Atreya's arm.

"Move," I growled, dragging her deeper into our green sanctuary.

The soldiers crashed past, close enough I could smell their sweat, see the dirt under their fingernails. But the magic held. They walked right by, blind to what was right under their noses.

When they were gone, I let out the breath I'd been holding. Atreya turned those silver eyes on me, and *Gods*—the fear in them made me want to—

"Your eyes," she whispered. "They're silver again."

Her heart was hammering against my chest, a trapped bird beating itself senseless. This wasn't the woman they whispered about in taverns, the one who could split the sky with a word. This was something else entirely.

Prey.

I could smell her terror, taste it on my tongue. Breaking her neck would be easy. Quick. Screw the Daylight ring.

But then she started shaking.

Something in my chest twisted.

Damn it all to hell.

"You're freezing," I muttered, shrugging out of my tunic and wrapping it around her shoulders. She didn't even blink, just kept staring at me with those huge, terrified eyes.

"He's going to find me."

I knew exactly who she meant. The Cruel King. I'd heard the stories—hell, I'd seen the evidence firsthand when Xaneth dragged me to Ember. That city was a gilded cage if I'd ever seen one, all gold spires and white marble hiding rot underneath.

Xaneth had bragged about the old ways, about how he'd get to "taste" the Furian Slayer. The sick bastard didn't just want her body—he wanted her power. As a Siphoner, he could drain every drop of magic from her, leaving nothing but an empty shell.

I couldn't let that happen. Not because I gave a damn about her, but because I needed that ring. That's what I told myself when I slipped the Adderdale poison into his wine.

She touched my face then, just a brush of fingers against my cheek. Such a small thing, but it sent electricity down my spine.

"We need to move," I said, scanning the forest. "Walk."

"But Siorsen—"

"Gone."

"But—"

"Is Ramses really what you're afraid of?"

She stood, magic crackling behind those silver eyes. "I'm not afraid of death."

And there it was—the predator beneath the prey. The monster wearing a pretty face.

"Some things are worse than death," I said.

Her eyes narrowed. "You would know."

I let my fangs show. "Damn right I would."

CHAPTER 10

Ronan

Her stomach growled like a caged beast. I bit back a sigh. At least she hadn't started complaining. Yet.

The stream gurgled nearby, the only sound breaking the heavy silence. My eyes swept the bank—rock to tree to shadow. Nothing. No soldiers lurking in the dark. I'd have caught their scent, heard the thunder of blood in their veins.

"Wait here," I whispered, already moving away.

Her grip on my arm tightened. "Don't leave me."

I met her eyes, saw the fear lurking in their depths. She was on the edge. "I have to," I whispered, "I'll be right back. I promise."

A promise. From me. Like I even remembered how to keep one of those anymore.

She nodded, but those fingers stayed locked on my arm. I had to peel them off one by one, like pulling thorns from flesh. "I *promise.*"

The trees opened up ahead, and there it was—a deer grazing in the clearing, head down, completely oblivious. My stomach clenched at the sight of that sleek coat, that strong neck. I dropped into a crouch, muscles coiling tight.

My fangs dropped, mouth flooding with need. Animal blood wasn't Fae or human, but it would do. I'd survived on worse.

I moved like lightning. The deer's head snapped up, eyes wide with terror, but too late. I slammed into it hard, pinning it down. My fangs punched through flesh, and hot blood exploded across my tongue.

I drank deep, feeling strength surge back into my dead veins. Drank until the deer went still, its life trickling away into nothing.

I pulled back, wiping my mouth with one hand. My thirst was quiet now, my hunger sated. Time to feed the girl.

Atreya was exactly where I'd left her, wound tight as a bowstring. Those silver eyes tracked my every move.

"Got one," I said, hefting my prize. She took it, fingers digging into the still-warm coat.

She went at it with her dagger, blade flashing silver in the moonlight. But her movements were all wrong, awkward and clumsy.

"You've never skinned anything in your life, have you?"

A blush crept up that pale neck. "No."

I took the blade from her hands. "Figures."

"I never needed to before."

"That's kind of my point."

My hands moved quick and sure, the blade sliding through hide like it was butter. Every now and then, I caught her mimicking my movements out of the corner of my eye.

I pretended not to notice.

"You make it look so easy," she murmured.

"It's not." I kept working, focused on the task. "Takes practice."

Finally, I handed her a strip of meat.

"Here. Eat."

Her fingers brushed mine as she took it. "Raw?"

I snatched the meat back, throwing the carcass over my shoulder. "*For f*—let's go."

"But—"

"We've wasted enough time. There's bound to be a tradesman nearby. We can trade this for real supplies."

She went quiet after that, falling into step beside me. I could feel her eyes on me, but I kept mine on the path ahead. "There's traders between here and Tifetown, through the mountains. Three days' walk to Tifetown. We'll find someone with supplies before then."

An hour dragged by, the moon climbing higher, casting silver light through the trees. The air had a bite to it now, and crickets chirped their midnight song. Atreya kept pace beside me, her eyes darting between the path and the dead weight over my shoulder.

"You sure about finding someone?" Her stomach growled again.

Maybe raw meat wasn't looking so bad now.

Building a fire wasn't an option. Too exposed. Might as well paint a target on our backs.

I nodded. "Traders work these routes. Villages need supplies."

"Ramses doesn't permit trade routes," she said.

"Oh. Wow. What will the people of Ferenz do? They absolutely won't break *any* laws Ramses pass." I rolled my eyes.

"And they'll want... that?" She jerked her chin toward the deer.

I shrugged. "Depends on what they have. Could be they need meat more than whatever trinkets they're hauling. They could have smoked meat already cooked for you. Fruit even."

Her stomach growled so loud that I winced.

The path twisted up into the mountains, shadows stretching like fingers across our path. Then I caught it—metal and sweat. Someone ahead.

My head snapped up, senses on high alert. Atreya noticed the change in me, her step faltering.

"What is it?" she whispered. "Is it Ramses?" Sparks of light sprang from her fingertips.

I held up a hand, signaling for quiet. I listened hard, trying to pinpoint the location. The scent grew stronger, and I could hear the faint clink of gear, the murmur of people—hopefully people.

I turned to Atreya. "Tradesmen," I said, adjusting the outer tunic I had given her to go over her head. "Up ahead. Stay behind me."

The path bent and there they were—three of them with loaded mules. Old guy in charge, two young muscle-heads flanking him. Armed like they were heading to war.

Had to be in these woods. Between the Boarux, thieves, and Hags? You'd be stupid not to be.

I stepped into view, the deer carcass held obvious in my hands. The tradesmen's attention turned to me, hands going to weapons.

"Hello," I said, trying to sound harmless. "Looking to trade."

The old man's gaze narrowed, flicking from me to Atreya behind. "What you got to offer?" he rasped. Human. He was human.

I hefted the deer. "Fresh meat. Looking for whatever supplies you can spare."

The old man eyed the deer, then me. "Already bled and skinned?" he asked.

"Yeah. My girl's hungry. Got anything worth trading?"

He grunted, giving Atreya another look. "What kind you after?"

"Food we can eat now. Fruit. Cheese. Dried meat. Bread if you've got it. Water too."

Old man scratched his chin. "Got dried meat. Apples. Cheese. All yours for the deer."

I hesitated. The deer was worth more than that. But Atreya's stomach growled again. I glanced at each of them, inhaling deeply. The strongest survive the woods. One was human—that I could smell. The other two were perhaps halflings.

I could kill all three of them, take what I want, and keep the deer. But my luck, they would have taken Nettleshade. Nettleshade serves as a natural protection against vampires. If a person has Nettleshade on them or has ingested it, a vampire cannot compel them or enter their home uninvited. Nettleshade also burns and weakens vampires upon contact.

Which is why I was keeping my distance. My only saving grace was that it's an incredibly rare plant.

But Atreya stepped in front of me, her hand extended. "Deal," she said.

The old man's eyes flicked to her, then back to me. He seemed to sense something, his gaze narrowing. But he just grunted, spitting to the side. He flashed browning teeth at her. "Fine. Girlie, bring the meat."

I hesitated, unsure. But Atreya was already taking the deer from me, her arms wrapping around it. She moved to the tradesmen, her movements stiff.

The old man took the deer, eyeing it. "Nice piece of work," he said. "You hunt it?"

I nodded. "Aye."

He grunted again, handing over a satchel. "This is all I got. You're welcome to it."

I took the satchel, peeking inside. Dried meat, a few apples, a wheel of cheese. A waterskin. It would do.

"Thanks," I said, tucking the satchel onto my shoulder. "Obliged."

"This meat is good, very well bled. Too good..."

The old man trailed off, his gaze fixed on me. I met his eyes, a growl rising in my throat. Something in his expression made my hackles rise.

"You're not..." He let the sentence hang, his gaze flicking to Atreya. "What are you?" he finished.

I went still, my heart sinking. I'd let my guard down, and now these men saw me for what I was. I could smell the fear rising off them, sharp and acrid.

The old man took a step back, his hand on the hilt of his sword. "You're one of them," he rasped. "A bloodsucker."

I didn't bother denying it. "Yes," I said, flatly. "I am."

The old man spat to the side. "Figures. You were too bleedin' handsome. Well, we can't let you just walk away."

I let out a sigh, rolling my eyes. "Must we do this?"

The old man's attention flicked to the satchel still clutched in my hand. "You want gold, boy? I got it. But I want something in return."

That surprised me. "What could you possibly want that *I* have?"

The old man's eyes glinted in the moonlight. "A vial of your blood. A vial, boy. That's all I ask."

"Why do they want that?" Atreya whispered behind me.

"Lady, vampire blood can do many things when consumed. Heal, give you strength, among other things," the old man nudged one of the men next to him and they shared in on the joke.

The other man spoke up with a chuckle, "Why not just kill him? You would have all the blood you needed then."

The old man scoffed. "Dead blood is useless. It loses its potency and healing properties when the body is dead."

Atreya inhaled sharply. I could feel that pull of static in her body.

I wish I could compel all three of them. But compelling required time and energy. Things I didn't have at the moment. And again, they could have Nettleshade.

"Fine," I said, a slow smile spreading across my face. "A vial of blood...for everything you have."

The old man's eyebrows shot up. "You drive a hard bargain, vampire."

I shrugged. "I'm not looking to die tonight. Are you?"

He grunted, seeming to consider. Then he nodded. "Deal," he rasped.

The old man rummaged through a pack, producing a vial. He held it out, his tongue flicking out. "A vial of blood, and you get everything. Food, water, gold...we'll even throw in a few trinkets."

I hesitated, but Atreya's stomach growled again, loud in the silence. And I could smell the fear rising off the tradesmen, sharp and coating my tongue. They wouldn't know how to kill a vampire, likely as not. They were bluffing. The old man might though.

"Fine," I repeated, rolling up my sleeve. I held out my arm, exposing my wrist. The old man's eyes fixed on it, gleaming with a hungry light. He took the vial, his movements quick and practiced. He tied a length of leather around my upper arm, the pressure making my hand tingle. Then he slid the point of a dagger into my vein.

I hissed, pain burning through my arm. But it was a clean wound, and I could feel my body already healing. The old man held the vial under the flow of blood, his face intent. It filled slowly, my blood gleaming red in the moonlight.

He pulled back, corking the vial with trembling fingers. "Vampire blood," he breathed. "Worth a king's ransom."

I flexed my wrist, feeling the skin knit back together. I rolled my sleeve down, covering the wound. "You have what you want," I said. "Now give us what's ours."

The old man grunted, handing over a larger satchel. "Food, water, gold...even threw in a few trinkets like I said."

I took it, peeking inside. More food than before, a few gold coins clinking at the bottom, leathers, some furs...and a small pouch of powder. I raised an eyebrow, looking at the old man. "What's this?"

The old man's gaze flicked away. "A little something extra," he rasped. "Healng powder. It speeds up the process."

I snorted. "You think I need that?"

The old man shrugged. "Thought it might come in handy. You seem the type to get hurt a lot."

I rolled my eyes, tucking the pouch away. "Thanks for your concern."

The old man just grunted, turning away. "Well, we're done here. Unless you want to buy something else?"

I glanced at Atreya, seeing the hunger still in her eyes. But we had what we needed. "No," I said. "We're good."

The old man nodded, clapping me on the back. "Well, safe travels then. May the road rise up to meet you."

I forced a smile, clapping him back. "And may your own road be smooth and level."

He just grunted, turning away. The tradesmen packed up what little remained, then continued on their way. We watched them go, then I turned to Atreya. "Well, that was fun."

She just stared at me, her eyes wide. "You just...let him take your blood."

I shrugged. "It was a fair trade."

"He said it was worth a fortune," she whispered.

"Would you rather we kill them?" I asked, turning my body toward their direction.

"No! Gods why do you always have to be so...so...diabolical," she snapped at me.

I curled my lip at her. "I didn't have anything else to give him. It was the only way to get you what you needed."

She was quietly chewing on her lip now, her arms crossed. After a moment, she asked, "How much further until you want to set up camp?"

"We need to find a cave at the very least," I said, scanning the mountainside.

I spotted a dark shape in the distance, partially hidden by trees. "There," I said, already heading towards it. "That cave should do for the night."

Atreya followed, her silence heavy with unspoken questions. I could feel her gaze on me, but I kept mine fixed on the cave. It was small, but it would provide some shelter from the elements. And any potential threats.

I ducked inside, my eyes adjusting to the dim light that filtered through the entrance. It wasn't that deep, and I would need to cover the entrance come sunrise.

The air was stale and filled with the scent of damp earth and mold. I moved to the side, making room for Atreya. She hesitated, then joined me, carefully moving around me.

I pulled the satchel forward, rummaging through it. "Here," I said, handing her a piece of dried meat and an apple. "Eat."

She took it, her fingers brushing mine. I could feel a spark of static at the touch, but I ignored it, passed her the waterskin. She drank like she'd found water in hell.

"You should rest," I said, leaning back against the cave wall. "We have a long journey ahead of us."

Atreya nodded, but she didn't move. She sat there, staring at me with an unreadable expression. I could feel her gaze like a touch, making my skin prickle.

I moved to the side, my hands already untying the furs from my pack. I shook them out, spreading them on the ground. "Here," I said, already turning away. "You can rest."

Atreya inhaled sharply, her gaze flicking from the furs to me. But then she moved, sinking down onto the makeshift bed. I could hear her sigh, feel the tension in her body begin to ease.

I didn't look, already moving to the entrance. I had to secure this place, make sure we were safe. I scanned the area, opening my mouth and clicking rapidly. Like a vampire bat, I used the clicks to locate things, to build a mental map of my surroundings. It was a power that came with being what I was, and it was one I relied on heavily.

But there was nothing, just the quiet of the mountains.

I moved back inside, my gaze finding Atreya. She was already curled up, her eyes closed. I could see the rise and fall of her chest, hear the soft sound of her breathing. She was asleep, finally.

I moved to sit beside her, my back against the cold stone wall. I could feel the weight of my gaze on her, but I didn't look away.

I reached out, my fingers brushing a strand of hair from her face. She didn't stir, didn't even flinch. I pulled my hand back as if I had burnt myself.

I let out a quiet gasp, then raised my palm to the entrance of the cave. I felt the surge of magic I had stolen from the Greenfolk Fae, and then plants and brambles began to grow, pushing their way through the entrance and filling it.

I sat there for a bit longer, watching quietly as a vine twirled around my finger. The vine slowly grew berries.

I could have grown her food this whole time.

CHAPTER 11

Ronan

I watched her sleep, my head a mess of things I couldn't sort out. This wasn't my territory—caring for someone else. Being *needed*. I'd spent my whole existence alone, surviving on instinct and selfishness.

Now? Now I caught myself counting the times she ate. Tracking her moods. Listening to her breathing change while she slept.

The nightmares had backed off lately. She woke up different—lighter, almost peaceful. That smile of hers, small and real, like sunrise after endless dark.

Sometimes I wanted to tell her why.

Tell her how I sat here night after night, slipping into her mind like a thief. Reshaping her dreams. Making them softer. Safer.

I was the reason she slept through the night now. The reason she could face Servat without breaking apart.

Part of me itched to confess. To watch that sunrise smile shatter into pieces.

Maybe she'd thank me.

Maybe she'd put a blade through my heart.

Both options had their appeal.

Night after night of being the good guy, of crafting pleasant dreams just to see her smile—it was starting to wear thin. She walked around with that holier-than-thou attitude, nose in the air like she was better than the rest of us.

Maybe it was time for a little fun.

I slipped into her mind like silk through water, finding those hidden corners she kept locked away. Everyone had secrets. Everyone had desires they wouldn't admit to themselves.

I found hers.

CHAPTER 12

Atreya

C orina materialized before me like a ghost stepping through the veil between worlds. The edges of her form wavered and distorted as though reality itself couldn't quite contain her presence, while the floor-length mirror behind her stretched and warped until its surface rippled like disturbed water in a midnight pool. She peeled off her leathers with slow movements, her body moving with a fluidity that made my breath catch in my throat. All the while her skin emanated an otherworldly glow that pulsed in time with my heartbeat. The room around us existed in a state of perpetual flux, its walls bleeding into floors that seemed to shift and change every time I tried to focus on them.

"Corina, I'm standing right here," I coughed, my voice echoing oddly in the space that seemed both vast and intimate at once.

She turned toward me with a predator's grace, her smile spreading across her face like blood seeping through white silk, dangerous and beautiful all at once.

"I know you are," she purred. Her finger traced my jawline with a touch that burned like hellfire and froze like ice.

The memories of how I'd arrived in this place slipped through my fingers like water through a sieve, disappearing into the ether every time I reached for them with desperate mental fingers. Corina had always been nothing more than my husband's irritating cousin—a constant thorn in my side who'd somehow become my reluctant confidante—but in this moment, she was something else entirely, something ancient and powerful that made my skin prickle with awareness and my blood sing with possibilities.

I had never dared to contemplate this.

Never. Not once.

"Corina," I began, but she silenced me with a gesture that brooked no argument.

"Shh," she whispered, pressing one perfectly manicured finger against my lips while her eyes burned through me. "Just feel everything I'm about to do to you."

Her lips were soft and warm, and they moved against mine with a confidence that left me breathless. I felt a rush of desire flood through me, my heart pounding in my chest.

My hands found her hips instinctively, muscle memory from countless encounters with men guiding my movements as I pulled her closer, while she rewarded me with a moan that vibrated through my entire body like a struck tuning fork. When her tongue teased at my lips, I opened for her without hesitation, exploring her mouth with a desperate hunger that surprised even me.

Corina's hands were everywhere, tracing patterns on my skin that left me shivering. She broke away from the kiss, her eyes locked on mine as she worked at my clothes. I helped her, shedding my layers until I stood before her as bare as she was.

The appreciation in her gaze as she devoured me with her eyes made me flush with equal parts embarrassment and arousal, but there wasn't a hint of judgment in her expression—only pure, unfiltered want that gave me the courage to look back at her with the same intensity.

I had never appreciated the female form like this before—all soft curves and smooth planes where I was used to hard angles and rough calluses—and the difference was intoxicating.

"Corina," I whispered, "I want you."

Alarm bells rang in my head. Why had I said that?

She smiled, her eyes sparkling with mischief. "I want you too," she said, barely above a whisper. And with that, she reached out and took my hand, leading me to the bed.

A bed?

Corina was gentle, and I mirrored her actions, my fingers dancing across her body as I marveled at the softness of her skin.

She let out a soft moan as I brushed against her nipple, and I felt a surge of desire at the sound. I leaned in, my mouth finding hers in a kiss that was both familiar and yet completely new.

She flipped me over onto my back, her body covering mine as she roamed her hand between my legs.

I arched into her hand, my breath coming in ragged gasps as she explored me with a gentleness I wasn't used to.

"The Queen is so wet," she chuckled, sinking her fingers in me. She removed her fingers and showed them to me, glistening and sticky.

I blushed at her words, but there was no shame in her gaze.

I reached down, my hand finding hers and guiding it back to where I ached for her touch.

She obliged, her fingers sinking into me once more. This time, there was no gentleness. Only a fierce hunger that matched my own. I arched into her touch, my body bowing off the bed as pleasure washed over me.

I moaned, my hands finding her hair and pulling her down into a kiss. I poured all my desire into that kiss, my tongue tangling with hers as I sought to get closer to her.

She groaned into my mouth, her fingers moving faster within me. I could feel my orgasm building, squelching noises filled the room as she violently crooked her fingers inside me.

When she crooked her fingers just right, hitting that spot that made the world fracture around the edges, my vision went white—

"Corina!" The name tore from my throat as I jolted awake in the cave's oppressive darkness, the fae light casting accusatory shadows on the stone walls. Sweat painted my skin like a guilty confession while my heart tried to punch through my ribs.

Ronan sat nearby, one eyebrow raised in that infuriating way of his, his hand resting on my ankle like a brand. "Was about to wake you," he drawled knowingly. "You were making quite the interesting sounds."

"Nightmare," I lied through my teeth, shame and lingering arousal warring for dominance in my blood. The cave mouth had been woven shut with vines and vegetation, trapping me here with my humiliation and a Vampire who could undoubtedly scent the truth rolling off me in waves.

I scrambled to my feet, trying to play it off despite the embarrassment burning in my cheeks. "Yeah, just a bad dream," I muttered, avoiding Ronan's gaze.

But I could feel his eyes on me, boring into my skin. He knew I was lying. I could smell the arousal clinging to me, heavy and musky. There was no way he couldn't scent it too.

I took a step back, trying to put some distance between us. But my foot caught on a rock and I stumbled, almost falling. Ronan was there in an instant, his hands catching my elbows and steadying me.

His touch sent a jolt of desire through me, and I felt my face heat even more. I tried to pull away, but he held tight.

"Are you okay?" he asked. His red eyes searched mine, and for a moment, I felt like he could see right through me.

I swallowed hard, trying to find my words. "Yeah, I'm fine," I lied again.

"You can tell me, you know," he said. "There's nothing to be embarrassed about."

"I'm going back to sleep," I snapped.

I reached the far wall of the cave and slid down to the ground, my back against the cold stone. I wrapped my arms around my knees and buried my face in my lap, trying to catch my breath.

The dream had felt so real. Corina's hands on my skin, her lips on mine. It had been like she was really there, like I could still feel her touch even after I woke up.

I groaned, running a hand over my face. Why did I have to have a dream like that now, when things were already so tense between us? And why did it have to feel so good?

I had never thought of Corina that way, nor ever desired her. It was the stupid conversation I had with Ronan that caused this.

I heard Ronan shift somewhere in the darkness, the soft rustle of fabric making me tense. My body was still thrumming with leftover energy from the dream, every nerve ending alive and aware.

CHAPTER 13

Ronan

The cave reeked of desire and shame—a heady cocktail that made my fangs ache. I'd had my fun playing in her dreams, but now I was paying the price, trapped in this stone prison with the evidence of my mischief hanging thick in the air between us. Her silhouette was a dark promise against the cave wall, barely visible in the weak fae light. She thought she was hiding it well—the racing pulse, the lingering arousal from the dreams I'd woven like poison through her mind. I savored her discomfort like aged wine, each wave of shame rolling off her sweeter than the last.

It had started innocently enough—well, as innocent as anything I do. Slipping into her dreams was child's play, my consciousness sliding through the cracks in her mental defenses like smoke through keyholes. I'd been curious what secrets the almighty Queen kept locked behind that pristine mask of authority. Turned out Her Majesty's mind was a treasure trove of deliciously dark desires.

The real art wasn't in watching her fantasies unfold—it was in reshaping them, each subtle manipulation like a brushstroke on canvas. The way her subconscious latched onto my suggestions, spinning them into elaborate scenes of pleasure and surrender... I barely had to guide her toward thoughts of Corina. That particular desire had been buried deep, waiting for someone like me to excavate it. Not even Corina particularly. That was just the face her dream had given her.

Dreamwalking is both gift and curse, but tonight it felt like pure torture. I hadn't meant to linger in her dreams—that's a lie, of course. What I mean is, I hadn't planned to stay quite so long, to weave quite such elaborate fantasies. But her mind called to me like a siren's song, and before I knew it, I was crafting scenes that now had her pressing herself against the cave wall like she could somehow disappear into the stone.

The thing about dreamwalking is that it's addictive. Once you've tasted someone's deepest desires, their hidden thoughts, it's hard to stay away. And Queen Atreya's mind was particularly... fascinating. I watched her rigid posture, satisfaction curling through my chest like smoke. She'd have to sleep eventually, and when she did... well. The night was young, and I had so many more dreams to share.

Truth is, I only started messing with her dreams because her nightmares were getting on my last nerve. Night after night, watching her thrash and moan, reliving Servat's death like some twisted infinite reel.

Annoying as hell.

"You should try to sleep," I said, not bothering to hide my amusement. "Long day of avoiding me tomorrow."

She made this little sound in the back of her throat—half growl, half something else entirely. If she only knew how long I'd been pulling her strings, playing puppet master with that pristine royal mind of hers. The real Queen Atreya would never dare let herself feel half the things I'd shown her. But in dreams? Baby girl was a whole different creature.

"Stop staring at me," she snapped, finally breaking the tense silence.

I didn't bother hiding my smirk in the darkness. "I'm not staring. I can barely see you."

"Liar," she muttered. "You can see perfectly well in the dark."

She wasn't wrong. Every flush creeping up her neck, every restless twist of her fingers against her shirt hem, every shiver she tried to suppress.

The dream still had its claws in her—and she was fighting it like her life depended on it. Spoiler alert: she was losing.

The power was intoxicating. Here was the mighty Queen, reduced to a flustered mess by dreams I had crafted. Each time she closed her eyes, I could slip back in, spin new fantasies, push her boundaries further. The possibilities were endless, and I intended to explore every single one.

After all, what was the point of having such a gift if you didn't use it to its full potential? And if my entertainment came at the cost of her composure... well, that was just a bonus.

"Want to talk about it?" I offered, sweet as poison. "Your dream, I mean. Might help to get it off your chest—"

"No!" The word exploded off the cave walls. She wrapped those royal arms around herself like armor. Like that could keep me out.

I let my voice drop low, honeyed with false concern. "Sounded intense. All that moaning in your sleep."

Her head snapped up so fast I heard her neck crack. Horror bloomed in those wide eyes. "What did you say?"

"Oh, nothing." I studied my nails, casual as you please. "Just noting your... sleep talking habits, Your Majesty."

The lie tasted sweeter than blood. Truth was, she hadn't made a sound—at least not where anyone could hear. But I'd been there, orchestrating every gasp, every whispered plea. Watching the blood drain from her face? Worth every second.

"You're lying." Her voice shook. Just a tremor, but it was there.

Perfect.

"Am I?" I let the question hang there like a noose. "You seemed pretty focused on someone specific. Corina, wasn't it?"

The way her breath caught was like music. Of course, I knew exactly how many times that name had fallen from her dream-lips—I'd written the whole damn script. But letting her think she'd betrayed herself? That was the real art.

"You don't know anything," she spat, but the fear in her scent sang a different tune.

I rose like smoke, stalking toward her corner of our little cave prison. She tried to melt into the wall, but her thundering heart gave her away. Fear, yes—but something darker too, something that made the air thick with possibility.

"Don't," she warned, but there was no steel in it.

"Don't what, Your Majesty?" I stopped just shy of touching her, close enough to feel the heat rolling off her skin. "Don't mention how your voice breaks when you say her name? Don't talk about those desperate little reaches for someone who isn't there?"

A sound caught in her throat, half-plea, half-protest. "Stop."

"But you didn't want to stop in your dream, did you?" I breathed the words against her ear. "In fact, you begged for—"

Her hand connected with my cheek before I could finish the sentence. The slap echoed through the cave, sharp and sudden. I caught her wrist before she could pull away, my grip firm but not painful. Not yet.

"Careful, love," I purred, running my thumb across her racing pulse. "All that pent up frustration isn't good for you."

Her pulse jumped beneath my thumb—a hummingbird trapped in a cage of bone and flesh. I could feel the heat radiating from her skin, smell the mix of anger and arousal that clouded the air between us.

"Let. Go." Each word was clipped, precise, every inch the queen she pretended to be. But I could hear the tremor underneath, the way her breath caught when I stepped closer.

"Make me," I whispered, letting my fangs graze her ear. She shuddered—not entirely in fear. "Your body betrays you, Your Majesty. Just like in your dreams."

"You know nothing about my dreams." But there was uncertainty there now, a crack in her armor.

I laughed softly, the sound low and dark in the confined space of the cave. "Don't I? Shall I describe them to you? How you arched into phantom touches, how you begged for—"

"Enough!" She tried to wrench away, but I held fast, spinning her until her back hit the cave wall. My other hand came up to cage her in, and I could see the rapid rise and fall of her chest, the way her pupils dilated in the darkness.

"It's fascinating, really," I continued, as if she hadn't spoken. "How the mighty Queen Atreya dreams of submission. Of surrender." I traced one finger along her jawline, feeling her tremble. "Of being taken apart piece by piece by someone who knows exactly what she needs."

"Fuck you," she hissed, turning her back to me and lying down.

I watched her rigid back, amused by her attempt to ignore me. The cave fell silent except for her uneven breathing and the distant drip of water from somewhere in the darkness. She was trying so hard to pretend she was asleep, but her body betrayed her—every muscle coiled tight as a bowstring.

"Sweet dreams," I murmured, just to watch her shoulders tense further.

The temptation to slip back into her mind was almost overwhelming. It would be so easy—she was exhausted, fighting sleep even now. One little push and I could be back there, weaving new fantasies, watching her come undone all over again. But that would be too easy, wouldn't it? No, the real game was here in the waking world, watching her struggle with the aftermath.

I settled back against the opposite wall, content to wait. She'd have to sleep eventually, and when she did... well. The night was still young, and I had so many more dreams to share.

Hours passed in tense silence. Her breathing gradually evened out despite her best efforts, and I watched with predatory patience as sleep finally claimed her. The moment her consciousness began to drift, I felt the familiar pull of her mind—stronger now, like a beacon in the dark. Her dreams called to me, sweet and tempting as blood.

But this time, I held back. Let her mind wander on its own, let her wonder if I was there, manipulating her thoughts. The uncertainty would drive her mad, and that was a different kind of power altogether.

Besides, I didn't need to enter her dreams to know what she was seeing. The way she shifted restlessly, the small sounds catching in her throat—her mind was doing my work for me now, replaying the scenes I'd planted there like seeds. They'd taken root, and now they were blooming all on their own.

"Ronan," she whispered in her sleep, and I smiled in the darkness.

Some dreams, after all, had a way of lingering long after the dreamer woke.

My name on her lips was the last straw. I couldn't resist.

"Having pleasant dreams?" I called out, loud enough to startle her awake.

She jolted upright, hair wild, eyes blazing in the darkness. "You—you're doing this to me. What are you doing to me?"

I held up my hands in mock surrender. "I've been sitting here the whole time, watching you writhe and moan. Though I must say, I'm flattered you were dreaming of me this time."

"I wasn't—" She cut herself off, running a hand through her tangled hair. "You're insufferable."

"And you're a terrible liar." I stretched languidly, making sure she caught the movement. "Tell me, Your Majesty, do all your subjects feature in your midnight fantasies, or am I special?"

She grabbed a small stone from the cave floor and hurled it at me. I caught it easily, rolling it between my fingers.

"Careful now," I chided. "Violence doesn't become you. Though after what I saw in your dreams earlier, perhaps I'm wrong about that."

"You have no right," she snarled, pushing herself to her feet. "No right to invade my mind, to—to plant these thoughts—"

"Plant them?" I laughed, "Oh, darling, I merely uncovered what was already there. Buried deep, perhaps, but very much yours."

She stalked toward me, every inch the predator she pretended not to be. "You think you know me so well, don't you? Think you can just walk through my thoughts like they're your personal game?"

"They're far more entertaining than any game I've ever seen." I rose to meet her, refusing to be intimidated. "And yes, I do know you. Better than anyone ever has, I'd wager. Better than you know yourself."

"You know nothing," she spat, but she was close now, too close. Close enough that I could see the pulse jumping in her throat, smell the lingering traces of arousal mixed with her anger.

"I know how you taste," I murmured, watching her eyes widen. "In your dreams, at least. I know the sounds you make when you're desperate. I know exactly how many times you've imagined my fangs against your throat."

A lie of course.

Her hand shot out to slap me again, but this time I was ready. I caught both her wrists, spinning us until she was pressed against the cave wall, my body caging her in.

"Always so violent," I tsked. "Is this how queens typically behave? Or is it just you?"

"Let go of me," she demanded. How cute.

"Make me," I echoed her earlier challenge. "You're stronger than me, remember? You could break free if you really wanted to."

She didn't move, her chest heaving against mine with each ragged breath. The air between us crackled with tension, thick enough to cut.

"I hate you," she whispered, but there was no conviction in it.

I leaned in close, letting my lips brush her ear. "No, you don't. That's what terrifies you, isn't it? Not the dreams, not even what I've seen in your mind. What terrifies you is how much you want it to be real."

She shoved me back with enough force to make me stumble. This time, I let her break free.

"You arrogant, insufferable, piece of—" She raked her hands through her hair, practically vibrating with rage. "You think because you can walk through dreams, you understand everything? You understand nothing!"

"Oh?" I couldn't help but goad her further. "Then explain why your heart's still racing."

"Because I want to kill you!" She whirled around, snatching up her cloak from the ground. "Every time you open your mouth, I imagine new ways to make you suffer."

I clicked my tongue. "Now that's not very queenly behavior."

"Fuck being queenly!" she shouted. "And fuck you, Ronan. Keep playing your little mind games. Keep thinking you're so clever, so in control." She yanked the cloak around her shoulders, movements sharp and jerky. "But remember this—I've killed better men than you for far less."

"Where are you going?" I asked, watching her storm toward the cave entrance. She slashed at the vines and greenery. "It's almost light out."

"Anywhere that isn't here with you." She paused at the threshold, silhouetted against the night sky. "And if you even think about following me or slipping into my mind again, I'll rip out your throat with my bare hands."

"Such violent fantasies," I called after her. "Sure you don't want to explore those in your dreams?"

Her response was a string of curses in at least three different languages, each more creative than the last. The sound of her boots crunching on gravel faded into the darkness, leaving me alone with the echo of her words and the lingering scent of her fury.

I smiled into the empty cave. She'd be back—she had to come back. But for now, let her rage at the stars. Let her try to convince herself that her anger was purely about invasion of privacy, about control.

We both knew better.

CHAPTER 14

Atreya

I stormed through the forest, branches whipping against my face as I pushed deeper. My blood was still boiling, electricity crackling beneath my skin with each furious step. Who did he think he was? Manipulating my dreams, acting like he knew me, like he had any right to—

"I don't need him," I snarled to the night air. "I can find Eldra myself. I'm the Queen of Ember. I don't need some arrogant, insufferable vampire playing games with my mind."

Dawn was approaching. Thank Gods. The forest seemed to pulse around me, shadows dancing in my peripheral vision. I welcomed the darkness, let it fuel my rage. Lightning sparked between my fingers, illuminating my path in brief, violent flashes.

"Should've fried him where he stood," I muttered, shoving through a thick patch of undergrowth. "Should've—"

A twig snapped behind me.

I spun, electricity already gathering in my palms, casting an eerie blue glow across the clearing. Three men emerged from the shadows, their grins gleaming dully in the darkness. Bandits. Because of course this night couldn't get any worse.

"Well, well," the largest one drawled, unsheathing a rusted blade. "What's a pretty thing like you doing out here all alone?"

I laughed, the sound sharp and bitter. "I am not in the mood for this."

"Hear that, boys?" He nudged his companions. "She's not in the mood."

They spread out, trying to circle me. Amateur move. They hadn't noticed the way the air was charging around us, how the leaves had stopped rustling, how every hair on their arms was starting to stand on end.

"Last chance," I warned, feeling the familiar surge of power building in my chest. "Walk away."

The first man lunged forward, blade swinging in a vicious arc toward my throat. I dropped into a crouch, feeling the wind of the blade passing over my head. As I rose, I drove my elbow into his solar plexus, channeling a spark of electricity through the point of contact. He stumbled back with a grunt, his muscles spasming from the shock.

His companion came at me from the left, wielding a crude club. I pivoted, letting his momentum carry him past me, but his weapon caught the edge of my cloak. The fabric yanked at my throat, nearly throwing me off balance. I rolled with the pull, using it to fuel my spin as I released a concentrated bolt of lightning from my fingertips. It speared through the first man's chest in a brilliant flash of blue-white light, the crack of thunder drowning out his final gasp.

The other two froze, finally registering what they were dealing with. Too late.

"Witch!" one of them spat, fumbling for a weapon.

The club-wielder recovered first, charging at me with a roar. I side-stepped, but my foot caught on a root, sending me stumbling. He seized the opportunity, his club connecting with my shoulder. Pain exploded through my arm, but the hit only fed my rage. Lightning coursed down my injured limb, leaping from my fingers to the club. The wooden weapon exploded in his hands, sending splinters flying.

"Wrong." I raised both hands, ignoring the throbbing in my shoulder, feeling the storm building inside me, demanding release.

The last bandit tried to flee, but I wasn't about to let him spread word of my location. Lightning split the night sky, channeling through my body and into the earth. It forked between the remaining bandits, striking them with enough force to lift them off their feet. The smell of ozone and charred flesh filled the air as their bodies hit the ground, smoke curling from their clothes.

I stood in the aftermath, breathing hard, watching the residual electricity dance across my skin. My shoulder ached where the club had struck, and I could feel a warm trickle of blood where a splinter had caught my cheek. The rage was still there, but it had shifted, become something colder, more focused.

"I don't need anyone," I whispered to the corpses at my feet. "Especially not him."

But even as I turned to continue my journey alone, a small voice in the back of my mind whispered that I was lying to myself. Just like he'd said. And with it being morning now, I would be stuck in that cave with him all day.

I hated that he was right.

I turned around to see Ronan standing there, panting, skin burning and flaking off. He looked worried, his flesh visibly sizzling in the morning light.

"What the hell are you doing outside?" I demanded. "It's daylight!"

He snarled, patches of his skin crackling and peeling away. "I saw lightning and I—" He cut himself off, jaw clenching against obvious pain. "Thought you might be in trouble."

"Get back to the cave, you idiot!" I grabbed his arm, trying to pull him toward the shelter. His skin was hot to the touch, blistering under the morning sun.

"I'm fine," he growled, but his legs buckled beneath him. I caught him before he hit the ground, ignoring the way his burning flesh seared my palms.

"Fine? You're literally disintegrating." I dragged him toward the cave entrance, his weight growing heavier with each step. "What kind of vampire runs into daylight?"

He laughed weakly against my shoulder. "The kind that heard you fighting and thought—" He broke off with a hiss of pain as another patch of skin blackened and peeled away.

"Thought what?" I snapped, finally hauling him into the blessed darkness of the cave. "That I couldn't handle myself? That I needed saving?"

He slumped against the cave wall, his usually perfect features a mess of burns and blisters. "That I couldn't bear to hear you die."

The words hung between us, heavy with implications neither of us was ready to face. I busied myself tearing strips from my cloak, trying to ignore how my hands shook.

"Well, as you can see," I said, gesturing to the scorched clearing outside, "I'm perfectly capable of handling a few bandits."

"I know." He was quiet, almost reverent. "I saw what you did. It was... magnificent."

I looked up from bandaging his burns to find his eyes fixed on me with an intensity that made my breath catch. Even half-burned, he managed to look devastatingly beautiful.

"Yes, well." I cleared my throat, focusing on wrapping another strip of cloth around his arm. "Next time trust that I can handle myself, okay?"

His hand caught mine as I finished the bandage, his touch gentler than I expected. "I didn't think," he admitted. "I just... reacted."

"Clearly." I tried to pull away, but his fingers tightened slightly.

"Atreya." The way he said my name made something in my chest twist. "About earlier. About the dreams."

I stilled, my pulse picking up speed. "Don't."

"No, let me finish." He shifted, wincing at the movement. "I crossed a line. Several lines. I won't do it again."

I stared at him, searching for any sign of deception. "Why should I believe you?"

He chuckled. "I mean it. But smart of you to be suspicious."

"Suspicious is my default state around you," I said, but there was less bite in my words than before. It was hard to maintain that level of anger when he was sitting there, half-burned because of his idiotic attempt to help me. "And you still haven't explained why I should trust you'll stay out of my dreams."

He leaned his head back against the cave wall, a slight smirk playing at his blistered lips. "Because, Your Majesty, reality has proven far more interesting than any dream I could craft."

I rolled my eyes, but felt heat creep up my neck. "You're deflecting."

"Am I?" His fingers were still wrapped around my wrist, his thumb tracing lazy circles against my pulse point. Even injured, he managed to make the simple touch feel dangerous. "Or maybe I'm realizing that watching you unleash lightning on those bandits was more exhilarating than any fantasy I could weave."

"Ronan." I tried to make it sound like a warning, but it came out more like a plea.

"The way the air crackled around you. How the lightning danced across your skin. The raw power radiating from you..." He pulled me closer, ignoring the way his burns protested. "Tell me, my queen, why would I waste time in your dreams when the reality of you is so much more intoxicating?"

I rolled my eyes, and wrapped the bandages a little tighter. "Shut your trap. Flattery gets you no where." I had years of experience with 'sorry's' from men—specifically Ramses. Always followed by ass-kissing and gifts and sweet nothings.

"Flattery?" He laughed, then immediately winced as the motion pulled at his burned skin. "I'm stating facts. You're absolutely terrifying when you want to be."

"Good," I muttered, finishing the last bandage with perhaps more force than necessary. "Then maybe you'll think twice before playing your little mind games."

"You think I burned half my flesh off for a game?" His tone had taken on that dangerous edge again, the one that made my pulse quicken despite myself. "That I risked final death for... what? Entertainment?"

"I think," I said carefully, "that you're used to being the one in control. And when you're not, you do stupid things to regain it."

"Like you running off into the forest alone?"

"That's different."

"Is it?" His thumb brushed across my bottom lip, feather-light. "You ran because you were losing control. Because I made you feel things you didn't want to feel."

I bit his thumb. Hard.

He didn't flinch, just smiled that infuriating smile. "Proving my point, Your Majesty."

"You're impossible," I growled, shoving away from him. "I should have let you burn."

"But you didn't." He settled back against the cave wall, looking entirely too pleased with himself for someone covered in third-degree burns. "Just like I couldn't let you face those bandits alone. Perhaps we're both impossible."

I turned away, unable to look at him any longer. "Get some rest. Your body needs to heal."

"Stay."

The word was quiet, almost vulnerable. It stopped me in my tracks.

"Why?" I asked, not turning around.

"Because," he said, and I could hear the smile in his voice, "I promise to behave. No dream walking, no mind games. Just… stay."

I should have kept walking. Should have told him exactly where he could shove his promises. Instead, I found myself sinking down beside him, careful not to brush against his injuries.

"If you try anything—"

"You'll electrocute me?" He chuckled. "I believe I've had enough physical trauma for one day."

Silence fell between us, not entirely uncomfortable. Outside, the sun climbed higher in the sky, sending thin shafts of light dancing across the cave entrance. Inside, we sat in the cool darkness, listening to each other breathe.

"Thank you," he said finally. "For the bandages. And for not leaving me to burn."

I snorted. "Don't get used to it."

"Let me make it up to you," Ronan said suddenly. "There's so many taverns. I'll find one along the way. We can go for drinks."

I stiffened at the suggestion, but couldn't deny the spark of interest that flickered through me. Taverns had always been forbidden territory—Ramses would have had a conniption at the mere thought of his queen mingling with commoners. *The crown must maintain its distance,* he'd always preached. *We are above them.*

"A tavern?" I tried to keep my voice neutral, but something must have betrayed my curiosity because Ronan's lips curved into that knowing smirk.

"Don't tell me the mighty Queen of Ember has never stepped foot in a tavern?"

"Of course I have," I lied, then immediately cursed myself for being so transparent when his smirk widened.

"Liar." He shifted closer, ignoring the way his burns protested. "You've never allowed yourself to be among the common folk, have you? Always kept apart, always above it all." He dropped to a whisper. "Always so *proper.*"

The way he said 'proper' made it sound like a sin. I swallowed hard, hating how easily he could read me.

"Ramses said—"

"Ramses isn't here," he cut in. "And from what I've seen in your dreams, you're quite tired of doing what Ramses said."

I shot him a warning look. "You promised. No more dream talk."

He held up his hands in surrender, though the gesture lost some of its impact given the bandages. "You're right, I apologize." But his eyes still danced with mischief. "So? What do you say? Ready to slum it with the commonfolk?"

The responsible thing would be to say no. To maintain the dignity of the crown, to keep that careful distance Ramses had always insisted upon. But then again, I'd already shattered most of my royal protocols by traveling with a vampire and sleeping in caves and cursing as much as I have been.

Never knew how liberating the word *fuck* could be.

"Fine," I said, trying to sound reluctant. "But only because I need a drink after dealing with your nonsense all the time."

His answering grin was bright enough to rival the sunlight he couldn't face. "Trust me, Atreya. You're going to love it."

CHAPTER 15

Atreya

It had taken us over two weeks of travel to finally discover a tavern that met Ronan's peculiar standards. We'd passed countless establishments, including several upscale inns that I'd naturally assumed would appeal to his refined tastes. But each time we approached one of the more respectable places, with their polished windows and well-dressed clientele, he'd find some fatal flaw. The prestigious Silver Crown was "insufferably pretentious," the Golden Chalice harbored "an alarming amount of holy symbols," and the Royal Oak—which had looked absolutely perfect to me—was dismissed with a curt "too many mirrors."

I wasn't stupid. After eleven nights of sleeping in ditches and abandoned barns, I'd figured out his game. Those fancy places? They weren't for our kind. Not anymore. Not with our faces plastered on every other tree and notice board in the kingdom. The hoods we wore could only hide so much, and those upper-class patrons? They actually read the wanted posters.

So we stuck to the shadows, pulling our hoods lower whenever we passed another wooden post with our likenesses nailed to it. The reward for our capture had doubled in the past week. Flattering, really, how badly Ramses wanted me back.

Ronan had a system for choosing our hideouts. He'd stop at each threshold like a predator scenting the air. But he wasn't looking for clean sheets or fresh bread. No, his blood-red eyes were mapping escape routes, counting potential threats, measuring just how much the owner would look the other way if things went sideways. Which was why this particular shithole—with its knife-scarred tables and clientele that looked one wrong word away from murder—got his stamp of approval.

Night had swallowed the last bits of daylight when we spotted the sign. "The Broken Barrel," it read, letters as faded as our chances of ever living normal lives again. Perfect name for a place as beaten down as its patrons.

Ronan's pace slowed as we approached, and I recognized his familiar assessment routine beginning. His head tilted slightly, nostrils flaring as he caught the mingled scents of smoke and spirits drifting from the entrance. A muscle in his jaw twitched as he studied the building's exterior—the worn stones, the shadows pooling in its corners, the position of its windows relative to the alley behind.

I held my breath, waiting for his verdict. We'd been walking since sunset, and my feet ached in protest. If he rejected this one too...

But then something changed in his expression. The tension in his shoulders eased, and a slight smirk tugged at the corner of his mouth. "This," he said, "might actually work."

I nearly sagged with relief. After two weeks of rejections, we'd finally found a place disreputable enough to meet his exacting requirements. Without waiting for further discussion, I started toward the entrance, eager to rest my weary feet and perhaps sample whatever passed for hospitality in such an establishment.

The door hit the wall with a bang that made my fingers twitch toward the knife at my hip. Even after weeks on the run, every loud noise still set my nerves on fire. I yanked my hood lower, scanning the room through the curtain of my hair.

The stench hit first—stale beer and sweat and something darker underneath. Smoke hung thick enough to choke on, drifting lazy circles in lamplight that barely penetrated the gloom. A dozen faces turned our way. I counted exits: front door, back hallway, probably a kitchen entrance. A habit I've casually adopted. When your face is worth its weight in gold to any bounty hunter with half a brain...

We'd passed three wanted posters on the way in here, our faces staring back at us from rain-soaked parchment. The reward number kept climbing. Ten thousand gold pieces now. Enough to set someone up for life—if they managed to take us alive.

Scattered patrons hunched over their drinks at the bar, while several scarred oak tables dominated the space, their surfaces polished to a warm sheen by generations of use. At one table, a group of men erupted in raucous laughter as one of their companions knocked over his tankard, the crash echoing through the room.

"Isn't this just bloody delightful?" Ronan's silver eyes swept the room with aristocratic disdain, his nose wrinkled at the common revelry. But I barely heard him. Every sight and sound was new to me—the crackling hearth, the musical clink of glasses, the bawdy jokes shouted across tables. It was overwhelming yet intoxicating.

The crash of a tankard hitting the floor made me jump. Laughter erupted from a table of men who looked like they killed people for fun. Just another night at your friendly neighborhood hellhole.

But Gods, it was beautiful.

I was in a tavern beyond the wall, and no one cared. No servants hovering at my shoulder. No whispered rumors following my every move. No suffocating weight of a crown I never asked for. Here, I was nobody. Just another shadow in a room full of them.

My hands shook as I remembered the palace walls closing in. The endless parade of servants managing my life down to which shoes I wore. The crushing certainty that I'd die in that gilded cage, every breath measured and approved by the court.

But here? Here I could tell them all to go fuck themselves. I could curse out loud, burp, and drink until vomiting. Ever since stepping out of Ember I've felt more wilder. Here, I could *breathe*.

I grabbed Ronan's sleeve, ignoring his theatrical sigh as I dragged him toward the bar. His resistance lasted exactly as long as it took the barkeep to slide two glasses our way. I watched, fascinated, as Mr. High-and-Mighty knocked his back like a common mercenary.

The barmaid appeared like smoke, all wild curls and dangerous curves. Her eyes fixed on Ronan like he was the last meal she'd ever need. "What's your poison, beautiful?"

I knew that look in Ronan's eyes—the one that said he was about to play with his food.

Ronan's lips curved into that deadly smile I'd seen him use right before things got bloody. "Wine sounds perfect." His voice was pure sin wrapped in velvet, the kind that made smart women do stupid things. "The finest you've got."

The barmaid practically purred as she leaned over the bar, giving us both an eyeful of what she was working with. "Oh honey, you should see what we keep downstairs." Her fingers traced patterns on the wooden counter. "I'd love to give you a private tasting."

I watched Ronan work his magic, that predator's grace that had probably dropped thousands to their knees over the centuries. His silver hair fell just right, those otherworldly eyes promising things that would make a succubus blush. Fuck, even I felt it—that pull, that electric current that screamed danger and desire in equal measure.

"Such a tempting offer," he said with honey-sweet poison. "But I've got this knife-happy Elf waiting on me. Rain check?"

She invaded his space like she owned it, one perfectly manicured nail trailing down his jaw. The air crackled with tension thick enough to choke on.

"Your loss, beautiful." She sighed, "But when you're done babysitting, come find me. I've got something sweeter than wine waiting."

Ronan's answer was pure sin. "Darling, when I need something intoxicating, you'll be my first stop."

She sauntered off, all swaying hips and knowing grin, leaving the scent of jasmine in her wake.

"Knife-happy Elf?" I muttered, grip tightening on my glass. "Real cute. And what am I, invisible? How come she didn't offer me any of the good stuff?"

"Sweetheart." Ronan's laugh was dark chocolate and razor blades. "Next to an *me*, most people don't notice the armed and dangerous runaway Queen." He ruffled my hair like I was some kind of pet. "And trust me, she wasn't offering anything that comes in a bottle."

Heat crawled up my neck as it clicked. "Oh. *Oh.*" I drained my glass, trying to drown my embarrassment. When had I become such a lightweight?

"What, no charm offensive for me?" The question slipped out before I could stop it.

One perfect eyebrow arched. "You want me to seduce you, Little Light?"

I snorted. "Please. I've seen too many bodies you've left behind to fall for your bullshit."

He spun toward me, all lethal grace and wicked promises. "Then tell me, dangerous creature, what brings you to this delightful establishment?" His fingers caught my chin, tilted my face up. "Not the watered-down piss they call ale, surely." The wine glass pressed against my lips. "Try this instead. Divine, isn't it? Like those eyes of yours."

I took a sip, fighting an eye roll. "Since when are you an expert on divine anything?"

"Little Light, I've tasted every pleasure this world has to offer." His thumb brushed my bottom lip. "I know quality when I see it."

This time I caught his meaning. "And how many bodies did those pleasures leave behind?"

He leaned in close enough I could feel his breath on my skin. "I've fucked in ancient ruins, killed in forgotten temples, and bedded creatures that would haunt your nightmares. But right now? You're the most dangerous and beautiful thing in this room."

We held each other's gaze for one heated moment before breaking into laughter that probably had half the bar thinking we were insane.

"Immune to my charms?" His eyes danced with amusement.

"Lucky me."

He ordered something that probably cost more than this whole damn tavern, and I watched him work his magic on the bartender. Centuries of practice made every gesture a weapon, every smile a loaded arrow.

"Special occasion?" I asked when the bottle appeared.

His eyes met mine, and for once the mask slipped. "Life's short, even for immortals. Especially the moments worth remembering."

My heart did something stupid in my chest. Because underneath all that carefully crafted danger, there was something real. Something that scared me more than all his sharp edges combined.

"Is this part of the act too?" I tried to laugh it off, but my wince betrayed me.

The moment shattered as three hundred pounds of drunk crashed between us, meaty fists slamming the bar hard enough to rattle glasses.

I saw Ronan's delicate silver eyebrow arch over the intruder's shoulder in annoyance. I gave Ronan a small shrug.

The giant's presence brought with it the pungent mix of stale ale and sweat. He swayed slightly, his massive frame blocking my view of Ronan entirely. When he spoke, his voice boomed across the bar like rolling thunder.

"Sweet little Elf bitch and her..." He swayed, squinting at Ronan like his bourbon-soaked brain couldn't process what it was seeing. "Pretty boy toy."

I caught a glimpse of Ronan's face—that dangerous stillness I'd come to recognize, like the surface of a frozen lake hiding treacherous depths beneath. His fingers drummed once, twice against his glass, the only tell of his growing irritation.

"Friend. You're pissing on what was, until now, a perfectly good evening," Ronan said darkly.

The giant made his first mistake—turning his back on the most dangerous thing in the room. His second was breathing his cheap whiskey stench in my face as he invaded my space.

"How 'bout you let a real man show you what—"

"I wouldn't finish that sentence," Ronan cut in. "My friend," he purred, each word dripping with centuries of cultivated menace, "you have exactly three heartbeats to remove yourself from our company. After that..." He grinned, and there was nothing friendly about it. "Well, let's just say I've acquired quite a taste for removing *obstacles* over the years."

The giant turned, perhaps finally sensing the predator at his back. His face drained of color as he met Ronan's gaze—those ancient eyes that had seen empires rise and fall, that held the weight of countless dark deeds.

One heartbeat.

Two heartbeats.

On the third, the giant stumbled backward, nearly upending an empty table in his haste to retreat. He disappeared into the crowd, leaving behind only the lingering stench of fear and cheap ale.

"Didn't need the rescue," I said, even as something warm and dangerous curled in my chest at how quickly Ronan had gone for the throat.

Just like that, the killer vanished behind that goddamn smirk. "Course you didn't. But I do so enjoy making the children behave." He swirled his wine like it was blood. "Got a reputation to protect. Can't let people think I've lost my edge."

"Heaven forbid," I drawled, but couldn't help matching his smile. "Though I notice you didn't actually have to *do* anything this time. Just looked at him all..." I waved my hand vaguely. "Vampire-y."

"Vampire-y?" He pressed a hand to his chest in mock offense. "Centuries of perfecting the art of intimidation, and you reduce it to 'vampire-y'? I'm wounded, truly wounded."

"Would you prefer 'spooky'? 'Dramatically brooding'? 'Gothically inclined'?"

His laughter, rich and genuine, drew more than a few appreciative glances from nearby patrons. "You know, most people would be a bit more rattled after an encounter like that."

I shrugged, reaching for my newly filled glass.

"Rattled? By that oversized ale barrel?" I took a deliberate sip of my drink. "After traveling with you for this long, my standards for 'rattling' experiences have significantly evolved. Remember the incident with that giant fish? The Boarux?"

"Forget that. What about the leeches? I've never heard anyone scream like that."

"Those weren't *normal* leeches," I protested, suppressing a shudder at the memory. "They were the size of my arm and had *teeth*. Actual teeth! And you—" I jabbed an accusing finger at him, "—you just stood there laughing while I flailed around!"

"Your dance moves were quite impressive. Very... interpretive." He demonstrated with a flowing hand gesture.

"I was helpless," I scowled. I took another sip of wine, letting its warmth chase away the phantom sensation of slimy creatures against my skin. "You could have at least pretended to be concerned."

"Darling, if I showed concern every time you stumbled into trouble, I'd have permanent worry lines. And that would be *tragic*." He ran a finger along his smooth forehead, as if checking for nonexistent wrinkles.

"Heaven forbid anything mar that perfect complexion of yours," I deadpanned.

"Perfect complexion that took centuries to achieve, I'll have you know," Ronan said, preening. His expression shifted suddenly, head tilting like a predator catching a distant sound. "All this wine has made me rather thirsty."

I caught onto his meaning, getting up to leave with him, but he stopped me. "You can wait here. Enjoy yourself a bit. Flirt. Be merry. Fuck a barmaid or something. I won't be long," he said. "I *promise*."

"And leave me to fend off more drunken giants?" I settled back into my seat with an exaggerated sigh. "Though I suppose that *would* give me a chance to practice my own intimidation techniques. I've been working on my glower." I demonstrated, scrunching my face into what I hoped was a menacing expression.

Ronan's lips twitched. "Adorable. Like an angry kitten." He ruffled my hair again—a habit I was beginning to suspect he maintained purely for my annoyance.

I watched as he glided toward the door, his movements liquid grace even after several bottles of wine. The crowd parted unconsciously before him—moths drawn to and simultaneously terrified of his flame. Just before he reached the exit, he turned back, silver hair catching the lamplight like spun moonbeams.

"Try not to start any revolutions while I'm gone," he called back, carrying that musical lilt that always seemed to emerge when he was anticipating a hunt. "And do keep that delightful glower of yours in practice."

I nursed my drink, watching the door swing shut behind him. The tavern felt different without his presence, as if the colors had dimmed just slightly. It was strange how quickly I'd grown accustomed to his particular brand of chaos, how empty spaces felt when he wasn't filling them with his centuries-old swagger and sharp wit.

The barmaid from earlier caught my eye and smirked, probably assuming Ronan had finally succumbed to her *exceptional vintage*. If only she knew he preferred his drinks significantly more... vital.

"Another round?" she asked, already reaching for a bottle.

I nodded, then remembered something. "Actually, I've been meaning to ask—what *is* that scent you're wearing? It's quite... captivating." I tried to channel some of Ronan's smooth charm, though I suspected I managed all the seductive power of a confused duckling.

She laughed—not the sultry chuckle she'd given Ronan, but something more genuine. "Oh honey, you're adorable. But stick to being yourself—it suits you better." She filled my glass anyway, adding with a wink, "This one's on the house. For entertainment value."

I slumped back in my seat, pride somewhat dented. "Is it that obvious I've been taking notes from him?"

"Let's just say there are those born to seduce, and those born to..." she gestured vaguely at my entire being, "...whatever this is."

"Charming," I muttered into my wine.

I sat there for a while, nursing my drink and watching the tavern's evening chaos unfold. The warmth of the wine was starting to make my head pleasantly fuzzy, and I found myself people-watching—a habit I'd picked up recently. A group of dwarves in the corner were getting louder with each round, their beards now flecked with foam. A pair of merchants haggled over some mysterious package, their whispers sharp and urgent. Just as I was considering calling it a night, a shadow fell across my table. I looked up to find another mountain of a man, this one somehow even broader than the last.

The second mountain of a man loomed over my table, his shadow swallowing the warm lamplight. "New blood in town? Or just passin' through for fun?" When he spoke it sounded like scraping boots on gravel, matching the weathered terrain of his face. As he leaned in, waves of stale whiskey and days-old sweat assaulted my senses.

Fighting the urge to recoil, I plastered on my most diplomatic face—the one I'd perfected during countless noble gatherings. "Just passing through," I managed, trying to breathe through my mouth. The wine's warmth in my belly had turned to ice.

"Passin' through, eh?" The way his tongue lingered on over his lip made my skin prickle. His eyes raked over me with the calculating hunger of a wolf sizing up its prey. "Business or... *pleasure*?"

My laugh came out brittle as I instinctively glanced toward where Ronan had been sitting. The empty chair mocked me. Of course he'd chosen now for his little hunting expedition.

"Actually, I'm here with someone," I said, my eyes sweeping the tavern for that familiar flash of silver hair. The crowd seemed to have swallowed him whole.

His mouth twisted into something that might have been a smile on a kinder face. "Funny, 'cause from where I'm standin', looks like you've been left all alone." His callused fingers ghosted across my cheek, bringing with them the acrid bite of stale cigar smoke. Every muscle in my body went rigid.

"He's just stepped out," I said, rising from my chair. "I should probably go find—"

His hand clamped around my wrist like an iron shackle, but his eyes weren't on me anymore. They'd locked onto the golden bracelet catching the tavern's dim light. "Now what's a pretty little thing like you doin' with somethin' this fine?" His grip tightened as I tried to pull away. "Caymen! Come look at this beauty!"

Terror slithered down my spine as a second figure approached. Caymen's face was a nightmare of burn scars, with a brand that twisted his lips into a permanent snarl, exposing teeth and gums on one side. His rounded ears marked him as human, though his appearance was anything but ordinary.

"Ain't she something?" Caymen's whistle cut through the tavern noise. The way his eyes crawled over me made me wish I could sink into the floorboards.

"The gold, you idiot," the first man growled. "Look at the craftsmanship. That's Elven work if I ever saw it. See that symbol on the clasp? Classic *Furian*."

The word hit me like a physical blow. Furian. *Aislinn* Furian.

My wedding gift—a golden collar that had once graced a lioness's neck. Before I'd killed her. The realization crashed over me like ice water.

I was wearing it. All this time, I'd been wearing a beacon of my identity right there on my wrist.

Caymen's scarred fingers hovered over the bracelet, his expert eyes dissecting every detail. "I ain't convinced, Stoff. That symbol's too warped—could be anything. Looks human-made to me."

"Listen, you stubborn bastard," Stoff leaned in, alcohol-soured breath hitting my face. "I've laid eyes on this mark before! Sure, it's distorted, but dragonfyre's the only thing that could've melted gold like this. Left that peculiar sheen, see?"

A derisive snort escaped Caymen. "Dragonfyre? And where exactly would that have come from? Ember's vaults?" His burned lips twisted. "Or perhaps King Eldra's mythical beasts?"

"Those whispers about Eldra's dragons might be just talk," Stoff conceded, his rough fingertips tracing the bracelet's curves with unsettling familiarity. His eyes slid to mine, glinting with dangerous curiosity. "But maybe our lovely friend here knows more than she's letting on. What's your name, sweetheart?"

"Joslynn," I blurted, heart thundering against my ribs. "And I recognize only one king—Ramses." The lie tumbled out, a desperate gambit.

Caymen's dismissive laugh sent chills down my spine. "Misguided little thing, aren't you? Beyond the wall, kings are nothing but fairy tales to us." His appraising gaze raked over me, followed by a conspiratorial wink. "Though that accent—pure Ember, isn't it? One of those loyalists, perhaps?"

"No." I jerked my wrist free from Stoff's grasp, taking an unsteady step backward. "I need to leave."

Their laughter followed me as I wove between tables, the wine making the floor tilt treacherously beneath my feet. I grabbed a nearby table for balance, their mocking chuckles echoing in my ears. Pushing off, I stumbled toward the exit, feeling their wolfish stares burning into my back.

The night air hit like a punch to the throat, shocking my senses awake. I sucked it down, desperate to clear the wine-fog that was making everything too soft around the edges.

"Ronan?" My call got swallowed by the darkness. Floating lanterns cast shifting shadows along the path, where drunk revelers staggered and swayed like leaves in a storm. I edged toward the forest's embrace, away from the press of unfamiliar bodies, only to find my path blocked by an old woman's cart, her caged birds echoing fragments of human speech into the night.

"Seems you're a bit lost, dear," she croaked, her face a canvas of deep wrinkles and creases. Time had not been kind to her; it had worn her down, bending her spine into a painful hump and leaving her frail body draped in threadbare cloth. Whatever Fae blood she might have had was hidden under the ravages of age. For if she were human, she would have been dead for a long time now.

"I'm just looking for my friend. Have you seen him?" I asked.

"Ah, the pretty silver one." Her grin cracked like old leather. "Down there." She pointed toward a stretch of darkness that looked like the Void itself. I took one step and heard her cart creak behind me—the sound of someone stepping on a thousand tiny bones.

I turned to find her grinning, teeth scattered like broken gravestones. "Such dangerous times," she cooed. "Better to walk together, wouldn't you say?"

Something primal screamed inside me to run, but I nodded, sparks dancing unbidden across my palms. Her caged birds took up an eerie chorus, their cries echoing through the trees like lost souls.

Minutes stretched like hours as we walked deeper into the suffocating darkness. My eyes adjusted enough to catch glimpses—twisted branches reaching like gnarled fingers, countless eyes reflecting my own fear back at me. Then suddenly, the bird-song ceased. The cart's death-rattle fell silent. Electric light bloomed from my hands, pushing back the darkness—

And finding something far worse waiting in it.

Where the old woman had stood, a nightmare now loomed. The creature before me defied nature itself—a grotesque fusion of human and beast that made me recoil. Its face was a pale, flat expanse of flesh stretched over a serpentine neck, eye sockets housing twin voids that leaked otherworldly light. What might have been hair writhed like living shadows, tangled with rotting vegetation and crawling things I didn't dare name.

The stench hit me then—decay and corruption so profound it turned my stomach. Twisted antlers crowned its massive head, each branch tipped with thorns that seemed to drink in what little light remained.

Lightning crackled between my trembling fingers. "Stay back!" The warning came out more desperate than commanding. I struck out, plasma arcing through the air to strike its chest. Flesh and fur ignited, but the beast barely seemed to notice. Its answering roar shook leaves from the trees while the abandoned birds screamed in their cage:

"Run! Run! RUN!"

Thunder answered my fear, rolling across the sky as rain began to fall in stinging sheets. The beast rose to its full height, towering over me like a mountain of nightmare-flesh.

"Little dove," it purred. Like a poison sliding into my mind. "Your terror seasons the meat so sweetly."

Raw power surged through me, and I channeled it into a desperate attack. Lightning split the earth, crawling over the monster's form in crackling rivers. But where my power should have reduced it to ash, its hide merely shimmered with ancient protection spells.

Again and again I struck, each bolt powerful enough to shatter stone, yet the creature remained. Worse—it smiled.

Its attack came with impossible speed. One moment I was standing, the next I was flying through the air until a tree halted my flight. The impact drove the breath from my lungs and sent agony racing through every nerve.

Through blurred vision, I watched it approach. Those burning void-eyes bore into mine, stripping away every defense, every pretense, until only my naked soul remained. It leaned close, breath like the wind through a tomb.

"I see you, little dove. Taste your fear. Taste the guilt that stains your spirit black."

My strength failing, I whispered a prayer to Naris. If this was my end, let the Goddess of Justice weigh my deeds fairly. Had the lives I'd taken in Ramses' name been balanced by those I'd tried to save? Or was this beast her instrument of righteous punishment?

Rain hissed against sudden flame as the forest began to burn. Lightning split the sky, painting everything in stark shadows and blinding light.

"Vryseris," I breathed my son's name like a final benediction, praying he would choose a better path than his father's. With the last of my power, I called down heaven's fire, hoping to split this horror in two—

The flash revealed Ronan standing atop a nearby rise, his silver hair a beacon in the darkness.

"My, my," he drawled, approaching with careful grace. "Tangling with a Hag? Your taste in dancing partners has certainly declined." The creature whirled to face him, its features contorting in confusion as it processed what it sensed.

"No soul," it hissed.

Ronan's crimson eyes blazed. "None whatsoever. I am all teeth and claws." He taunted the beast, wiggling his fingers near his face.

"Run, Run!" the imprisoned birds squawked in terror.

Ronan clicked his tongue in mock disappointment. "Running is so dull. You know, I've never faced a Hag before. This should be entertaining."

The excitement on his face made my blood run cold.

"Shall we waltz?" He extended his hand with mock courtesy, and the Hag answered with a bone-rattling roar, lunging with terrifying speed. But Ronan was liquid shadow, flowing around the attack with inhuman grace. His laughter, sharp and wild, cut through the night air as he spun away from those deadly claws.

I dragged myself behind a gnarled oak, every movement sending fresh waves of agony through my battered body. From my shelter, I watched their deadly dance unfold.

"Come now, grandmother," Ronan taunted, dodging another vicious swipe. "Surely you can do better than that? I've seen drunken pixies with better aim."

The Hag unleashed a barrage of strikes, each powerful enough to shear through stone. Ronan wove between them as if they were falling leaves, his movements more poetry than combat. "Tsk tsk," he scolded, wagging a finger. "Patience, dear. The best dances build slowly."

Fury blazed in those hollow sockets as the creature launched into a frenzied assault. Moonlight caught on fangs and claws while Ronan danced through death with infuriating ease.

"Points for enthusiasm," he purred, ducking beneath a strike that splintered the ancient tree behind him. "But your technique needs work. And honestly—" he slashed out, opening a deep gash across its mottled hide, "—when was the last time you groomed those claws?"

The Hag circled him now, recognizing a predator that wouldn't be easily felled. Her eyes gleamed with ancient cunning as she assessed her opponent.

Then her head snapped toward me.

I was the easier prey.

She charged with explosive force, reducing my hiding place to kindling. Before I could summon even a spark of power, she was upon me. That ancient face contorted, jaw unhinging to reveal rows of needle-sharp teeth.

Pain exploded through my shoulder as those teeth sank deep, tearing through flesh and muscle like paper. The world began to fade, reality crumbling at the edges as my mind sought escape from the agony...

CHAPTER 16

Atreya

Sacred flutes wove their ethereal melody through incense-laden air, priestesses' chants rising and falling like gentle waves. My mind gratefully retreated into this sanctuary, away from the Hag's fetid breath and tearing fangs. Here, surrounded by the familiar scent of night-blooming jasmine and temple smoke, I was safe.

"Lady Atreya." The greeting came soft as silk beside me. Priestess Andes stood there, her presence both comforting and unsettling—like seeing a beloved face in a dream, knowing it can't truly be there. Her hands rested on my shoulders, their weight too real for this illusion.

"You seem troubled," she murmured, her eyes holding mine.

"I come here often," I whispered, the words tasting of copper and lies. "For prayers, for offerings—"

"No." It carried the finality of a temple bell. "This is not your place anymore." She gestured toward the towering statue of Nexus, the ebony goddess's serene face caught in eternal lamplight. At her feet writhed her children—vampires, werewolves, creatures of shadow and hunger. The in-between ones. The cursed ones.

Like Ronan.

Like the thing that wore an old woman's skin.

His name escaped my lips—"Ronan"—and pain bloomed in my chest like a poisoned flower. Something dark and heavy pressed against my thoughts, a memory trying to surface through murky waters.

Her grip tightened. "The companions we choose shape our fate, Lady Atreya." Her words echoed strangely, as if spoken from the bottom of a well. "Even the tamest beast may turn. Even the most trusted friend may—"

But when I turned, she was gone. In her place loomed Nexus herself, obsidian skin gleaming with inner fire, one stone finger pointing inexorably toward a shadowed archway. A path I knew, yet didn't know. A door that should remain closed.

The Shrine of Tespar waited below, calling with a siren's song of brimstone and ancient power. Here dwelt the Mother of All, first defier of gods, she who chose the abyss and made it her throne. The air itself seemed to pulse with malevolent life, magma threading through black stone like blood through veins.

Her statue rose before me—not cold marble but living darkness, roots and tendrils forever writhing, eyes burning like the hearts of dying stars. This was no benevolent goddess demanding flowers and fruit. Tespar required essence, truth, the raw beating heart of mortal fear and desire.

She who bore the Forgotten Ones, who balanced the world's order with necessary chaos. She who understood that light needs shadow, that creation demands destruction.

In this place, where reality wore thin as autumn frost, I could almost hear her whispers. Almost grasp the truth that slithered just beyond my reach—

Thunder shattered the vision, hurling me back into the nightmare. Not temple walls but arena stands surrounded me now, packed with hungry eyes and baying screams. Not incense but blood filled my nostrils, my own blood pooling on the filthy ground.

The lioness above me snarled, death gleaming in her eyes.

Wrong. This was wrong. I wasn't meant to be here, not again, not now—

The crowd's roar built to a crescendo, and I looked up to find my husband watching, his face a mask of cold disdain. He would not help. He never had.

"Ronan!" The name tore from my throat, a desperate prayer to a darker god.

Then blessed darkness claimed me, and I knew no more.

CHAPTER 17

Atreya

"Wake up." Ronan's command pierced through the darkness, pulling me from the depths of unconsciousness. For a moment, I wrestled with my heavy eyelids, my consciousness ebbing and flowing like the tides washing over a sandy beach.

"Get up!" His sharper tone cut through the haze, but exhaustion still weighed me down. My shoulder throbbed, a dull ache sapping the last of my strength. The shrieking of the birds had fallen silent, as had the rasping screech of the Hag.

"N-no," I croaked, my throat raw and sore from screaming. It felt as if I had swallowed handfuls of sand and glass.

"Listen, I need you to at least drink this." Annoyance, but he wasn't unkind. There was a note of assertiveness there that I hadn't heard from him before.

At the mention of water, my dry mouth flooded. I opened my lips, seeking the cool liquid. It trickled down my chin, but I swallowed greedily, trying to take in as much as possible. He didn't bring the canteen directly to my lips, instead holding it just above me, allowing the liquid to stream down into my throat.

The taste was a peculiar combination of sweetness, like honey and berries, followed by an odd, salty aftertaste. It brought to mind the restorative potions and remedies I had at home. Gradually, I noticed my shoulder pain and breathing issues improving. "When did you acquire these tonics?" I managed to ask, a little stronger now. Was it one of the tonics the traveling men had given us?

A brief pause, then the sound of a bag being rummaged through. I shifted onto my side, struggling to open my eyes. Ronan's back faced me as he searched through my deer skin satchel, his silver eyebrows knit together in concentration. The crackle of a fire and the smell of burning wood filled my nostrils. We were somewhere in the mouth of a dark cave, just sheltered enough from the outside elements. Our things were neatly placed around the campfire, a pot of something simmering over the flames, the scent of it permeating the air.

I was safe, far away from the Hag and my past.

Had Ronan heard me screaming his name?

"What happened?" I asked, sounding much louder and sharper than I would have liked.

"You just had to run off and make a new friend," he huffed. "The Hag made you its own personal chew toy, and I had to come to your rescue." He tossed the bag and went digging in another, a chorus of low growls coming from him.

"You killed it?" I asked, astounded.

He snorted derisively, tossing the bag aside and moving on to another, all the while maintaining his air of nonchalance. "Of course I did," he responded with an air of self-importance. "Made quite the mess, I must say." He wiped his hands on a rag for affect.

"The Hag—I've never encountered anything like it," I said.

"Not surprising." Ronan shrugged. "There are many types. That one was a Mimic. I'm actually impressed you survived. Never felt curious about what lurks beyond the wall?"

"I know it's dangerous out there. Creatures, Fae, humans—all manner of beings. But a Hag..."

"A Hag is a soul-eater," he explained. "She would have consumed your flesh and trapped your essence, using your form while imprisoning your soul within one of her birds."

"Those birds—they were... Oh Gods!"

"Save the tears," he muttered, tossing another bag aside as he searched through our last pack.

"What are you looking for?"

He shifted back onto his heels with an annoyed sigh, head tilting upward. The firelight carved deep shadows across his sharp features. "You're bleeding," he said, concern crossing his face.

I touched my shoulder, wincing as I sat up. "It's painful, but I'll survive."

"No," he shook his head, "*bleeding*." The word dripped with venom.

My hand drifted down, eyes widening in dread as understanding dawned.

"You don't have any supplies," he sighed. "A female without supplies."

"I didn't expect it so soon," I admitted, wishing we'd reached an inn where I could purchase essentials.

"Stress likely triggered it. Fabric?"

"What?"

He tore the sleeves from his beige tunic, working the material into strips. "I used all the bandages on your shoulder while you were unconscious. This will have to do."

I touched my shoulder reflexively. The pain had faded significantly, replaced by spreading warmth. He braided the fabric into makeshift thick bandages before offering them to me. I hesitated.

"Place them in the lining of your undergarment and tie it."

"I know how it works," I huffed.

I'd always had prepared materials; creating them myself was foreign. The fact that Ronan possessed this skill and I did not, flustered me. It was something I should know how to do, and proves his point that I have been pampered...

"How did you learn this?" I wondered what woman he learned this from. What woman had he cared enough about to learn this? Ramses would have cut off his own hands.

His expression hardened, eyes narrowing. "I had a mother once. And a sister. I wasn't conjured from nothing." The last words came barely audible.

I started to speak, but he cut me off. "No. I won't discuss them."

Pain laced his words and he tried to hide it by clearing his throat. The subject clearly wounded him, and I hesitated before responding. But there was vulnerability in his eyes, a longing to be understood that this boundary was a serious one.

"I won't pry," I said softly, touching his arm. "But I'm here if you ever want to talk, Ronan." His skin felt cool beneath my palm.

Our eyes met briefly, his stern facade softening. His hand covered mine in silent thank you before he turned back to the fire as if nothing had happened.

The river rushed ahead through the trees. "I'll keep watch," Ronan said flatly, not looking at me as he pulled off his ruined shirt with obvious annoyance.

I gathered my things—a towel and a plain underdress. The moon hung high, lighting my path to the river that cut through the dark woods.

At the tree line, I stopped, the memory of the Hag's teeth making my shoulder throb. But when I glanced back, Ronan sat unmoved by the fire, completely calm.

It hit me then—how easily he had defeated what I couldn't touch. My lightning, my power that had made me feared in Ember, had done nothing. The truth settled cold in my chest: I'd been fooling myself about my own strength. Here, beyond the wall, I walked a thin line between control and chaos.

I found a smooth boulder by the water's edge and settled there. My ruined clothes—bloody and torn—fell away. The river bit at my feet with ice-cold teeth, but I made myself go deeper.

That's when the strange warmth began again, spreading from my shoulder like honey. The pain vanished completely. Curious, I peeled back the bandages. Dried blood flaked away, revealing perfect skin—not even a scar remained. The healing was faster than anything I'd ever known.

This wasn't like Ramses' healing tonics. Those had knocked me out. This was different. This was—

The feeling hit like lightning, stealing my breath. "Oh!" My knees buckled as memories flooded in—phantom hands on my skin, dark eyes burning with hunger. My heart slammed against my ribs as Ronan's face filled my mind.

He wasn't here, but my mind conjured him anyway—shirtless, moonlit, pressing close with deadly grace. His lips, usually wielding insults like weapons, now trailing fire down my neck.

The cold river couldn't cool the heat building inside me. The tingling spread lower, and my hand followed. Lost in fantasy, I imagined Ronan's touch replacing my own—those dangerous hands learning every secret my body held.

I barely noticed what I was doing as my fingers sought deeper pleasure, but it wasn't enough. I needed more, needed him—

The slick moss betrayed me. Water closed over my head, shocking me back to reality.

I stormed back to camp, mud squelching between my toes.

"You gave me blood! Your blood!" I jabbed an accusing finger at his calm form. Surely Naris would see this as blasphemy.

Another wave of pleasure crashed through me, buckling my knees. The cry that escaped was equal parts ecstasy and horror. Nothing in my years with Ramses had prepared me for this—this deep, pulsing need.

Ronan grimaced, running fingers through his hair, a rare blush coloring his cheeks. I clutched my clothes tighter, burning with shame.

"It's a side effect," he explained, avoiding my eyes. "Vampire blood does many things—healing, strength, regeneration. And... this." He gestured vaguely at my trembling form.

"And what exactly is 'this'?" I demanded, desperate to escape the feeling.

"It causes euphoria. Makes certain... activities more intense." He cleared his throat, composure returning like a shield. "But it will pass. I promise."

My face burned hotter than the campfire. "How long?" The question came out strangled.

"A few hours. Maybe until dawn." Ronan's voice was carefully neutral, but I caught the slight twitch at the corner of his mouth. Was he *amused*?

"This isn't funny!" Another wave hit, and I grabbed a nearby tree trunk for support. The rough bark beneath my fingers felt electrifying. Even the cool night air against my skin was almost too much to bear.

"I never said it was." He stood, crossing his arms. "But you needed healing, and my blood was the quickest solution. Would you have preferred I let you die?"

"No, but—" I broke off as he approached, my heart thundering in my chest. The firelight played across the planes of his bare chest, and I forced myself to look away. "A warning would have been nice."

"Ah yes, because there was plenty of time for a detailed explanation while you were bleeding out. Besides, you're handling it better than most."

I laughed, though it came out more like a desperate gasp. "This is 'handling it well'?"

"You should see what happens to *humans* who aren't prepared for it at all." Something dark and knowing flickered in his eyes. "They tend to become... rather uninhibited."

The implication sent another shock of pleasure through me. I pressed my thighs together, trying to maintain what little dignity I had left. "And you? Does your own blood affect you this way?"

The question slipped out before I could stop it. Ronan went very still, his expression unreadable in the shadows. For a long moment, only the crackling of the fire and my ragged breathing broke the silence.

"No," he finally said roughly. "But your reaction to it..." He trailed off, taking a deliberate step back. "You should try to rest. I'll keep watch."

I nodded, not trusting myself to speak. As I made my way to my bedroll, I could feel his eyes on me, heavy as a physical touch. Sleep would be impossible, but at least I could pretend to try.

Behind me, Ronan's chuckle carried softly on the night air: "Next time, I'll warn you."

Next time.

I shifted on my bedroll, trying to find a comfortable position that didn't make my skin feel like it was on fire. That's when the gold bracelet caught the firelight, gleaming like a mocking reminder. I twisted my wrist, watching it slide against my skin without giving even a millimeter of space.

"Fuck," I muttered, sitting up and yanking at the metal band. The more I pulled, the tighter it seemed to get, like it was alive and determined to stay exactly where it was.

Ronan's eyes flicked to my struggle. "Problem?"

"This fucking thing won't come off." I held up my wrist, the gold catching the firelight again. "It was a wedding gift." I finished bitterly.

He raised an eyebrow. "So?"

"So?" I let out a harsh laugh. "You weren't there when they brought Aislinn Furian into the arena. She was transformed—a lioness. But around her throat..." My voice caught. "There was a collar. Gold, just like this."

Understanding darkened Ronan's expression. He crossed to me in two fluid strides, taking my wrist in his cool hands. His touch sent another wave of pleasure through me, and I bit my lip to keep from making a sound.

"This is Aislinn's collar," he said. It wasn't a question. His fingers traced the intricate patterns etched into the metal. "Reforged into a bracelet. Clever bastards."

"Can you get it off?"

He examined it from every angle, his crimson eyes narrowed in concentration. Then he tried to slide it over my hand—gently at first, then with more force. The metal wouldn't budge.

"Shit," he muttered, releasing my wrist. "It's sealed with magic. Old magic." His jaw clenched. "Ramses may be the only one who can remove it."

I jerked my wrist away, cradling it against my chest. "I'm not going back to him," I said sharply. "There has to be another way."

"There's always another way," Ronan said, his tone dropping to that dangerous velvet that made my blood—his blood—sing through my veins. "But you might not like it."

The fire crackled between us, throwing shadows across his face that made him look more predator than man. I forced myself to meet his gaze, fighting against the waves of pleasure that still coursed through me at his proximity.

"Tell me."

"We cut off your hand."

I swatted his arm and he laughed.

"It hasn't been a bother this whole time. Just leave it. Maybe Eldra can figure out how to get it off."

The mention of Eldra made something shift in Ronan's expression. He moved back to his position by the fire, but there was a new tension in his shoulders.

I couldn't wait for this to be over.

CHAPTER 18

Atreya

D awn crept over the horizon like spilled wine, painting the cave entrance in shades of purple and crimson. I didn't sleep much, my eyes burned with the need to sleep.

The effects of Ronan's blood had finally faded, leaving me hollow and strangely bereft. My body felt both stronger and more sensitive, like a newly-healed wound. Every rustle of fabric against my skin reminded me of the previous night's moments by the river.

I kept my eyes fixed on the cave wall, unable to look at Ronan. He moved around our makeshift camp with practiced efficiency, organizing our belongings as if nothing extraordinary had happened. But there was a new tension in his shoulders, a careful distance in the way he avoided brushing against me when he passed. He left the bedroll out and the fire burning low.

"We should reach the trading post by midnight tonight," he said, "You can replenish your supplies there."

I nodded, grateful for the mundane topic. "And perhaps find proper lodging? A real bed would be welcome after..." I trailed off, heat creeping up my neck.

"After your encounter with the Hag," he finished smoothly, though the slight quirk of his lips told me he knew exactly what I'd meant to say. I turned over.

The firelight caught his silver hair, creating a cruel, beautiful halo effect. I found myself studying the way his muscles moved beneath his new shirt—one retrieved from his pack to replace the one he'd sacrificed for my sake.

"Stop that," he said without turning around.

"Stop what?"

"Your heart rate increases when you look at me now. It's... distracting." His words carried an edge of strain I hadn't heard before.

I jerked my gaze away, mortified. Of course he could hear my heartbeat. What else had he sensed during the night? How much had he known about my activities by the river?

"The blood bond will fade," he continued, more gently now. "Give it time."

"Blood bond? You didn't mention that part."

Ronan finally turned to face me, his expression grave. "My blood in your veins creates a temporary connection. It's why the healing was so effective. It's also why..." He gestured vaguely between us. "Why everything feels more intense."

"How temporary?" I demanded, remembering the phantom sensations, the way his face had filled my mind unbidden.

He hesitated, and in that pause, I heard everything he wasn't saying. "Ronan?"

"It depends on the amount consumed and the... compatibility of the individuals involved. Some bonds fade within days. Others..."

"Others?"

"Can last considerably longer." He turned back to his packing, but not before I caught the flash of something hungry in his eyes.

My stomach twisted at his words. "And ours?" The question hung between us like smoke.

Ronan's movements stilled, his hands frozen in the act of rolling up a blanket. "You're different," he admitted quietly. "Your magic, your blood—they're unlike anything I've encountered." He straightened, finally meeting my gaze. "I can't predict how long this will last." He turned to me, his hands full of clothes. "You can bathe and change..."

A sudden cramp doubled me over, forcing a hiss of pain through clenched teeth. The sound had barely left my lips before Ronan was moving. He retrieved an earthen pot from beside the fire. Steam curled like phantom fingers as he poured its contents into a roughly carved wooden cup.

"Here." He was softer than usual, almost gentle. "Willow bark and chamomile, with a touch of honey. For the pain."

I stared at him, momentarily forgetting my discomfort. "You knew this would happen?"

The firelight caught his profile as he turned away, but not before I glimpsed something vulnerable in his expression. "The blood bond... it allows me to feel echoes of your pain. I don't sleep anyway, so I gathered herbs before dawn."

The tea was bitter but soothing, warming me from within. As I sipped, Ronan busied himself laying out the fresh clothes he'd prepared—including, I noticed with a mixture of embarrassment and gratitude, the makeshift supplies he'd crafted. He had made more of them. Significantly more.

How many of his tunics did he shred?

The next wave of pain struck harder, stealing my breath. I curled inward, pressing my palm against my abdomen. Before I could protest, Ronan's hand replaced mine, his touch cool as mountain snow through the fabric of my shirt. The relief was instantaneous—like plunging into a cold stream on a scorching day.

"There are advantages," he murmured, "to having a body temperature significantly lower than yours." His lips quirked slightly. "And this method has considerably fewer... side effects than my blood."

I should have pulled away. The intimacy of the moment, combined with the lingering effects of the blood bond, made my skin tingle where he touched me. But the relief was too powerful to resist.

"Thank you," I whispered, letting my head fall back against the cave wall. "Though I have to wonder how many other women you've helped through their monthly cycles."

His hand stiffened slightly against my abdomen. "Just my sister," he grimaced, tight with old pain. "Before..."

I covered his hand with mine, offering silent comfort. For a moment, we sat there, connected by touch and silence. Then he cleared his throat and withdrew, the walls coming back up behind his eyes.

"The trading post has an herbalist," he said, returning to his practical tone. "We can get you proper supplies there. For now..." He gestured to the clothes and materials he'd prepared.

The day crawled by with excruciating slowness. I changed into fresh clothes, grateful for the privacy the cave's shadows provided, while Ronan kept the fire burning low—more for my comfort than necessity. Each hour seemed to stretch endlessly, the forced proximity making me acutely aware of his every movement, each unnecessary breath he took out of habit.

"We'll leave at sunset," he said, extinguishing the fire as the last rays of daylight began to fade. "The Hag may be dead, but her territory won't stay vacant long. Others will come to claim it."

"Others? More Hags?"

"Or worse." He shouldered both our packs despite my protests. "The forest keeps most creatures contained, but the truly dangerous ones..." He paused, scanning the darkening treeline. "They're drawn to power. And you, my dear, are practically a beacon."

We emerged from the cave into twilight, the forest taking on an ethereal quality as shadows lengthened. Ronan moved with renewed energy, his supernatural grace more pronounced in the growing darkness. At my questioning look, he smiled—a rare, genuine expression that transformed his severe features.

"This is my time," he explained, gesturing to the dusky landscape. "Everything becomes clearer, sharper. Even the air tastes different."

The path ahead wound through dense forest, barely visible beneath years of accumulated leaves. Ronan set a brisk pace, though I noticed how he shortened his stride to match mine. The blood bond thrummed between us.

"About last night," I began, then immediately regretted speaking when he stumbled—actually stumbled. I hadn't thought vampires could be caught off guard.

"Perhaps we shouldn't—"

"No," I interrupted, surprising us both with my firmness. "We need to discuss it. This bond... you said I'm different. What exactly does that mean?"

Ronan was quiet for so long I thought he might ignore the question entirely. When he finally spoke, he was carefully controlled. "Normally, sharing blood creates a temporary connection. The human or Fae gains strength, healing, enhanced senses. The vampire gains... insight. Access to memories, emotions...Usually only happens that way if both parties share blood. It's strong even though I haven't tasted you."

My steps faltered. "You can read my mind?"

"Not exactly." He caught my elbow as I tripped over a root, his touch sending sparks across my skin. "It's more like... catching fragments of a dream. Images, feelings. Nothing coherent unless—" He cut himself off abruptly.

"Unless what?"

His jaw tightened. "Unless more blood is shared. The bond strengthens with each exchange. The Vampire sees even more if it is combined with sex."

Something he said reminded me of something. I just couldn't place it.

The implications of that statement hung heavy in the night air between us. I thought of the previous night's fantasies, the way his face had filled my mind. Had he seen those too? The thought sent heat rushing to my cheeks.

"Your heart is racing again," he noted quietly.

"Stop listening to it," I snapped.

"I might as well try to stop breathing. Though I suppose I could do that, technically," he laughed.

A branch snapped somewhere in the forest, and Ronan's demeanor changed instantly. He pushed me behind him, scanning the darkness with intense focus. Several moments passed before he relaxed slightly.

"Just a deer," he murmured. "But we should be more careful. The trading post may be our destination, but we're not the only ones who hunt at night."

"What do you mean?"

His expression darkened. "News travels fast beyond the wall. A powerful magic user, The Furian Slayer, traveling with a vampire? We're bound to attract attention—wanted or otherwise."

As if to emphasize his point, a distant howl echoed through the trees. Not a wolf's cry—something deeper, more guttural. Something hungry.

Ronan's hand found mine, cool fingers interlacing with my own. "Stay close," he whispered. "And whatever you hear, whatever you see—don't let go."

"I—" Whatever I was going to say died on my lips as another howl split the night, closer this time. Ronan's grip on my hand tightened.

"We need to move," he hissed, "Though your... distraction isn't making it easier to focus."

"*My* distraction?" I challenged, finding strength in indignation. "You're the one who failed to mention these rather significant details about blood bonds and—and—"

"Sex?" The word rolled off his tongue like dark honey, making me stumble again. This time when he steadied me, his touch lingered longer than necessary. "Would you have preferred I listed every possible outcome while you were bleeding out?"

A rustle in the undergrowth had us both freezing. Ronan's nostrils flared, scenting the air. He opened his mouth and a series of sharp, rapid clicking filled the air. After a moment, he pulled me forward again, our pace quickening.

"Besides," he continued as if we hadn't paused, "I didn't expect the bond to take hold so... thoroughly. Your magic seems to amplify everything."

"Everything?" The word came out breathier than I'd intended.

He shot me a sideways glance, his sudden silver eyes gleaming in the darkness. "*Everything.*" His thumb traced a small circle on my palm, sending shivers up my arm. "Your emotions, your desires—they echo through the bond like ripples in still water. It's... distracting."

"Then let go of my hand," I challenged, though I made no move to pull away.

His lips curved into something between a smile and a grimace. "I told you—don't let go. Unless you'd prefer to face whatever's hunting us alone?"

Another howl, this one answered by several more. The sound seemed to come from all around us now.

"What are they?" I whispered.

"Shadow Wolves," he replied grimly. "They hunt in packs, using darkness itself as their weapon. They're drawn to power—and right now, we're glowing with it."

I swallowed hard. "The blood bond?"

"Among other things." His eyes flickered to me meaningfully. "Your magic, my nature, our... connection. We might as well be ringing a dinner bell."

A shadow detached itself from a tree trunk, taking solid form as it moved. I caught a glimpse of gleaming eyes, too intelligent for any natural beast, before Ronan yanked me behind him.

"Don't look directly at them," he warned with a low growl. "They use your gaze to anchor their magic."

The clicking sound came from him again, faster now, almost angry. Answering clicks emerged from the darkness, accompanied by the soft pad of paws on dead leaves.

"The trading post," I whispered. "How much further?"

"Too far." His hand tightened on mine. "There's a shrine nearby—consecrated ground. They won't be able to follow us there."

Another shadow-shape materialized to our left, then another to our right. The wolves were herding us, I realized with growing dread. But toward what?

"Ronan—"

"I know." His expression shifted, something primal and desperate flashing across his features. "Remember what I said about your magic amplifying everything?"

"Yes?"

"Good." Without warning, he spun me around and pulled me against his chest. His eyes, bright silver in the darkness, locked onto mine with an intensity that stole my breath. "Because I'm about to do something incredibly stupid."

His mouth claimed mine in a fierce, desperate kiss. The blood bond exploded between us like a struck match, and suddenly I could *feel* everything—his hunger, his fear for my safety, the razor's edge of control he walked every moment we touched. Power surged through me, raw and electric, making my skin buzz and my vision blur.

"Now," he gasped against my mouth, "push it out. All of it. Like throwing a net."

The forest erupted in silver fire.

CHAPTER 19

Ronan

The silver fire blazed through the clearing, but it wasn't the flames that made my dead heart stutter. Through our kiss, I felt it—a current of power so vast it made my own supernatural strength feel like a candle flame beside a forest fire. The wolves shrank back, their shadow-forms rippling with uncertainty, but I barely noticed them. Something was wrong.

The magic flowing through our bond had changed. What had started as pure argentine light now carried threads of oily darkness, like ink dropped in clear water. It coiled through her power, through *her*, familiar yet utterly foreign. My first thought was that it was some taint from my own nature—I was, after all, a creature of shadow and blood. But no. This was something else. Something older. Hungrier.

"Atreya," I managed, with effort. The darkness felt like smoke in my lungs, though I hadn't needed to breathe in centuries. "Pull back. Something's—"

She didn't seem to hear me. Her eyes had gone completely silver, but in their depths, I caught glimpses of that same writhing darkness. Her power poured out of her in waves, and with each pulse, the shadow-threads grew stronger.

The wolves weren't just retreating now—they were cowering, pressing their bellies to the ground in submission. They recognized this power, I realized with growing dread. They knew what it was, what it meant.

"Atreya!" I spun her to face me, breaking our connection. The sudden absence of her power left me reeling, but I forced myself to focus on her face. "Look at me."

For a moment, those silver eyes stared through me, ancient and terrible. Then she blinked, and I watched awareness flood back into them.

"Ronan?" Her voice was small, confused. "What... what was that?"

I pulled her closer, scanning the treeline. The wolves were gone, but their departure brought no relief. They'd run not from our combined strength, but from something far worse.

"We need to move," I said, avoiding her question. "Now."

But as I led her toward the shrine path, my mind raced. That darkness in her magic—it had felt like the void between stars, like the spaces where even creatures like me feared to tread.

Like something that should have stayed buried.

The shrine path twisted upward through ancient pines, their branches creaking like old bones in the wind. Atreya stumbled twice, her usual grace deserting her. Each time I caught her, I felt echoes of that strange power humming beneath her skin.

I kept my eyes on the path ahead, tracking the worn stone steps that led to the shrine. In eight hundred years, I'd seen magic twist and corrupt and destroy. But this... this was different. This was *wrong* in a way that made every instinct I'd honed over centuries scream in warning.

The shrine loomed ahead, its weathered stone facade a stark silhouette against the star-strewn sky. In daylight, the ancient structure might have seemed peaceful—just another forgotten temple slowly being reclaimed by the forest. But now, with that corrupted power still crackling in the air, every shadow looked like a mouth ready to swallow us whole.

Atreya's fingers dug into my arm. "The voices," she whispered. "Do you hear them?"

I didn't, but the way she said it made my skin crawl. "What are they saying?"

"I don't... it's not words, exactly. More like..." She pressed her free hand to her temple. "Like something scratching at the inside of my skull."

Great. Now she was hearing shit.

The steps ended at a circular courtyard. Moss-covered statues lined the perimeter, their features worn smooth by centuries of rain and wind. I'd been here before, decades ago, but something was different. The air felt thick, charged—like the moment before lightning strikes.

"We shouldn't be here," Atreya said, but her voice had changed. That same ancient resonance I'd heard in the clearing crept back in, making her words echo strangely. When I turned to look at her, silver light leaked from the corners of her eyes like rivers.

I grabbed her shoulders. "Fight it, Atreya. Whatever this is—"

"It's already here," she said, and this time the voice wasn't hers at all. It was older than the stones beneath our feet, older than the mountains themselves. "It's been here all along, waiting. And now..." A smile curved her lips, terrible in its serenity. "Now it's awake."

The statues around us began to weep black tears.

I'd seen enough.

Fuck this.

The black tears from the statues had reached the ground, forming pools that seemed to drink in what little moonlight remained. As I watched, the liquid began to move against gravity, creeping up the courtyard's stones in spiraling patterns that made my vision blur.

Before that ancient thing wearing Atreya's face could speak again, I wrapped my arms around her.

"Back to sleep you go, love."

With a swift motion born of centuries of practice, I pressed my fingers to the pressure point at the base of her skull. Her eyes rolled back, and she collapsed into my arms—a trick I'd learned from an assassin over a hundred years ago. Usually, I tried not to think about the fact that I'd learned it by killing him.

But Atreya's unconsciousness didn't stop what was happening. The black liquid continued its upward crawl, and now I could hear it—a soft, wet sound like thousands of tiny mouths sucking at stone. The sound brought back memories of things I'd spent centuries trying to forget, of caverns deep beneath Maradi where—

No. Focus.

I gathered Atreya's limp form closer, trying to ignore how her skin burned fever-hot against mine. The black liquid had nearly reached the top of the nearest statue, and the sucking sounds grew louder, more deliberate. Like something learning to speak.

My options were shit. The forest behind us crawled with shadow-wolves, and ahead... well. I'd rather face a hundred wolves than whatever was waking up in this place. But there was nowhere else to go except—

My eyes caught on a half-hidden archway between two of the weeping statues. The shrine's inner sanctum. In my experience, running deeper into ancient, possibly cursed temples was a spectacular way to get yourself killed. But the alternative was standing here watching that black tide rise, and I'd survived eight centuries by knowing when to take calculated risks.

I shifted Atreya's weight and moved. The black liquid seemed to track our movement, changing course to flow toward us. By the time I reached the archway, I could smell it—old copper and something else, something that reminded me of the spaces between worlds.

Of Death.

The sanctum beyond was circular, its domed ceiling lost in darkness. Moonlight filtered through holes in the ancient stone, creating pools of silver that somehow made the shadows deeper. At the center stood an altar, its surface carved with symbols that hurt to look at.

"Interesting choice," came Atreya's voice from my arms—except she was still unconscious, her face slack and peaceful. The sound came from everywhere and nowhere. "Bringing her closer to us."

Laughter echoed off the walls, and the shadows began to move. They peeled away from the corners like old paint, revealing glimpses of what lay behind reality's thin skin. Things with too many eyes. Things that shouldn't exist.

"Poor young thing," the voice said, and now it came from the altar itself. "So certain. So *ignorant*. Did you think your little death-magic made you special? Did you think hundreds of years made you old?"

The shadows pooled at the base of the altar, coalescing into a form that made my ancient bones ache with recognition. A woman—or something wearing the shape of one—emerged from the darkness. Her movements were liquid grace, each step leaving ripples in reality itself. But it was her face that stopped me cold. Or rather, the absence of one.

Where features should have been, there was only smooth, obsidian darkness. Yet somehow, I knew she was smiling.

She extended one long-fingered hand toward Atreya's unconscious form. "Mother," she called, and the word echoed with the weight of eons. "We've waited so long."

I tightened my grip on Atreya, backing toward the archway. But the darkness had sealed it off, leaving us trapped with this thing.

"She doesn't know, does she?" The figure tilted her featureless head. "What she truly is? What she carried inside her all these years, sleeping, growing, waiting to be awakened?" Her laugh was the sound of glaciers cracking. "But you suspected, didn't you, death-walker? You felt it in her power, that echo of the void. That taste of *home*."

The word 'home' hit me like a physical blow, carrying with it memories of a place I'd tried desperately to forget—a realm of endless night where even vampires feared to tread. A place where things like this... woman... were merely the smallest of its horrors.

"She's not your mother," I said, but even as the words left my mouth, I remembered the threads of darkness in Atreya's magic, the ancient resonance in her voice. The way the wolves had recognized her power.

"Oh, but she is," the figure purred, taking another step closer. "She's carried us since before your kind learned to walk upright. We are her children, her legacy, her true nature." She spread her arms wide, and the shadows rippled. "And now, at last, we're ready to come home."

In my arms, Atreya began to stir.

I acted on pure instinct, leaning down and pressing my lips to Atreya's. Not a kiss of passion, but of desperation. My fangs extended, piercing the soft flesh of her neck, and I drank deeply. Her blood hit my tongue like liquid starlight, carrying that same terrible power I'd felt before—but now there was something else. Something ancient that made my very soul recoil.

The figure by the altar hissed, the sound like steel on stone. "Clever boy," she said, but there was rage beneath her tone.

The magic in Atreya's blood coursed through me, raw and wild, more than I'd ever dared to take before. It burned like sacred fire, threatening to tear me apart from the inside. I lifted my palm toward the faceless woman, toward the writhing shadows that surrounded her, and *pushed*.

The power burst from my hand in a wave of silver-white light shot through with threads of that same darkness that had corrupted Atreya's magic. But now, having passed through me—through the filter of eight centuries of death-magic and blood rituals—it was something else entirely. Something new.

The faceless woman screamed, and for the first time, there was fear in her ageless voice.

The silver-threaded darkness tore through the faceless woman's form like lightning through smoke. Where it touched, reality itself seemed to fray, revealing glimpses of that endless void I remembered—but this time, *I* was the one controlling it. The power sang through my veins, a symphony of light and shadow that threatened to unmake me with every heartbeat.

"Impossible," the figure snarled, her form rippling as she tried to maintain cohesion. "You're nothing but a parasite, a shadow-drinker. You cannot—"

I pushed harder, letting more of Atreya's power flow through me. The transformation of her magic through my blood felt like dying and being reborn with each pulse. "Eight centuries," I ground out, "of drinking power from creatures like you. Did you really think I never learned anything?"

But even as I spoke, I felt Atreya growing colder in my arms. I'd taken too much, pushed too far. The faceless woman saw it too, and the sound she made sounded like broken glass shattering. "Stop! You're killing her!" she shrieked, and for a moment, it was like there was true emotion on her faceless form.

"That's the point," I lied through gritted teeth, even as panic clawed at my chest. The magic was killing me too, burning through my undead flesh like holy fire, but I held on. I had to make this creature believe I'd destroy everything—including Atreya—rather than let whatever dark destiny she had planned unfold.

The faceless woman's form flickered like a candle in a storm. "You fool," she hissed, her voice fracturing into multiple tones. "Kill her, and you'll tear open the veil between worlds. Everything she's contained within herself—all of us—we'll pour out uncontrolled. Is that what you want? To unmake reality itself?"

My arms trembled. Atreya's skin had gone grey, her lips blue. The power flowing through me started to stutter, like a dying heartbeat.

"Then help me," I snarled. "Help me save her, or I swear by every dark god that I'll burn us all to ash right here."

The faceless woman went still. The shadows around her stopped their writhing dance, and for a moment, the only sound was the wet rattle of Atreya's failing breath.

"You love her," the figure said, and this time her voice held something almost like wonder. "A creature of shadow and blood, and you *love* her."

"Don't be stupid," I snapped. "Now are you going to help, or should I see what happens when I push this power past its breaking point?"

She moved then, liquid-swift, reaching out with those too-long fingers. I tensed, ready to unleash everything I had left—but her touch when it came was gentle. She pressed one hand to Atreya's forehead and the other to my chest, right where my heart had stopped beating eight centuries ago.

"The old ways demand sacrifice," she murmured. "Blood freely given, death freely chosen. But perhaps..." Her featureless face turned toward me. "Perhaps there are new ways."

Power surged through her touch—not the corrupted darkness from before, but something older, purer. It felt like falling into a well of stars, like touching the space between heartbeats. My vision went black, then silver, then exploded into colors I had no names for.

The last thing I heard before consciousness fled was the faceless woman's whisper: "Let's see what happens when we rewrite the rules, shall we?"

CHAPTER 20

Ronan

I woke to the sound of cursing and the acrid smell of burnt wood. My eyes snapped open, every muscle tensed for a fight—but instead of cosmic horrors and faceless women, I found Atreya crouched by a sad pile of twigs, trying to light a fire with what appeared to be her third match.

"Mother*fucker*," she muttered as another match sputtered and died.

I sat up slowly, my head spinning like I'd downed an entire brewery. The shrine looked... normal. Weathered stone, moss-covered statues, morning sunlight filtering through the pines. I was safely placed in the darkest areas of the shrine. No black tears, no reality-bending shadows, no—

Wait.

Brackium flowers. They were everywhere, their violet petals scattered across the courtyard like drops of wine. I knew those flowers. More importantly, I knew what they did to Fae, humans and vampires who got too close to them when they released their spores.

"Oh good, you're awake," Atreya said, not looking up from her fire-starting attempt. "I was starting to worry you'd sleep through the whole day. Though after last night's performance, I wouldn't blame you."

I rubbed my temples. "Last night's...?"

"Mm-hmm." The match caught, and she carefully fed the tiny flame with dried leaves. "You know, when you started dancing with the statues and telling them they had beautiful faces? Right after you tried to convince me that my magic was actually the birth canal for ancient shadow beings." She glanced up at me, her lips twitching. "The part where you tried to exorcise a particularly suspicious-looking pine tree was my favorite."

I stared at her. "I did not."

"Oh, you absolutely did. Complete with dramatic hand gestures and everything." The fire finally caught, and she sat back with a satisfied smile. "The tree remains suspiciously evil-looking, in case you were worried."

I looked around again, taking in the perfectly ordinary shrine, the scattered Brackium flowers, and Atreya's completely unphased expression. "But the wolves—"

"Ran off when you started howling at them in what you claimed was 'ancient wolf language.'" She made air quotes with her fingers. "I've got to say, for an eight-hundred-year-old vampire, you're a surprisingly light-weight. One faceful of Brackium spores and you went full cosmic horror conspiracy theorist."

I dropped my head into my hands and groaned. "Fuck."

Her laughter echoed off the shrine walls—the completely normal, not-at-all-weeping shrine walls. "Don't worry," she said, patting my shoulder as she passed. "I won't tell anyone that the great and terrible Ronan got high as hell and tried to save reality from my allegedly void-spawned magic."

I peeked through my fingers at her retreating form. "You're never going to let me live this down, are you?"

"Not a chance," she called back cheerfully. "Now come on, help me with this fire. Unless you need to perform any more exorcisms first?"

I got to my feet, carefully avoiding the scattered Brackium flowers, and tried to salvage what remained of my dignity. I couldn't quite shake the memory of that faceless woman's voice, or the feeling of ancient power burning through my veins.

But that was ridiculous. Obviously.

"How are you feeling?" I asked carefully.

"Fine. I could use a bath," she said pointedly.

I watched her gather kindling, trying to spot any lingering signs of that otherworldly power I'd sensed—or thought I'd sensed—the night before. Her movements were fluid and graceful as always, but entirely Fae. No silver light leaked from her eyes, no darkness threaded through her aura.

Still, something nagged at me. "The wolves really just... ran away?"

"Mm-hmm." She straightened up, arms full of dry branches. "Right after you started quoting what you *insisted* was some ancient rite, but sounded more like someone having a stroke."

I pinched the bridge of my nose. Brackium spores were notorious for causing vivid hallucinations, especially in vampires. Our enhanced senses made us particularly susceptible to their effects. The whole thing—the corrupted magic, the faceless woman, the cosmic horror of it all—had probably been nothing more than a very bad trip.

Probably.

But when Atreya dropped the kindling by the fire, I caught a glimpse of something on her neck. Two perfect puncture marks, already healing.

"Atreya," I said carefully. "Did I... bite you last night?"

She touched the marks, her expression unreadable. "Oh, that? Yeah, right after you declared yourself the 'Guardian of Reality' and before you started slow-dancing with that particularly menacing pine tree." She grinned. "Don't worry, you were a perfect gentleman about it. Asked permission and everything, though your exact words were 'I need to filter the void through my ancient blood magic to save the universe.' Very *romantic*."

I stared at the bite marks. They looked real enough, but everything else about last night felt like a dream filtered through smoke and shadow. "And you just... let me?"

"Not at first," She sat down beside me, close enough that I could smell woodsmoke in her hair. "I figured giving you blood might fix whatever the hell was wrong with you."

She laughed and shook her head. "Not exactly. You just got *more* dramatic about saving me from my apparent destiny as mother of the void." Her fingers brushed against the bite marks on her neck. "Though I have to say, for someone high out of their mind on Brackium spores, you were surprisingly gentle."

I winced. "About that... why weren't you affected?"

A slight blush colored her cheeks. "We have Brackium flowers in the Elrathilion," she said, not quite meeting my eyes. "I built up a tolerance years ago."

"Did I..." I hesitated, watching her face carefully. "Did I kiss you at any point during this... episode?"

The blush on her cheeks deepened, and she busied herself with arranging branches in the fire. "Wow, you were *really* high, weren't you?"

Something in the way she spoke made my dead heart do an interesting little flip. "That's not an answer."

"You also proposed marriage to a rock that you said had, and I quote, 'very trustworthy grooves,'" she deflected, poking at the fire with perhaps more force than necessary. "So maybe we shouldn't do a full inventory of your greatest hits from last night."

I caught her wrist gently, stilling her assault on the innocent firewood. "Atreya."

"You did," she admitted softly. "Right before you bit me. You said something about how if we were all going to die in the void anyway, you didn't want to go without knowing what starlight tasted like." Her lips curved in a small smile. "It was actually kind of sweet, in a completely deranged sort of way."

"Ah." I let go of her wrist and leaned back, trying to process this information with whatever dignity I had left. "Well. That's..."

"Mortifying?" she suggested helpfully. "Hilarious? Further proof that eight-hundred-year-old vampires should stay away from hallucinogenic flowers?"

"All of the above," I muttered, dropping my head back into my hands. "I'm sorry I didn't get you to the trading post before this happened."

She shrugged. "It's fine. You made me enough supplies that I can wait until night again."

I looked away from her, to the treeline behind her.

But just for a moment, in the space between one breath and the next, I could have sworn I saw something move in the shadows between the trees. Something with too many eyes, watching us with ancient patience.

I blinked, and it was gone.

Probably just the last of the Brackium working its way out of my system. Probably.

The sun bled out across the horizon, painting the clouds in shades of violet that reminded me uncomfortably of Brackium flowers. We'd spent the day recovering—well, *I'd* spent it recovering while Atreya alternated between tending the fire and finding new ways to remind me about my "ancient wolf language."

I stood, stretching muscles that felt like they'd been put through a meat grinder. The last traces of Brackium-induced madness had faded, leaving behind only fragments of memory that felt more like fever dreams than reality. But something still felt... off. Like a word caught on the tip of my tongue, or a shadow glimpsed in a mirror.

"You're doing it again," Atreya said.

"Doing what?"

"That thing where you stare into the middle distance like you're trying to solve the mysteries of the universe." She stepped closer, studying my face. "Are you sure you're okay?"

I was about to assure her that yes, I was fine, when something moved in my peripheral vision. I turned sharply, but there was nothing there. Just trees and lengthening shadows and—

A whisper. So faint it might have been the wind, but it carried that same otherworldly resonance I remembered from last night: *"Soon."*

"Ronan?" Atreya touched my arm, and I nearly jumped out of my skin. "Okay, you're officially freaking me out now."

I forced a smile. "Just the last of the Brackium playing tricks on me," I said, though I wasn't entirely sure I believed it. "Come on, we should get moving before full dark."

She didn't look convinced, but she nodded and started toward the shrine's entrance. I followed, trying to shake off the persistent feeling that we were being watched.

Just before we left the courtyard, I glanced back one last time. The statues stood silent and still in the fading light, their faces weathered but distinctly present. No tears of darkness, no cosmic horror.

But there, at the base of the largest statue, a single Brackium flower remained. As I watched, its petals turned to face me, like a tiny purple eye tracking our movement.

And just for a moment, I could have sworn it winked.

CHAPTER 21

Atreya

Was it cruel to keep messing with Ronan? Yes. But he deserved it. Did he do all those things I said he did while high off his ass? No, not all of it. Was it satisfying watching him suffer? Absolutely.

Sure, he did have a bad reaction to the Brackium flowers.

The truth was, he'd mostly just passed out after mumbling something about shadows. I'd spent the night watching over him, making sure he didn't choke on his own tongue or whatever vampires did when they got high on flower spores. But teasing him was... easier. Easier than admitting I'd spent hours checking his breathing, easier than acknowledging the way my heart had clenched when he'd collapsed.

Served him right.

Play in my head and I'll play in yours.

I was still smirking at his discomfort when we rounded a bend in the path and I saw them—purple orchids climbing up an old oak tree. My steps faltered, the smile dying on my lips.

"Purple orchids for my love," Ramses used to say, presenting them with that charming smile that never quite reached his eyes. I'd thought it was romantic at first, the way he'd fill my chambers with them. Until the day I tried to give some away to a servant.

The bruises had taken weeks to fade.

There had been other moments, so many of them bleeding together in my memory: The time he'd thrown a vase at my head for speaking to another noble at a feast. The nights he'd lock me in my room with nothing but those damned orchids for company, their sickly-sweet scent choking me until I begged for forgiveness for imagined slights. The way he'd stroke my hair afterward, telling me he only did these things because he loved me so much.

"Atreya?" Ronan's voice cut through the memories. He'd stopped a few paces ahead, watching me with a frown. "What's wrong?"

I realized I'd wrapped my arms around myself, nails digging into my sides. Forced them to relax. "Nothing," I said, too quickly. "Just... tired."

But my eyes kept drifting to those purple blooms, and suddenly I could smell them—that cloying sweetness that had always meant pain was coming. My stomach churned.

"My beautiful, delicate flower," Ramses would coo, right before he showed me just how delicate I wasn't. How much pain I could take before I broke. Always with those orchids watching, their purple heads nodding in approval of my tears.

"It's not nothing." Ronan stepped closer, careful, like he was approaching a wounded animal. Maybe I was. "You're shaking."

The worst part? Sometimes I still caught myself checking my behavior, measuring my words against his rules. Don't laugh too loud. Don't draw attention. Don't make him angry. Like he still owned pieces of me, even now.

"We can take another path," Ronan said quietly. He hadn't touched me, hadn't moved any closer. Just stood there, solid and present, blocking my view of the orchids.

I swallowed hard against the lump in my throat. "No," I managed. "No, it's fine. They're just flowers."

But they weren't. They were shackles made of petals, and their purple shadows had followed me out of that gilded cage, all the way here to this forest path.

I forced my feet to move, each step an act of defiance. *They're just flowers,* I told myself again. *He can't hurt you anymore.*

But as we passed the oak tree, I kept Ronan between me and those climbing blooms. Just in case.

Some days the memories ambushed me without warning. A scent on the breeze, a particular shade of purple, even the way shadows fell across a room—any little thing could send me spiraling back. My body would react before my mind could catch up: heart racing, palms sweating, muscles tensing for a fight that wasn't coming. Time became fluid in those moments, reality blurring at the edges until I couldn't tell if I was in the present or trapped in the past.

The worst part was how my mind played tricks on me. I'd find myself checking over my shoulder constantly, jumping at innocent sounds, my nerves raw and exposed like stripped wire. Sometimes I'd catch myself spacing out, lost in memories I couldn't quite grasp, only to snap back to awareness minutes or hours later with no recollection of where the time had gone. The constant vigilance was exhausting, but I couldn't seem to turn it off. Every cell in my body remained coiled tight, ready for danger, even in moments of relative safety. Servat had taught me to be aware of my surroundings, but this was different—this was surviving, not living. The weight of everything—Ramses's abuse, Servat's death, the endless running—sat heavy in my bones, making even the simplest tasks feel like wading through deep water.

The loneliness hit me in waves, some days stronger than others. I felt it most in quiet moments like this—when the world slowed down enough for me to remember everything I'd lost. Sometimes I'd wake up feeling invincible, ready to take on whatever the day threw at me. Other times, the weight of survival pressed down so hard I could barely breathe. It was strange, feeling both weak and strong at the same time, like a sword that had been tempered but could still shatter if struck just right. And then there was Ronan. I hadn't meant to let him get close—hadn't meant to feel anything beyond irritation for the vampire who'd forced his way into my life. But somehow, between the arguments and the life-or-death moments, something had shifted. Maybe it was the way he never pushed when I flinched from touch, or how he kept finding ways to make me laugh despite myself. Or maybe it was simpler than that—maybe it was just that he saw me, really saw me, not as something to be protected or possessed, but as someone who could stand beside him, sharp edges and all. It terrified me, this growing comfort in his presence. Because comfort meant vulnerability, and vulnerability meant risk. But there were moments, like now, when I caught myself wondering if some risks might be worth taking.

We'd barely made it another mile when I heard it—the low rumble of rushing water. The path ahead curved sharply, revealing a gorge that cut through the forest like a wound. A rope bridge, ancient and weathered, swayed gently in the evening breeze.

Below, at least fifty feet down, white water crashed over black rocks.

I stopped at the bridge's edge, eyeing the frayed ropes and weathered planks. The gorge was deep enough that the mist from the rapids below didn't quite reach us, but I could feel the cool dampness in the air, taste the mineral tang of wet stone.

"Well," I said, aiming for lightness I didn't feel, "I guess we know why no one uses this trading route anymore."

Ronan moved past me to test one of the anchor points. The rope creaked under his touch, ancient fibers straining. "It's not ideal," he admitted, "but it's our best option. Unless you'd prefer to backtrack several miles and try to find another crossing?"

The thought of going back past those orchids made my skin crawl. "No," I said quickly. Too quickly, judging by the way his eyes flickered to my face. "This is fine. It's just a bridge."

Just a bridge, like they were just flowers. I was getting very good at lying to myself.

Ronan stepped onto the first plank, testing his weight carefully. The wood groaned but held. "I'll go first," he said. "If it can hold me, it can hold you."

I heard him mumbling something about hating water.

I wanted to protest—I wasn't some delicate thing that needed protecting—but the protest stuck in my throat. Because wasn't that exactly what I'd been, earlier? Frozen by the sight of a few purple flowers, trapped in memories I should have been strong enough to overcome by now.

The bridge swayed as Ronan made his way across.

I watched the muscles in his back tense with every creak and groan of the ancient structure, ready to move at the first sign of collapse. But he made it to the other side without incident, turning back to face me with an encouraging nod.

"Your turn," he called. "Just take it slow."

I placed one foot on the first plank, then the other. The bridge shifted under my weight, and my stomach lurched. Below, the rapids seemed to roar louder, hungry for a mistake.

"So fragile," Ramses whispered in my memory. *"So easy to break."*

I gripped the guide ropes until my knuckles went white, forcing myself to take another step. Then another. The wind picked up, making the bridge sway more dramatically, and I had to bite back a curse.

"You're doing fine," Ronan's shout carried across the gorge, "Just keep moving. Don't look down."

Naturally, I immediately looked down.

The world tilted sideways as vertigo hit me full force. The rapids below seemed to reach up, their white foam fingers beckoning. My legs went weak, and for one terrifying moment, I was sure I was going to fall.

"Atreya." Ronan's call cut through the panic. "Look at me. Not the water, not the bridge. Just me."

I dragged my eyes up to meet his across the distance. His expression was intense, focused entirely on me, as if he could keep me safe through sheer force of will.

"That's it," he said. "Now keep walking. You're halfway there."

I was? I resisted the urge to check my progress, keeping my gaze locked on Ronan instead. One step at a time, I told myself. Just like escaping Ember. Just like leaving Ramses. One step at a time until you're free.

The bridge gave an ominous crack.

My heart stopped. Beneath my feet, I felt something shift—not the normal sway of rope and wind.

Ronan must have heard it too, because his expression changed from encouraging to alarmed in an instant. "Run," he said, "Now!"

I ran.

The world exploded into splinters and screams.

One moment I was running, the next I was falling. The ropes snapped with a sound like thunder, planks disintegrating beneath my feet. Ronan's shout followed me down, but the roar of the rapids swallowed everything else.

I saw the bridge collapse in sections, wooden shards catching the last rays of sunlight like falling stars. Saw Ronan's face transform from alarm to horror. Saw the white water rushing up to meet me, hungry and endless.

"Fragile little bird," Ramses echoed in my head. *"What happens when you finally fall?"*

The impact drove the air from my lungs in a violent rush. Cold wrapped around me like a fist, dragging me under. The current seized me, tossing me against rocks that felt like hammer blows. Up became down became sideways—I couldn't tell which way led to air.

Not like this, I thought fiercely. *Not after everything I survived.*

"Atreya!"

I caught glimpses of Ronan running along the gorge's edge, keeping pace with the river.

I tried to call back, but another wave crashed over me, filling my mouth with water. The magic under my skin flickered, weakening. How long could I keep this up? How long before—

Something snagged my arm, yanking me sideways. A branch, half-submerged and sturdy enough to hold my weight. I clung to it, muscles trembling with effort as the river tried to tear me away.

"Hold on!" Ronan was closer now, scaling down the gorge wall with inhuman speed. "Just hold on!"

Easy for him to say. He wasn't the one with a raging river trying to—

The branch creaked.

Oh no.

"Ronan!" I screamed, just as the wood gave way.

The last thing I saw before the river claimed me again was his face, twisted in a fury I'd never seen before. Then the current dragged me under.

My body slammed against another rock, and stars burst behind my eyes. The current spun me like a leaf, each impact stealing what little air remained in my lungs.

"Poor little Fae. Always needing someone to save you."

Anger flared hot in my chest, burning against the river's cold. No. I wasn't that person anymore. I wasn't helpless.

I threw everything I had into one brutal stroke, fighting against the current. My fingers brushed stone—another rock, smoother than the others. I grabbed it, muscles screaming as I fought to hold on.

Without hesitation, Ronan dove into the churning rapids.

I could see him now, a dark shape moving against the white foam, faster than any human or Fae could swim. My grip on the rock was failing, fingers numb from cold and impact. Just a little longer, I told myself. Just—

The current ripped me away again.

This time when I went under, the world went quiet. Peaceful, almost. The rage of the river seemed distant, muffled. My lungs burned. The magic inside me flickered like a dying candle.

"This is how it ends," Ramses whispered. *"This is what you get for thinking you could be strong."*

Strong hands seized me, yanking me against a solid chest. Ronan. Even through the water's cold, I could feel the unnatural chill of his body as he wrapped one arm around my waist, the other fighting against the current.

We broke the surface together, me gasping for air, him snarling with effort as he tried to keep us both afloat. The river fought him for every inch, desperate to drag its prey back under.

"Hold onto me," he growled in my ear. "Whatever happens, don't let go."

I locked my arms around his neck as he twisted in the water, positioning himself to take the brunt of impact as another rock loomed ahead. We hit hard enough to drive what little air I'd managed to catch from my lungs.

But Ronan didn't let go.

He took impact after impact, using them to gradually work us toward the shoreline. Every collision would have broken human bones, but he just grunted and held on tighter, his face a mask of determination and barely contained fury.

Finally, his feet found purchase on the riverbed. With one last surge of strength, he half-dragged, half-carried us onto a narrow strip of pebbled beach.

We collapsed together on the stones, me coughing up river water, him absolutely still except for the arm still locked around my waist. For a long moment, the only sounds were my ragged breathing and the continued roar of the rapids.

"*That*," Ronan said roughly, "was incredibly stupid."

I turned my head to look at him, ready to point out that the bridge collapsing wasn't exactly my fault—and stopped. His eyes were solid black, pupils blown wide with adrenaline and fear. Water streamed from his hair, making him look younger somehow. More vulnerable.

"You hate water," I said, remembering his earlier mumbling. "You could have—"

"Died?" He barked out a laugh that held no humor. "I'm already dead, remember? You, on the other hand..." His arm tightened around my waist. "Don't do that again."

"Don't do that again?" I pushed myself up on my elbows, ignoring the way every muscle screamed in protest. "What exactly was I supposed to do? Sprout wings?"

He made a small sound of annoyance.

"You should have run faster."

"Run faster?" I sat up fully, ignoring the way the world spun. "Oh, I'm sorry, next time a bridge collapses under me, I'll be sure to outrun gravity."

"You know what I mean." Ronan pushed himself up too, water still dripping from his hair. "You hesitated at the start. If you'd just—"

"If I'd just what?" Heat rose in my cheeks, and not from embarrassment. "Been less *fragile*?"

His eyes narrowed. "That's not what I—"

"No? Because it sure sounds like you're suggesting I somehow *chose* to fall into that river." My pitch rose with each word, powered by a cocktail of leftover adrenaline and building anger. "Like I thought, 'hey, you know what would be fun? A nice swim with some rocks!'"

"That's not—" He raked a hand through his wet hair in frustration. "I'm trying to say you should have—"

"Should have what?" I was fully shouting now. "Please, oh ancient and wise vampire, tell me exactly what I should have done differently! Because clearly, you know everything about—"

"You should have let me carry you across!" he shouted.

I put my hands on my hips. "At what point did you offer that?"

"I knew you would say no so I didn't. But you should have let me."

"Let you..." I blinked. "Are you insane?"

"It would have been safer."

"It would have been *patronizing*."

"It would have been *smart*."

"Oh, because I'm clearly too stupid to walk across a bridge by myself?"

"Because I can't die!" He surged to his feet, water cascading off him. "Because if that bridge was going to collapse, better it happen with someone who can't drown! Because watching you fall was—" He cut himself off, jaw clenching.

"Was what?" I stood too, swaying slightly but too angry to care. "Inconvenient? Annoying? Another example of how *fragile* I am?"

He slapped a hand over my mouth. "You're insufferable."

I bit his hand.

He yanked it back with a curse, more surprised than hurt. "Did you just—"

"Yes," I snapped, "I did. Because contrary to what you might think, I'm not some delicate flower that needs to be protected."

"That's not—" He made a sound of pure frustration. "I know you're strong. I *know* that. I know you can fight back. But strong doesn't mean invincible, and watching you fall..."

Fight back.

Suddenly I wasn't mad anymore. I felt hot tears burn behind my eyes. Servat didn't think I was some precious thing that would break. He always told me to fight back and I did. I fought with everything in me.

And Servat was dead and I was here.

The fight drained out of me all at once, leaving me cold and shaking. I sank back down onto the rocky shore, wrapping my arms around my knees.

"Hey. Stop that. It's no reason to cry," Ronan snapped.

"I'm not crying," I said, even as traitorous tears spilled down my cheeks. "It's this stupid Hellscape."

Ronan made a sound somewhere between a sigh and a growl. He stood there for a moment, water dripping from his clothes, looking like he was fighting some internal battle. Finally, he dropped down beside me, careful to leave space between us.

"Look," he said, softer now. "I didn't mean to... I'm not good at this."

"At what? Nearly drowning?"

"Just tell me what's wrong. Really wrong. Not the bridge, not the flowers. Something's been eating at you."

I stared at the rushing water, its roar somehow quieter now, or maybe I was just too tired to care. "Nothing's wrong."

"Atreya. Let it out. Whatever anger, whatever pain you're carrying—let it out. It's killing you slowly, I can see it."

The tears came faster now, hot against my cold cheeks. "I can't."

"You can."

"I *can't*," I insisted, "Because if I start, I don't know if I'll be able to stop. And I can't—I can't fall apart. Not here. Not now."

"Why not?"

"Because—" I swallowed thickly. "Because Servat would want me to be stronger than this."

Ronan was quiet for a long moment. Then he said something that surprised me.

"Tell me about him," he said finally.

I turned to look at him sharply, searching his face for any hidden motives. "Why do you want to know about Servat?"

"Because you just nearly drowned mentioning his name," Ronan said, "And because every time you talk about being strong, it sounds like you're quoting someone else's words."

My hands clenched into fists. "Don't do that."

"Do what?"

"That thing where you act like you can see right through me." I stood up, ignoring how my legs shook. "I'm not some puzzle for you to solve, Ronan. And Servat isn't some tragic backstory for you to pick apart."

"I never said he was." He remained seated, but his eyes tracked my movement. "I just asked you to tell me about him."

"Why?" The question came out harsher than I intended. "So you can judge how I failed him too?"

Something flickered across his face—understanding, maybe, or pity. I hated both options equally.

"Is that what you think?" he asked quietly. "That you failed him?"

The tears threatened again, but I forced them back. "I don't think anything. I know what happened."

"Do you?" He stood now, water still dripping from his clothes. "Or do you know what you've convinced yourself happened?"

I laughed, and it sounded bitter even to my own ears. "You're one to talk. Every time I got close to asking you about your past you shut down."

"Nice deflection," he said, unmoved. "Try again."

"Why are you pushing this?" I took a step back, suddenly needing distance. "What do you *want* from me?"

"I want you to tell me about him. All your great moments. Talk about them."

"I don't talk about him," I snapped, "because it hurts too much. Because every good memory is tainted by how it ended. Because—" I cut myself off, wrapping my arms around myself.

"Because what?" He asked.

"Because we were supposed to have forever! He was supposed to be here! He fucking promised me! He promised!" The confession burst out of me like a dam breaking. "Because he taught me everything—how to fight, how to survive, how to be *strong*. He never treated me like I was fragile or precious or... or *owned*. He just..." I had to stop, choking on memories.

"He just what?"

"He just believed in me," I whispered. "Even when I didn't believe in myself."

CHAPTER 22

Ronan

I watched her break apart, this fierce creature who'd spent so long holding herself together. Her words hung in the air between us, raw and honest in a way that made my dead heart ache. I knew that pain—the weight of promises broken not by choice but by fate's cruel fucking hand.

"Tell me one thing about him," I said softly. "One good memory. Not how it ended, not what was lost. Just... one moment when he made you feel strong."

Atreya stared at the rushing water, tears still tracking down her cheeks. For a moment, I thought she wouldn't answer. Then:

"He taught me to fight with a sword," she said. "Everyone else—the other instructors—they'd hold back, afraid of hurting the precious Queen. But Servat..." A ghost of a smile touched her lips. "He knocked me on my ass multiple times. Then he helped me up and said, 'Good. Now you know what it feels like to fall. Next time, make me work harder for it.'"

The smile grew stronger, more real. "So I did. Every day, I made him work harder. And one day..." She laughed, and this time it held genuine joy. "One day I finally knocked *him* down. He looked up at me from the ground, blood running from his split lip, and he had the biggest grin I'd ever seen. He said—" Her voice caught. "He said he'd never been prouder."

I moved closer, careful not to touch her. "He was right to be proud."

"Was he?" She turned to face me, and there was something desperate in her eyes. "Because I'm still running. Still falling. Still—"

"Still fighting," I cut in. "Still getting back up. Still making people work harder to knock you down." I gestured to the river. "You nearly drowned, and your first response was to bite me for suggesting you needed help. If that's not what he taught you, I don't know what is. Stubborn ass."

She laughed again, watery. "I can't believe I actually bit you."

"Neither can I." I rubbed my hand theatrically. "I think you broke skin this time."

"You deserved it."

"Probably."

We stood in silence for a moment, watching the last rays of sunlight paint the rapids gold. Finally, Atreya spoke again:

"I miss him," she whispered. "Every day, I miss him so much it feels like drowning. And I'm so angry—at him for dying, at myself for surviving, at the whole world for just... continuing like nothing happened. Like he didn't matter."

I knew then what she needed to hear. Not platitudes about strength, not assurances that it would get better. Just truth. About me.

"My mother died during my Rite of Passage," I said quietly, "In my tribe, we sent young males into the wilderness with nothing but a knife—barely more than a sharpened piece of metal, really." I could feel Atreya's eyes on me but kept my gaze fixed on the rushing water. It was easier that way.

"Six months. I was only gone six months." My hands clenched involuntarily. "I got lost early on, hit my head badly enough to forget why I was even out there. By the time my memories returned and I found my way back..." The words stuck in my throat like thorns.

"When I finally made it home, I expected to find my mother and sister waiting. Instead, I found Isla, my childhood friend. She told me my mother had taken the mourning shroud—a declaration that she had no men left in her life. No mate, no sons." I swallowed hard. "No protection."

The reddish moonlight that came caught the rapids, turning them blood-red. "The rival tribe came three months after I'd left. They always targeted the mourning women first—they were seen as easy prey. My mother..." My voice cracked slightly. "My mother fought them. Fought until she couldn't anymore. My sister survived, at least. But I was only gone six months. Six months that cost me everything."

"The worst part is, I can't remember her face. I remember her nose. She would always swipe a finger along my nose. Say how sharp it was. Like hers." I made the gesture.

Atreya reached out hesitantly, then seemed to think better of it and let her hand drop. "I'm sorry," she said softly. "About your mother. About... all of it."

"It was a long time ago." The words came out automatically, a shield I'd worn for centuries.

"Time doesn't always help," she said, and there was understanding there that cut deeper than pity ever could. "Sometimes it just gives you more space to remember what you lost."

After a long moment, she asked, "What happened to your sister?"

I stiffened, the old guilt rising like bile in my throat. Decades of regret. "I wasn't around much. After... after what happened to our mother, I couldn't handle the guilt. Knowing I should have been there. Should have protected them both." My hands clenched at my sides, nails biting into palms. "Eventually there came a point where I would never see her again."

The river's roar seemed to grow louder, as if trying to drown out the echoes of old wounds laid bare. But it couldn't wash away the memory of my sister's face the last time I saw her—how young she'd looked, how lost. How much she'd needed her brother to stay. I fought hard to remember those features—and still, they slipped away like sand in my hands.

And I'd failed her, just like I'd failed our mother.

The silence stretched between us, heavy with shared grief and understanding. I needed to break it before I drowned in centuries of regret. My eyes caught on her still-soaked clothing, and I latched onto the first distracting thing I could find.

"I can see your nipples through your tunic," I said.

CHAPTER 23

Atreya

My eyes snapped wide. "I'm sorry, *what* did you just say?"

"Your clothes," Ronan gestured vaguely at my soaked tunic, his expression carefully neutral. "They're... rather transparent. I thought you might want to know."

Heat flooded my cheeks as I crossed my arms over my chest. "Were you—were you actually looking at my—"

"Would you really like me to answer that?" A hint of amusement crept over him, the corner of his mouth twitching upward. Something about that almost-smile sent a shiver through me that had nothing to do with my wet clothes.

"No," I said quickly. Then, softer, "Maybe."

Tell me. Please tell me.

He just shrugged and settled himself on the beach, peeling off his own sodden shirt to wring it out. I tried not to stare. I failed miserably.

I found a deep enough pool in the sand, guarded by two giant rocks that protected it from the wilds of the river. I crept behind one and took off my wet clothes, shaking them out and bringing them with me in the water to clean.

I peeked around the rocks at Ronan.

Moonlight painted silver trails across his skin, highlighting the lean muscle of his shoulders, the elegant line of his throat. He was beautiful in the way ancient statues were beautiful—all clean lines and perfect symmetry, too flawless to be quite real. The expanse of black tattoos and crisscrossed white scars danced along his pale skin. I found myself wondering if his skin would be cold to the touch, like marble, or if—

His eyes met mine, dancing with mischief. "Now who's looking?"

I jerked my gaze away, but not before catching his satisfied smirk. "I wasn't—I mean—it's different."

"Oh?" He leaned back on his elbows, making no move to put his shirt back on. "Do explain how it's different."

"Because you're—" I gestured vaguely at him, heat creeping up my neck. "And I'm—"

"I'm what?" He was definitely enjoying this now, the insufferable man. "Strikingly handsome? Irresistibly charming?"

"Impossible," I muttered, sinking deeper into the water until only my eyes remained above the surface. The cool water helped soothe my burning cheeks, but did nothing for the flutter in my stomach.

Ronan laughed, the sound rich and warm in the night air. "Fair enough." He lay back on the sand, folding his hands behind his head. "Your secret's safe with me, though. I won't tell anyone you were admiring the view."

I sent a small wave of water in his direction, but he just chuckled again. The teasing light in his eyes slowly faded as he gazed up at the stars, replaced by something more contemplative. Something almost... peaceful.

I found myself drifting closer to shore, drawn by the quiet vulnerability of the moment. He looked different like this—less the dangerous vampire, more the man who'd just shared stories of his past. The man who'd jumped into rushing rapids to save me without hesitation.

The man who was still, technically, my captor.

Get it together. This isn't real. You're just lonely. You were literally just crying to him about Servat. Are you sick?

But when I finally emerged from the water, shivering slightly, he was already holding out a dried tunic from our pack. His fingers brushed mine as he handed it over, and that brief contact sent electricity racing up my arm.

As I sat down next to him on the cool sand, I found myself drawn to his profile, the way the moonlight highlighted his strong jawline and the soft curve of his lips. I shook my head, trying to rid myself of these thoughts. This was Ronan, a vampire, not some abstract figure to be ogled at.

He was a viper with his words. He knew how to play with people. He could be so charming one minute, then go off the next.

After all, this was the same man who helped me with Xaneth.

Also the same man who ripped me away from my son.

I glanced at Ronan, at his silver, silk hair that was still damp from our swim. He was running his fingers through the strands with a scowl.

"Can I..." I hesitated, then gathered my courage. "Can I braid your hair?"

He turned to look at me, surprise flickering across his features. For a moment, I thought he'd refuse. Then his expression softened into something I couldn't quite read.

"Have at it," he said quietly, shifting to sit in front of me.

I scooted forward until my chest was almost touching his back and reached up, my fingers brushing against his hair. His hair was silk between my fingers, still damp from the river. I worked slowly, carefully, hyper-aware of every point where my hands brushed against his neck or shoulders. I gathered a section from the top of his head, beginning to weave it in a simple three-strand braid.

If I leaned forward just slightly, I could press my lips to the curve of his shoulder...

Halfway through, I paused, my fingers still tangled in his hair. "Does it feel strange?" I asked.

He shook his head slightly. "No, it's... nice." The admission seemed to surprise him as much as it did me.

When I finished, he reached back to touch the neat plait, something thoughtful in his expression. "You know," he said slowly, "in my culture, braiding someone's hair has many meanings."

"Oh?" I tried to ignore how my heart sped up at the word 'meanings.'

"Masters would braid their slaves' hair, weaving gold through it as a sign of status." His voice was distant, lost in memory.

I remembered the night I had met him, through the fog of drink, how gold trinkets had been woven into his hair. How well he had been dressed. I kept my thoughts to myself.

"And in marriage ceremonies, couples would braid their hair together before making their vows. They'd cut the joined braids afterward, keep them as symbols of their bond."

"Well then," I said, aiming for lightness, "I suppose I should feel honored that you let me braid yours."

His laugh was soft, almost gentle. "You should. It's quite the privilege."

A shiver ran through me—from the cold this time, though the way he was looking at me didn't help.

"You're freezing," he said, frowning. "I'll get a fire started."

He rose in one fluid motion and walked away, his braid swaying slightly with each step. I watched him go, trying to ignore the way my fingers still tingled from touching his hair, the way my heart seemed to have forgotten its proper rhythm.

This is dangerous, I told myself firmly. *He's dangerous.*

But as I watched him gather firewood, his movements graceful in the moonlight, I wondered if the real danger wasn't him at all—but the way he made me feel like maybe, I wasn't alone anymore.

I hugged my knees to my chest, watching as Ronan arranged the wood with practiced efficiency. His hands moved with that inhuman grace that still caught me off guard sometimes—too quick, too precise. A reminder of what he was, as if I needed one.

"You're staring again," he said without looking up.

"I'm observing," I corrected, though heat crept up my neck. "There's a difference."

The corner of his mouth lifted. "Is there?" With a slight gesture, he ignited the wood—another casual display of power that made my breath catch. The flames cast dancing shadows across his face, turning his silver hair to molten gold where it escaped the braid.

"Show-off," I muttered.

"You weren't complaining about my abilities when I pulled you from the river." He settled beside me, close enough that I could feel the warmth radiating from his skin. So much for the marble statue theory.

"That's different. That was…" I trailed off, remembering the terror of being swept away, the solid strength of his arms around me. "That was you saving my life."

"Again," he added softly. "I don't make it a habit of saving damsels in distress unless I'm trying to kill them myself."

"I'm not a damsel in distress," I scoffed.

"Sure looked like it to me."

Okay, so he had a point.

"At this rate, we won't ever get to Eldra's," I sighed.

"Eldra's." Ronan stiffened slightly. "You're still determined to go through with this?"

"I have to. You saw what Ramses did to Tor. What he continues to do to the people. You were right. He is the best chance. Plus I have some questions I need to ask him."

Like why Joslynn drew his symbols in her journal.

Ronan's face became pinched.

"Questions." Ronan's tone had taken on that careful neutrality again, the one that usually meant he was hiding something. "About what, exactly?"

I traced patterns in the sand, debating how much to reveal. The firelight made the grains glitter like tiny stars. "Just some things I wanted to ask. Private things."

"Private things," Ronan repeated, taking on an edge I hadn't heard before. He turned to face me fully, firelight casting harsh shadows across his features. "Planning to get *very* private with Eldra, are you?"

I recoiled at the venom in his tone. "Excuse me?"

"Oh, come now." His laugh was bitter, nothing like the warm sound from earlier. "Young, beautiful woman seeking the protection of the most powerful man in the region? I'm sure he'll be *very* interested in helping you." His eyes raked over me in a way that made me feel suddenly exposed, despite being semi-clothed. "Especially given your… particular charms."

"Is that what you think of me? That I'd—that I would—"

"I know about how Ramses shared you with other men. Some of whom were married. Just so he could gather intel and prestige. It would be something you are familiar with."

For a moment, I couldn't breathe, couldn't think past the roaring in my ears. Then fury crashed through me, hot and violent as wildfire.

"How *dare* you." My voice shook. "How *dare* you throw that in my face. You have no idea—" I broke off, choking on rage and something dangerously close to tears. "You have no idea what I had to do to survive. What Ramses made me—"

"I didn't mean—" Ronan started, his expression shifting from anger to horror.

"No." I scrambled to my feet, needing to put distance between us. The tenderness of moments ago felt like a cruel joke now. "You meant exactly what you said. You think I'm some kind of—that I would willingly—" A harsh laugh tore from my throat. "Gods, I was actually starting to trust you."

Ronan stood too, reaching for me. "Listen—"

"Don't touch me!" I jerked away from his hand. "Clearly, you think I just want to add another powerful man to my list of conquests."

"Atreya." He said through gritted teeth. "That's not what I—"

"Save it." The blood bond thrummed between us, a discordant melody of anger and regret and something deeper, darker. I could feel his emotions bleeding into mine, making it hard to tell where my fury ended and his began. "I don't want to hear your excuses."

"If you would just *listen*—"

"To what? More accusations? More reminders of what I've done?" The bond pulsed with each word, making me dizzy with its intensity. "When will this cursed thing go away?" I pressed a hand to my chest where the connection burned brightest. "I'm so tired of it. Tired of feeling everything you feel. Tired of being around you."

His expression went perfectly, terrifyingly blank. "Tired of me already? And here I thought we were having such a lovely moment by the fire."

"That's exactly the problem!" The words burst out before I could stop them. "I was actually starting to—" I cut myself off, but it was too late.

Something flickered in his eyes. "Starting to what?"

"Like you," I whispered, hating how vulnerable the admission made me feel. "Despite everything, I was starting to like you. And then you had to go and ruin it with your cruel words and your assumptions about—"

His hand shot out, grasping my chin with surprising gentleness. The touch sent the blood bond singing, a bittersweet harmony that made my knees weak. His face was a mask of cold control, but I could feel the storm of emotions raging beneath the surface.

"I *ruin* everything I touch," he said, flat and final.

The words hung in the air between us, heavy with the weight of old wounds and bitter truths. Through the bond, I caught glimpses of memories—fragments of pain and loss that stretched back centuries. The rawness of it stole my breath.

I wanted to pull away. I wanted to lean in. I wanted to scream at him until my throat was raw. I wanted to—

The blood bond surged, and suddenly I couldn't tell which desires were mine and which were his.

So I bit him. Right on his lip.

CHAPTER 24

Ronan

The sharp sting of her teeth against my lip sent electricity coursing through my veins. For a moment, I froze, caught between the instinct to retaliate and the overwhelming urge to pull her closer and fuck her. The blood bond flared between us, a wild current of desire and anger and fear that threatened to drag us both under.

I jerked back, tasting copper on my tongue. "What the hell was that?"

She glared up at me, defiant despite the tremor in her hands. "Now we're even for what you said."

A laugh bubbled up in my throat—harsh, surprised. Of course she'd find a way to draw blood, this maddening woman who refused to cower even when she should. Who kept making me feel things I had no business feeling.

"Even?" I touched my lip, the small wound already healing. "You think a little bite makes us even?"

"No," she shot back. "But it made me feel better."

The bond hummed between us, telling me that was both truth and lie. She was still angry—*gods*, was she angry—but there was something else there too. Something that made her pulse quicken when I stepped closer, that made her eyes drop to my mouth despite her fury.

"Did it?" I murmured, letting my fingers trail along her jaw where I'd held her moments ago. "Did it really make you feel better? Or did it just make you want—"

She slapped my hand away. "Don't. Don't you dare try to—to *seduce* me out of being angry with you. You don't get to say those horrible things and then act like this."

She was right. Of course she was right. I had no business touching her, wanting her, not after what I'd implied. The accusations I'd thrown at her like weapons—gods, what had I been thinking? I hadn't been thinking at all, had I? Just reacting to the surge of possessive rage that had coursed through me at the thought of her going to Eldra, of her letting him—

The bond pulsed with echoes of her pain, showing me exactly how deeply my words had cut. Showing me memories I wished I hadn't seen: her shame, her fear, the things she'd endured at Ramses' hands. Things no one should have to endure.

And pain. A great deal of pain.

"I'm sorry," I said, the apology feeling inadequate even as it left my mouth. "What I said was unforgivable. I didn't mean—" I ran a hand through my hair, forgetting about the braid until my fingers caught in it. Her braid. The intimacy of that moment felt like a lifetime ago now.

"Then why did you say it?" Her question was quiet, dangerous. "Why did you try to hurt me like that?"

Because I'm terrified of how much I care. Because everyone I've ever cared about has been destroyed. Because you make me feel things I haven't felt in centuries, and it's easier to push you away than to admit that.

But I couldn't say any of that. Couldn't admit how much power she already had over me. So I just stood there, silent, while the bond tried to transmit everything I couldn't say anyway. I quickly shut it down, willing the bond to quiet.

How fucking inconvenient.

"You want to know why?" I finally said, rougher than I intended. "Because you make me forget myself. Because every time I think I have control of this—" I gestured between us, encompassing the bond, the tension, everything unsaid "—you do something that makes me lose my mind."

"So it's my fault?" She took a step forward, closing the distance I'd tried to maintain. "You say cruel, horrible things because I make you *forget yourself*?"

"No." I caught her wrist as she moved to shove me, my thumb pressed against her pulse point. Her heart was racing. "I say cruel things because I'm a cruel creature. Because that's what I am—what I've always been."

"That's not true," she said, "I'm trying to be your friend here, Ronan, but you're making it so damn difficult."

Friend.

My grip tightened on her wrist before I could stop myself. Through the bond, I felt her pulse jump—not from fear. Something I refused to examine too closely.

"Friend?" I tested the word, tasting its unfamiliarity. It's been years. "Is that what you think this is?"

She yanked her wrist from my grip. "What else would it be?"

I wasn't sure how to answer. What were we? Captor and captive? Allies of convenience?

Friend.

"You tell me," I said finally. "Friends don't usually bite each other."

"You bit me first," she shot back.

"Fair."

"Yet here we are."

I couldn't help the dark laugh that escaped me. "Here we are indeed." I stepped closer, watching the way her breath hitched. "And where exactly is that, Atreya?"

She lifted her chin, defiant as ever. "Somewhere we shouldn't be."

"Shouldn't we?" I brushed a strand of hair from her face, letting my fingers linger against her skin. The bond sang at the contact, a symphony of want and warning. "Then why aren't you moving away?"

"Why aren't you?" she breathed.

I swiped my thumb across her lips, catching the edge where she'd drawn my blood. Her eyes darkened, and before I could react, she bit me again—this time on my thumb. Sharp pain mixed with something far more dangerous, sending heat coursing through my veins.

"You really need to stop doing that," I growled, but my body betrayed me. My free hand shot out, gripping her waist and pulling her down with me as I fell back onto the sand. She landed with her legs on either side of my bare stomach, her hands braced against my chest.

Through the bond, I felt her surprise spike, followed by a wave of... Something that made her fingers curl against my skin, made her breath catch in her throat.

"Make me," she challenged, but she trembled slightly.

The bond thrummed between us, a desperate melody of desire and denial.

This is madness, I thought. *This is exactly what I was trying to avoid.*

But with her weight settled against me, her pulse racing beneath my hands, avoidance seemed like a distant memory. A fool's errand. Especially when she was looking at me like that, like she wanted to bite me again, like she wanted to—

She's not wearing pants.

She's bare. On my stomach.

And so fucking warm.

I sucked in a sharp breath as the realization hit me. The tunic I'd given her earlier—it barely reached her thighs. And now, with her straddling me like this...

"Atreya," I warned. The bond was overwhelming now, a thundering cascade of shared sensations that made it impossible to think clearly.

She must have felt it too, because her eyes went wide. A blush crept across her cheeks as she seemed to realize her position, but she didn't move. If anything, her fingers pressed more firmly against my chest.

"I should—" she started.

"Yes." But my hands stayed at her waist, betraying me.

The firelight painted her skin gold, catching in her damp hair like a crown of flames. She was beautiful in a way that hurt to look at—wild and fierce and so achingly alive. And still very much my prisoner, a fact that sobered me instantly.

"We can't," I said, forcing myself to loosen my grip. "This isn't—"

"Right," she finished, but there was something like disappointment coloring her face. Or maybe that was just the bond, mixing up her emotions with mine until I couldn't tell the difference anymore.

She moved to climb off me, but in her haste, her knee slipped in the sand. I caught her instinctively, and suddenly she was pressed fully against me, her face inches from mine. Her breath fanned across my lips, still stained with my blood from her bite.

For one endless moment, we stayed frozen like that, caught in the space between what we wanted and what we knew was right. The bond pulsed between us like a living thing, urging us closer, closer...

"Ronan," she whispered, and my name on her lips sounded like both prayer and curse.

That's what finally broke me. I sat up abruptly, setting her aside with more gentleness than I felt capable of. "We should get going. Trading post is still a bit away."

She stared at me for a long moment, hurt and confusion warring in her expression. Then she nodded once, sharply.

This was all Eldra's fault.

I stalked away from her, my hands clenched into fists at my sides. Every step felt like warfare—part of me desperate to turn back, to finish what we'd started, while another part wanted to grab her by the throat and shake her until she understood how dangerous this was. The violence and desire tangled together in my chest until I couldn't separate them anymore, couldn't tell if I wanted to kiss her or kill her. Both options would probably destroy us. The bond throbbed like an open wound, feeding me fragments of her confusion, her hurt, her own answering desire.

I slammed my mental walls up higher, trying to block it out. This is what I am—what centuries of blood and death and power have made me. A monster wearing the skin of a man, pretending at civilization. And monsters don't get to have gentle things. Don't get to have *her*, no matter how much every cell in my body screamed for it. Better to be cruel now than to let this progress until I inevitably tainted her too. Until I broke her, like I broke everything else I touched.

CHAPTER 25

Atreya

The walk to the trading post was torture.

Every step felt like walking through molasses, the silence between us thick enough to choke on. The bond wasn't helping—if anything, it seemed determined to remind me of every heated moment by the fire, every accidental brush of skin against skin.

I kept my distance, trailing a few steps behind Ronan. His braid was coming undone, silver strands escaping to catch the moonlight. My fingers itched with the memory of weaving it.

Stop looking at his hair.

"There." Ronan startled me from my thoughts. He pointed to a cluster of lights in the distance, barely visible through the trees. "Trading post's just ahead."

I quickened my pace to catch up, forgetting my resolution to keep my distance. "Will they be open this late?"

"They're always open." His mouth quirked up slightly. "Places like this cater to those who prefer to travel after dark."

Right. Vampires.

As we got closer, I could make out more details—a sprawling wooden building with a wraparound porch, lanterns casting pools of warm light. Several horses were tied up outside, their breath steaming in the cool night air.

"Stay close," Ronan murmured as we approached. "Some of the clientele can be... unpredictable."

I was about to remind him that I could handle myself when the door burst open, spilling lamplight and raucous laughter onto the porch. A group of men stumbled out—no, not men. Their eyes gleamed too bright in the darkness, their movements too fluid to be human.

One of them spotted us and nudged his companion. "Well, well. Look what we have here."

Ronan's hand found the small of my back, urging me forward. The touch sent sparks through the bond, but I forced myself to focus on the potential threat ahead.

"Evening, gentlemen," Ronan said smoothly as we passed. His tone was pleasant enough, but I felt the way his muscles tensed, ready for trouble.

The vampires' eyes followed our movement, and I caught fragments of their whispered conversation:

"—traveling with a Fae—"

"—heard rumors about a silver-haired—"

"—thought he was dead—"

I glanced at Ronan, but his expression revealed nothing. He guided me through the door, his hand never leaving my back.

The trading post's interior was warm and smoky, packed with an eclectic mix of travelers. Humans clustered near the central fireplace, while the darker corners held shadowy figures that made me want to look anywhere else. The air smelled of tobacco, leather, and something metallic that I tried not to think too hard about.

"Charming place," I muttered.

Ronan's laugh was barely more than a breath against my ear. "Wait until you see the rooms."

The rooms.

Right. We'd need somewhere to sleep. Or at least, I would. The thought of sharing a room after what had happened by the fire made my pulse spike.

Through the bond, I felt Ronan's awareness of my reaction, followed by a wave of... something that made my cheeks burn.

"I'll see about lodging," he said, his voice rougher than usual. "Don't wander off."

As if I would. The clientele alone was enough to keep me rooted to the spot. I watched as Ronan made his way to the counter, where a weathered woman with striking violet eyes was cleaning glasses with a suspicious-looking rag.

Left alone, I became acutely aware of the attention we'd drawn. Several pairs of eyes tracked my movements as I edged closer to the fire, trying to look like someone not worth bothering.

"Ain't often we see your kind in here."

I turned to find a human man watching me from his seat by the hearth. His clothes marked him as a merchant, though the quality suggested business hadn't been good lately.

"My kind?"

He gestured vaguely. "Faeries. Least, not ones what ain't property. They tend to steer clear of vampires." His eyes flicked to my neck, searching for a claiming mark. "You *are* free, ain't you?"

Before I could answer, a familiar hand settled on my shoulder. "She's with me," Ronan said, carrying a warning that made the merchant pale.

"Meant no offense," the man mumbled, suddenly very interested in his drink.

Ronan's grip tightened slightly. "We should go. Room's ready."

I nodded, letting him guide me toward a narrow staircase. The bond hummed between us, a constant reminder of everything we weren't talking about.

One room, I thought. *This should be interesting.*

The room was exactly what I'd expected from a place like this—small, dusty, with a single narrow bed pushed against the far wall. A threadbare rug covered most of the wooden floor, and a cracked mirror hung at an angle beside a wash basin.

"Cozy," I said, trying to ignore how the space seemed to shrink with both of us in it.

Ronan shut the door behind us, the click of the latch unnaturally loud in the quiet room. "I'll take the floor."

"Don't be ridiculous." I gestured at the rough wooden boards. "That can't be comfortable."

"I don't sleep much anyway." He moved to the window, peering out at the darkness. "And after what happened by the fire—"

"We're not talking about that," I cut in quickly.

He turned to look at me, moonlight silvering his profile. "Aren't we?"

"No." I busied myself with examining the bed's questionable blanket. "We're going to pretend none of that happened. That's what you want, isn't it?"

Through the bond, I felt his frustration spike. "Is that what you think I want?"

"I don't know what you want!" The words came out sharper than I intended. "One minute you're—" I gestured vaguely, heat creeping up my neck at the memory of his hands on my waist, "—and the next you're acting like I'm poison."

"Maybe you are," he said softly, dangerously. "Maybe that's exactly the problem."

Before I could respond, a commotion erupted from downstairs—raised voices, the crash of breaking glass. Ronan was at the door in an instant, his entire demeanor shifting.

"Stay here," he ordered.

"Like hell I will." I moved to follow him, but he blocked the doorway with his body.

"Atreya." My name was a growl on his lips. "For once in your life, do as you're told."

It made me hesitate just long enough for him to slip out and shut the door. I pressed my ear against the wood, straining to hear what was happening below.

The voices were clearer now, anger carrying through the floorboards:

"—saw him come in here—"

"—silver-haired bastard thinks he can—"

"—kill him this time—"

My heart stuttered. They were looking for Ronan. And judging by the snarls mixing with the shouting, they weren't human, maybe Fae. Maybe vampire.

Maybe Ramses and his soldiers.

Gods damn it! I cannot catch a break.

I glanced around the room, searching for anything I could use as a weapon. The wash basin was ceramic—it would break easily enough. And the mirror, if I could get it off the wall...

Stay here, he'd said.

Like hell.

CHAPTER 26

Ronan

I took the stairs two at a time, my mind racing. Those voices—I knew them. Of course I knew them. The same ones that had haunted me for centuries, belonging to the only others who'd survived Xaneth's "training."

As I reached the bottom of the stairs, three figures materialized from the crowd like wraiths. Selene, with her shock of white-blonde hair and cruel amber eyes, flanked by the twins, Marcus and Domini. My siblings in blood, if not by birth.

"Well, if it isn't our wayward brother," Selene purred, her delicate features twisted in a sneer. Before I could react, her hand cracked across my face with supernatural speed. "You absolute fool."

Marcus, the broader of the twins, stepped forward. His dark hair was pulled back severely from his face, highlighting the sharp angles of his cheekbones—so like Xaneth's it was unsettling. "Do you have any idea what you've done?"

"Several things, apparently," I drawled, tasting blood where Selene's ring had cut my lip. "Care to be more specific?"

Domini, leaner and more elegant than his twin, let out a harsh laugh. "He jokes. Our master is ready to tear the realm apart, and he *jokes*." His silver eyes—so different from my own—flashed dangerously. "Tell us it isn't true, brother. Tell us you didn't steal the Queen of Ember."

"I didn't steal the Queen of Ember," I mimicked.

Selene's hand shot out again, but this time I caught her wrist. "Now, sister, you know how I hate it when you mark up my face."

"You arrogant, reckless—" She yanked her arm free. "Xaneth will skin you alive for this. All for some Fae whore?"

"Watch your mouth, Selene."

"Or what?" Marcus stepped closer, using his bulk to crowd me against the bar. "You'll run away again? That's all you're good at, isn't it, Ronan? Running when things get difficult?"

I felt my fangs lengthen, a growl building in my throat. "You have no idea why I left."

All three of them went still. Then Selene's face split into a vicious grin. "Oh, brother," she breathed. "Tell me you haven't been stupid enough to fall for her."

"Don't be stupid Selene. You know as well as I that Vampires do not love."

Her eye twitched.

Selene's past flickered through my mind—her own desperate attempt at love, centuries ago. A human merchant with kind eyes and gentle hands. I'd never seen her so alive as she was during those brief months.

"You're right," Selene said, brittle as winter frost. "We don't love. Xaneth made sure of that, didn't he? Made sure we understood exactly what happens when we try."

The twins shifted uncomfortably. They'd been there too, that day. We all had.

"I remember how you smiled," I said quietly, knowing the words would cut deep. "When Xaneth found out you'd turned him. He pretended to be just as happy."

"Shut up." Her fingers curled into claws at her sides.

"You actually thought Xaneth would let you keep him. Thought he'd understand your love for Kain."

"I said shut up!"

"Instead, he made us all watch. Made us stand there while he drove that stake through Kain's heart at dawn. Made us watch him burn in the sun, screaming your name until his vocal cords turned to ash."

Selene's composure shattered. With a feral snarl, she launched herself at me, fangs bared. I caught her mid-leap, using her momentum to spin us both. We crashed into a table, sending glasses shattering across the floor.

"I needed out! I hate Xaneth! So do you! So do all of you!" I snarled.

Marcus and Domini exchanged glances—quick, but telling. We all knew the truth of it, even if none of us had dared speak it before.

"Hate him?" Selene laughed, the sound sharp as broken glass. "You think that matters? You think your petty feelings change anything?" She shoved away from me, straightening her clothes with trembling hands. "We belong to him. Forever. That was the deal."

"That was his deal. I never agreed to an eternity of—"

"Please," she begged. "He's livid. He may actually kill you this time."

"Let him try," I said, but it lacked conviction. We all knew what Xaneth was capable of. "I'm not going back."

"Then you'll die," Marcus said quietly. "And so will she. Ramses is not a kind male, brother. There is wickedness in him beyond the scope of Xaneth."

I heard movement on the stairs behind me—familiar footsteps that made my heart stutter. *No. No, no, no. Stay upstairs. Please, for once, just listen.*

But when had Atreya ever done what I wanted?

"Well, well." Someone new spoke—melodic, dangerous. "What a touching family reunion."

I didn't need to turn to know who it was. It had haunted enough of my nightmares.

Raya emerged from the shadows like she was born from them, her white-gold hair a stark contrast to her black leather armor. Where Selene was ice, Raya was poison—beautiful, lethal, and utterly without mercy. Xaneth's second favorite child, and the one who'd always hated me most for being first.

"Sister," I said flatly. "I was wondering when you'd show up."

Her laugh was like breaking glass. "Did you really think you could run without me coming to collect?" Her crimson eyes flickered to the stairs where Atreya stood. "And with such interesting company."

I moved before conscious thought, placing myself between Raya and the stairs. "She's not part of this."

"Oh, but she is." Raya's smile showed too many teeth. "Father sends his regards, by the way. He's quite eager to see you again. Both of you."

Through the blood bond, I felt Atreya's spike of fear—quickly replaced by determination. *Don't do anything stupid*, I silently pleaded. *Not now.*

The twins shifted again, and I caught the way Domini's hand brushed against Marcus's arm—a gesture so subtle, so ingrained after centuries together, neither of them seemed aware of it. They'd always been like that, even before Xaneth's "training." Two halves of the same broken soul.

"You remember how it was in the beginning," Domini said softly, his silver eyes holding mine. "When he first brought us all together. Before the blood and the pain, when we actually believed we could be a real family."

"Shut up," Selene snapped, but there was a tremor in her words that betrayed her.

I remembered. Of course I remembered. Those first few months when Xaneth played the role of benevolent father, gathering his "children" one by one. Selene had been first after me, then the twins, and finally Raya. We'd been so young, so desperate to belong somewhere. To someone.

"We used to sneak out at midnight," Marcus said, his deep voice thick with memory. "All of us. Remember that abandoned cathedral on the hill? Domini would play that old pipe organ while Selene danced."

"And Raya would sing," I added, watching my sister's face contort at the reminder. "You had such a beautiful voice before he made you swallow glass that night. What was it he said? 'Beauty is weakness, and I will burn every weakness from you until only strength remains.'"

Raya's hand went unconsciously to her throat, where the scars still lingered beneath her high collar. "He made us strong."

"He made us monsters," Domini countered, earning a sharp look from his twin. "Don't pretend you've forgotten what he did to us that first year. The 'lessons' in the basement. The way he'd pit us against each other, promise his love to whoever drew the most blood."

"And you always won, didn't you, brother?" Selene's smile was razor-sharp. "His perfect firstborn. The only one of us who could transform. The rest of us were just... practice dummies for your training sessions."

The guilt hit me like a physical blow. How many times had I torn into them under Xaneth's command? How many bones had I broken, how much blood had I spilled, all to earn a father's twisted approval?

"I never wanted—" I started, but Marcus cut me off.

"Save it," he growled. "You were his favorite, his precious weapon, while the rest of us scraped by on whatever scraps of attention he deigned to give us. Do you know what he did to Domini after you left? How he punished us all for your betrayal?"

Domini's hand tightened on his twin's arm. "Marcus, don't."

"No, let him speak," Raya purred, her crimson eyes gleaming. "Let our dear brother know exactly what his freedom cost us."

But I already knew. The blood bond between siblings—another of Xaneth's cruel gifts—had carried echoes of their pain across continents. Their screams had haunted my dreams for decades.

"I hear them sometimes," I admitted quietly. "In the dark. All of you. Calling for me. Begging me to come back."

"And yet you never did," Selene whispered, ancient hurt bleeding through her icy facade. "You left us there with him. Your family. Your blood."

"You were never just family to him," I snarled. "We were weapons, tools, pretty puppets to dance on his strings. And you know what happens to tools that break his rules."

The memory of Kain's execution hung heavy between us—a stark reminder of the price of defiance. But there was more. So many more broken bodies, shattered souls, centuries of calculated cruelty disguised as love.

"Selene," Raya commanded without taking her eyes off me, "seal the exits."

Purple magic shimmered across the windows and doors as Selene complied. The remaining patrons scattered, leaving only our twisted family in the suddenly too-small room.

"I'll bring Father your head myself," Raya purred, drawing twin blades from her back. "I've waited centuries for this, brother."

"You always were jealous," I taunted, buying time as I assessed our options. Five against two—no, against one. I had to keep Atreya out of this. "Father's second best. Never quite good enough, were you?"

Raya's beautiful face contorted with rage. "I am his true heir!" She launched herself at me, blades singing through the air.

I caught her first strike on my forearm, letting her momentum carry her past me.

The other siblings backed away, forming a loose circle around us. This was between Raya and me—an ancient rivalry finally coming to blood.

"True heir?" I laughed, the sound harsh and cold. "Is that what he told you while I was gone? Did it help you sleep better, sister, thinking you'd finally earned his favor?"

Raya's blades were a silver blur as she attacked, each strike precise and lethal. I dodged the first, caught the second with my bare hand, ignoring the bite of steel into flesh. Through the blood bond, I felt Atreya's sharp intake of breath at my pain.

"You abandoned him," Raya snarled, breaking free of my grip. "Abandoned us. And for what? Some Fae witch who'll never love you?"

I moved like shadow, like death, like all the things Xaneth had taught us to be. My fist connected with her jaw, sending her staggering back. "Better than being his puppet for eternity."

She spat blood, her crimson eyes blazing. "At least I know what I am. You?" She circled me, blades catching the lamplight. "You pretend at nobility, at redemption. But we both know what lives in your heart, brother. The same darkness he put in all of us."

"You're right." I felt that darkness rising now, ancient and hungry. "Let me show you exactly what he made me."

We clashed again, faster than human eyes could follow. Her blade opened a gash across my chest; my elbow cracked against her ribs. We were mirror images of destruction, everything Xaneth had crafted us to be.

"I saw what you did to his soldiers," Raya panted, blood dripping from a split in her lip. "Fifteen of them, torn apart. Was that your nobility at work?"

Through the bond, Atreya's shock hit me like a physical blow. I hadn't told her about that night, about what I'd done to ensure our escape. Some truths were better left buried.

"Everything we love belongs to him. Everything we are belongs to him. When will you learn?"

"Never." I caught her wrist, twisted until I heard bones crack. "That's why he hates me most."

She didn't scream—Xaneth had trained that out of us centuries ago. Instead, she drove her knee into my stomach, following with a slash that would have opened my throat if I hadn't moved in time.

"He doesn't hate you," she spat. "He's disappointed."

"Better disappointment than slavery." I drove forward, matching her speed with raw power. "Better exile than another century of his 'love.'"

"His favorite son, his perfect weapon, reduced to this—playing protector to some Fae queen. Tell me, what do you get out of this? Is her cunt sweet?"

My fist connected with her sternum, sending her crashing into a table. She rolled, came up with a throwing knife that embedded itself in my shoulder. I yanked it free and sent it back, pinning her sleeve to the wall.

"I'll tell you what *we* did to Kain," she snarled, ripping free. "Every detail, every scream. I'll tell her too." She jerked her chin toward Atreya. "Let her know exactly what happens to those we dare to care about."

Something in me snapped. The careful control I'd maintained for centuries cracked, letting the darkness beneath surge forward. My vision tinged red as ancient power coursed through my veins—the gift Xaneth had unwittingly given only me.

Spawns aren't meant to transform.

The first time it happened, I thought I was dying.

We were training in the underground chambers, as we did each night. Blood—my blood—painted the stone floor black in the torchlight. Xaneth circled me like a predator, each movement a study in lethal grace.

"Again," he commanded, his black eyes gleaming with something I couldn't name. "Show me what you're truly capable of."

I was stronger than the others, had been from the beginning. But strength wasn't enough. It would never be enough for him.

The change started in my core—a sickening crack that sent me to my knees. My spine twisted, vertebrae shifting and elongating with wet pops that echoed off the chamber walls. Black veins spread across my skin like spilled ink, pulsing in time with my thundering heart.

"Interesting," Xaneth murmured, watching me convulse with clinical detachment. "Very interesting."

I lunged at him without conscious thought, moving faster than I ever had before. My talons raked across his chest, drawing first blood—something none of his other children had managed in three centuries.

His laughter echoed off the stone walls. "Beautiful," he breathed, touching the wounds with something like reverence. "Perfect."

Then his hand was around my throat, slamming me into the chamber wall hard enough to crack stone. "How long?" he demanded. "How long have you been able to do this?"

I snarled, the sound inhuman, and tried to break free. My wings beat frantically, powerful enough to create gusts that whipped his hair around his face. But I was still untrained in this form, still weak compared to his centuries of power.

He began to squeeze.

"Weeks," I choked out finally. "Maybe... months."

His grip tightened until I felt cartilage begin to give. "And you didn't tell me?"

"Because... I knew..." My talons dug into his wrist, drawing blood that ran black in the torchlight. "Knew you'd... use it."

"Use it?" His laugh was soft, almost gentle. "My boy, I'm going to perfect it."

The next hours were a lesson in pain I would never forget. He broke each wing methodically, watching how they healed. He tested the limits of my transformed strength, my speed, my endurance. And when I tried to revert back to my normal form, he forced me to maintain the transformation until blood ran from my nose and ears.

By the time dawn approached, I lay broken on the chamber floor, wings shredded to ribbons, scales flaking off to reveal raw flesh beneath. The transformation had finally given way, leaving me small and vulnerable in a way that made my teeth ache.

He gathered my limp body into his arms with uncharacteristic tenderness. "You understand now, don't you?" he murmured, brushing blood-matted hair from my face. "Everything you are belongs to me. Every power, every breath, every drop of blood in your veins—it's all mine."

I tried to speak, but only managed a wet cough that spattered crimson across his chest.

"Shhh." His lips pressed against my forehead, tasting of copper and salt. "Rest now, my perfect weapon. Tomorrow, we begin again."

And we did. Night after night, he forced me to transform, then broke me down until I could barely remember my own name. Until the very thought of changing made me shake with terror and remembered pain.

Until I was exactly what he needed me to be—his masterpiece, his monster, his most beloved nightmare.

Three centuries later, I can still feel his hands on my wings, still hear him whispering praise even as he tore me apart. And now, standing in this tavern with my transformation pending body, I see the same fascination in Raya's eyes that I saw in his.

The same hunger to break something beautiful.

It began at my core, a sickening crack of bone and sinew as my spine elongated. Black veins spider-webbed across my skin like ink in water, pulsing with each thundering heartbeat. My jaw distended with an audible snap, fangs bursting from my gums in gleaming ivory daggers. The pain was exquisite—a symphony of breaking and remaking that I'd denied myself for so long.

Membrane and bone erupted from my shoulder blades in a spray of blood, unfurling into massive bat-like wings. They stretched translucent and white in the dim light, each vein and sinew visible like delicate lacework. My fingers lengthened into razor-sharp talons, skin hardening into armor-like scales that rippled with iridescent darkness.

I moved faster than thought, catching her throat in one hand and lifting her off her feet. My transformed voice was a guttural growl, barely recognizable as speech. "You won't speak his name," I snarled, feeling my fangs lengthen further, venom dripping from their points. "You won't speak to her at all."

My wings mantled around us both, casting shadows that seemed to writhe with a life of their own. The monster Xaneth had crafted was fully awakened now—ancient, terrible, and thirsting for blood. Every movement was liquid grace wrapped in lethal intent, power thrumming through newly transformed muscle and bone.

Raya's smile was all blood and triumph, even as she struggled for air. "There you are, brother. There's the monster he made you to be."

I could feel Atreya's horror through the bond, taste her fear on my tongue. This was what I really was—what I'd always been, beneath the thin veneer of civilization. My wings pulsed with each thundering heartbeat, the membrane so thin it was almost transparent, yet strong enough to shred steel.

A monster. A weapon. A thing of darkness and death.

Xaneth's perfect son.

CHAPTER 27

Atreya

I couldn't breathe.

The creature before me—because surely this couldn't be Ronan—was something out of ancient nightmares. His wings cast writhing shadows across the tavern floor, their translucent membrane revealing a delicate network of veins that pulsed with each beat of his heart. silver scales rippled across his skin like liquid metal, and when he turned his head slightly, I caught a glimpse of eyes that burned like molten silver with pupils that were pits of red.

His face had transformed into something both beautiful and terrible—sharp planes and harsh angles where there had once been softer features. Pronounced ridges swept along his brow bone like gothic architecture, casting deep shadows over those burning silver eyes. His cheekbones had become razor-sharp, stretching his alabaster skin into an aristocratic mask that belonged in the halls of ancient vampire lords. The bridge of his nose bore delicate ridges that traced up to his forehead, like the markings of some long-forgotten royal bloodline. I caught glimpses of long fangs that seemed too elegant to be mere weapons.

"Ronan." I took a step forward, ignoring the way Selene and the twins tensed. "Look at me."

He didn't move, didn't acknowledge me at all. Through the bond, I felt his consciousness slipping further into darkness, into the monster Xaneth had crafted him to be.

"*Ronan.*" I reached out, letting my fingers brush against the membrane of his wing. It was warm, impossibly soft despite its strength. "Come back."

The wing twitched under my touch. Slowly, so slowly, his head turned toward me. Those silver eyes fixed on my face, wild and ancient and not quite sane.

"There you are," I said softly, as if soothing a spooked horse. "I see you."

A shudder ran through his massive frame. The bond pulsed with confusion, with fear—not of me, but *for* me. He thought I would run from him now that I'd seen what he truly was.

"I'm not afraid," I told him, though my heart raced. "Not of you."

"No! Not in my tavern!" The barkeep's groan cut through the tension, his weathered hands gripping the edge of the bar until his knuckles went white. But even as he protested, he was already ducking behind the counter—he'd seen enough supernatural fights to know when to make himself scarce. "Take it outside, for gods' sake!"

Raya made a choked sound that might have been a laugh. "You should be. You should be terrified." Her fingers clawed at Ronan's grip, drawing blood that ran black down his scales. "This is what loving him gets you, little queen. Death and darkness and—"

The crack of her spine echoed through the tavern like a thunderclap.

Ronan's hand tightened with supernatural strength, and in one fluid motion, he snapped Raya's neck. Her body went limp, eyes wide with surprise even as the light faded from them. He let her corpse fall to the floor with a dull thud.

The silence that followed was absolute.

Then, one by one, the other vampires—including his siblings—dropped to their knees. Selene was the first, her white-blonde hair falling forward to hide her face as she bowed her head. The twins followed, their movements synchronized even in submission.

"My lord," Selene whispered.

I felt Ronan's surprise war with something darker, more primal. His wings spread wider. "No. Stand. I am not Xaneth.

They stood, but kept their heads bowed. Even Selene, who had struck him earlier with such contempt, now radiated deference.

"Swear it," Ronan commanded, carrying that otherworldly resonance. His wings mantled wider, casting the kneeling vampires in deeper shadow. "Swear you never saw us here. That you never saw what I've become."

"Brother—" Selene started, but his growl cut her off.

"Swear it on your blood. On your bond to Xaneth himself." His talons flexed, Raya's blood still dripping from their points. "Or join our sister."

The twins exchanged glances—a silent conversation born of centuries together. Finally, Marcus spoke, "I swear it. On blood and bond, I swear we never found you."

"As do I," Domini echoed.

Only Selene hesitated, her amber eyes fixed on Raya's cooling corpse. "He'll know," she said softly. "He always knows."

"Then lie *better*." Ronan's wings shifted, sending dancing shadows across the walls. "You're good at that, sister. Tell him we were already gone when you arrived. Tell him whatever pretty story will keep your head attached to your shoulders."

Through the bond, I felt his fear for them—these broken siblings who'd suffered alongside him for centuries. Despite everything, he didn't want them to face Xaneth's wrath.

"I swear it," Selene finally whispered. "On blood and bond, I swear we never saw you or the queen." She raised her head, meeting his transformed gaze. "But brother... he won't stop hunting you. Either of you."

"I know," he said.

"Is she worth all this?"

Ronan didn't answer Selene's question. His wings trembled slightly, and through our bond, I felt something shifting—like sand slipping through an hourglass, like water trickling away.

The connection that had hummed between us since he shared his blood was slowly fading, its melody growing fainter with each passing second. I pressed a hand to my chest where the bond had burned brightest, feeling its absence like a physical ache.

His transformation began to reverse, scales melting back into skin, wings folding into nothing as if they'd never existed. But his eyes—they stayed that molten silver, pupils still ringed with red, as he turned to look at me.

I knew then, with a certainty that scared me, that this was the last time I'd feel his emotions bleeding into mine. The last time I'd know his heart as clearly as my own.

"Get some sleep," he said roughly. He wouldn't meet my eyes now, wouldn't answer the question still hanging in the air. "We have a long journey ahead tomorrow."

Tell me, I wanted to say again. *Please tell me if I'm worth all this.*

But he never answered that question. Maybe he couldn't. Or maybe the answer scared him as much as it scared me.

I watched him walk away, his silver hair catching the moonlight streaming through the window. The bond gave one final, feeble pulse—like a goodbye—and then it was gone, leaving only echoes of what had been.

And questions that would remain unanswered.

CHAPTER 28

Ronan

The tavern came back to life.

None of the other vampires acknowledged the violence that had just occurred outside of bowing their respects. They were too old, too jaded for that. When you've lived for centuries, death becomes as commonplace as breathing is to mortals. A young vampire in a velvet coat dealt cards at a corner table, his victims' rings still adorning his pale fingers. Two female vampires in elaborate dress whispered and giggled over some private joke, their fangs glinting as they smiled. The scene was almost peaceful—if you could ignore the predatory gleam in their eyes, the way they watched the few human patrons like wolves eyeing sheep.

This was our world. Violence followed by civility. Death followed by drinks. The endless waltz of immortality.

I could feel my siblings' presence behind me—their fear, their reverence, their horror. All of it scraped against my nerves like steel on bone.

Marcus stepped forward, his boots scraping against the wooden floor. "You think that will protect her? Sending her to bed? Brother, you just killed one of our own. In front of witnesses."

"The witnesses swore—"

"Oaths mean nothing to Xaneth," Domini cut in. "You know this better than any of us. He can cut truth out of stone."

I did. Gods help me, I did. My hands clenched into fists, and I watched as silver scales rippled beneath my skin before fading again. The transformation wasn't fully settled yet. Maybe it never would be.

I turned to face them fully, these broken pieces of my past that refused to let me go. The candlelight caught Marcus's face, highlighting the scar Xaneth had given him centuries ago—a reminder of what happened to those who failed our maker. Domini stood rigid, his hands clenched at his sides, still wearing the military bearing from his human life that even immortality hadn't erased. And Selene... Selene watched me with eyes that had seen too much, understood too well.

Selene was my favorite. I would never say such a thing out loud, but they knew it.

I found her in the carnage of Bone Isle. Seventeen. Covered in other people's blood. Beautiful in the way broken things can be beautiful.

She'd tried to save her sister. Stupid. Brave. The kind of thing that made me pause with my blade already wet with the village's death. The little one was already cooling in the root cellar when I found them. Selene didn't beg. Didn't cry. Just looked at me with eyes that promised violence.

"Let me close her eyes," she said. Steady voice. Steady hands. Even with my knife against her throat.

Xaneth had rules about who we could turn. Pretty faces. Strong souls. The ones who could become monsters worth keeping. Selene? She was already halfway there.

I delivered her to him like a gift. No clothes. No tears. Nothing but rage wrapped in smooth skin and sharp bones. Xaneth's tongue flicked out when he saw her. Snake-like. Hungry. "Exquisite," he called her.

The change nearly broke her.

Three days of screaming. That's what it took for Xaneth's venom to burn through her humanity. I watched her writhe on the stone floor, her skin growing paler with each passing hour until it was like polished bone. Her hair turned white as death itself, bleached of color by the change, spreading around her head like fresh snow on burial ground. When she finally opened her eyes, they blazed with an unholy amber fire. The hunger that followed was exquisite in its violence. She tore through five villagers before her mind returned, before she could form words again. But when she did speak, her voice carried the weight of centuries she hadn't lived yet. No trace remained of the girl from Bone Isle. In her place stood something eternal. Something perfect.

When it was over, she looked at me with new eyes. Immortal eyes. "Thank you," she said, "for making it quick. For my sister."

Mercy's a funny thing. She hated me for sparing her life more than for taking her sister's. That hatred kept her sharp. Kept her alive. While others begged their way into immortality—plague victims, war refugees, desperate souls—Selene came to us baptized in the blood of everyone she'd ever loved.

She wore her trauma like a crown. Made Xaneth nervous sometimes, the way she'd look at him. Like she was counting his weaknesses. Cataloging the ways she might one day make him pay.

That's why she's my favorite. Because she understood the truth: Sometimes living is the cruelest punishment of all.

"You can't protect her forever," Marcus said, moving closer. His shadow stretched across the floor like spilled ink. "Xaneth will find out. He always does."

I met his gaze, letting him see what the change had done to my eyes. "I'm not the same creature he made anymore. Neither are you."

A bitter laugh escaped Domini. "Different enough to murder Raya? She was one of us for three centuries."

I waved a hand flippantly. "Is that really a loss though?"

"Ramses is going to lay waste to this land. We are to move on from it," Selene said.

"Then move on from it. I'm not leaving."

Not until I finished what I started.

"What is the end game here?" Selene huffed. "Xaneth won't stop looking for you. He will eventually create more spawns with blind faith like Raya." She waved her hand at our dead sister's body crumpled on the floor. "This is a plague."

"It does not concern any of you."

Selene threw her hands up in the air. "This is the Water City all over again—"

"Don't."

"You are doing this blind and with your cock. She has a pretty face, I can find you another! Please, brother, I beg you, reconsider this. Her scent is wrong. All wrong. She is already married to the Cruel King—"

"Enough," Marcus sighed. He spoke to Domini and Selene then. "He's made up his mind."

Selene opened and closed her mouth like a fish. "But—"

Marcus cut her off with a look.

He turned to me. "We are coming with you."

"Like hell you are."

He shrugged. "It's either we come with you, or we go back to Xaneth empty-handed and get tortured. And I'll make sure you feel everything down our blood bonds."

Domini moved to stand beside Marcus, his military precision making the motion look like a battle formation. "Think logically. Four of us stand a better chance than one, especially now that you've... decided on leaving."

Selene was silent, her lip curled into a snarl.

They weren't wrong—having them with me would increase our chances of survival. But it would also multiply the risks. More bodies meant more tracks to cover, more minds for Xaneth to probe, more weaknesses to exploit.

Besides that, I highly doubt Eldra would be privy to let in four vampires into New Solara. And I doubt they would be happy about it either. His fucking surname literally meant *Sunlight* in the Old Tongue.

Still. They were mine. My blood. My burden.

"Fine," Selene said.

"Fine," I growled. "But we do this my way. No questions. No arguments. And if any of you even think about betraying her location to Xaneth—"

"We know, we know," Domini interrupted, rolling his eyes. "You'll tear out our hearts and feed them to us. Your threats were more creative when you were younger."

"You are only to come with me to the Port of Ambrose. That's it."

"Fine by me. We can take a boat to get the hell off this godsforsaken place," Selene snapped.

I motioned to the other barkeep, a weathered vampire with skin like cracked leather, Not the one who yelled at us earlier. "Bloodwine. The good stuff. Four glasses."

The barkeep's yellowed eyes flickered between us before he nodded, reaching beneath the counter for a dusty bottle with a black wax seal. The liquid inside gleamed like rubies in candlelight.

Marcus smirked as the glasses were poured. "So... Atreya." He drew out her name like a blade being unsheathed. "Quite the beauty. Those silver eyes alone would make any man—or monster—lose his head."

"Don't," I warned, but Domini was already grinning.

"Oh, come now, brother. You can't blame us for being curious." Domini lifted his glass in a mock toast. "Did you bed her yet? Or is the mighty Ronan actually playing the gentleman this time?"

Selene's sharp laugh cut through my anger.

"Gentleman?" She took a long drink, her amber eyes gleaming over the rim of her glass. "Our brother? The same one who once seduced an entire convent just to spite a cardinal?"

"That was different," I growled.

"Was it?" Marcus leaned forward, his scar catching the light. "Or is it that this time you actually care? That's why you're being so... careful."

"My relationship with Atreya is none of your concern."

"So there is a relationship," Domini pounced on the words. "Beyond just wanting to save her pretty neck from Xaneth?"

Selene muttered something that sounded suspiciously like "or bite it" into her glass.

I drained my bloodwine in one swallow, letting the rich taste of it wash away the urge to strangle them all. "If you're quite finished..."

"Not even close," Marcus grinned, showing fang. "But we'll save the rest for the road. After all, it's a long way to the Port of Ambrose."

The others laughed, and I wondered, not for the first time, if killing Raya had been the easier part of my night.

The bloodwine hit different tonight.

Maybe it was the stress of killing Raya. Maybe it was the weight of my siblings' judgment. Or maybe it was just that the barkeep had been holding out on us with the good stuff all along. Whatever the reason, by the fourth glass, the room had taken on that peculiar tilt that usually preceded very bad decisions.

"You know what's funny?" I announced to no one in particular, watching the candlelight dance through my empty glass. "Her eyes... they're like liquid moonlight. And that black hair... like shadows coming alive. Dancing shadows."

Domini choked on his drink. "Oh gods, he's actually gone and fallen in love."

"Have not," I growled, but the effect was somewhat ruined when I missed the edge of the bar with my elbow and nearly face-planted into the counter. "I just appreciate... aesthetics."

"Aesthetics," Selene repeated dryly. "Is that what we're calling it now?" She grabbed at her breasts and made kissing sounds.

Marcus was practically vibrating with poorly contained glee. "Remember when he tried to write poetry that one time? In Odath?"

"Don't you fucking dare—"

But Domini was already clearing his throat dramatically, adopting a horrible impression of my voice: "'Your blue eyes pierce like starlight through darkness, your smile deadlier than any blade—'"

"I will end you."

"'Your beauty strikes me like a stake through the heart—'"

"That's it." I lunged across the table, but in my current state, I miscalculated spectacularly. Instead of grabbing Domini's throat, I managed to knock over three glasses, upend a chair, and somehow get my coat caught on one of Selene's ridiculous sleeve ruffles.

The resulting tangle sent us both sprawling to the floor in a heap of leather and lace.

"Your coordination," Selene observed from beneath me, "is like a newborn foal learning to walk. But dead. A dead foal. That's also drunk."

"Shut up," I muttered, trying to extract myself with what remained of my dignity. The room wouldn't stop spinning. "This is your fault. All of you. With your... your faces. And your judging. And your remembering things I specifically told you to forget."

Marcus was actually wiping tears from his eyes. "Oh, but brother, how could we forget? Especially the part where you compared her gaze to 'twin moons that guide lost souls to their doom—'"

I managed to get to my feet, swaying only slightly. "I'm leaving. To check on Atreya. Because I'm responsible. And none of you appreciate my literary genius."

"Your what now?" Domini wheezed.

I pointed at them accusingly, though I might have been pointing at a coat rack. "Stay. Here. All of you. I mean it."

"Of course," Selene said solemnly. "We wouldn't dream of following you to witness whatever catastrophic attempt at romance you're about to commit."

I turned with all the dignity I could muster, which wasn't much, and promptly walked into a support beam.

The last thing I heard before stumbling up the stairs was Marcus's voice: "Ten gold pieces says he tries to serenade her."

"Twenty says he falls down the stairs first," Selene countered.

I made it up exactly three steps before proving her right.

CHAPTER 29

Atreya

Sleep was a stranger that night.

I lay in the tavern's narrow bed, my thoughts as restless as shadows dancing across the rough-hewn ceiling beams. Moonlight painted silver stripes on the wood above, but every time I closed my eyes, all I could see were Ronan's wings casting those writhing shadows, Raya's body falling like a puppet with cut strings. The crack of her spine echoed in my memory—a sound I knew would join the collection of horrors that already haunted my dreams.

But worse than the violence was the silence in my mind.

The severed bond felt like a phantom limb—ghost sensations of emotions that weren't mine anymore, echoes of a connection I'd barely begun to understand before it was ripped away. My hand pressed against my chest, searching for even the faintest whisper of Ronan's presence, but found only the steady drum of my own heartbeat.

A floorboard groaned in the hallway.

I sat up, my hand automatically reaching for the iron dagger beneath my pillow. But the footsteps passed my door without pausing, their cadence too light to be Ronan's. Probably one of the twins, I thought, though I couldn't tell which.

Dawn was still hours away when I finally gave up on sleep. I dressed quietly in the dark, lacing my boots with fingers that trembled more than I wanted to admit. The mirror above the washbasin showed me a stranger—a girl with shadows under her eyes and steel in her spine. I barely recognized myself anymore.

The floorboards creaked outside my door again—not the light steps from before, but heavy, stumbling ones that made the ancient wood groan in protest. I reached for my dagger, but before I could grasp it, the door swung open with all the grace of a wounded bear.

Ronan stood—or rather, swayed—in the doorway, his usual predatory grace replaced by something decidedly more... mortal. His silver hair was mussed, falling across those impossible eyes that couldn't quite seem to focus on any one spot. The same creature who'd snapped Raya's neck hours ago now appeared to be having an intense argument with my doorframe.

"You're drunk," I said, amazed. The mighty vampire, was thoroughly, utterly trashed.

"No," he replied with grave dignity, then promptly walked into my washbasin. "Maybe. Slightly. It's the bloodwine's fault. Marcus started it."

I bit back a laugh. "Did he force it down your throat?"

"He quoted my poetry." Ronan's face twisted like he'd tasted something foul. "From *Odath*."

"You write poetry?"

"Wrote. Past tense. Very past. Ancient history." He finally managed to find the chair, though it took him two attempts to actually sit in it. "It was terrible poetry. About eyes like moons and... other things that shouldn't be spoken of."

The mighty creature who'd had me terrified of his power hours ago was now slumped in my chair, looking more like a dejected schoolboy than an immortal being. It was... oddly endearing.

"But you know what?" Ronan straightened suddenly in the chair, nearly toppling it backward. "They're wrong. My poetry was... *is*... magnificent. Listen—" He cleared his throat with theatrical gravity.

"In shadows deep and moonlight pale,

Your beauty makes my dead heart quail,

Like silver stars in midnight skies,

I drown within your perfect—hiccup—eyes."

I pressed my lips together, trying desperately not to laugh. The fearsome vampire who'd torn through Raya like tissue paper was now gesturing grandly with each verse, nearly smacking the washbasin off its stand.

"That's not even the best part," he declared, standing up with such sudden enthusiasm that he had to grab the wall for support. "I also wrote songs. Many songs. Brilliant songs."

"Oh no," I whispered, but it was too late.

"MY HEAAAART BEATS NOT BUT FOR YOUUUU!" His voice boomed through the tiny room, managing to be both incredibly loud and impressively off-key. "LIKE BLOOD IN MOONLIIIIGHT, MY LOVE IS TRUUUUE!"

"Ronan—"

"THOUGH CENTURIES PAAAASS LIKE GRAINS OF SAAAAND—"

Selene's voice cut through the catastrophic serenade as she passed the open door: "Ten gold pieces, Marcus!"

Ronan spun toward her so fast he nearly fell over. "You're supposed to be downstairs!"

"And you're supposed to be dignified," she called back, her laughter echoing down the hallway. "We're both disappointed!"

He turned back to me with an expression of profound betrayal. "Nobody appreciates art anymore."

"Is that what we're calling it?" I asked, unable to hold back my grin any longer.

"Everyone's a critic," he muttered, slumping back into the chair. "Just wait until I get to the verse about your hair being like... like..." He frowned deeply. "What's black and also beautiful?"

"Maybe we should save the rest of your artistic repertoire for another time," I suggested gently.

"Probably wise," he agreed, his eyes starting to drift closed. "The room's spinning anyway. Makes the words all... swooshy."

"Swooshy?" I chuckled.

"Wait!" His eyes flew open suddenly. "I remembered another one. This is... this is my masterpiece." He attempted to stand again, swaying like a tree in a storm. "I wrote this in... somewhere. A place. With trees."

"That narrows it down," I said dryly.

"Shhhh. Art requires silence." He raised one finger dramatically, nearly poking himself in the eye. "Ahem...

'Oh crimson drops that stain my lips,

Like rubies caught in moonlight's grips,

No vintage fine could taste as sweet,

As when our immortal hearts did meet—'"

"TWENTY MORE GOLD PIECES!" Marcus shouted from downstairs.

"WOULD YOU ALL JUST—" Ronan spun toward the door again, lost his balance, and had to catch himself on the bedpost. "—stop interrupting genius at work!"

"Is that what we're witnessing?" Selene's call drifted up. "I thought someone was torturing a cat."

Ronan's face scrunched up in indignation. "I'll have you know I once performed for a queen!"

"Was she deaf?" Domini chimed in.

"She was very appreciative of my talents!" Ronan shouted back, then lowered his voice to a conspiratorial whisper. "Though, now that I think about it, she might have been trying to have me executed the next day. The details are fuzzy."

I couldn't help it—I burst out laughing.

"Nobody understands artists," he muttered. "We suffer for our craft."

"We're all suffering for it right now," Selene called up.

"That's it!" He straightened, wobbling only slightly. "I'm going to prove my artistic worth once and for all. The ballad of the silver-eyed maiden needs a proper chorus!"

"Please don't—"

"WHEN MOOOOONLIGHT STRIKES YOUR RAVEN HAAAAIR—"

"THIRTY GOLD PIECES!" Three voices shouted in unison from below.

I was beginning to understand why some vampires chose to sleep in crypts.

"I think you need some fresh air" I laughed, helping him up straight.

Before I could stop him, he lurched toward the window, fumbling with the latch.

"Ronan, wait—"

But he was already climbing out, his usual grace completely abandoned as he nearly fell headfirst onto the slanted tiles. I rushed to the window, heart in my throat, only to find him sprawled on his back, staring up at the stars with an expression of profound confusion.

"The roof," he announced gravely, "is very tilted tonight."

"That's generally how roofs work," I said, trying not to laugh. "Come back inside before you fall off."

"The stars are dancing," he mumbled, making no move to get up. "Like your eyes. But... in the sky."

I sighed, keeping careful watch over his prone form.

"Just let me sleep here for an hour," he slurred. "Just one hour. The sun's not up yet."

I glanced at the eastern horizon—still dark, but I knew dawn wasn't far off. The thought of him burning in the sun sent ice through my veins. "Absolutely not. Inside. Now."

"One hour," he repeated, his eyes already closing. "Promise I'll wake up. Vampire's honor."

"That's not a thing."

But he was already drifting off, his face softening in a way I'd never seen before.

Because Vampires didn't need sleep. Unless they were drunk as fuck I guess.

I settled by the window, my eyes fixed on the horizon. One hour. I could stay awake for one hour, counting every minute to make sure he didn't burn when dawn broke. The night air was cool against my skin, carrying the salt-tang of the distant sea and the musty scent of the tavern's old wood. From below, I could hear his siblings still laughing, carrying up through the thin floors.

I watched the stars wheel overhead, each one a bright reminder of how much time was passing. Every few minutes, I checked the eastern sky, my heart racing faster as the darkness ever so slowly began to fade.

Ronan didn't stir, his chest rising and falling in a rhythm that seemed too human for what he was. One strand of silver hair fell across his face, moving slightly with each breath. The mighty vampire, laid low by bloodwine and bad poetry, completely at my mercy.

And here I was, keeping vigil to make sure he survived his own drunken foolishness.

The irony wasn't lost on me.

Is she worth all this?

He eventually stirred awake, stretching his limbs, a silhouette cut sharp against the star-strewn sky. No wings now, no scales catching moonlight—just a man who looked too young to carry the weight of centuries. He didn't turn as I climbed out onto the roof, but his shoulders tensed, acknowledging my presence.

"You should be resting," he said, his voice carrying that same roughness from earlier. Sober.

"So should you." I settled beside him, letting my legs dangle over the edge. The night air was cool against my skin, carrying the scent of pine and distant rain. "But I guess neither of us are very good at doing what we should."

A muscle ticked in his jaw. "No. We're not."

"What happened to the bond?" I asked, because someone had to break this fragile silence between us. "Why did you—"

"It ran its course." His words cut through the night air like steel. "What you saw tonight... that power comes with a price. And I won't let you pay it."

I shifted closer, ignoring how he tensed. "That's not your choice to make."

"Isn't it?" Bitterness crept over him. "I've watched Xaneth's blood bonds destroy everything they touch for centuries. They start as chains of gold and end as nooses." His hands clenched into fists. "I won't be your executioner."

"You're not Xaneth."

"No." A laugh scraped from his throat, harsh and hollow. "I'm worse. What he did to create me—" He broke off, shaking his head.

The space between us felt vast suddenly, though we sat close enough that I could feel the unnatural heat radiating from his skin. I thought of Raya's body hitting the floor, of the way his siblings had knelt before him like supplicants before an altar.

"Show me again," I whispered.

His head snapped toward me. "What?"

"Your wings. Show me."

"No." He started to stand, but I caught his wrist.

"Please." I held his gaze, refusing to look away from the conflict warring in those red depths. "I need to see you. All of you."

For a long moment, he didn't move. Then, slowly, like ice cracking in spring, something in him yielded. The air around us grew heavy, charged with that same electric energy I'd felt in the tavern. His skin rippled, moonlight catching on scales that emerged like stars breaking through clouds.

The wings unfurled with a sound like silk sliding over steel, their span blocking out the sky above us. This close, I could see patterns in the membrane—swirls and whorls that looked almost like writing in a language too ancient to name.

I reached out, letting my fingers trace one of the veins that pulsed with his heartbeat. He shuddered but didn't pull away.

"Beautiful," I breathed.

His laugh this time was softer, tinged with wonder and fear in equal measure. "You truly aren't afraid, are you?"

"I told you before—not of you." Then I smacked his arm. "You could have flown us across that damn bridge! You son of a bitch!"

His wings shuddered, then disappeared as suddenly as they'd appeared. "You really aren't afraid."

"You sound disappointed."

"Kind of am."

"Disappointed that I'm not running screaming into the night?" I leaned back on my hands. "A little late for that."

"You saw what I did to Raya. What I *am*."

I let out a heavy sigh. "Ronan. My hands are not clean of blood. I know the feel of a neck breaking in my hands. What you did does not frighten me."

His eyes flashed in the darkness, that impossible silver catching starlight. "There's a difference between killing to survive and what I am. What I was made to be."

"And what exactly were you made to be?" I challenged, turning to face him fully. "Xaneth's weapon? His perfect monster?" I reached up, ignoring his flinch as my fingers traced the line of his jaw. "Because from where I'm sitting, you've already proven him wrong. You protected your siblings tonight, even after everything. A true monster wouldn't care."

Ramses had used me has his weapon countless times. Used me without so much as a second thought. My husband was a cruel thing. He was the monster.

"I was married to one."

Ramses didn't need wings or scales to be monstrous.

A shiver ran through me at the memory of those nights in the palace—of being dragged from my bed, of fighting against iron grips while my pleas echoed off stone walls. Of standing naked and exposed in an arena, blood running down my thighs, while thousands watched. No, Ramses hadn't needed supernatural power to inflict terror.

"He used fear like a weapon," I said softly, my fingers still resting against Ronan's jaw. "The anticipation of pain can break someone just as effectively as the pain itself. Sometimes more so."

"That's why I can't maintain it," Ronan said suddenly, his voice rough. "The transformation. It—" He broke off, and I felt him struggling to find the words. "Each time I change, it drains something vital. Something that takes days, sometimes weeks to replenish."

I thought of the way the bond had faded, how his energy had seemed to slip away like water through cupped hands. "The blood magic?"

"More than that." His fingers traced absent patterns on the roof tiles. "Xaneth's experiments... he wanted weapons that could level cities. But even his power had limits. The transformation tears at the fabric of what I am. Too many changes too quickly, and there might not be enough of *me* left to come back."

A chill ran through me that had nothing to do with the night air. "You mean you could lose yourself? Like you almost did downstairs?"

"Or worse." His voice dropped to barely a whisper. "I've seen it happen to others. Xaneth's failed attempts. They'd change one too many times, and their bodies would just... collapse. Like houses built on rotting foundations."

I remembered the wild, ancient look in his silver eyes, the way his consciousness had slipped toward darkness. "the bond—" I started, but he cut me off.

"The bond linked us. If I pushed too far, if I lost control or..." He swallowed hard. "Your mind would shatter alongside mine."

"So we can't rely on your wings to escape," I said, trying to keep myself steady despite the horror of what he was describing. "We do this the hard way."

"The hard way," he agreed, and I caught the ghost of a smile at the corner of his mouth. "How disappointing for you."

"I've managed this long without flying." I bumped his shoulder with mine. "Though I still say you could have mentioned it before I climbed across that damn bridge."

His laugh was soft but genuine. "And miss watching you curse every plank? Never."

Once when I was young, looking out over the balcony of my bedroom at the clouds, I felt the sky crack open, and a deluge of water fell from the sky the whole day. It was cold.

Ramses had been particularly unforgiving. My dress had wrinkled. I had dared showed myself in such a state at the dinner table. Vryseris wasn't even a thought yet.

I thought I had known cold then. No.

He dragged me out into the night air, dress and all, and made me sit in the courtyard while the heavens wept. My bones had been made of ice then, threatening to shatter. I remember seeing the birds scrambling for cover out of the rain, and how I wished I had wings.

I learned something that night, as the rain soaked through layers of silk and pride. Ramses hadn't just been teaching me a lesson about proper dinner etiquette—he'd been showing me what power truly meant. The ability to make someone else feel small, to turn nature itself into a weapon of discipline.

The courtyard stones had patterns I'd never noticed before, whorls and ancient cracks that became rivers in the downpour. I traced them with

numb fingers, counting seconds, minutes, hours, until they blurred together like ink in water. Time moves differently when you're at the mercy
of someone else's cruelty.

If Vryseris had existed then, perhaps things would have been different.
But that's the trouble with looking back at memories through the lens
of what came after—we paint them with colors that didn't exist at the
time. No, that night belonged solely to Ramses, to rain, and to the girl I
was, learning that some lessons leave frost in your marrow that never quite
thaws.

And Servat, he had been sweet kindling in that Hellfrost. Ronan—did
he have someone like that?

Like how Selene had Kain, however brief?

Did he ever love and lost?

CHAPTER 30

Ronan

T he dawn brought with it the kind of headache that made me question several centuries of life choices.

I found my siblings sprawled across various surfaces of the tavern's main room, looking about as dignified as drowned rats. Marcus was face-down on a table, one arm dangling limply over the edge. Domini had somehow wedged himself between two barrels, his usually pristine military posture replaced by something that resembled a broken marionette. And Selene, my dear sister, was curled up in a corner, using her elaborate dress as a makeshift nest while muttering curses in at least three dead languages.

"I hate everything," she announced to no one in particular. "Especially you, Ronan."

"Noted," I managed to croak, sounding like my throat had been dragged through gravel. The bloodwine that had seemed so excellent last night now felt like liquid regret coursing through my veins. "Though I believe this was Marcus's idea."

"Was not," came Marcus's muffled protest from the table. He didn't bother lifting his head. "I merely suggested we drink. You're the one who decided to perform your entire collection of terrible poetry."

Domini groaned from his barrel prison. "Please don't remind me. My ears are still bleeding."

"It wasn't terrible," I insisted, though fragments of last night's impromptu performance were starting to surface in my memory with horrifying clarity. Had I really tried to compose a new verse about Atreya's hair being like 'midnight's sweetest kiss'? Gods help me.

"It was worse than terrible," Selene said, finally managing to sit up. Her white hair looked like it had been styled by a hurricane. "It was memorable. Now we'll never be able to forget it, no matter how much we drink."

"Speaking of drinking," Marcus finally lifted his head, revealing an impressive imprint of wood grain on his cheek, "remind me never to touch bloodwine again. I think I can taste colors."

"You say that every century," Domini pointed out.

"And I mean it every century."

I started to respond, but movement from the stairs caught my attention. Atreya descended, looking frustratingly alert and put-together. The sight of her made fragments of last night crash back into my consciousness—climbing onto the roof, my wings, our conversation about Ramses...

And before that, oh gods, the singing.

She caught my eye and smiled, a hint of mischief playing at the corners of her mouth. "Good morning, my artistic friend. Any new verses you'd like to share with the class?"

My siblings' collective groans could probably be heard in the next town.

"I'm going back to Xaneth," Selene declared, pulling her dress over her head like a shroud. "It would be less painful."

"Don't you dare," I warned, then immediately regretted it as my head throbbed in protest.

Atreya's laugh was like silver bells—beautiful, but currently far too loud. "Don't worry, I won't ask for an encore. Though I have to admit, the part about my eyes being 'twin moons that guide lost souls to their doom' was... memorable."

"Kill me," I muttered. "Someone please just kill me now."

"Can't," Marcus said cheerfully, despite looking like death warmed over. "We need you alive to remind us of this moment forever. The great and terrible Ronan, brought low by bloodwine and bad poetry."

"I hate all of you."

"No, you don't," Atreya said softly, and it made me look up. She was watching us with an expression I couldn't quite read—something between amusement and understanding, with perhaps a touch of envy. "This is what family looks like."

The words hung in the air, heavy with meaning. I thought of her marriage to Ramses, of cold palace halls and calculated cruelty. Of how different this must seem – four immortal beings, sprawled around a tavern in various states of dishevelment, bickering like children despite our centuries of existence.

"Yes," I said finally, meeting her gaze. "I suppose it is."

Marcus was the first to recover, straightening his coat with exaggerated dignity despite the wood grain still imprinted on his cheek. He swept into an elaborate bow that only swayed slightly.

"My lady Atreya," he purred, taking her hand before I could stop him. "I don't believe we've been properly introduced. I'm Marcus, the handsome one of the family." He pressed a kiss to her knuckles, letting it linger just a moment too long. "I must say, our brother's poetry hardly does your beauty justice."

I growled low in my throat, but Domini was already stepping forward, his military bearing somehow intact despite his obvious hangover.

"Domini," he said simply, offering a crisp bow. "Former general of the Third Legion, current babysitter to these three disasters." He shot me a pointed look. "Though some require more supervision than others."

"You tried to duel a statue last night," Selene muttered, finally emerging from her dress-cocoon. Her white hair stuck up at impossible angles, but she managed to make it look intentional. "I'm Selene. The only one with any sense, though you wouldn't know it from last night." She fixed Atreya with an appraising look. "Also, since my idiot brother hasn't told you yet – we're coming with you to Port Ambrose."

"You're what?" Atreya's eyes widened, darting to me.

"Oh, he didn't mention that part?" Selene's smile was sharp. "Typical. We're your new traveling companions. At least until the port. Then we're getting on the first ship out of this godsforsaken place."

"I was going to tell her," I grumbled.

"When? After another poetry recital?" Marcus grinned, then turned back to Atreya with a look that made me want to throw him through a wall. "I do hope you'll allow me to walk beside you on our journey. I'd love to hear more about the woman who inspired such... passionate verses."

"Touch her hand again," I said pleasantly, "and you'll be walking with broken fingers."

"So possessive," Marcus sighed dramatically. "My lady, I do apologize for my brother's barbaric manners. Perhaps over our journey, I can show you what true refinement looks like."

Domini snorted. "You once ate an entire deer raw because you were too impatient to cook it."

"That was one time!"

"It was last week," Selene said flatly. "Bled it dry and ate it. Barbaric."

Atreya's laugh cut through their bickering—bright and genuine, with none of the careful restraint I'd heard in her voice at the palace. "Well," she said, looking at each of my siblings in turn, "this should be an interesting journey."

"Interesting," I muttered, watching Marcus straighten his cravat with renewed purpose. "That's one word for it."

Selene's amber eyes narrowed as she studied Atreya's face, a knowing smirk playing at her lips. "Those are quite the dark circles under your eyes, my dear. I trust my brother kept you up all night with his... poetry?"

"I was making sure he didn't burn to death in the dawn, actually," Atreya replied dryly. "Someone had to keep watch while he was busy composing verses on the roof."

"The roof?" Marcus perked up, his hangover momentarily forgotten. "Oh, this keeps getting better."

"Someone owes me forty gold coins, I'm not sure who. So in light of that, all four of you should cough up ten," Domini said, his hand stretched out.

"Fuck off," I ground, pinching my nose.

"Sun is out," Atreya said, glancing toward the tavern's grimy windows. "We can't travel until night anyway." Her stomach chose that moment to growl loudly, making her cheeks flush.

Marcus's face lit up. "Breakfast! That's exactly what we need. And perhaps a touch of bloodwine to ease the—"

"Didn't you *just* say you were swearing off bloodwine forever?" Domini interrupted, raising an eyebrow.

"Did I?" Marcus looked genuinely puzzled. "That doesn't sound like something I'd say. Besides, hair of the dog and all that." He flagged down the tavern keeper. "A tray of your finest fruits, and another bottle of the good stuff!"

"Gods help us," Selene muttered.

Once the food arrived, they gathered around the scarred wooden table. Marcus was already pouring generous measures of bloodwine, ignoring Domini's disapproving stare.

"So," Marcus said, leaning forward with predatory interest, "tell us, dear Atreya – what's the worst thing you two have encountered in these charming woods so far?"

"The Hag," Atreya answered without hesitation, reaching for a bright red apple.

"The Kolqua fish," I said at the exact same time.

She turned to me, surprise evident on her face. "The fish? Really? After everything we've seen?"

"You didn't see it from underwater," I muttered, suppressing a shudder at the memory. "Those teeth... and the way it moves..." I took a long drink of bloodwine.

"More terrifying than the Hag?" Atreya challenged. "The one who literally tried to wear my skin?"

Marcus's eyes were gleaming with fascination. "Oh, this is going to be a delightful journey. Do tell us more about this skin-wearing Hag."

CHAPTER 31

Atreya

Ronan's family is utterly insane. I loved every minute of it. We exchanged stories at the table, Marcus already getting a little tipsy. He said he didn't have shit to do until night anyway, might as well have fun.

But I was exhausted, and Ronan knew it to. He ordered some meats and cheese on a tray then excused us to retire to the room.

In the soft glow of the dimly lit room, Ronan paused mid-chew, his eyes flicking up to meet mine.

"Why did you choose to stay with Ramses for such a long time? What was it that kept you there?" His question hung in the air as he took a bite of the lamb, chewing slowly, each movement of his jaw deliberate and measured.

His eyes squinted slightly as he exhaled a deep sigh, a grimace pulling at the corners of his mouth as he forced himself to swallow the well-cooked meat. He coughed lightly, clearing his throat before grimly noting, "This lamb... it's cooked far too much for my liking."

I watched him, a bemused smile playing on my lips. "You don't have to force yourself to eat it, you know. I can't imagine it's something you actually need, considering... well, you know," I gestured vaguely with a dismissive wave of my hand, "your vampiric status and all."

At this, his face fell into a solemn expression, a hint of disappointment clouding his features. I quickly cleared my throat, attempting to dispel the awkward tension that had suddenly descended upon us. Turning my back to him, I found my confidence again. "As for your question, it was my son. He was my reason, the driving force that made me endure Ramses for so long. I could have chosen to end it all at any point."

"But I couldn't. I had to stay, for my son's sake. I had to ensure he was safe, that he would have a future. Ramses, despite his faults, is a-a powerful man. He could provide protection, a sense of stability and safety—he's never hurt Vrys... And in our world, that was more valuable than anything else."

I could feel Ronan's gaze on me, his silence urging me to continue. "I couldn't let my son grow up without a mother, without someone to guide him, teach him, and watch over him. I can't imagine what he would be like without me. So, I made a sacrifice. I stayed with Ramses, withstood his cruelty, his indifference. All for my son."

The memories of those years were like a sharp blade, stabbing at my heart with each passing thought. But I pushed through, determined to get my point across.

"But now, things are different. I am different." I turned to face him. "Things are different now." My nails dug crescents into my palms. "I wake up, and I don't immediately check if Ramses is in a good mood. I speak, and I don't measure every word against his temper. I breathe, and for the first time in years, the air doesn't feel like it's choking me. I won't let *anyone*, not even Ramses, control my life anymore. I will fight for my freedom, for my son's freedom. And I will win."

"You sound a lot like a rebel leader," Ronan said.

A laugh bubbled from my throat, the sound echoing off the cave walls. "Perhaps I am," I replied, sincerely. "Perhaps that's exactly what I need to be."

I held his gaze, letting the weight of my words hang in the silence between us. I had never identified as a leader, much less a rebel. But my experiences had shaped me, hardened me. I was no longer the naive girl who had fallen in love with Ramses, who had placed her trust in the wrong hands.

"I'm tired of being a pawn in someone else's game," I continued in a harsh whisper. "I'm tired of living in fear. I want to take control of my own destiny, and if that makes me a rebel, then so be it." Years of being at the mercy of Ramses and whoever he had me bed. Of being forced to do whatever he wanted, no matter how monstrous. Of listening to my maidservants beg for their lives.

Strange how only a few days outside of his control, and I was ready to fight for my freedom, now that I had a taste of it. I could feel the anger building in me.

The memory of the arena and the screams of the crowd still rang in my ears.

If I did manage to get Vrys, we would not go back to Ember.

Ronan's gaze softened, a hint of admiration flickering in his eyes. He didn't say anything, but he didn't need to. His silence spoke volumes. In the dim light of the cave, I saw a new side of Ronan—a side that understood, that empathized.

A moment of silence passed between us before Ronan broke it, full of false cheer. "So, how about that fork? Or do you prefer using your hands?"

I stammered slightly, taken aback by the sudden shift in conversation. "I-I'll manage with my hands," I managed to respond, memories of our previous argument about eating utensils filling my mind. He had craftily whittled a small fork out of stone for me back then, a crude jest at my supposed 'pampered' lifestyle. I had no intention of giving him another opportunity for such mockery.

"You know, I've spent countless centuries shrouded in darkness, never expecting to find anything that would make this existence worthwhile. After all, I am technically dead." His words were punctuated with a light chuckle, his lips curving into a wry smile.

I stiffened at his laugh, my back still turned to him. "That sounds... quite lonely," I admitted quietly. I heard him sigh, and then felt his presence behind me. He reached over my shoulder, his fingers easily tearing through the leather straps I had been struggling to cut with my knife.

"You have claws, why do you not use them?" He queried, a note of amusement seeping into his question.

My response was sharp and defensive. "I've never really needed to use them." It was a partial truth; I did indeed possess claws, but their use was reserved for when Ramses required it.

Ronan's tone was laced with skepticism as he responded. "So, the tales I've heard of the formidable and ruthless Queen... they've been exaggerated?"

"I am not ruthless."

"Didn't you kill many of your own maidservants?"

"Never. I never laid a finger on them," I argued, not hiding my disgust. He laughed lightly, shaking his head in disbelief.

"What about the tale of you burning down an entire sector of Ember just to eliminate a few insignificant servants?"

I faltered, my grip on the leather straps loosening as they slipped from my grasp and fell to the floor. I turned to face him, my gaze meeting his towering figure.

"Oh come on. I showed you my monster. Now you show me yours."

"Do you want me to confess that every single rumor about me is true? Would that satisfy you? Would that bring me peace?" I asked.

"Did you actually burn it down? Because slaves fled to your temple for safety?"

"They didn't run fast enough! I had no choice. I offered them an escape! I provided explicit directions."

He tilted his head, a strand of silver hair tumbling over his brow.

"I told them to seek refuge in the temple, promising them sanctuary and safety. But what did they do instead? They went looking for their loved ones!" My eyes locked onto his, my confession reverberating through the darkened room. He remained silent, patiently waiting for me to continue.

"Ramses learned of my actions and dispatched guards all over the city in pursuit of them, causing a massacre. I was aware of their hideout; they made the mistake of confiding in me. Ramses knew it too. He ordered me to track them down or else he would continue killing indiscriminately. So, I went out, found them and their families... and slaughtered them all." My throat tightened as I recalled the pungent scent of blood and the sheer horror that unfolded. The way the sky cracked with thunder and lightning—the smoke that shrouded the city. However, my act had been merciful; if they were caught alive by Ramses' men, they would have suffered unspeakable torture along with their families for weeks on end.

"What atonement does your deity, Naris, demand for such a grievous transgression?" he questioned.

I bit the inside of my cheek, my face contorting as I struggled to find an answer. "I suppose some things are irredeemable," I murmured, my eyes flicking to his. "Naris does not demand *atonement* for actions taken under command or force," I stated, repeating the mantra Priestess Andes had preached to me when I flung myself at her feet the night I killed those people. "In our faith, we believe in the necessity of *balance* and the inevitability of *consequence*. Spend one hundred and twenty days in temple to rid ourselves of guilt, does not erase the crime, we have to accept the repercussions they bring—because it will catch up to us."

"So, do you believe you've paid for your...crimes?"

"Yes and no," I said. "I live with the consequences every day. The *knowing*, the memory of what I did, is a constant reminder of the choices I've made. It's a burden I bear alone."

He was silent for a moment, his eyes thoughtful. "That's a heavy burden to carry," he finally said.

"Yes, it is. But it's also a reminder of the lengths I'm willing to go to protect those I care about."

"Even if it means becoming a monster in the eyes of others?"

"Even then," I confirmed. "Because at the end of the day, I know who I am and what I stand for. And I won't let anyone else define that for me."

"Except your Goddess," he mused. "You have strange Gods."

I shrugged. "You are not from around here, so I assume we have different Gods?"

"I have no Gods. I am not religious. I believe in the things I can feel and the things I can see."

"We have a Goddess for your kind. Nexus," I said, my tone clipped. He blinked, his expression momentarily confused. He frowned, searching for the right words.

"Nex-is? A Goddess for Vampires?" he asked.

"She who loves the unloved," I said, reciting the scripture of her temple. His eyes narrowed, his expression dark.

"I have had many who loved me," he said, a wry smile on his face.

"Have you ever loved anyone?" I asked before I could stop myself.

He paused, his smile fading. "It's a complicated question," he replied after a moment. His gaze fell to the floor, his expression inscrutable.

"Isn't it always?" I responded, softer than I intended. I watched as he contemplated my question, the silence in the room becoming almost palpable.

After what felt like an eternity, he finally looked back up at me. His eyes were filled with an emotion I couldn't identify. "I suppose... I suppose I have loved. In my own way."

"In your own way?" I echoed, my curiosity piqued.

He shrugged. "Love is a strange thing. It's different for everyone. For me... It's been a mixture of fascination, obsession, desire. It's not something I've ever tried to define."

I tilted my head, studying his face. "And have you ever been in love?"

"*In* love?" he repeated, as if the phrase was foreign to him.

"Yes, *in* love. Where you care deeply for someone else, where their happiness matters as much as your own, if not more." I said, trying to explain the complex emotion. "To want to kiss them. Marry them even."

He was quiet for a long moment, his gaze distant. I could see the cogs turning in his head as he considered it. "I'm not sure," he finally admitted. "I've cared for people, yes. But to say that I've been *in* love in the way you describe it... I don't know."

"Well, perhaps Nexus is not a Goddess for you after all. Maybe Elenaria—she is said to have many lovers. Goddess of fertility and beauty."

He chuckled lightly at that. "Perhaps. But perhaps... perhaps I just haven't found the right person yet."

As the silence stretched between us, I realized something had shifted. The dynamic between us had long ago changed. I'd exposed a part of myself, a vulnerability I'd kept hidden for so long. And in doing so, I'd allowed Ronan a glimpse into who I truly was beneath the armor, beneath the title of Queen.

And for the first time, I felt understood. I felt seen. And it was a feeling I hadn't realized I'd been craving.

"You keep stopping to help people along your way...Why?" he asked.

I laughed a short and bitter sound. "No one knows who I am. I am not a queen out here, beyond the wall. I am just a nobody. Without Ramses to control my every move, I suppose this is who I would *choose* to be."

He seemed to consider this for a moment, and scrunched up his nose at this as if my answer was inadequate.

"You're a rather interesting female," he said, bending down to the leather straps I had dropped and handing them to me.

"Thank you, I think?" I replied, accepting the leather straps from him. "And you're a rather interesting vampire."

He shrugged nonchalantly. "Perhaps. But as you've noted, I'm not most vampires."

"Perhaps we're not so different after all, Ronan," I mused aloud.

"You think so?"

"I do. We're both creatures of our circumstances, striving to define our own paths. And we both carry burdens that others may not understand," I said, my gaze meeting his.

I had never asked him about his past, I just assumed. I remember his reaction when I mentioned that he was Xaneth's slave.

His eye twitched, his expression hardening. His gaze fell to the floor.

I bit my lip, immediately regretting it. The silence stretched between us, heavy and tense.

"Ronan, I—" I began, but he held up a hand, silencing me.

"It's fine," he said quietly, his tone carrying its usual humor. "You are curious. I can't begrudge you of that. I am rather fascinating. It's not something I wish to discuss right now."

His false cheerfulness hung in the air like smoke, the forced lightness in his tone doing nothing to mask the shadows that flickered behind his eyes. I recognized that darkness—it was the same one I saw in my own reflection, the kind that comes from wounds too deep to ever fully heal.

"I understand," I said softly, meaning it. Because I did. Some demons weren't meant to be dragged into the light, some stories weren't meant to be told until the teller was ready. I knew that better than most.

He shifted his weight, the movement causing his silver hair to catch the dim light. For a moment, he looked otherworldly—ancient and untouchable. But then his eyes met mine, and I saw something painfully human in them.

"Do you?" he asked, rough like gravel. "Do you really understand what it's like to—" He cut himself off, jaw clenching. His hands curled into fists at his sides, the tendons standing out like steel cables beneath his skin.

"To be owned?" I finished for him, "To have your choices stripped away until you're nothing but what *they* want you to be?" My fingers traced the phantom weight of chains I'd worn for far too long. "Yes, Ronan. I understand."

Something shifted in his expression then—a crack in that carefully maintained facade. He took a step toward me, and another, until I could feel the chill radiating from his immortal flesh.

"You were a queen," he said, but there was no accusation there. Just a quiet sort of recognition.

"I was a glorified whore. And you were a warrior of your tribe," I countered. "But chains are chains, whether they're made of gold or iron."

He exhaled sharply, the sound almost like a laugh but too bitter to truly be one. "Quite the pair we make, aren't we? A runaway queen and a—" He stopped again, that muscle in his jaw jumping.

"A survivor," I finished for him. Because that's what we both were, beneath all the titles and masks we wore. Survivors of different hells, perhaps, but survivors nonetheless.

His eyes locked onto mine, crimson meeting silver, and for a moment, I saw everything he couldn't say reflected in them. The pain, the rage, the desperate fight to reclaim what had been stolen. I saw it all, and I understood.

"Another time," he said finally, "Perhaps another time, I'll tell you *that* story."

I nodded, accepting it. Some tales needed darkness to be told, and some wounds needed time to be ready for the light.

"Another time," I agreed, and watched as something like relief flickered across his face.

CHAPTER 32

Ronan

Night had descended like a velvet shroud, and I couldn't take my eyes off her. Atreya's exhaustion was written in every line of her body, each step becoming heavier than the last. The desert of Calazan stretched before us like an endless sea of darkness, but first, we needed to make it through Vanhyn.

Marcus, the bleeding heart, stepped closer to her. "Come on, little queen. Up you go." He crouched down, offering his back like some kind of noble steed. The sight made something twist in my chest—something that felt dangerously close to jealousy.

"Don't spoil her, brother," I drawled, forcing lightness into my tone. "She's tougher than she looks." My eyes met hers across the darkness, and for a moment, I saw that familiar steel in her gaze—the same fire that had drawn me to her in the first place.

But then she swayed, just slightly, and my hands twitched with the urge to steady her. To pull her against me and carry her myself. The thought had ambushed me, unwelcome and dangerous.

"I can walk," she insisted, but her voice trembled with fatigue. "I'm not some pampered noble who needs—"

"Get on my back before you face-plant in the sand," Marcus interrupted, his tone brooking no argument.

"Consider it payment for letting me win that card game earlier."

I narrowed my eyes at him. Always the protector, even when it wasn't his place to be.

Her answering smile, tired as it was, had lit up the night. Finally, she relented, climbing onto his back. Something in my chest tightened as I watched her arms wrap around my brother's neck, her head resting against his shoulder.

"Vanhyn's about four hours away," I said, forcing myself to focus on the path ahead. "We'll rest there before tackling Calazan." The desert's dangers weren't something to take lightly. A big glowing ball of death and heat.

The night air grew colder as we trekked forward, and I caught the exact moment Atreya surrendered to exhaustion. Her head dropped against Marcus's shoulder, her breath evening out into the deep rhythm of sleep.

"She's out cold," Marcus announced, adjusting his grip carefully. His voice carried that annoying hint of fondness I'd come to expect from him. "Like a kitten after a feast."

Selene snickered from behind us. "A drooling kitten," she added, and I shot her a warning glare over my shoulder. "What? Look—she's actually drooling on Marcus's jacket."

"Both of you, quiet," I snapped, but there was no real heat in it.

Snow began to fall, delicate flakes catching in Atreya's dark hair like stars against the night sky. Marcus shifted her weight again, and I had to fight the urge to take her from him. To carry her myself.

"You know," Marcus said, low enough not to wake her, "for someone who's supposedly the most dangerous queen in Ember, she looks remarkably innocent right now."

I thought of the fire in her eyes when she had spoken of rebellion, of freedom. Of the steel in her spine when she had confessed to burning down that sector. Nothing innocent about that. But here, wrapped in exhaustion and trust, she looked like someone else entirely.

"Appearances can be deceiving," I muttered, picking up our pace. The sooner we reached Vanhyn, the better. "And she's not some curiosity for you two to coo over."

"Aww, is someone jealous?" Selene teased, falling into step beside me. "You know, brother, you could just admit that you—"

"Finish that sentence," I warned, "and I'll tell Marcus about that time in Dame Persa when you—"

"Point taken," she cut in quickly, but her knowing smile made me want to bare my fangs.

The snow fell harder now, and I shrugged off my cloak, draping it over Atreya's sleeping form. She burrowed deeper into the warmth, a small sound of contentment escaping her lips.

Dangerous. This was all so incredibly dangerous.

"What do you need in Ambrose anyways?" Marcus asked.

"I told you before. The less you know."

"Right." Marcus's tone dripped with sarcasm. "Because that's worked out so well for us in the past."

I kept my eyes fixed on the horizon, where the first hints of Vanhyn's lights pierced the darkness like tiny daggers. "You're alive, aren't you?"

"Barely," Selene muttered, kicking up snow with each step. "Remember Orit? When your 'need-to-know' basis nearly got us all executed?"

The memory hit like a punch to the gut, but I refused to let it show. "That was different."

"Different how?" Marcus shifted Atreya's weight again, and her fingers curled tighter into his jacket. "Different because this time you're carrying precious cargo?"

My jaw clenched. "She's not cargo."

"No?" Selene's voice turned razor-sharp. "Then what is she, brother dear? Because from where I'm standing, you're playing a very dangerous game with a very dangerous woman."

I whirled on her, my patience snapping like a brittle bone. "You think I don't know that? You think I don't—" I cut myself off, aware of Atreya's steady breathing just feet away. "There are things in motion that you can't understand. That even I don't have a clear understanding of. I am doing my part. Then I'll be done with her."

She snorted. "Is that what you're telling yourself?"

Domini had halted.

Vanhyn Lake spread before us like shattered obsidian, its partially frozen surface reflecting what little starlight pierced through the heavy clouds.

The mountain air bit at our exposed skin, carrying the promise of more snow.

"We'll rest here," I announced, already scanning the shoreline for shelter. "The trees will provide some cover from—"

"From what? The elements, or those who hunt us?" Selene's breath clouded in the frigid air as she paced along the water's edge. "Because I'm not sure which is worse at this point."

A sharp intake of breath drew my attention. Marcus had finally set Atreya down, and she curled against the base of a frost-covered pine, still wrapped in my cloak. Still sleeping. Still trusting.

"I'll take first watch," Selene volunteered, waving off my protest. "You look like death warmed over, brother. Both of you do."

She was right—exhaustion pulled at my bones like lead weights. I settled against a nearby tree, close enough to Atreya to reach her if needed, far enough to maintain the illusion of distance.

The crack of ice splitting the silence was our only warning.

"Selene!" Marcus's shout tore through the night as something dark and sinuous wrapped around our sister's ankle. The water erupted in a spray of ice and darkness, and then she was gone—dragged under with barely a scream.

I was on my feet in an instant, weapons drawn, but what good were blades against water wraiths? The lake's surface had already begun to re-freeze, sealing our sister beneath.

"No!" Atreya's scream rang out behind me, sharp with panic. She was awake—when had she woken?—and before any of us could move, she was running.

"Atreya, don't—!" The words barely left my mouth before she plunged into the water, disappearing beneath the dark surface.

For one heartbeat, nothing happened. Then the lake exploded with light.

Lightning coursed through the water like liquid starfire, illuminating the depths in brilliant, terrible clarity. Through the ice, I saw them—hundreds of wraiths, their elongated bodies twisting like smoke underwater, their hollow eyes fixed on their prey. On Selene. On Atreya.

The lake turned into a storm contained, every bolt of lightning revealing more horrors lurking in the depths. Wraiths scattered like startled fish, their ethereal forms dissipating under the assault of pure energy.

"Marcus!" I shouted, already moving. "Break the ice! We need to—"

Another explosion of light, this one so bright it burned shadows into my vision. Through the spots dancing in my eyes, I saw two figures break the surface—Selene gasping for air, Atreya's arms locked around her waist, both of them crackling with residual energy.

I reached them first, hauling them onto solid ground as Marcus shattered more ice to clear a path. Selene collapsed onto her hands and knees, coughing up lake water, while Atreya...

Atreya stood there, dripping and magnificent, her eyes still glowing with power. Lightning danced across her skin like a living thing, and in this moment, she looked every inch the queen she truly was.

"You," Selene managed between coughs, "are full of surprises."

The glow faded from Atreya's eyes, replaced by something more vulnerable. She swayed slightly, and this time, I didn't fight the urge to steady her. My hands found her shoulders, and she was ice-cold, trembling.

"That was incredibly stupid," I told her, even as I wrapped her in my cloak again. "Reckless. Dangerous."

She looked up at me, water dripping from her lashes, and managed a weak smile. "You're welcome."

One by one, the wraith bodies floated to the surface of Vanhyn Lake, their ethereal forms now blackened and twisted. The smell of ozone and charred flesh hung thick in the air.

Marcus prodded one of the floating corpses with a branch. "You think wraith meat's any good? Might save us some hunting time."

"Why don't you fish one out and find out?" Domini suggested sarcastically. "I'm sure they taste like chicken. Everything does, right?"

"You're not feeding that to her," I hissed. "Marcus, Domini—gather wood. Now. We need to move fast if we want to reach Vanhyn before morning."

They scattered to follow my orders, and within minutes, a pile of relatively dry wood lay at my feet. I stretched out my hand, letting my magic flow. Fire sparked between my fingers, then leaped to the kindling, hungry and eager.

The flames cast dancing shadows across Atreya's face as she huddled closer to the warmth. Her hair was still dripping, and her lips had taken on a concerning bluish tinge. But her eyes—they stayed fixed on the floating wraith corpses, a mixture of horror and satisfaction in their depths.

I didn't want to think about what that look meant. About how much more powerful she was than any of us had imagined. About how she'd jumped into that freezing water without hesitation to save my sister.

"We need to move," I said, watching Atreya's trembling intensify despite the fire's warmth. "The wraiths never hunt alone. Where there's one nest, there's usually—"

"More," Selene finished, still coughing up bits of lake water. "Much more. And I, for one, don't fancy another swim."

Domini kicked one of the charred wraith corpses back into the water. "Shame about dinner, Marcus. Though I suppose watching our little queen turn them into lightning rods was entertainment enough."

"Your priorities continue to astound me," I growled, already gathering our scattered supplies. The wind had picked up, carrying with it the distinct scent of approaching storm. "Vanhyn's less than an hour away if we push hard. We can find proper shelter there."

Marcus helped Atreya to her feet, and I pretended not to notice how she swayed. How pale her skin had become. How her eyes kept darting back to the lake, as if expecting more wraiths to emerge at any moment.

"That was quite a light show," he murmured to her, quiet enough that I had to strain to hear. "Didn't know you had that in you."

"Neither did I," she whispered back, and something in her tone made me turn. Made me really look at her.

Fear. That's what I saw in her eyes. Not of the wraiths, not of the cold—but of herself. Of what she'd done. Of what she was capable of. A remnant of that dream I had of that shadowbeing inside of Atreya came forth then.

"Move," I ordered, harder than necessary, because softness wouldn't serve any of us now. "Unless you all fancy becoming wraith food after all."

The lake's surface had begun to freeze again, sealing away the evidence of what had happened here. But I couldn't shake the image of those hundreds of hollow eyes, all fixed on our little queen.

On what she carried.

On what she was.

Vanhyn's streets glistened with fresh snow, the cobblestones slick beneath our feet. Dawn hadn't quite broken, but already the city stirred with early risers—merchants setting up their stalls, guards making their rounds, old women shuffling to the temple for morning prayers.

And everywhere, the wanted posters.

They were fresh, the ink barely dry, plastered across every surface like a macabre decoration. Atreya's face stared back at us, rendered in harsh black strokes that somehow still captured the defiance in her eyes. Next to hers, my own portrait sneered at passersby, the reward amount beneath it enough to feed a family for ten lifetimes.

"Well," Selene muttered, tugging her hood lower, "at least they got your good side, brother."

I shot her a dark look as we huddled deeper into our cloaks. Atreya walked between Marcus and me, her head bowed, still shivering from her swim in the lake. Every few steps, her shoulder brushed against mine—whether for warmth or reassurance, I couldn't tell.

An elderly woman shuffled past, her basket full of fresh bread. The scent made Atreya's stomach growl, reminding me how long it had been since she's eaten. Selene's eyes followed her, a familiar glint appearing in them.

"No," I started to say, but she was already moving.

"Excuse me, grandmother," Selene called out, honey-sweet. The old woman turned, and I watched my sister's pupils dilate, her power reaching out like invisible tendrils. "Do you live alone?"

The woman blinked slowly, her weathered face softening. "Yes, dear. Just me since my Harold passed."

"Perfect." Selene's smile widened. "You should take us home with you. Invite us in for tea."

Marcus leaned close to my ear. "Old people blood always tastes like death and disappointment."

"Don't you dare," Atreya hissed, but there was a hint of amusement in her tone. "She's someone's grandmother."

I couldn't help the laugh that escaped me, earning surprised looks from both of them.

The old woman led us through winding streets to a modest house tucked between a bakery and an herbalist's shop. The moment we stepped inside, she began fussing over us like we were her long-lost grandchildren.

"Come with me, dears," the old woman said, leading Atreya and Selene toward a back room. "I've got some of my daughter's old clothes that should fit. Can't have you catching your death in those wet things."

I watched them disappear around the corner, my eyes lingering perhaps a moment too long on Atreya's retreating form. When I turned back, Marcus was smirking at me.

"Not a word," I warned.

In the adjacent room, I could hear rustling fabric and the old woman's gentle fussing. Selene, ever shameless, was the first to change. Through the partially open door, I caught Atreya's sharp intake of breath as Selene stripped down without ceremony.

"Oh, don't be shy, little queen," Selene's said. "We're all friends here."

There was a pause, then the soft sound of wet fabric hitting the floor. I kept my eyes firmly fixed on the fire, but noticed Atreya stealing a quick glance through the doorway. Her cheeks flushed pink when she realized I'd caught her looking, and I couldn't help but arch an eyebrow, a smirk tugging at my lips.

"Really?" I mouthed, enjoying the way her blush deepened.

She turned away quickly, but not before I saw the ghost of a smile on her face. It was... endearing, how someone who could turn wraiths to ash could still be flustered by such a simple thing.

"These should do nicely," the old woman's voice broke through my thoughts as she returned, Selene and Atreya now dressed in simple but warm clothing. The deep blue of Atreya's borrowed dress made her eyes look almost violet in the firelight.

"Look at you all, soaked to the bone! Sit, sit by the fire. I'll fetch some blankets." She clucked her tongue at Atreya's damp clothes on the floor. "You would have caught your death, dear. Let me make you some hot tea."

Something caught my eye as she bustled around—a plant in the window, its silver leaves unmistakable even in the dim light.

Nettlesbane.

My spine stiffened. Nettlesbane was rare, used primarily for one purpose: breaking compulsion spells and repelling vampires. Vampire poison. I looked at the old woman with new eyes, noting the clarity in her gaze, the purposeful way she moved.

She wasn't compelled. She never had been.

"The wanted posters went up yesterday," she said casually, setting a tray of tea and bread before us. "Five million crowns for the Queen of Ember. Seven for the traitor who stole her." Her eyes met mine, knowing and fierce. "But there are still those of us who remember what it means to fight for something greater than gold."

Atreya's head snapped up. "You..."

"Word travels, Your Majesty, even here in Ferenz. We hear things. About a king who treats his queen as cruelly as he treats his people." She poured tea with steady hands. "About a queen who dared to stand against him. Who refused to kill rebels in an arena."

"I killed Aislinn Furian," Atreya pointed out darkly.

"Aye. At nothing more than a youngling. What choice did you have?"

Atreya's hands tightened around her teacup. "That doesn't change what I did."

"No," the woman agreed. "But intention matters. Choice matters." She reached for something beneath her chair—a folded piece of parchment, worn at the edges. "Just as it matters that you chose to spare my family, even when the king demanded his head."

There was a silence. On the parchment was a name. The old woman tapped her finger on the paper.

"Who is Cairn Dryer?" Domini asked.

"My son." The old woman's words crackled like dry leaves as she pointed a long, knobby finger at Atreya. "He was one of those rebels that you spared in the arena."

The firelight caught the tears gathering in her eyes, but there was steel in her spine as she stood straighter. "When they brought him before you, he was certain he would die. They all were. But you..." She shook her head, wonder creeping over her. "You looked the king in the eye and said *no*."

Atreya's hands trembled around her teacup.

"My boy was nineteen when he decided to fight for a better world. When you saved him...for however long you saved him." She pressed a weathered hand to her heart. "Well, let's just say there are more of us out here than you might think. People who remember kindness. People who would rather die than see you back in that monster's hands."

"Then they must have forgotten how I have killed hundreds of rebels in that arena," Atreya whispered.

"Hundreds?" Marcus let out a low whistle. "And here I thought I was impressive with my body count." He paused, then added cheerfully, "Though mine were mostly accidents. Did you know you can actually kill someone with a badly cooked meat pie?"

"Marcus," Domini and I growled in unison.

The old woman's eyes never left Atreya. "You gave them a chance to live."

"And look how well that turned out," Atreya said bitterly. "Your son—"

"Made his own choices," the woman cut in firmly. "Just as you made yours."

Selene, who had been unusually quiet, leaned forward. "So you're helping us because of one act of mercy? Seems a bit risky, considering the price on our heads could set your grandchildren's grandchildren up for life."

"Some things are worth more than gold, vampire," the woman replied, making Selene startled at the casual use of the word.

"Well, this is cozy," Marcus declared, reaching for another piece of bread. "Nothing brings people together quite like shared trauma and high treason. Speaking of treason, that meat pie story I mentioned—"

"If you finish that story, I will personally feed you to the next wraith we meet," I threatened.

"Really?" Domini raised an eyebrow at me. "You'd waste perfectly good wraith bait?"

The old woman watched our exchange with knowing eyes. "You're an odd group," she said finally, "but then again, the best rebellions usually are."

CHAPTER 33

Atreya

The roar shattered the morning peace like glass.

I bolted to the window of the grandmother's cottage, my fingers gripping the weathered sill. The sound was unmistakable—I'd know it anywhere. That peculiar screech-growl that had haunted my nightmares for months.

Siorsen.

His massive red form blotted out the sun as he circled overhead, scales gleaming like fresh blood in the morning light. Those distinctive black ridge spines that ran down his neck, the way his left wing dragged slightly from an old battle wound—there was no doubt. This was Ramses's mount, the dragon who'd tried to burn me alive in the Battle of the Crimson Vale.

His wings spread wide enough to cast half of Vanhyn in shadow. Buildings crumbled beneath his tail as he landed, stone and wood splintering like kindling. The sound of screaming filled the air, and the acrid smell of smoke and dragon-fire drifted through the open window.

"Mother!"

Oh. No. Gods above.

My heart stopped. There, perched atop Aegis's silver back, was my son. The second dragon's scales shimmered like moonlight on water, making Vrys's small form even more stark against them. His black hair whipped in the wind, his small face a mirror of his father's determination. Of my fear. He couldn't be more than fifty feet above the ground, close enough that I could see the tears on his cheeks.

I pressed my hand against the glass, a sob catching in my throat. My baby. My beautiful boy.

"Bring forth the Queen of Ember!" Ramses's command boomed. He sat astride Siorsen like a dark god of war, his black armor absorbing the sunlight. The dragon's claws dug into the cobblestones, leaving deep gouges in the stone. "Surrender her, and your pathetic town remains standing!"

The grandmother yanked me back from the window just as Siorsen's tail demolished the baker's shop next door. "The catacombs," she whispered, already moving. "Quickly!"

She yanked back an ornate rug, revealing a trapdoor beneath. The wood was worn smooth with age, the metal hinges well-oiled. This wasn't the first time she'd helped people escape.

"The tunnels run beneath all of Vanhyn," she explained, thrusting a weathered map into my hands. Her fingers trembled but she remained steady. "Follow them east. They'll take you straight to Calazan."

Another explosion rocked the building. Dust rained from the ceiling.

"Mother!" Vrys called again. "Please! I want to go home! I want you to come home."

The pain in his cry nearly brought me to my knees. Domini caught my arm as I swayed.

"He's using him," Marcus snarled, his fangs dropping in rage. "Using your own child as bait."

"Of course he is," Selene's hissed. "It's what monsters do."

I could barely breathe. My son was up there, probably terrified, definitely confused. And here I was, about to run. Again.

Ramses' call carried over the chaos: "You have until sundown, Atreya! After that, well..." Siorsen's roar punctuated his threat. More screams. More crumbling stone.

"How?" I choked out. "How is he here?"

"Who cares," the grandmother cut in. "Now move!"

"Mama, please!" Vrys's pleaded, "I miss you. I miss you so much."

Something in me snapped. Before anyone could stop me, I was already moving toward the door, my hand reaching for the iron handle. My son needed me. What kind of mother was I, hiding while he begged?

"Atreya, no!" Domini grabbed my wrist, his grip like steel. "You know what Ramses will do—"

"He's my son!" I wrenched against his hold, tears streaming down my face. "My baby boy is up there crying for me!"

Marcus stepped between me and the door. "And what happens when Ramses has both of you? When he uses Vrys to control you? When he forces you to watch as he—"

"Don't," I whispered, but the fight was already draining from me. Because he was right. Because I knew exactly what Ramses would do.

He was right. We had to go. Had to run. Had to leave my son behind.

Again.

The trapdoor opened to reveal rough-hewn steps disappearing into darkness. The grandmother pressed a torch into my hands, her eyes fierce with determination.

"Your son needs a free mother more than a dead one," she said, as if reading my thoughts. "Go. Live. Fight."

Another explosion, closer this time. The windows rattled in their frames.

"Mother!" Vrys's called me. "Please come back!"

I stumbled toward the stairs, each step feeling like betrayal. The others followed, Marcus taking up the rear, his expression grim.

The last thing I saw before the trapdoor closed was the grandmother's face, set with steel determination. The last thing I heard was my son's cry, breaking my heart all over again.

Then darkness swallowed us whole, and all that remained was the sound of our breathing and the echo of my failure as a mother.

The catacombs waited, promising escape.

And somewhere above, my son called for me, not understanding why his mother kept running away.

The torch cast dancing shadows on the ancient stone walls. Water dripped somewhere in the darkness, a steady rhythm that matched my broken heartbeat. The air was thick with the smell of wet earth and decay.

Rats scurried across our path, their red eyes reflecting the torchlight. I could hear them squeaking in the shadows, hundreds of them, maybe thousands. The sound of tiny claws on stone made my skin crawl.

"At least we won't go hungry," Selene said, trying for levity. "Though I prefer my meals less... furry."

My laugh came out like broken glass. "Is this funny to you? My son is up there, being used as bait by his father, and you're making jokes about rats?"

The silence that followed was deafening. Even the rats seemed to pause.

"You think you're the only one who's lost someone?" Selene asked softly. "The only one who's had to run while someone they loved screamed their name?"

I whirled on her, torch flame dancing wildly. "Don't you dare—"

"I had a sister once." The words fell like stones into still water. "Her name was Lily. She was six."

Something in her tone made me stop. Made me really look at her. In the torchlight, her white hair gleamed like fresh snow, her amber eyes holding centuries of pain I'd never bothered to see before.

"Xaneth came to Bone Isle like a storm. Dragons aren't the only monsters who can rain fire from the sky. I hid her in the root cellar. Told her to be quiet. To be brave." She smiled, but it was all teeth and old wounds. "She was so good at following instructions. Even when the flames started. Even when the screaming began. She didn't make a sound."

Marcus and Domini had gone still behind us. Ronan's presence was a heavy shadow, silent as the grave. They knew this story. Had lived parts of it.

"I thought—" Selene's words caught, just for a moment. "I thought if I could just keep her hidden, keep her safe... But he found us. He always finds us." She met my eyes then, and I saw the truth of it. The weight of survival. "So yes, Atreya. I know what it's like to hear someone you love cry for you. To know you'll never answer that cry again."

The torch guttered in my grip. Somewhere above us, a building collapsed. The sound was muffled down here, like thunder from a distant storm.

"I'm sorry," I whispered. The apology felt inadequate.

Selene just nodded, then turned and continued down the tunnel. Her boots splashed through shallow puddles, the sound echoing off the stone walls. The rats scattered before her, as if they too could sense the old violence that lived beneath her skin.

We walked in silence after that, each lost in our own private hells. The vampires moved like shadows behind me, their footsteps unnaturally quiet even on the wet stone. Above us, my son's cries had faded to memory, but they echoed in my head with each step.

The catacombs stretched endlessly before us, promising either escape or damnation.

I wasn't sure which I deserved anymore.

The map was useless in the dark.

"Left," Marcus muttered, his vampire sight picking out details I couldn't see. "There's an inscription here—old merchant routes."

My thighs burned from hours of walking. The torch had burned down to almost nothing, the flame casting weird shadows that made the rats look like writhing masses of darkness. My feet caught on something—probably bones. I didn't look down to check.

A distant roar vibrated through the stone above us. Dust and pebbles rained down.

"He's still searching." Domini said. "Siorsen will level the whole town."

My fingers clenched around the torch. More deaths. More destruction. All because of me.

The tunnel opened into a vast chamber, the ceiling disappearing into darkness. Ancient columns rose like tree trunks, carved with symbols I didn't recognize. The air felt different here—older, heavier with secrets.

"Wait." Ronan's command cracked through the darkness.

We all froze. Even the rats went silent.

That's when I heard it. A soft scratching sound, like claws on stone. But not rat claws. Something bigger.

Something hungry.

"Run," Ronan whispered.

The torch sputtered out.

Darkness crashed over us like a wave, and the scratching got louder. Closer.

I couldn't see, but I could feel the others moving. The vampires' natural grace made them silent even at full speed. I wasn't so lucky. My boots slapped against wet stone as I sprinted blindly forward.

The thing behind us shrieked—a sound like metal tearing through flesh.

"Left!" Marcus shouted. "Left, now!"

I slammed into a wall, shoulder screaming in protest, before finding the turn. The creature's breath was hot on my neck, smelling of rot and old blood.

Selene appeared beside me, grabbed my arm, yanked me forward. "Move faster, or I swear by all the gods I'll throw you to it myself."

The threat in her tone wasn't entirely playful.

We ran through the dark like souls fleeing hell itself. Maybe we were. Above us, my son called my name. Below us, ancient horrors wanted to eat me alive.

Just another fucking day in my life.

The creature burst into the torchlight, and my stomach dropped through the floor. Eight legs, each thicker than my waist. Eyes like black diamonds, reflecting our terror back at us. Its mandibles clicked together, dripping venom that sizzled when it hit the stone.

We crashed through something sticky and thick. Webbing. Of course there was webbing. Because this day wasn't already perfect enough.

"Hold on!" Ronan spun around, cupping his hand to his mouth. He exhaled, and flame erupted from his palm like dragon's breath, illuminating the horror show around us.

Hundreds of smaller spiders, each the size of a housecat, scattered across the walls and ceiling. Their bodies gleamed wetly in the firelight, eight-legged nightmares straight out of a madman's fever dream.

The webbing melted away under Ronan's flame, but more spiders kept coming. The vampires started clicking—that weird echolocation thing they did—trying to map our escape route.

All four of them suddenly stopped dead in their tracks.

"What?" I demanded, heart hammering. "What is it?"

Domini's face said it all. "You're not going to like this."

They led us into a chamber larger than all the others, and I immediately understood why. The entire space was draped in thick, ropey webbing. Egg sacs the size of wine barrels hung from the ceiling like grotesque party decorations.

And there, suspended above it all like some unholy queen, was the biggest spider I'd ever seen. Its body alone was the size of a wagon, legs spanning the width of the chamber.

"Oh, fuck this." Lightning crackled between my fingers, and I let it fly.

The bolt struck true, frying the monster where it hung. Unfortunately, I hadn't considered one tiny detail—gravity.

Eight tons of dead spider queen came crashing down, exploding on impact. We were instantly drenched in... well, let's just say I'd never be eating soup again.

"Really?" Selene wiped something unspeakable from her face. "Lightning? That was your solution?"

"I don't see you coming up with any better ideas!" I shot back, gagging as something dripped into my mouth. "Oh gods, I can taste it. Why can I taste it?"

A deep rumbling cut through our bickering. We all looked up to see cracks spreading across the ceiling, right where my lightning bolt had struck.

Marcus summed it up perfectly: "Well, shit."

"Move!" Ronan's command sent us scrambling through spider guts and webbing. Above us, stone groaned like a dying beast.

The first chunks of ceiling crashed down behind us, each impact sending shockwaves through the chamber. Egg sacs burst as they fell, releasing hundreds of baby spiders that rained down like some twisted parody of confetti.

"Left tunnel!" Domini clicked rapidly, the sound bouncing off the walls. "It leads up!"

We dove for the opening just as a massive section of ceiling gave way. Marcus yanked me forward by my collar, my feet barely touching the ground as we ran. The thunder of falling rock chased us up the tunnel, along with a wave of dust and—yes, more spider babies.

"I hate this," I panted, brushing tiny arachnids off my shoulders. "I hate this so much."

"At least you're not wearing white," Selene shot back, her usually pristine hair now a horrifying mess of spider innards and web fragments.

The tunnel curved sharply upward, the incline nearly vertical. My boots slipped on the slick stone, but Domini grabbed one arm while Marcus took the other. They practically flew up the shaft, dragging me between them like a rag doll.

"This is undignified," I muttered.

"Would you prefer dignified and dead?" Ronan called from behind us, where he was still occasionally shooting bursts of flame at any spiders that got too close.

The collapsing chamber below us sent vibrations through the entire tunnel system. Cracks spider-webbed across the ceiling—and wasn't that just a delightfully appropriate metaphor?

"Almost there!" Domini's shouted, "The surface is—"

The ceiling chose that moment to give up entirely.

We burst through the collapsing tunnel like cork from a wine bottle, launched by the force of the explosion below us. I had just enough time to think, 'Oh, this is going to hurt,' before we all crashed onto the cobblestones of what appeared to be Vanhyn's market square.

In broad daylight.

Covered in spider guts.

Right in front of a group of very startled merchants.

"Good morning," I managed, trying to maintain some dignity while picking baby spiders out of my hair. "Lovely day for a walk, isn't it?"

A woman screamed. Several people dropped their baskets. One man just stood there, mouth open, holding a half-eaten apple that slowly slipped from his fingers.

"Could be worse," Marcus groaned from somewhere to my left. "At least Ramses isn't—"

A familiar roar cut through the air.

"You just had to say it, didn't you?"

"The sun!" I gasped, spinning toward my vampire companions. But instead of bursting into flame, they were just... standing there, dripping with spider innards and looking mildly annoyed.

Domini wiped a glob of goo from his face, examining it with scholarly interest. "Well, this is peculiar. The queen's viscera appears to ward off the sun's burning touch."

"Are you telling me," Selene said slowly, "that we're being saved from burning to ash because we're covered in spider guts?"

Marcus actually laughed. "Nature's blessing in the foulest form. Disgusting."

"If we survive this," Ronan muttered, "we are never speaking of it again."

Another earth-shaking roar interrupted our moment of horrified revelation. Siorsen's massive shadow passed overhead, and the market square erupted into chaos.

"You know," I said, watching people flee in terror from both the dragon and our spider-soaked appearance, "I'm starting to think the gods just really enjoy tormenting us."

"Less talking," Marcus grabbed my arm, "more running!"

Siorsen's tail smashed through a fruit stall, sending apples and oranges bouncing across the cobblestones. The red dragon's roar shattered windows, raining glass down on the fleeing townspeople.

"There!" Domini pointed toward the tannery district. "The old bell tower—we can lose them in the narrow streets!"

We sprinted through the chaos, spider-soaked boots slipping on crushed fruit and broken glass. A blast of dragon-fire turned the marketplace behind us into an inferno.

"Atreya!" Ramses' scream boomed across the square. "Still running, my love? And here I thought you'd want to see your son!"

My heart clenched at Vrys's distant cry. But Marcus's grip on my arm was iron, keeping me moving forward.

"Hard left!" Ronan called. "Now!"

We dove into an alley just as another gout of flame scorched the street where we'd been standing. The narrow passage between buildings was barely wide enough for two people, forcing us to run single file.

"The spider blessing's wearing off," Selene hissed, smoke rising from her exposed skin where the guts had started to dry.

"Through here!" Domini kicked open a door, revealing the tannery's workspace. The stench of curing leather hit us like a wall. "The vats will mask our scent!"

We wove between hanging hides and steaming pools of who-knows-what, the vampires now moving faster as their protection from the sun faded. Above us, wood creaked as Siorsen's weight settled on the roof.

"Come out, come out," Ramses sang. "You're only making this harder on everyone. On Vrys."

My fingers crackled with lightning. "I'm going to kill him."

"Later," Marcus promised, yanking me toward a back window. "First, we need to—"

The ceiling exploded inward.

Wooden beams and roofing tiles rained down as Siorsen's massive head burst through the ceiling. Sunlight streamed in, forcing the vampires to dodge between patches of shadow. The dragon's nostrils flared, steam rising from them as he scented the air.

"The vats!" Domini screamed.

I didn't think—just acted. Lightning arced from my fingers into the nearest tanning vat. The liquid exploded upward, showering Siorsen's face with scalding, putrid fluid. The dragon reared back with a shriek of pain and fury, taking most of the roof with him.

"This way!" Marcus shoved me toward a half-hidden door between two massive drying racks. The leather hanging above us caught fire as Siorsen's wild breath weapon set the tannery ablaze.

We burst through the door into what looked like a storage room. Barrels of tanning solution lined the walls, and the stench was even worse here.

Selene's skin was starting to smoke in earnest now, the spider's protection almost gone.

"There's a trap door," Ronan kicked aside a barrel, revealing iron rings set in the floor. "Used to smuggle leather past the tax collectors."

"How quaint," Selene drawled, "More tunnels. Because the last ones worked out so well."

The building shuddered as Siorsen landed fully on what remained of the roof. Wood groaned in protest. Through gaps in the ceiling, I could see Ramses dismounting, his boots hitting the charred beams with deliberate slowness.

"Found you," he called in a sing-song sound that made my blood run cold.

Domini and Marcus heaved the trap door open just as the storage room's door burst into splinters. I caught a glimpse of Ramses' face—beautiful and terrible as always—before Ronan shoved me down into darkness.

The last thing I heard was Vrys calling my name again, "Mother!"

Then we were falling, tumbling through blackness, the smell of leather and smoke replaced by the dank breath of yet another underground passage.

The drop wasn't as far as I'd feared. We landed in what felt like hay—old and moldy, but better than stone. The vampires recovered instantly, their night vision giving them the advantage.

"Ronan," Domini whispered urgently. "Light."

A small flame bloomed in his palm, casting eerie shadows on walls that looked different from the catacombs. These were finished stone, with metal tracks running along the floor.

"The old mining tunnels," Marcus breathed. "They connect to the river."

Above us, Ramses's laughter echoed down through the trap door. "Running again, my love? And here I thought we could have a civil conversation about custody arrangements."

Selene's skin was blistering now, the last of the spider's protection gone. She pressed against the tunnel wall, seeking shadows that weren't there.

"The river's half a mile east," Domini said, tight with pain as sunlight streamed through the opening above. "If we can reach it—"

A thunderous crash cut her off as something massive slammed into the floor above. Dust and debris rained down. The ceiling groaned.

"He's going to bring the whole building down on top of us," Marcus snarled.

"Good." I grabbed Selene's arm, supporting her as we started running. "Let him. Maybe he'll bury himself in the process."

We sprinted through the darkness, Ronan's flame lighting the way. The tracks beneath our feet were slick with age and moisture, making each step treacherous. The sounds of destruction followed us, growing closer as Ramses and Siorsen tore through the tannery above, hunting.

The tunnel curved sharply right, then dropped into a steep decline. The tracks disappeared into black water.

"The river must have flooded this section," Domini said, "We'll have to swim."

Another crash from behind, closer now. The tunnel shook, ancient support beams creaking in protest.

"Atreya!" Ramses' shout carried through the stone. "I can smell you down there. All of you. Bring her to me, vampires, and I might let you live!"

"Charming offer," Selene muttered through clenched teeth. "I vote we drown instead."

The water looked like ink in the dim light of Ronan's flame. Something splashed in the darkness ahead—something big.

"Please tell me these tunnels don't have water spiders," I whispered.

Marcus's laugh was grim. "Worse. Cave eels."

"Of course there are cave eels. Why wouldn't there be cave eels?"

A silvery shape slithered past my legs, crackling with blue energy. Another followed, then another, their bodies lighting up the flooded tunnel like living lightning.

"Electric eels," Domini breathed. "The mining companies used to harvest their power for the drills."

I felt the familiar tingle of electricity dancing across my skin as more eels emerged from the darkness. Their bodies pulsed with power, creating strange patterns in the black water.

"Well," I said, letting my own electric current flow through my fingers and into the water. "This might actually work in our favor."

The eels responded immediately, drawn to my energy like moths to flame. Their bodies lit up brighter, creating a brilliant display of blue-white light that illuminated the tunnel.

"Cover the others," Marcus urged. "Quick!"

I reached out with my power, wrapping each vampire in a protective field of electricity that matched the eels' signature. The creatures swam closer, curious about these new entities that felt like their own kind.

"They think we're one of them," Selene said, wonder replacing the pain as an eel brushed against her leg without attacking.

Above us, stone cracked and groaned as Ramses and Siorsen continued their destruction. But down here, in this strange underwater world of living lightning, we had found an unexpected sanctuary.

"The eels know every underwater passage," Domini said. "They'll lead us to the river."

We moved through the water, surrounded by our glowing guides. The electric field I maintained around us made the vampires appear to pulse with the same bio-luminescent rhythm as the eels. More of the creatures joined our odd procession, until we were swimming in the center of a living constellation.

Ramses's frustrated roar echoed through the stone, growing fainter as the eels led us deeper into their domain. The sound of destruction faded, replaced by the gentle swish of water and the soft crackle of electricity.

The river spat us out into blinding sunlight. The water churned around us as we surfaced, gasping, our electric eel escorts disappearing back into the depths with final crackles of farewell. Before us stretched the endless expanse of the Calazan Desert, its red sands burning under the midday sun.

"The banks," Selene hissed through clenched teeth, her skin already starting to smoke. "Quickly!"

We dragged ourselves onto the muddy shore, the vampires immediately dropping to their knees and clawing at the wet earth. Their movements were desperate, primal—survival instinct taking over as the sun seared their flesh.

"Help us dig," Domini commanded with a wince. "Deep enough to shield us completely."

I joined them, my fingers sinking into the cool mud. Within minutes, we'd carved out four crude graves along the riverbank, deep enough to completely cover a body.

"You'll need to dig us out at sunset," Selene said, already lowering herself into her makeshift sanctuary. Her silver hair was caked with mud, her pale skin angry with burns. "Don't forget about us down here."

Marcus managed a weak laugh as he settled into his own hollow. "Yes, that would be rather unfortunate."

"I won't leave you," I promised, helping Domini pack the wet earth around himself. "I'll be here."

Ronan was the last to be buried, his amber eyes meeting mine before the mud covered his face. "Stay safe. And remember—"

"I know," I cut him off, packing the final layer of earth over him. "Don't do anything stupid while you're sleeping."

The desert wind picked up, hot and dry, already beginning to crack the mud around their makeshift graves. In the distance, I could just make out the spires of Vanhyn, smoke still rising from where Siorsen had wreaked his havoc.

Somewhere in that chaos was my son.

But for now, all I could do was wait for sunset and pray the vampires' mud cocoons would hold.

I settled against a twisted tree trunk, its branches offering meager shade from the relentless desert sun. The river gurgled beside me, a constant reminder of the four bodies buried in its banks. Every so often, I checked the mud graves, making sure they hadn't cracked too severely in the heat.

The desert stretched endlessly before me, waves of heat distorting the horizon into a shimmering mirage. Red sand dunes rolled like frozen waves, their edges sharp against the merciless blue sky. In the distance, Vanhyn's smoke had finally begun to thin.

My son's cry echoed in my memory, replaying like a torture device of my own making. *Mother! Please come back!* Each remembered cry was a knife in my chest, twisting deeper with every passing hour.

I pulled my knees to my chest, feeling smaller than the grains of sand that dusted my spider-gut-crusted boots. The smell was horrific now, baking in the sun. I'd tried washing it off in the river, but some stains, it seemed, were determined to stick.

"Some mother I am," I whispered to the empty air. "Some queen."

A scorpion scuttled past my feet, its stinger raised like an accusation. I watched it disappear into a crack in the mud, seeking shelter from the sun's assault. Even the creatures of the desert knew better than to stay exposed.

The mud over Domini's grave cracked slightly. I crawled over, using my sleeve to drip river water onto it, sealing the fissure before sunlight could reach his vulnerable skin. The wet earth smelled like copper and decay—fitting, given what lay beneath.

"I could go back," I said aloud, testing. "Right now. While they sleep. They couldn't stop me."

But Marcus's words haunted me: *And what happens when Ramses has both of you? When he uses Vrys to control you?*

He was right. They were all right. And I hated them for it.

A shadow passed overhead—just a vulture, but my heart still stopped until I confirmed it wasn't Siorsen's massive form. The bird wheeled lazily above me, perhaps hoping I'd eventually become carrion.

"Sorry to disappoint," I told it, "but I'm not dead yet. Though gods know Ramses is trying his best to change that."

The sun crawled across the sky with agonizing slowness. I dozed fitfully, jerking awake at every sound, my hands crackling with defensive lightning. But nothing came—no dragons, no spiders, no armies. Just the wind, the river, and the weight of my choices.

When the sun finally began to set, painting the desert in shades of blood and gold, I started digging.

Domini was first, his usual pristine appearance now a mess of dried river clay and tangled hair. The others followed, shaking off earth like dogs after rain.

"Well," Selene said, attempting to salvage what dignity she could while picking mud from her ears, "that was an experience I hope never to repeat."

Marcus stretched, his joints cracking like old wood. "Agreed. Though I must say, it beats burning to death."

"Barely," Ronan muttered, scraping mud from his arms.

His eyes found mine, and something in them had changed during the day's rest. Something had hardened into resolution.

"We need to split up," he said, "We're too easy to track as a group now that Ramses has seen us."

"No. We stay together. We're stronger—"

"We're slower," Domini cut in gently.

My throat tightened. "But if Xaneth catches any of you—"

"We already swore not to tell," Selene said.

"That's not what I meant."

"That's exactly what you meant," Marcus said softly. His mud-caked face was grave in the fading light. "You're worried he'll torture our location out of us."

"He will," Ronan said. "That's why you can't get caught."

I stared at my companions—these people who'd become so much more than allies in such short time.

"Which is precisely why we must separate. Four trails instead of one. Three chances to lead them away from you," Domini said.

"I won't let you—"

"Let us?" Ronan's laughed. "Since when do you let us do anything, Your Majesty?"

The use of my title made me flinch.

"North," Domini said, already moving. "I'll take the route back toward Tor. The sun there is brutal enough to mask any vampire traces."

"East," Marcus nodded. "Through the Wrenwood. Ramses won't expect us to return there."

"West," Selene's smile was sharp. " Go to the port and sail off. The Bone Isles remember me. And my sister's grave could use some company."

They were really doing this. Really leaving. My chest felt too tight, like someone had wrapped iron bands around my ribs and was slowly squeezing.

"If any of you die," Ronan said, "I'll personally hunt down your corpse and kill you again." His eyes met each of theirs in turn. "Stay alive. Stay hidden. And for fuck's sake, stay away from spiders."

They chuckled at the joke.

I didn't laugh.

I lurched forward and wrapped my arms around Selene. She went rigid, clearly as surprised by the contact as I was. For a moment, we just stood there, awkward and uncertain, like two people who'd forgotten how hugs worked. Then, slowly, her arms came up to return the embrace. She smelled like river mud and lightning and something uniquely her—like fresh snow.

"Keep my brother safe," she said in my ear.

CHAPTER 34

Atreya

Three nights of trudging through endless dunes had worn us both paper-thin. My feet were blistered, my throat raw from thirst, and the constant wind had scoured my skin until it felt like sandpaper. We'd taken shelter in an abandoned termite mound—a massive clay structure that rose from the sand like some ancient temple. Before that, Ronan dug us tunnels into the ground, that would collapse on top of us every time the wind shifted.

Ronan had explained the termite mounds could withstand decades of desert storms. Right now, though, I didn't care about its architectural significance. It was the only thing between Ronan and the approaching dawn.

I watched him pace our tiny sanctuary, his movements getting more erratic with each passing minute. The dried blood Domini had given us was down to a pathetic dusting in the bottom of the pouch, and Ronan's eyes had taken on that glassy sheen of hunger I'd learned to recognize. He stuck his finger in the remaining red powder and rubbed it on his teeth with a grimace that would have been comical if we weren't both so desperate.

"Would you stop that?" I snapped, my own thirst making me irritable. The cut on my wrist from feeding him yesterday still stung. "You're going to bring the whole thing down on us moving around like that."

"I'm sorry," he bit back, scraping his tongue against his teeth to get every particle of dried blood, "is my attempt to not burst into flames disturbing you?"

"You're not going to burst into flames. We've got at least an hour before sunrise." I watched a termite crawl across my boot, wondering if they tasted as bad as they looked.

He ran a hand through his hair, leaving it standing up at odd angles. Sand fell from the dark strands, adding to the growing pile at his feet. "Fifty-three minutes, actually. But who's counting?"

"Oh, for fuck's sake." I shifted against the packed clay wall, trying to find a comfortable position on the hard ground. "At least sit down. Your pacing is making me dizzy."

"I don't need to sit. I need to—" He stopped abruptly, nostrils flaring. His whole body went still in that unnaturally perfect way only vampires could manage.

"Need to what?" I challenged. "Brood more intensely? Is that even possible?"

"You're bleeding."

I looked down. A sharp piece of clay had cut my palm, a thin line of red welling up. "It's nothing."

His laugh was strained, almost hysterical. "It's not nothing. Not when we're both—" He swallowed hard, throat bobbing.

"Both what? Hungry?" I stood up, angry now. "At least you got some blood yesterday." I thrust out my wrist where I'd slit it and let him feed from me, much to his chagrin. The wound was an angry red line against my skin. "I haven't had a proper meal since Vanhyn."

"That's different—"

"How? Because you're a vampire?" I picked up one of the crawling termites and popped it in my mouth out of pure spite. The crunch was satisfying, but the taste made me want to gag. I swallowed anyway. "Eat some termites," I snapped.

"I could hurt you!" The words exploded from him, making the walls of our shelter tremble.

A crack appeared in the clay above us. Then another. Sunlight started to seep through, and Ronan pressed himself against the far wall, his skin already starting to smoke. The scent of burning flesh filled our crumbling sanctuary.

"No," I whispered, watching our shelter crumble. "No, no, no."

The termite mound collapsed around us. Morning light flooded in, harsh and merciless. Ronan made a sound I never wanted to hear again—something between a scream and a prayer.

"No!" I scrambled toward him as his skin began to blister. We'd been through too much, survived too many collapsed tunnels and shifting sand traps, dragon fire, spiders, a hag—to lose him like this. "Hold on!"

I reached for my power, but panic made it slip through my fingers like water. The sun climbed higher, and Ronan pressed himself against what remained of the clay wall, trying to find any shadow to hide in. The smell of burning flesh filled the air.

"Atreya," he gritted out, "run. Get to the next shelter—"

"Shut up!" I threw my hands up, desperately searching the clear desert sky. Not a cloud in sight. Just like the last three days of endless blue that had forced us to dig those useless tunnels, had driven us into this termite mound that was now betraying us too.

Think. Think.

Lightning crackled under my skin, responding to my fear. I made it rain once, in the arena when I was a child. When my powers first came to me.

I sent my power straight up, electricity arcing from my fingers into the sky. The air began to ionize around us. One mile up. Two. Three. Higher.

"Come on," I snarled, forcing more power into the atmosphere. Sweat dripped down my face as I pulled moisture from the earth itself, from the clay, from my own body. Static made my hair stand on end.

The first cloud formed, small and pitiful against the sun. Not enough. Ronan's skin was blackening as he duck himself into the hot sand to try and escape.

I screamed in frustration, in fear, in rage. Lightning answered my call, striking the ground around us in brilliant forks. The thunder that followed shook the earth, and finally—finally—the clouds began to grow.

"More," I gasped, though my legs were shaking. "More!"

I reached out in all directions, calling to every particle of moisture, every temperature difference, every potential for storm within a hundred miles. My vision blurred. Blood trickled from my nose.

The sky darkened as thunderheads boiled into existence. One storm cell crashed into another, building, growing, until the sun was just a memory. Lightning danced between clouds, thunder rolling continuous now. The pressure dropped so suddenly my ears popped.

The first heavy drops hit my face just as my knees gave out. Then the rain truly began—sheets of it, drenching us instantly, turning the desert to mud. Each drop sizzled against my electrically charged skin.

I tried to stand but couldn't. Every part of me trembled with exhaustion. Through the curtain of rain, I saw Ronan straighten, his burned skin already beginning to heal in the artificial night I'd created.

"You..." he started, rain streaming down his face, washing away the blood and char.

"Saved your ungrateful ass?" I panted, pushing wet hair from my eyes. "Yeah, I did. Maybe next time—"

His mouth crashed into mine, cutting off whatever smart remark I'd been about to make. He tasted like blood and lightning, and his hands tangled in my hair like he was drowning and I was air. I kissed him back just as fiercely, all our hunger and fear and desperation pouring into something else entirely. A small voice in the back of my mind wondered if he could feel what I was feeling—if my blood running through his veins had created a one way bond like previously. It would explain the way his kiss felt like completing a circuit, like lightning finding its way home.

Ronan jerked back suddenly, as if my lightning had shocked him. For a moment, we just stared at each other, rain streaming down our faces. His eyes were wide, the hunger in them now mixed with something else entirely.

"That was..." he started, then stopped, taking three deliberate steps backward. His hand went to his mouth, fingers touching his lips like he couldn't quite believe what had just happened.

I stayed on my knees in the mud, too exhausted to stand, too stunned to speak. The storm above us rumbled, almost like it was laughing at the situation.

"We should..." Ronan ran a hand through his wet hair, making it stick up even worse than before. "We should find better shelter. Before the storm passes."

"Right," I managed hoarsely. "Shelter."

He wouldn't look at me as he offered his hand to help me up. I noticed he dropped it the instant I was steady on my feet.

"Calazan isn't much farther," he said, carefully neutral. "Another day's journey, maybe less if we push through the night."

The way he said it made it clear he intended to pretend the last five minutes hadn't happened. Fine. I could play that game too.

The storm I'd conjured lasted long enough to get us moving, but by nightfall, the clouds had dissipated like they'd never existed. Just like Ronan and I were pretending that kiss had never happened.

We walked in silence, the kind that felt like a living thing between us. Every time our shoulders brushed, he jerked away like I'd burned him. Maybe I had. The residual electricity still crackling under my skin made my hair stand on end, and I caught him watching me from the corner of his eye when he thought I wasn't looking.

"There." Ronan's voice was rough from disuse as he pointed to lights flickering in the distance. "Calazan."

The city rose from the desert like a mirage, its ivory towers catching the starlight. Market fires dotted the outer walls, and even from here, I could smell spices and cooking meat. My stomach cramped painfully.

"Thank fuck," I muttered, picking up my pace. My legs felt like lead, and the power drain from the storm had left me light-headed. I stumbled, and Ronan's hand shot out to steady me, wrapping around my bare arm.

The contact sent a jolt through us both. His fingers tightened for a fraction of a second before he yanked his hand back like I was poison. The hunger in his eyes when he looked at me wasn't just for blood anymore, and we both knew it.

"Don't," he pleaded with a sigh.

"Don't what?" I snapped. "Trip? Breathe? Exist within ten feet of you?"

"You know what I mean."

"Actually, I don't." I stopped walking, planting my feet in the cooling sand. "Use your words, Ronan. What exactly am I not supposed to do?"

He whirled on me, all coiled tension and barely contained whatever-this-was. "This isn't—we can't—" He made a frustrated sound. "What happened back there—"

"Was a kiss," I cut in. "A fucking kiss, not a blood bond. Though maybe it's both, isn't it? Is that why you can barely look at me? Because you can feel what I'm feeling?"

His jaw clenched. "We should focus on getting to the city."

"Right. The city. Where you'll probably try to ditch me first chance you get now."

"I wouldn't—" He stopped, raking both hands through his hair. "Atreya, please."

The way he said my name made something in my chest crack. Please what? Please stop making this harder? Please pretend I couldn't feel his hunger echoing through whatever connection we'd forged? Please forget how his mouth felt against mine?

"Fine," I said, turning back toward the distant lights of Calazan. "Let's focus on the city. On getting food and real shelter and forgetting any of this ever happened. I'm good at pretending. Are you?"

I started walking again, not waiting for his answer. After a moment, I heard his footsteps following, maintaining that careful distance he'd kept since the storm.

The silence between us felt different now—less like a living thing and more like a tomb. By the time we reached Calazan's gates, I wasn't sure which was worse: the hunger that had driven us into that termite mound, or this new hunger that seemed determined to tear us apart.

Calazan's gates stood open to the night, merchant caravans still trickling in and out despite the late hour. We slipped through with a group of traders, our dusty clothes and travel-worn appearance drawing no special attention. Inside the city walls, the streets were a maze of ivory and sandstone, market stalls still doing business under lamplight. The scent of saffron and grilled meat made my mouth water, but Ronan led us past the food vendors, deeper into the winding alleys.

"Where are we going?" I asked, trying to keep my tone neutral despite my growing irritation. "The inns are back that way."

"I know a place," he said, his first words to me since we'd entered the city. "Somewhere safe."

We turned down narrower and narrower streets until we reached what looked like an ancient library, its walls stained with age. Carved symbols decorated the stone archway—protection wards, I realized, though they were so old they'd lost most of their power.

Inside, the library smelled like decay and forgotten things. Dust motes danced in what little moonlight filtered through the grimy windows, and our footsteps echoed off marble floors that had seen better centuries. I half-expected something to crawl out of the shadows and try to eat us—it would've been on brand for how this day was going.

"Up here," Ronan said, heading for a narrow staircase tucked between towering shelves. The stairs creaked under our weight, and I caught myself counting the steps to distract from how close he was in the tight space. Seventeen. Eighteen. Nineteen—

He stopped so abruptly I almost slammed into his back. The door in front of us was solid oak, reinforced with iron bands that looked newer than everything else in this place. Ronan's fingers traced a pattern on the metal, and something clicked inside the lock.

"After you," he muttered, pushing the door open.

The apartment beyond was small enough to feel claustrophobic, but somehow still managed to be bigger than the tunnels we'd been sleeping in. A bed hugged one wall, its sheets dusty but intact. There was a kitchen area that might've been cozy once, before time and abandonment got their hands on it.

"Whose place is this?" I asked, running a finger through the dust on a nearby shelf. The gesture left a clean line in the gray coating, like a scar.

Ronan's shoulders went rigid. "Someone who's dead."

"Yeah, I figured that part out." I turned to face him, crossing my arms. "Want to be more specific, or should I add it to the growing list of shit you won't tell me about?"

His laugh was bitter, barely more than an exhale. "You really want to do this now?"

"Do what? Ask questions? Talk about literally anything real?" The exhaustion and hunger and whatever the fuck was crackling between us since that kiss made my tone sharper than I intended. "Sorry, I forgot—we're pretending everything's fine and normal and you didn't just bring me to some dead person's secret apartment."

"They were a friend." Each word sounded like it was being dragged out of him. "From before. When I was... different."

"Different how?"

"Alive." He moved to the kitchen area, his movements too precise, too controlled. "There's preserved food in here somewhere. You should eat."

I wanted to push harder, to demand real answers about who this friend was and why we were standing in their apartment and what the hell we were doing here at all. But the way his hands shook as he opened cabinet doors told me I'd already pushed too far.

"Fine," I said, dropping onto a chair that protested my weight. "Feed me. But this conversation isn't over."

His back was to me, but I saw the tension in his shoulders ease just slightly. "With you," he said, "it never is."

Ronan moved toward another door I hadn't noticed, hidden in the shadows of the apartment's far corner. When he pushed it open, the hinges protested with a screech that made me wince. But what lay beyond made me forget the noise entirely.

A massive stone tub dominated the washroom, its surface etched with the same symbols I'd seen on the library's entrance. Dust and grime coated everything, but I didn't care. The mere sight of it made my eyes burn.

Ronan took one look at the filthy state of things and rolled his eyes. With a lazy wave of his hand, the dust vanished, leaving the stone gleaming as if it had just been scrubbed. He reached for the ancient taps, and by some miracle—or magic—water began to flow.

I didn't wait for an invitation. Didn't care that I still had my clothes on or that Ronan was right there. The moment steam started rising from the water, I was in it, boots and all. The heat hit my aching muscles and I had to bite back what might have been a sob.

"You're going to ruin your clothes," Ronan said, but there was something gentle in his tone I hadn't heard since before the kiss.

"Don't care." I dunked my head under the water, coming up gasping. Three days of sand and sweat and blood began to dissolve away. "Holy fuck, this feels good."

He moved behind me, and I tensed, but his fingers were careful as they found the tie in my hair. "Let me help," he said softly, working at the knots that had turned my braid into a rat's nest. "Before you end up having to cut it all off."

While he worked, he reached for various bottles on a nearby shelf, uncorking each one to smell them. "Lavender," he murmured, setting one aside. "Sage... rose... ah, this one." He held a blue bottle close to my shoulder. "Jasmine and something else. It was her favorite."

The 'her' slipped out before he could catch it, and I felt his hands go still in my hair.

"You don't have to tell me," I said, even though curiosity was burning through me. "But you can. If you want to."

His fingers resumed their gentle work on my tangled hair, and for a long moment, I thought he wasn't going to answer. Then: "Her name was Mira. She was a witch. And she saved my life, once. A very long time ago."

The silence stretched between us, broken only by the gentle splash of water and the soft tugging of his fingers in my hair. I wanted to ask how she'd saved him, what had happened to her, why her apartment still felt like a shrine. But for once, I kept my mouth shut, letting him work through whatever memories were playing behind his eyes.

He poured something from the blue bottle into his palm—the scent of jasmine filled the air, mixed with something deeper, earthier. His fingers worked the soap into my hair with careful, methodical movements that made my scalp tingle.

"You're good at this," I murmured, trying not to lean into his touch like some touch-starved cat.

"Mira used to say I had magic fingers." He swallowed on her name. "She'd come home from healing work with migraines. This helped."

I closed my eyes as he massaged my temples, not trusting myself to look at him. The water had turned murky with desert grime, but I couldn't bring myself to care. Every point of contact between us felt charged, like the lightning from earlier had taken up permanent residence under my skin.

"Tell me about her," I said softly as his fingers worked through another knot. "About Mira."

His hands stilled for a moment, then resumed their gentle work. "It was... a different time. Back when same-sex couples were more than just frowned upon." He reached for more of the jasmine soap, the scent wrapping around us like a memory. "I'd taken a blow to the head in a fight I can't remember. Somehow got myself on a ship, ended up here—half a world away from where I was supposed to be."

The water sloshed gently as he tilted my head back to rinse.

"I was living under the docks," he continued, "No memories, no purpose. Just... existing. That's where Mira found me. She and her lover, Sianna, they took me in. Brought me here."

"To their library," I murmured, pieces clicking into place.

"Mm." His fingers worked at a particularly stubborn tangle. "They had to be careful. Secret. This place was their sanctuary." He paused, and I felt his hands tremble slightly against my scalp. "Until the Elder Sparrows found out about them."

"Elder Sparrows?"

"Religious fanatics. They'd sweep the streets, looking for anyone they deemed... unnatural." His words turned to ice, but his touch remained gentle. "They dragged Mira and Sianna into the street. Cut their throats right there in the open."

I reached back blindly, finding his wrist with my wet hand. He let out a shaky breath.

"I didn't get there in time. But seeing them like that—it shocked everything loose. All my memories came flooding back. Who I was, where I was supposed to be, the Rite of Passage I was meant to be going through. I remembered everything while kneeling in their blood."

The jasmine scent suddenly felt heavier, more significant. Sacred.

"I buried them together," he said, barely above a whisper. "Then I left. Couldn't stay here after that. But I've maintained the wards, kept their sanctuary safe." His fingers resumed their work, combing through my now-untangled hair. "Sometimes I think Mira knew, even then, that I'd need this place someday. She was good at seeing things like that. Futures that might be."

"I've never heard of the Elder Sparrows," I said, frowning. "Not in any history book, not even in whispered stories."

A dark smile played at the corners of Ronan's mouth. "Good," he said, fingers still working through my hair. "That means I did it right."

Something in his tone made me turn slightly, water sloshing against the tub's sides. "Did what right?"

"Culled a plague. Every last one of them. Their temples. Their texts. Their bloodlines." His fingers stilled in my hair. "Their memory."

A shiver ran through me that had nothing to do with the cooling water. The kind of power it would take to eradicate an entire religion from history... I thought about the casual way he'd cleaned this room with a wave of his hand, and suddenly that simple act felt different. Heavier.

His hands resumed their work, but there was something methodical about it now, like he was remembering other, less gentle movements. "They took something precious from me. So I took everything from them."

The thrill that went through me should have been fear. Should have been horror at the scale of such vengeance. Instead, I felt something closer to awe. To hunger.

"Good," I said, and felt him go still behind me.

"Tilt your head back," he instructed softly. When I complied, warm water cascaded over my hair, his hands following to rinse away the soap. "There. Better?"

I made a sound that might have been agreement or might have been something else entirely. The exhaustion of the past few days was catching up with me, made worse by the heat of the water and the gentleness of his touch.

"Don't fall asleep in there," he said, and I could hear the smile in his voice. "I'm not fishing you out if you drown."

"Liar." I opened my eyes to find him closer than I expected, his face just inches from mine. The hunger was still there in his eyes, but it was softer now, mixed with something that made my chest ache. "You'd save me."

His hand, still tangled in my wet hair, stilled. "Atreya…"

"I know," I said quickly. "We're not talking about it. Any of it." I pulled away, water sloshing against the tub's sides. "You should go check the perimeter or whatever it is you do when you're avoiding me."

He stood so abruptly it was like I'd shocked him again. "There are clean clothes in the bedroom. I'll… I'll find us something to eat."

This time when he fled, I didn't stop him. Just sank deeper into the cooling water and tried not to think about the way his fingers had felt in my hair, or how the scent of jasmine seemed to linger long after he was gone.

CHAPTER 35

Ronan

The man's skin was fever-hot against mine, his pulse a drumbeat in the dark alley. He thought this was just another hookup, just another moment of desperate pleasure against cold stone walls. His hands traced my chest, hungry and eager, completely unaware that this hunger was nothing compared to mine.

"Fuck," he gasped as I pressed him harder against the wall. "You're so—"

I caught his mouth with mine, not wanting to hear whatever he thought I was. His blood sang beneath his skin, calling to me like a siren. Three days in the desert had left me ravenous, and the pathetic amount I'd taken from Atreya wasn't enough. Not nearly enough.

His fingers tangled in my hair as I moved to his neck, teeth grazing his pulse point. The steady thrum of his heartbeat was a countdown he didn't know was ticking. Five minutes of life left. Four. Three.

"Wait," he panted, trying to push me back. Maybe some animal instinct was finally kicking in, warning him that predators don't usually play with their food quite like this. "Someone might see—"

I laughed against his throat. "No one will see." No one ever did. Not in alleys this dark, not when I didn't want them to. "No one will hear you either."

He relaxed at that, mistaking my words for discretion rather than the promise they were. His hands resumed their exploration, and I let him have his last moments of pleasure. It was the kindest death I could offer—better than what I'd given the Elder Sparrows. Better than what they'd given Mira and Sianna.

When my fangs finally sank into his throat, he didn't even struggle. Just made a small sound of surprise that quickly turned to pleasure as my venom hit his bloodstream. They always did. His blood flooded my mouth, hot and rich and exactly what I needed. Each swallow felt like coming back to life, like power returning to dead limbs.

His heartbeat began to slow. Four minutes had passed. Then three. Two. I could feel him growing weaker, his hands no longer urgent against my skin but fluttering like dying birds.

One minute.

"Shh," I whispered against his throat, though he hadn't made a sound. "It's almost over."

His pulse stuttered once, twice, then stopped altogether. I held him up for a moment longer, making sure I hadn't missed a single drop. When I finally stepped back, his body crumpled to the ground like a puppet with cut strings.

I wiped my mouth with the back of my hand, already feeling the borrowed life burning through my veins. My skin tingled with renewed strength, and for the first time since the desert, I felt truly alive.

The body at my feet would be ash before sunrise. They always were. No evidence, no questions, no loose ends. Just another missing person in a city too big to care.

But as I turned to leave the alley, Atreya's words echoed in my head: "Good." That's what she'd said when I told her about destroying the Elder Sparrows. Not horror, not fear. Just... acceptance. Understanding.

I wondered what she'd think if she could see me now, with someone else's blood still warm on my lips. Would she still look at me with that mix of awe and hunger? Or would this finally be the thing that made her realize what I truly was?

Before leaving, I knelt beside the cooling body, methodically checking his pockets. Old habits died hard, and money was money. My fingers found a leather pouch that jingled promisingly.

Gold and silver coins spilled into my palm. The silver made my skin prickle unpleasantly. But Atreya could use it. She'd need supplies, food, things I no longer required except as pretense.

I pocketed the pouch, ignoring the way the silver burned through the leather against my thigh. Better to keep playing at being something closer to human than monster, even if we both knew it was a lie.

Even if part of me wondered if maybe that was why she wasn't afraid—because she recognized the monster in herself, too.

The cramped room felt smaller when I returned, arms laden with bread, cheese, and a full waterskin. I tossed the remaining coins onto the threadbare blanket beside Atreya, but froze mid-motion when I finally noticed what she was wearing.

Mira's dress.

The sight of it hit me like a physical blow. I'd spent weeks on that piece—intricate embroidery along the neckline, careful pleating at the waist. Each stitch had been a meditation, a way to repay Mira's kindness when she'd taken me in. Now it draped across Atreya's frame like a ghost, a reminder of everything I'd lost.

"We'll get you something else tomorrow," I said, my voice rougher than intended. "The market stalls should have—"

"Is that safe?" Atreya's fingers worried the fabric, and I had to look away. "The wanted posters—"

I crossed to the window, retrieving a sand scarf and hood from a hook on the wall. The fabric was worn soft from use, stained the color of the desert itself. I tossed them to her, watching as she caught them with those too-quick reflexes of hers.

"Everyone looks the same here," I said, gesturing to the window where countless figures moved through the streets below, all wrapped against the endless sand. "There are thousands of people in this city, all of them hiding from something or someone. A few wanted posters won't matter when you're just another ghost in the crowd."

Despite my grim words, Atreya's face lit up with an almost childlike excitement. She wrapped the sand scarf around her shoulders, testing its drape, her earlier hesitation forgotten.

"A whole city to explore," she breathed, moving to the window beside me. Her fingers traced the weathered windowsill as she peered down at the bustling streets below. "I've never... I mean, before all this, I was always..."

She didn't finish, but she didn't need to. I recognized that hunger in her voice—not the dark kind that drove us to kill, but the simple desire for normalcy. For freedom. The markets would be overwhelming with their riot of colors, sounds, and smells. Merchants hawking their wares, children darting between stalls, the mingled aromas of spices and sweat and life.

"Just stay away from the temple district," I warned, though I couldn't bring myself to dampen her enthusiasm entirely. "And be back before sunset."

She nodded, already pulling the hood up to frame her face. The heavy fabric transformed her into just another shadow in a city full of them.

CHAPTER 36

Atreya

I left Ronan as soon as the sun rose. I could use the space to breathe and try to work out what I was feeling. I wandered through the bustling throngs, my gaze drinking in the myriad stalls and their treasures. The market of Paladin was alive with sound and color—merchants hawking their wares in a dozen different languages, the scent of spiced meats and sweet incense mixing in the air. Ronan was right. Everyone looked the same here.

A stall caught my eye, set apart from the others. Unlike the bright awnings and flashy displays of its neighbors, this one was draped in rich, dark velvets that seemed to absorb the light. Amidst the luxurious fabrics, something glinted. The merchant—tall and otherworldly, with eyes like pearls and a smile that didn't quite reach them—beckoned me closer.

"My lady," he purred, "I see you have discerning taste. Perhaps you'd be interested in this?" He gestured to a mirror, its silver frame adorned with intricate patterns that seemed to shift when I wasn't looking directly at them. "It can show you anything you desire, anything at all."

I quirked a brow, studying the unusual merchant as much as his wares. "A mirror that shows more than just a reflection?"

"Indeed." He lifted it with reverent hands. "Ever wonder what you'd look like with golden hair and hawk-like eyes? Or perhaps..." His pearl-white eyes studied me knowingly. "Perhaps there are other things you wish to see?"

The mirror looked ordinary enough at first glance, but there was something about it that made my skin prickle with awareness. Magic, old and powerful, hummed beneath its surface. I took it from him, surprised by its weight. As I turned it over, my breath caught—there, on the back, was a small, faded mark: a downward-pointing triangle with curved top and bottom. The symbol of Elenaria

"Where did you acquire this?" I demanded, sharper than intended.

The merchant's smile widened, showing teeth that were just a bit too white, too perfect. "The mirror has passed through many hands, my lady. Each owner adding to its enchantment, each leaving their mark upon its magic. It has witnessed empires rise and fall, crossed the boundaries between realms, and now..." He spread his hands. "Now it finds itself here, awaiting its next keeper."

"How does it work?" I asked, my fingers tracing the intricate patterns in the frame. Under my touch, they seemed to writhe like living things.

"Simply hold the mirror and speak your desire," he said, his voice dropping to a whisper. "It will show you what you seek—not the future, nor the past, but anything you wish to see in the present moment."

I studied him over the mirror's edge. "Such a thing would be hidden away in some noble's vault or a temple's sacred chambers. Not here in a market stall."

His face faltered for just a moment, like a candle flickering in a draft. He quickly composed himself, giving way to his polished demeanor once more. "Indeed, my lady, many have sought to possess the mirror for its powers. Yet, its magic is not for the faint of heart, and it seems to find its way to those who truly understand its worth."

"Tell me, merchant," I said, unable to shake the feeling that there was more to this exchange than simple commerce. "Why part with such a treasure? Why not use its powers for yourself?"

He leaned forward slightly, those unsettling eyes boring into mine. "A mirror such as this is a reflection of the soul, my lady. It requires a keeper with a pure heart and clear intentions. My path lies in the trade of wonders, not in their wielding."

"And how do you know my heart is pure?"

"Goodness isn't always obvious to the eye," he smiled, "It's found in the questions one asks, in the choices one makes. You question the mirror's purpose rather than blindly seeking its power. That alone tells me much."

I nodded slowly, understanding dawning. "And what would you ask in exchange for such an item?"

His gaze fixed on my wrist, where Ramses' golden bracelet caught the light. "That would be a fair trade, I think. Its beauty is matched only by its value—a worthy price for an item of such unique enchantments."

My hand went to the bracelet instinctively. The gift Ramses had given me after I defeated Aislinn Furian. Once, I had worn it with pride. Now it felt like the last remaining shackle of a life I wanted to forget.

"I... I can't remove it. It's sealed with magic."

He reached out, his long fingers barely brushing the gold. At his touch, the bracelet loosened effortlessly, sliding off my wrist as if it had never been bound there at all. I stared at my bare wrist, stunned.

The weight difference was immediate, both physical and symbolic. My last tie to being the Furian Slayer, gone. My eyes burned as he took the bracelet from my trembling hands.

He frowned, fingers curling around the gold. "My lady, if this trinket holds such meaning—"

"Take it," I cut him off, my voice rough. "I don't want it anymore."

He bowed his head. When he opened his hand again, the bracelet had vanished as if it had never existed. "May you continue to prosper, my lady."

"Show me Vryseris," I whispered to the mirror. It vibrated and glowed, but then died out with a spark. The surface turned dark, almost as if ink had been poured across it, before clearing again to show only my own reflection.

"It doesn't work if there is other magic at play," the merchant said.

"How convenient," I murmured, running my fingers along the mirror's edge. Whatever magic concealed Vryseris was powerful enough to resist even Elenaria's ancient enchantments. The thought sent a chill down my spine.

I turned my back to him, holding up the mirror to my face. "Show me Ronan." There was a low vibration in my palm, and the mirror began to glow again.

The surface of the mirror shimmered like the surface of a still pond disturbed by a gentle breeze. Then, as if a veil had been lifted, the glass cleared to reveal a scene of Ronan. He was seated in the library, a book open before him, the dim light of a single candle flickering against his ageless features.

My breath hitched in my throat. His finger was following along the words of his book, and he was quietly mouthing the words as he read. I tentatively touched the mirror's surface, tracing the edges of the image, trying to read his lips.

He stretched his limbs, the muscles rippling through his body. His eyes closed, and he began to hum, a soft, soothing melody that I recognized as one I had hummed many times before. When my heart thudded in my chest, I lowered the mirror and whirled on the merchant to ask him if the person you view in the mirror can sense you, but when I did, he was gone.

No trace of him remained, the stall empty and old, broken down the middle.

I glanced around, half expecting to catch a glimpse of him slipping through the crowd. I waved to the neighboring stall, a woman and her daughter selling candles. "Excuse me. Have you seen where the man at this stall went?" The woman shook her head, her brow furrowed.

"There was no man at this stall. It's been empty for years," she said, then turned to her daughter, saying something in another language I didn't catch.

"It is the worst spot for a stall, no one sets up there," the daughter scoffed.

Had the merchant been a specter, a trick of magic or the mind? The mirror in my hand was undoubtedly real, its weight and coolness against my skin.

I hadn't imagined it.

"Sorry to have bothered you," I said to the woman, turning to leave.

"If a spirit has visited you, the gods must be watching over you," the daughter called out to me.

Her words hung in the air as I walked away from the stall. Could it be that the gods, or a particular goddess represented by the symbol on the mirror, had indeed orchestrated this encounter?

I clutched the mirror closer, a sense of reverence mingling with my bewilderment.

I sought out Ronan in the library, my heart thundering against my ribs. The corridors were quiet save for the whisper of my footsteps and the gentle clink of the mirror against my hip. When I found him, he was exactly as I'd seen in the mirror—bent over his books, candlelight dancing across his features, lost in whatever ancient text had caught his attention.

For a moment, I just watched him. This creature of darkness and power, this being who had lived through centuries, sitting there looking almost peaceful. Almost human. The sight made my chest ache with something I wasn't ready to name.

"Ronan," I called softly.

He looked up, his eyes finding mine in the dim light. A gentle smile graced his lips. "Atreya, you've returned sooner than I expected. Did you find what you were looking for?"

I stepped into the room, the door closing behind me with a soft click. "In a way, I found more than I bargained for," I replied. "Paladin is huge."

I drew the mirror from my cloak, the silver frame catching the light of the candles.

"A mirror? You really are vain aren't you?" He chuckled.

"It's for you, actually." I slid the mirror across the table toward him.

"Very funny. You know as well as I do that I can't see myself in mirrors." He went back to reading, dismissing me.

I watched him dismiss the gift, smirking to myself. "Not this one, Ronan. This is no ordinary mirror. It's *enchanted*."

His eyes flicked up to meet mine, and his lips twitched. "Conned into buying a magic trick? I left you alone for a few hours and you get scammed?"

I sighed in exasperation, leaning my elbows on the table. "I saw you reading in here. Using the mirror, I *saw* you."

"You knew I was in the library. I have been here since you left." He flipped through a few more pages.

I started humming the same song he had been singing. It was a simple melody, lulling and soothing. He put the book down and leaned back in his chair. He narrowed his eyes at me, his face thoughtful.

"Spying on someone who is peacefully reading is quite rude."

"So, you believe me then?" I smiled, sliding the mirror closer to him. His red eyes flicked to my bare wrist and then back to the mirror.

"Your bracelet is gone."

"I traded it for the mirror."

"I gave you gold," he murmured.

"And I still have your gold."

"You didn't need to part with your things." He frowned.

"It was mine to part with. I wanted to part with it." I tapped the mirror impatiently. He frowned harder.

Ronan uncrossed his arms and leaned forward, the skepticism in his eyes softening as he considered the possibility that I wasn't jesting about the mirror.

I waved my hand at him. "Don't. The bracelet means nothing. It is nothing." I walked over behind him, leveling at his shoulder. "Go on."

He hesitated for a moment longer before finally picking up the mirror. Holding it before him, I watched his face. There was a tick in his brow, as he prepared himself for that familiar absence of his reflection.

"I see nothing," he sighed.

"You're not doing it right." I grasped my hand over his, ignoring how it sent a jolt through me. I fixed the mirror to his eye level. "Show me Ronan."

The mirror vibrated gently under our touch, and once again, it began to glow with the same soft, ethereal light I had witnessed at the market. Ronan's eyes widened as his visage slowly materialized within the glass.

It was him—undeniable and clear. His reflection gazed back with a mixture of astonishment and a trace of something deeper, something that had been locked away for centuries. His breath was shallow, and he blinked, eyes glazing over.

"There," I whispered, "It's no trick, Ronan. It's magic."

He didn't respond at first, too caught up in the sight of himself. Ronan's hand, the one not held by mine, reached up to touch his own face, his fingertips brushing against the surface of the mirror as if to confirm the reality of his reflection.

"By all the night's stars..." he breathed out with a mix of wonder and a poignant sort of grief. "I had forgotten—"

"What you looked like?" I offered softly.

"Yes," he murmured, barely audible. "I'd forgotten the man who used to stare back at me. The one who walked in the sunlight, who..." he trailed off.

There was a profound silence as Ronan continued to study his face, to rediscover the contours and lines that had defined him, to reconnect with the visage that had been stolen by his vampirism.

"I had blue eyes," he finally said. "My mother's eyes. They used to say the river of Midorai ran through us."

I remained silent, letting him explore his memories. "She was beautiful, so very beautiful. My sister, Misanda, looked just like her too," he whispered.

"You must have loved them," I prompted for him to continue, should he wish to share more.

Ronan nodded, his gaze still fixed on the mirror, though he was now looking beyond his own reflection, into the depths of a time long gone. "Misanda and I were inseparable. We shared everything—thoughts, dreams, even our mischief," he said, "But when I turned, everything changed. I became a child of the night, and she remained a child of the day. Our paths diverged, and I... I lost track of her."

"Have you ever thought about finding her?"

Ronan's smile faded, and a shadow seemed to pass over his face. "I have," he admitted, with a mixture of regret and resignation. "But so many years have passed, Atreya. Misanda's life would have been lived in full by now. She would have grown old in a world that I could no longer inhabit, and then she would have passed on as all mortals do."

"You are not of Fae?" I asked in disbelief, scanning his elven traits over.

"I am—was. She was my half-sister. We shared the same mother, but different fathers. A halfling's life would have been a long one, long enough to have grown old. His mortal blood cursed her to that fate. It's a cruel twist of fate," he continued, "To be left behind, to remember, while those you love... they just become echoes."

I braced myself for his next question, knowing where this was headed.

"C-can it show me her? Her life?" He swallowed thickly.

I shook my head. "The mirror does not show the past of another. But perhaps, it can show you your own memories? You were there for parts of her life, I don't see how that wouldn't work?"

He took a deep breath and held the mirror up once more, his gaze intense and focused. "Mirror, show me my memories of Misanda, my sister, as we were in our youth," he commanded. I smiled at his need to be so specific.

A soft luminescence emanated from within, growing brighter until it was almost blinding. I squinted against the glare, but Ronan remained steadfast, his eyes never wavering from the glass.

Slowly, the light began to fade, coalescing into shapes and colors that took on the form of a sun-dappled glade. Two children appeared within the mirror's frame, a young Ronan with eyes as blue as the sky and a girl whose silver hair carried in the breeze. They were chasing one another, laughing and running.

Ronan's breath hitched, and a tear escaped down his cheek. "Misanda," he whispered. The children in the mirror were oblivious to our gaze, lost in the happiness of their moment. "That's her," Ronan whispered, tears brimming in his eyes. "That's my Misanda."

I wanted to shrink away, to hide. To give Ronan his privacy, but I was glued to his side, my hand holding his over the mirror.

The scene shifted, transitioning through snippets of memories—them fishing by the banks of a river, studying under the tutelage of their Fae mother, celebrating the changing seasons with their mixed heritage community, and sharing secrets when they should have gone to bed.

"When I am of age, I am going to marry a faerie, and I will have lots of children, and they will have lots of children. That way, you won't be alone when I am gone," Misanda told him, braiding his hair into a long plait. He was lanky, younger than he was now, but not by much.

"Disgusting. I don't want to think about that," younger Ronan said.

The memory elicited a brief, melancholic chuckle from present-day Ronan. "She always had such grand plans," he sighed.

In the mirror, young Misanda playfully tugged on the braid, her eyes sparkling with mischief. *"Oh, come now. You'll be a handsome elf lord one day. All the maidens will be vying for your attention."*

As the images flickered past, Ronan's face was a canvas of emotions, each memory painting strokes of joy, laughter, and the inevitable onset of sorrow as they grew older and their paths began to diverge.

Finally, the mirror stilled, the last image fading away to leave only Ronan's reflection staring back at him.

He lowered the mirror, his grip on the frame tight, "Thank you," he said in barely more than a rasp. "Seeing her, our life together... it has brought her back to me, if only for a moment."

Slowly, Ronan released the mirror, his gaze lingering on the glass before turning to meet mine. "I can never repay you for this, Atreya. This gift..."

"There is nothing to repay, nothing at all. Besides, I've gained as much from this as you have. I've seen a part of you that few have the privilege to witness."

I looked up at Ronan, his form backlit by the fading light that tried to break through the thick curtains and realized that the feelings I had for him had shifted, deepened into something I could no longer deny.

The silence stretched on, and in that quiet, my heart spoke a truth I had been reluctant to admit, even to myself.

I was falling in love with Ronan.

"I should put this somewhere safe," he said, carefully wrapping the mirror in a piece of velvet cloth from his desk drawer. His hands trembled slightly as he secured it. "Such magic should be protected."

I watched him tuck the mirror away, noting how his fingers lingered on the cloth-wrapped bundle before he finally closed the drawer. When he turned back to me, there was a vulnerability in his eyes I'd never seen before.

"Why did you really trade your bracelet for this? It is the only proof you have outside of Ember that you are the Furian Slayer..."

I swallowed hard, caught between honesty and self-preservation. "Because some chains are worth breaking," I finally said. "And some gifts are worth more than gold."

CHAPTER 37

Ronan

Later that night, when Atreya's breathing had settled into the gentle rhythm of sleep, I found myself drawn back to the mirror. My hands trembled slightly as I unwrapped it from its velvet shroud, memories of our earlier conversation by the river still echoing in my mind—her pain over Servat, my confession about Mother and Misanda.

"Show me my mother," I whispered, the words catching in my throat like thorns. "Show me Lyria of the River Tribe, from my memories before I turned."

The mirror hummed beneath my touch, its surface rippling like disturbed water. For a moment, I thought of Atreya's words from earlier—how time doesn't help, it just gives you more space to remember what you lost. She understood that kind of pain, the way it hollows you out from the inside.

The surface cleared, and there she stood in my memory—my mother, tall and graceful, her silver hair cascading down her back like moonlight on water. Those eyes—the same ones I once had—sparkled with wisdom and warmth as she tended to her garden of night-blooming flowers. I could almost smell the sweet perfume of the moonflowers she loved so much.

My chest tightened as I watched these fragments of memory play out. She had always preferred the twilight hours, saying they held a magic all their own. I wondered what she would have thought of what I'd become—this creature of eternal night, so far removed from the son she'd known.

The scene shifted, showing her reading to Misanda and me by candlelight. I touched my nose unconsciously, remembering how she would swipe her finger along it, commenting on its sharpness. Like hers. These fragments of memory—they were all I had left, and even they seemed to slip through my fingers like water.

"I wish you could have guided me through what I became," I whispered to her image. "Though perhaps it's better you never saw what your son turned into."

A single crimson tear traced down my cheek, falling onto the mirror's surface. The image wavered, then cleared to show my own reflection—red eyes where blue ones had been, pale skin that would never again feel the warmth of the sun. I thought of Atreya's words by the river, about how time gives you more space to remember what you lost. She was right, but perhaps it also gave you space to find something new.

Down the hall, I heard her shift in her sleep, murmuring something unintelligible. The sound drew a smile to my lips despite the weight of old memories.

I carefully rewrapped the mirror, each fold of the velvet deliberate and gentle. Mother would never know what I'd become, and perhaps that was a mercy. But Atreya—she saw me as I was and didn't flinch. Didn't run. Instead, she shared her own broken pieces, showing me that even the deepest wounds could heal, given time and trust.

Perhaps that's what drew me to her—not just her strength or her beauty, but the way she carried her scars with grace, the way she understood that some wounds never truly heal. And somehow, in sharing our broken pieces, we'd both found something worth holding onto.

I closed my eyes, listening to her steady heartbeat down the hall. My mother might not have lived to see what I became, but maybe she'd be proud of who I was trying to be now.

Someone worthy of the light I'd found in the darkness.

Rising from my seat by the mirror, I moved to the window, drawn to the silver-kissed gardens below. The night air carried the sweet scent of jasmine, reminding me of how Atreya had paused to smell each flower during our walk earlier, her face lighting up with simple joy at each new discovery.

That was what made this... whatever was growing between us... both precious and painful. Every time she looked at something with fresh eyes, every moment of wonder at things I'd long since taken for granted, I felt it—this pull toward her that grew stronger with each passing day. But it was that very innocence, that untarnished view of the world, that made me want to step back.

I'd lived through centuries, seen empires rise and fall, watched countless seasons change. Atreya... she was just beginning to spread her wings, to discover who she was beyond the walls that had confined her. The way her eyes had widened at the sight of fireflies dancing over the river, how she'd gasped at the taste of wild berries—these were the experiences she deserved to savor, to discover at her own pace.

My fingers traced patterns on the cold glass, following the path of a moonbeam. Yes, I felt something for her—something that made my ancient heart stir in ways I'd thought impossible. But I'd seen too many young souls rush headlong into the darkness, thinking they were ready for its depths, only to lose themselves in its embrace.

"Let her bloom," I whispered to myself, the words both a promise and a reminder. "Let her discover the world's wonders before she chooses its shadows."

A soft sigh drifted from her room, and I smiled, imagining her lost in dreams of all the adventures yet to come. She deserved that time—to taste freedom, to make mistakes, to learn who she was when no one was watching. And if my role in her story was to be the guardian of that journey rather than its destination... well, perhaps that was exactly as it should be.

Still, as I turned away from the window, I couldn't help but wonder if Mother would have liked her—this brave, broken, beautiful soul who'd wandered into my darkness and somehow made it feel less lonely. I had a feeling she would have loved Atreya's garden-wild spirit, her fierce determination to grow despite the shadows of her past.

Time had taught me patience, but patience was a bitch when everything in me screamed to take, to own, to destroy. Some flowers only bloom in darkness—but Atreya? She deserved the sun.

Even if watching her reach for it killed me.
Because that's what I do. I ruin. I corrupt. I destroy.
And God help me, I wanted to ruin her most of all.

The days that followed our night at the mirror blurred together, each one bringing me closer to an edge I hadn't known existed. The change happened so gradually, I almost didn't notice it at first. Like watching a shadow lengthen across the floor as the sun sets, my noble intentions began to twist into something darker, more possessive. Each day brought a new test of my resolve—the way she'd look at me with those trusting eyes, how she'd lean into my touch when I adjusted her clothes or braided her hair.

I told myself I was protecting her, guiding her. But with every lesson in proper dress, every tutorial in social graces, I was really marking her as mine. Teaching her to move through my world, molding her into something that belonged in my shadows rather than her light.

The mirror scene haunted me—how I'd shared my memories of Mother, bared my soul in a moment of weakness. I'd promised myself then to let Atreya bloom in her own time, to be nothing more than a guardian on her journey. But guardians don't feel this burning need to possess, this maddening desire to corrupt.

This inexplicable urge to corrupt her gnawed at me, growing stronger with each passing day. I found myself watching her more intently, noting every graceful movement, every innocent gesture that spoke of her sheltered past. What had started as a desire to protect her innocence was transforming into something darker, more primal.

Perhaps it was inevitable. After all, I ruin everything I touch. And Atreya, with her garden-wild spirit and fierce determination, was too tempting not to ruin. The question wasn't if I would corrupt her, but when—and how completely she would let me.

CHAPTER 38

Ronan

"Y ou're not fucking wearing that," I said, eyeing Atreya's outfit.

Atreya had the nerve to look offended. "What's wrong with my clothes?"

"What isn't wrong with them? You are *not* coming out with me like that."

She blushed angrily. "These are the clothes you got me!"

"For traveling, not for a night out in Calazan. I said get something nice, not something that screams 'I have no taste'." I shook my head, already seeing the disaster this could be.

"So?" She crossed her arms, a petulant look on her face.

"I told you to buy yourself something nice, Atreya." I reminded her, trying not to lose my patience.

"I bought the mirror." She muttered, looking down.

I pinched the bridge of my nose. "You want to go to Calazan then you need to dress up. Inconspicuous—not *poor*."

"I don't have anything else!" She threw up her hands.

I turned to her, looking her up and down. "Turn around," I ordered.

She huffed but complied. My gaze traveled from the oversized green tunic to the ill-fitting leather pants. "You know, you do have a nice ass. Maybe we can work with that." I said, a plan forming in my mind.

She spun back around, scowling. "What's that supposed to mean?"

"It will draw attention away from whatever is happening here." I waved a hand over her chest.

She crossed her arms over her chest. "What's wrong with my breasts?"

"Nothing. As a matter of fact, I should look just to make sure." I teased, trying to get a rise out of her.

She swatted my arm, blushing.

I chuckled and held up my hands in a defensive gesture. "I was just going to check if they were worth showing off."

"Well, they're not," she muttered, looking down.

That struck a nerve in me. I liked teasing her. I liked making her blush. I liked watching her get flustered. What I didn't like was how she said that. Like she really meant that about herself.

"You have nice breasts," I deadpanned, trying to reassure her.

Atreya looked taken aback. "You think so?"

I nodded. "I do. And I think you should show them off."

Her cheeks flushed pink. "I don't know…"

I stepped closer to her. "I do. Trust me."

She bit her lip, looking uncertain. But then she nodded. "Okay."

I grinned. "That's the spirit." Then I brought a knife out and slashed the green tunic open from the hem to the neckline.

"Ronan!" She shouted covering herself with her arms.

"Relax. I know what I'm doing." I soothed, already turning to the task at hand.

She eyed me warily, but didn't stop me as I got to work. I quickly got to it, my hands moving with practiced ease as I cut away the excess fabric, turning the ill-fitting tunic into something that would actually flatter her figure. I worked fast, but I worked carefully, making sure everything was perfect.

As I worked, I pulled out the gold trinkets I had hidden in my hair and set them on the table. They sparkled in the light, and I knew they would be the perfect accent for her outfit.

As I stepped back to admire my handiwork, Atreya looked at herself in the mirror. Her eyes widened in surprise, and then a smile spread across her face.

"Where did you learn to do this?" she asked, turning herself this way and that.

"I've had to make my own clothes for years," I answered with a sniff. I liked the way she grinned at herself in the mirror. It made me want to tear up the rest of her clothes. Maybe I would, later. Right now, I just wanted to enjoy the sight of her in all her glory.

"You look good." I said, feeling a strange sense of pride.

She blushed and looked away, "Thanks."

"Would you like me to braid your hair?" I asked.

She blushed more furiously and nodded.

I gestured for her to sit on the edge of the bed. "Come here then."

She settled down, and I moved behind her, running my fingers through her dark hair. It was softer than I expected, and I found myself enjoying the simple act of touching it.

"Your hair is nice," I commented, separating it into sections. "Thick. Good for hiding things in."

She laughed softly. "Is that all you think about? Hiding things?"

"Among other things." I began weaving the strands together, incorporating the small golden trinkets I'd set aside. They caught the light as I worked them in, creating a pattern that would draw attention without being obviously valuable. "Like how to make you look expensive without actually being expensive."

"Is that what we're doing?" She tilted her head slightly, and I tugged it back into position.

"Stay still," I chided. "And yes, that's exactly what we're doing. Calazan isn't just about looking rich—it's about looking like you don't care if people know you're rich."

"That makes no sense."

"Neither does most of high society." My fingers moved quickly, years of practice making the complex pattern almost automatic. "But if you want to blend in, you need to learn their rules."

"And you know all their rules?"

I smirked, though she couldn't see it. "I know how to break them properly."

She was quiet for a moment, and I could feel her relaxing under my touch. "Why are you helping me?"

The question caught me off guard, and my hands stilled for a moment before resuming their work. "Because I want to," I said simply, not ready to examine my motivations too closely.

"That's not really an answer."

"It's the only one I have right now." I secured the last piece of gold into her braid and stepped back. "There. Take a look."

She stood and moved to the mirror, turning her head to see the intricate pattern I'd woven. The gold pieces caught the light, creating a subtle shimmer that made her hair look like it was threaded with starlight.

Her eyes met mine in the mirror. "It's beautiful."

"You're beautiful," I said before I could stop myself. The words hung in the air between us, too honest for comfort.

She turned to face me, and for a moment, I thought she might say something that would make this all too real. Instead, she beamed at me and said, "So, are we ready for Calazan now?"

I cleared my throat, grateful for the return to safer ground. "Almost." I reached into my pocket and pulled out a small vial of perfume. "One last touch."

"What is it?"

"Something to make sure all eyes are on you. Even though your face would be hidden, it is nice to be admired." I stepped closer, uncorking the vial. "Close your eyes."

She did, and I carefully dabbed the perfume on her pulse points—wrists, neck, behind her ears. The scent was subtle but intoxicating, a blend of night-blooming flowers and something darker, more dangerous.

"There, now you're ready to break some hearts."

Her eyes opened, and the look in them made my breath catch. "Just hearts?"

I stepped back before I could do something stupid. "Let's start with hearts and work our way up to breaking everything else."

I held out my arm. "Shall we go?"

She took it, and I could feel the weight of her gaze on me. "You clean up nice yourself."

I chuckled and led her out the door. Maybe this night wouldn't be a total loss.

I don't know what it is. I don't know why I feel this way. Why?

This inexplicable urge to corrupt her gnawed at me.

I could see the darkness churning within her, a snake straining against its cage.

I was drawn to it. Would the snake strike if set free?

Occasionally, a flicker of the wild, untamed woman I'd glimpsed within Ember's walls would surface. My instincts would roar to life, yearning to claim her, to possess the storm that danced in her eyes.

I remembered the soft whisper of my name as I swept her onto the dance floor, her body pliant with desire—courtesy of what ever Ramses had given her.

Her curiosity about the world beyond Ramses' carefully constructed prison tantalized me. It stirred something deep within my soul.

I craved witnessing her downfall, her fiery rise from the ashes of the kingdom he'd built around her and becoming something else.

I longed to see her wield her power to destroy those who hurt her, not heal. These people wouldn't lift a finger to aid her if she ever needed it, wouldn't sacrifice a crust of bread if she hungered.

It infuriated me, how she offered herself with open arms to a world that would devour her without hesitation.

Selfishness was the key to survival. It had sustained me thus far.

The conflicting desires were maddening. I wanted what was best for her—for me.

But soon, none of it would matter. Once I possessed the Daylight Ring, I would be free to abandon this place.

To abandon her. Because Gods only knew that beings like me don't get to live happy endings. I ruin everything. That was my curse.

But before I did, I wanted to see her. Raw, unguarded, unspoiled. I wanted to see her as she truly was. I wanted to see her blood, her soul, her essence.

And she walked beside me without knowing the thoughts that consumed me. How she consumed me—

Her scent, her sweet scent, her graceful swaying, the way she held her head, all drove me fucking nuts.

Her beauty made my fingers itch to touch her, to wrap my hands around her waist.

No.

Her silver eyes took in the sights around her. The air pulsed with the rhythmic thump of drums, the sharp clang of cymbals, the wild trill of flutes. Dancers spun and leaped, their brightly colored skirts and sashes fluttering like exotic birds in flight. Tambourines shook and rattled in time with the beat.

Singers' songs rose and fell in haunting melodies, the lyrics of which I had only distant memories of. The smell of sweat, incense, and spilled wine hung heavy over everything, intoxicating.

Ember's hand tightened on my arm, her body swaying unconsciously to the rhythm of the music. Her silver eyes sparkled with excitement, her lips curled up into a delighted smile. She was a vision of ethereal beauty, a shining star amidst the gaudy decadence of the festival. I felt a pang in my chest, a squeezing in my lungs. I wanted to drag her close, to claim her lips, to never let her go. No. I pushed the thoughts aside, focusing on the sights and sounds around us. We pressed through the crowd, the music and laughter growing louder with each step.

A female dancer pulled her into the opening that formed, her scarf around her neck. Atreya looked back at me, uncertain.

I gave her a reassuring nod and a gentle push. "Go on. I'll be right here."

She bit her lip, then nodded and let herself be pulled into the whirl of color and movement. I watched, mesmerized, as she lost herself in the rhythm of the music and the swirl of the dancers. Her laughter rang out, a joyous, carefree sound.

I felt a pang in my chest, a burning desire to join her, to lose myself in the magic of the moment. But I pushed the feelings aside—she wouldn't want that.

I wonder what she would want?

CHAPTER 39

Atreya

A s we walked through the winding streets of Calazan, the sounds of the city grew louder around us. The music and laughter from the festival faded into the distance, replaced by the hawking calls of vendors and the clanging of pots and pans from the nearby market. The air was thick with the smells of exotic spices and fresh bread, making my stomach growl with hunger. I hadn't eaten since morning, and the aromas wafting from the food stalls were teasing.

But as we turned a corner, the sights and smells of the market gave way to something entirely different. A large stone building loomed ahead of us, its entrance guarded by heavy iron doors. The sign above the door read 'The House of the Red Wyvern' in bold red letters.

"Ronan," I said, tugging on his arm. "What's that?"

"It's a brothel," he answered.

"Really? And people pay to... you know?" *Fuck.*

"That's how it works, yes." He said it like it was the most normal thing in the world.

I raised an eyebrow. "Have you, you know?" I pointed to the Brothel and then back at him.

He narrowed red eyes at me. "Are you trying to ask me if I've paid for sex?"

Oh great. Now he is offended.

"Because I absolutely have," he finished.

I gaped at him, unsure how to respond.

"Oh, don't look so shocked," he teased. "I am a charitable man, after all. I do my part for the economy. Plus it would be absolutely criminal for a man of my charm and good looks to not be willing to share the pleasure of his company with those in need of it."

I looked from the bold sign to him.

"You want to go in?" he asked.

"No!" I said a little too loudly.

He looked down at me, a smirk playing on his lips. "Oh, come now," he said, low and persuasive. "I promise you'll find it...enlightening. Besides, I'm not going to let anything happen to you."

I bit my lip, unsure. But he just gave my hand a reassuring squeeze and led me forward. The guard at the door eyed us up and down, but he just nodded at Ronan and stepped aside. "Welcome," he greeted.

Ronan led me inside, his hand firm on my lower back. The entrance hall was dimly lit, the only light coming from a few flickering torches on the walls. The air was thick with the smells of smoke and perfume, and I could hear the distant sounds of laughter and music. A woman greeted us, her dress barely covering her body. "Welcome to the House of the Red Wyvern," she said. "How may I assist you tonight?"

I didn't know how to respond.

"This is Atreya," Ronan said, his hand still on my back. "I want to show her a good time. Take us to one of the...busier rooms."

The woman's eyes flickered to me, then back to Ronan. "Of course," she said with amusement. "Right this way."

She led us through a winding corridor, the walls decorated with erotic tapestries. I could hear the sounds of the house growing louder around us—the thumping of music, the clinking of glasses, the sounds of...other things. Gods they were loud. My heart was racing in my chest, and I could feel a flush rising to my cheeks.

This was a bad idea. Leave it to me to get too curious.

The woman stopped in front of a heavy wooden door, a smirk still playing on her lips. "Enjoy your night you two," she said, then reached out and flung the door open.

Ronan's hand on my back urged me forward, and I stepped through the doorway, my eyes widening as I took in the sight before me. The room was large, the walls lined with plush couches and chairs. The whole place was laden with the smells of wine and sweat. But it was what was happening on the couches that made my eyes go wide and stumble back.

There were people...together. And they weren't wearing sand scarves to hide their faces. Everywhere. Men with women, men with men, women with women. They were kissing and touching, some even more than that. Heads were bobbing in laps and legs were straddling faces. I didn't know which end was which. I felt a flush rise to my cheeks. I had heard of such places, but I had never imagined I would ever see one firsthand. Ramses spent many nights in pleasure houses. He loved them.

The last time I witnessed other people together was when my husband taught me a lesson on our wedding night.

"Ronan," I whispered, tugging on his arm. "I don't know if I can do this."

He looked down at me, his eyes gleaming with amusement. "Just watch," he whispered back. "You don't have to do anything you don't want to. Just enjoy the show."

I bit my lip, unsure. But he just gave my hand a reassuring squeeze and turned me back to the room. I watched, mesmerized, as the people around us lost themselves in pleasure. It was...new. The sounds and smells and sights all combined to create a heady, overwhelming sensation. No one paid us mind. It was shameless.

And as I watched, I began to feel...things. My skin felt too tight, my heart was racing in my chest. I could feel a heat building in my lower belly, a tingling sensation in my...other places. I was getting...aroused. Wet.

Ronan's hand was still on my back, and I could feel his eyes on me, watching me. He could probably smell it on me, the scent of my arousal. I felt a flush rise to my cheeks, sweep over me again, but I couldn't tear my gaze away from the sight before me.

Suddenly, a woman was in front of me. She was...stunning. Her hair was long and curly, her eyes a deep shade of brown. She was smiling at me, her full lips curled up in a inviting way. "Well, hello there," she said sweetly. "My name is Elara. What's yours?"

I just stared at her, blinking. But then Ronan was in my ear. "Go on," he whispered. "Talk to her."

"I don't have any money," I stuttered out.

Elara's eyes flickered to Ronan, then back to me, and she laughed. "You have already been paid for tonight," she said with a sly smile.

I turned to look at Ronan, who winked at me. "This is Atreya," he introduced me.

Elara just laughed, a throaty sound, then reached out and took my hand. "It's nice to meet you, Atreya. Why don't you and I get to know each other better?"

"Oh-oh okay," I stuttered out. Elara was leading me to the other side of the room, where curtains draped and a private area was waiting. Ronan followed behind like a shadow.

Elara sat me down in plush green cushions and leaned against the couch opposite me. "So," she said, her eyes locked on mine. She spread her legs and leaned forward, so close to me that her breath tickled my skin. "Tell me about yourself, Atreya."

I said the first thing that came to mind. "I like bread."

Ronan snorted from where he was sitting on the couch opposite of Elara. I shot him a look. Elara laughed and leaned forward some more, tracing her fingers along my jaw.

Then she was leaning in, her lips pressing against mine. I froze, but then something...shifted. The kiss deepened, her tongue sliding against mine. It was...nice. More than nice. It was...good.

I felt myself getting lost in the sensation, my hands coming up to twine in her hair. I was...enjoying myself. The realization sent me reeling, but I couldn't bring myself to care. It felt too...good.

As we kissed, I could feel Ronan's eyes still on me, watching me. He could probably see exactly how aroused I was. I felt a pang of self-consciousness, but then Elara's hands were on my breasts, and I was lost in the sensation once again.

I didn't know what was happening to me. I didn't know why I was letting this woman touch me, kiss me. But as I looked up at her, I saw something in her eyes...something that made me want to give in to this, to see where it would go. Even if it meant losing myself in the process.

Elara hand cupped my breast, her thumb brushing against my nipple. I gasped, and she leaned in to kiss me harder, her tongue probing deeper. I tried to let instinct guide my movements, mimicking her, rubbing her nipples.

"Let her work, Atreya," Ronan said gently.

It was like being pulled into warm water.

Elara moaned into my mouth, her body pressing closer against mine. I could feel her heat, her desire, and it only fueled my own. I had never felt this way before, never imagined I could feel this way. It was like a dam had burst inside me, unleashing a torrent of sensations I had no idea how to navigate.

But she seemed to know exactly what she was doing. Her hands roamed my body, touching me in ways that made me gasp and tremble. Her mouth never left mine, her tongue dancing with mine in a rhythm that was both familiar and yet completely foreign.

I couldn't think, couldn't reason. All I could do was feel, and oh gods, the feelings were overwhelming. I was on fire, my skin burning with a desire I had never known I was capable of.

"Elara," I moaned, her name a plea on my lips.

"Yes, love," she whispered back, her breath hot against my skin. "Let go. Let me show you how good it can feel."

I opened my eyes, acutely aware of Ronan watching us, his eyes glued to me. A man was on his knees before him, his hands untying Ronan's pants. Even as the man obscured my vision, I could see the precise moment the man's mouth closed on Ronan's cock. Ronan's eyes snapped to mine, and I could feel his gaze burning into me. We were dancing on something dangerous.

I wanted him to look at me like that—with fire in his eyes, his fangs slightly bared. Elara moved down my body, her hands stroking my skin, undoing the laces of my breeches.

The whole time I never looked away from Ronan.

And then her tongue was slipping through my folds.

I gasped, my hips jerking off the couch, closing my eyes. It was...different. Not bad, but different. Her touch was softer than a man's, her mouth gentler, smoother, But there was something about it, something that made me want more.

"Elara," I moaned again, my hands fisting in her hair.

"Yes, love," she mumbled against me. "Just relax. Let me make you feel good."

She licked me gently, with light pressure, entering one finger inside of me experimentally, then two. She crooked her fingers and sucked.

I started grinding against her face, I couldn't help it.

It was building in me, a slow burn that threatened to consume me. Her tongue was moving in a steady rhythm, her fingers playing with me.

I could feel myself getting closer, could feel the pressure building. And then I was there, my body shuddering as my orgasm washed over me. I cried out, my hips jerking against her mouth. It was...intense. The most intense sensation I had ever felt.

As I came down, I opened my eyes to see Ronan still watching me. His eyes were burning with desire, his chest heaving with ragged breaths. The man before him had moved away, and now Ronan was stroking himself, his hand moving in a fast rhythm. He was *large*. Larger than any man I had seen. I bit my bottom lip. His eyes never left mine as he worked himself toward his own release.

I felt a pang of...something. Desire? Jealousy? I didn't know. But as I watched him, I knew I wanted him to feel what I just had. I wanted him to feel that kind of pleasure, that kind of release.

"Ronan," I whispered, his name coming out shaky.

He groaned, his head falling back against the couch. "Atreya," he moaned. "Gods, Atreya."

And then he was coming, his body shuddering violently. I watched, mesmerized, as he worked himself through it. His eyes were glued to mine, and I could see the feral gleam in them, the satisfaction. And then his eyes cleared and he was standing.

"We've wasted enough time here," he said gruffly.

But I was tired and confused.

"Now," he snapped, grabbing my arm and pulling me off the couch.

I didn't understand where his ire came from. I thought we were—I don't know what I thought, but I suddenly felt dirty and in the wrong as he dragged me out of there.

I stumbled after him, my mind reeling as I tried to process what had just happened. We had barely stepped out of the House of the Red Wyvern before Ronan was dragging me down the street, his long strides forcing me to almost run to keep up with him. I didn't understand what had changed, didn't understand where this anger was coming from.

"Ronan," I tried again, tugging on his arm. "What's wrong?"

But he just kept walking, his jaw clenched in a tight line. We didn't stop until we had reached the city gate, and then he was spinning me around to face him. His eyes were blazing with something I didn't understand, his face twisted in a scowl. He shoved me up against the nearest wall, inhaling me.

"Do you realize how good you smell when you come? I can taste it in the air."

My knees wobbled. I glanced up at him, standing on my tiptoes to kiss him, but he was pulling back.

His pupils were blown wide. "Careful, love. You don't want your first time with me to be in an Alleyway like some common whore."

"It's okay—"

"I don't want to," he breathed. He stepped back. "Now if you will excuse me, I need to find someone or something to bite. I suggest you fetch yourself dinner." He turned from me, walking away.

I felt a sting at his words, but before I could respond, he was turning and striding away from me. I watched him go, confusion and frustration warring within me. I didn't understand what had just happened, didn't understand where his anger had come from. Hadn't we just...shared something?

I took a deep breath, pushing aside the pang of disappointment that threatened to overwhelm me. I wouldn't let myself dwell on it, wouldn't let myself feel hurt by his callous words. I had known what I was getting myself into, had known that this was all just a fleeting moment of pleasure. And pleasure it had been. I couldn't deny that.

But as I turned and made my way back through the winding streets of Calazan, I couldn't shake the feeling that I had just made a grave mistake. That in letting myself feel something for Ronan, in allowing myself to be vulnerable, I had opened myself up to a kind of pain I wasn't sure I could overcome.

CHAPTER 40

Ronan

I stalked through the darkening streets of Calazan, my fangs aching, body burning with a hunger that had nothing to do with blood. The image of Atreya—flushed and wanting, eyes locked on mine as another woman touched her—was branded into my mind like a curse.

What kind of fool was I, thinking I could maintain control while watching her come undone? The scent of her arousal still clung to my senses, sweet and maddening. I'd orchestrated my own torture, letting my perverse desire to corrupt her innocence override my better judgment.

She was young, pretty enough—dark hair that could almost pass for Atreya's in the shadows. That thought made me grip her harder than necessary, and she gasped. The sound was wrong, too breathy, too eager. Nothing like the soft, surprised catches in Atreya's breath that had tortured me all evening.

The woman's pulse fluttered beneath my fingers as I tilted her head, exposing the smooth column of her throat. She melted against me, mistaking my predatory intent for passion. How easy humans were to fool, seeing only what they wanted to see. Their minds filled in the blanks with romantic fantasies, never imagining the monster waiting to strike.

I sank my fangs into her flesh, and warm copper flooded my mouth. Her blood was... adequate. Common. Nothing like the intoxicating scent that had been driving me mad all night. But it would serve its purpose. Each swallow was a reminder of what I was, what I would always be. A creature of shadow and hunger, taking what I needed in dark corners while the rest of the world slept.

When I finished, I compelled away her memory and any evidence of my feeding. The ritual was familiar, practiced. Simple. Unlike everything else about this cursed night. She would wake tomorrow with nothing but a vague memory of a passionate encounter, perhaps a slight weakness she'd blame on too much wine. Another faceless meal in an endless procession of them, forgotten before her feet carried her from the alcove.

Gods, the way Atreya had looked at me while that man serviced me—curious, wanting, completely unaware of how close I'd come to throwing aside centuries of control and taking her right there. She had no idea what she was playing with, how dangerous this game had become.

I'd meant to teach her a lesson about desire, to show her the pleasures her body was capable of experiencing. Instead, I'd taught myself how thoroughly she could undo me with nothing more than a heated glance and the sound of my name on her lips.

The memory of her moans echoed in my mind, and I slammed my fist into the nearest wall. The stone cracked, pain shooting through my knuckles. Good. I deserved it for my weakness, for letting this go too far.

I could still taste her disappointment in the air when I'd left her at the gate. She'd wanted me to kiss her, to touch her, to claim her as mine. And gods help me, I'd wanted to. But I wouldn't take her like some common whore in an alley. She deserved better than that.

She deserved better than me.

But that truth didn't stop the possessive rage that had coursed through me watching another's hands on her body, another's mouth bringing her pleasure. Even though I'd arranged it, even though I'd wanted to see her fall apart, something primitive inside me had roared mine with every gasp that left her lips.

I needed to end this. Get the Daylight Ring and leave before I ruined her completely. Before I gave in to this maddening urge to corrupt every last inch of her innocence, to mark her as mine in ways that would leave no doubt about who she belonged to.

But as I made my way back to the inn, I knew it was already too late. The damage was done. I'd crossed a line tonight, and there was no going back. The only question that remained was how completely I would damn us both before this was over.

Because one thing had become crystal clear in that brothel—I didn't just want to corrupt Atreya anymore. I wanted to possess her, body and soul, until there wasn't a single part of her that didn't belong to me.

And that terrified me more than anything else had in centuries.

From the shadows of a merchant's awning, I watched her window high above the street. A single candle still burned behind the curtains, casting her silhouette in amber light. My enhanced vision caught every detail—the way she paced, how her fingers combed through her hair, the moment she paused to press her palm against the glass. Even from this distance, I could hear her heartbeat, its rhythm as familiar to me now as my own dead silence.

I'd followed her scent here, tracking it through the maze of city streets like a wolf on the hunt. The trail of lavender and warm skin led me past the sleeping houses, around the corners where her hand had brushed stone walls, through the exact spots where her feet had touched cobblestones hours before. Each lingering trace of her presence was a breadcrumb drawing me closer, though I had no right to follow.

Three stories up, Atreya's shadow moved again. She was restless—good. Let her feel a fraction of the torment she'd inflicted on me. I shifted position as a drunk stumbled past, moving deeper into the darkness. No one would notice me here, just another piece of the night's architecture. I'd had centuries to perfect the art of going unseen while watching my prey.

But Atreya wasn't prey, was she? No, she was something far more dangerous. The predator in me recognized her as both quarry and hunter, her innocence a weapon that cut deeper than any blade. Every movement of her shadowed form pulled at something primitive in my chest, something that demanded I scale these walls, shatter that window, and claim what my instincts insisted should be mine.

The sound of her window latch clicking open froze me in place. Atreya leaned out into the night air, her dark hair falling loose around her shoulders, and for one mad moment, I thought she'd sensed my presence. But her gaze swept past my hiding spot without pause, searching the empty street with the kind of desperate hunger I recognized all too well.

"Where are you?" she whispered, the words carrying to me on the night breeze.

My fingers dug into the stone wall behind me, leaving shallow grooves in the masonry. The sight of her in nothing but a thin nightdress, skin glowing in the moonlight, tested every ounce of restraint I'd managed to rebuild since leaving the brothel. The fabric clung to her curves, nearly translucent where it caught the light from her room. She'd never looked more like prey.

She shivered in the cool air, but didn't retreat inside. Instead, she closed her eyes and tilted her head back, exposing the elegant line of her throat. Whether the gesture was unconscious or deliberate provocation, it sent a wave of hunger through me that had nothing to do with blood.

"I can feel you out there," she said softly, and my dead heart seemed to stutter in my chest. "You're watching me, aren't you?"

I remained perfectly still, though everything in me strained toward her. She couldn't possibly know I was here. This was nothing more than the fantasy of a young woman caught up in the lingering heat of the evening's entertainment.

"You left me wanting." The words fell from her lips like an accusation. "Is that what you intended? To work me into such a state and then abandon me to burn?"

A low growl built in my throat before I could stop it. She was playing with fire, this innocent who thought she understood desire. She had no concept of what real burning felt like—the kind that had consumed me for centuries, that threatened to reduce everything I was to ash.

"Come to me," she breathed, and the invitation was more potent than any compulsion I could weave. "I know you want to. I saw it in your eyes when she touched me. When I—"

I was across the street and scaling the wall before conscious thought could intervene, moving faster than any human eye could track. I caught myself just below her window, fingers digging into the stone, my face mere inches from her bare feet on the sill.

The gasp that escaped her lips was pure satisfaction. "I knew you'd come."

I met her eyes, letting centuries of power flood my gaze. Though she was Fae, my vampiric compulsion had been honed over countless years, and I poured every ounce of it into my command. The force hit her like a wave, and I saw her body sway, her ethereal features flickering as my power wrestled with her innate magic.

"Sleep, Atreya," I commanded. "Go to bed. Now."

She fought it, but I was stronger. Her eyes began to glaze, the light in them dimming under the weight of my will.

"No," she whispered. "Ronan..."

I pushed harder, wrapping my compulsion around her like chains. "Sleep until morning. Forget this moment."

Her resistance crumbled. She swayed backward, and I caught her before she could fall, careful to minimize our contact. Even through the compulsion, magic sparked against my fingers like static electricity.

With more gentleness than I thought myself capable of, I guided her to her bed. Her dark hair spilled across the pillow, and in sleep, her features softened into peaceful surrender.

"Ronan," she murmured again, fighting even in sleep.

I pressed my palm to her forehead, sending one final wave of compulsion through her. "Sleep deeply."

Only when her breathing settled did I withdraw. The compulsion would hold—at least until morning—but I knew this game had just become infinitely more complex. I was a fool for not recognizing the truth sooner.

As I slipped back into the night, I couldn't shake the feeling that I'd just sealed both our fates. Because while I could compel her to sleep, to forget, I couldn't compel my own dead heart to stop wanting her. And wanting her was more dangerous than any game I'd played before.

Night draped itself over Calazan like black silk, stars piercing through gaps in the clouds above. Atreya walked three paces ahead of me, her spine rigid with anger, each step a deliberate percussion against the street. The silence between us was a living thing, heavy with unspoken accusations and desires neither of us dared to say.

"We should reach the Port of Ambrose by dawn," I said, watching her shoulders tense at the sound of me speaking. "If we maintain this pace." And if we found shelter before the sun could turn me to ash, but I left that part unspoken.

She didn't respond, just quickened her steps. The night crowd—thieves, courtesans, and others who made darkness their trade—parted around her like water around a stone, sensing perhaps that her grace carried an edge of danger. Or maybe they simply recognized the fury radiating from her small frame.

"The silent treatment?" I couldn't help the mocking edge that crept into my tone. "How delightfully juvenile."

That got a reaction. She spun to face me, her eyes flashing with that otherworldly light that reminded me she wasn't as soft as she sometimes appeared.

"You don't get to mock me," she hissed, closing the distance between us. Her finger jabbed into my chest, magic crackling where she touched me. "Not after what you did."

I caught her wrist, my grip firm but careful. Even angry, I couldn't forget how easily I could break her. "And what exactly did I do, little Fae? Give you what you wanted? Show you pleasures you'd never known?"

"You used me." He face cracked on the words. "Set me up like some kind of game piece, watched me fall apart, and then—" She yanked her hand free. "Then you treated me like I was nothing. Like I was *dirty*."

The accusation hit harder than it should have. "Is that what you think?"

"What else should I think?" Her eyes glistened with unshed tears, but her chin remained lifted in defiance. "You arranged for another woman to touch me, watched me like I was your personal entertainment, and then couldn't get away fast enough when it was over."

I moved before she could react, backing her against the nearest wall. My hands planted on either side of her head, caging her in. "You think I left because I was disgusted?" I leaned in close, letting her feel the full weight of my presence. "You have no idea how close I came to taking you right there in that brothel. To showing everyone exactly who you belong to."

Her breath hitched, pupils dilating. "I don't belong to anyone."

"No?" I dragged my nose along her neck, inhaling the intoxicating mix of her arousal and fear. "Then why can I smell how wet you are right now? Why does your heart race every time I get close?"

"If you want me, then take me," she challenged.

CHAPTER 41

Atreya

"If you want me so badly," I spat, shoving past him into the dense forest that bordered Calazan's outskirts, "then stop playing these ridiculous games."

The branches whipped against my face as I stormed ahead, but I didn't care. Anything was better than looking at him right now, than remembering how he'd watched me in that brothel, how he'd left me aching and confused.

"Games?" Ronan's laugh was cruel, cutting through the night air. "You think this is a game to me?" He caught up easily, his supernatural speed making my angry retreat look childish. "You have no idea what you're asking for."

I spun to face him, leaves crunching under my boots. "Then enlighten me, oh wise one. Because from where I'm standing, you're the one who keeps pushing me away then pulling me back like some kind of toy."

His eyes flashed red in the darkness. "A toy?" He moved closer, backing me against a massive oak tree. "Is that what you think you are to me?"

"What else should I think?" My voice cracked embarrassingly. "You paid someone else to touch me while you watched. You—"

"I watched," he growled, "because if I had touched you myself, I wouldn't have been able to stop." His hand slammed into the tree trunk beside my head. "Do you understand what that means? What I would have done to you?"

Heat pooled low in my belly at his confession. "Maybe I wanted you to."

"No." He pushed away from the tree, running a hand through his hair. "You don't know what you're asking for. You're young, inexperienced—"

"Don't you dare patronize me." I followed him, refusing to let him retreat this time. "I'm not some innocent child who needs protecting. I've been married before, remember? I know exactly what I'm asking for."

His laugh was bitter. "Your marriage? To a man who treated you like property? Who hurt you?" He turned back to me, eyes blazing. "That's exactly why I can't—won't—touch you. You deserve better than another monster's hands on your body."

"You're not a monster."

"I am," he said, dropping to a dangerous whisper. "I'm the worst kind of monster, little Fae. The kind that wants to possess you completely. The kind that wants to mark you, claim you, ruin you for anyone else."

My breath caught. "Then do it."

For a moment, the forest went completely still. Even the night creatures seemed to hold their breath, waiting to see what would happen next.

"You don't mean that," he said finally, but I could hear the strain in his voice.

"I do."

He flung himself away from me, snarling.

"Where were you?!" Ronan's shout shattered the night's silence like breaking glass. Shadows danced across his face, making the sharp angles of his jaw more pronounced, more dangerous. "Where were you when my heart still beat? When my soul was young?"

Moonlight filtered through the canopy above, casting silver patterns on his skin. He stalked toward me with predatory grace, each step deliberate, measured. The air crackled with tension, thick enough to choke on.

"Half a millennium ago, when I was pure." His laugh was bitter wine, dark and potent. "When I was untainted, like those pathetic mortals you now show such *affection* for." He spat the word like poison.

"For centuries, I've been alone. I've watched time pass like water through my fingers, pretending that this curse—this immortality—was anything but a very long way to lose everything I've ever cared about."

"And then I met you," he whispered. "It was like watching the sun rise for the first time in eight hundred years. And it terrifies me, Atreya, because I'd forgotten what it felt like to want to keep something. To want to stay." His fingers twisted into his hair as he growled his frustration.

The bark of the ancient oak bit into my back as I retreated. Autumn leaves crunched beneath my feet, their dying whispers a counterpoint to my thundering heart. His presence overwhelmed me—winter frost and night-blooming jasmine, death and desire wrapped in one intoxicating package.

"Atreya, where were you when I was Fae? Bursting with aspirations? The audacity of your absence—to miss out on my better days. How dare you invade my existence *now*, as I am enveloped in darkness, consumed by rage and loathing, with nothing left to give? When I could never become anything beyond this monstrous form that I am? How *dare* you shatter all that I've built? How dare you evoke these unbearable *emotions* within me?"

"I'm not making you feel anything—" The protest died in my throat as Ronan's shadow fell over me, dark and consuming as midnight itself.

"You make me feel *everything!*"

The ancient oak behind me shuddered as his fist connected with the bark, sending splinters cascading over my shoulders. The scent of crushed wood and his rage-tinged magic filled my lungs.

My body remembered before my mind could catch up. Head tilted back. Throat bared. A dance as old as prey and predator—but which was I? The forest held its breath, waiting to find out.

Submit Submit Submit.

His exhale painted ice across my skin. The press of his lips against my pulse point sent electricity arcing through my body, and his nose traced the shell of my ear like he was memorizing my scent. Like he needed it to survive.

"Ronan." His name escaped me as his fingers found my throat—not squeezing, just... holding. Claiming.

The familiar fog tried to descend, that cotton-wool blanket of dissociation Ramses had taught me to crave. But Ronan's touch was different.

Every point of contact blazed with clarity, anchoring me firmly in my skin. In this moment.

His grip vanished. I turned, slow as honey dripping, and found myself drowning in eyes like fresh-spilled blood. His breath came in sharp bursts, stirring the loose strands of hair around my face.

"I don't wish to cause you pain," the plea scraped raw from his throat. His gaze flickered, uncertain for the first time since I'd known him. "I don't want to hurt you."

Truth rang in every syllable, and something in my chest cracked open.

"Then don't." I reached up, letting my fingertips ghost over the sharp cut of his cheekbone. Such a simple touch, but it made him shudder like I'd struck him with lightning.

The space between us vanished. His eyes had softened somehow, midnight bleeding into dawn, but the intensity behind them sent shivers racing down my spine. His hand found my face, thumb tracing my cheekbone like I was spun sugar, like I might dissolve if he pressed too hard.

"Atreya." My name on his lips was a spell and a prayer. Each letter dripped with power that skittered across my skin like static electricity.

"Yes?" The word barely made it past my thundering heart.

His exhale shook. "Is this..." Confusion creased his brow, an expression so human it made my chest ache. "Is this what love feels like?"

The question knocked the air from my lungs. This creature of shadow and steel, asking about love like a child reaching for fire for the first time. My heart cracked wider, bleeding light.

"Love is..." I caught his hand against my cheek, held it there like an anchor. "It's wanting someone else's happiness more than your own. It's terror and triumph and everything in between."

His eyes never left mine. "My heart is ice. Dead things don't feel warmth except when they feed."

"And now?" I whispered. "What do you feel now?"

His other hand slid into my hair, cradling my skull. "With you?" A broken laugh escaped him. "With you, I *burn*."

The forest fell silent. We stood suspended between heartbeats, between breaths. Between what was and what could be.

"I've bathed in blood," he murmured, rough as century-old stone. "I've torn apart kingdoms. How could someone like you—pure as starlight, fierce as wildfire—ever love a monster wearing a man's skin?"

The self-loathing that took over him made me ache. Made me brave.

"Maybe," I whispered, "I see past the monster to the man beneath. Maybe I see *you*, Ronan. All of you. The darkness and the light. The cruelty and the kindness. And maybe—" I pressed my palm flat against his chest, where his heart hadn't beat in centuries. "Maybe I choose both."

He was afraid. He was asking me—asking me if I *could* love him. If I *did* love him. The laugh that bubbled up in my throat was bitter as nightshade. He'd placed me on a crystal pedestal, fragile and pure, when my soul was just as scarred as his. My fingers found his cheek, tracing the sharp edge of immortality etched into his skin.

"Love isn't a ledger, Ronan." A truth I'd learned through blood and tears. "It doesn't tally sins or measure worth. It strikes like lightning—wild, devastating, impossible to control." I pressed harder, feeling the marble-cold of his skin. "I see *you*. Not the monster you wear like armor, but the man beneath. The one who brings me water when I'm parched. The one who watches over me in darkness. That man deserves to be loved."

Could I say it? Could I say the words that he wanted to hear? The confession clawed at my ribcage, desperate to break free. Three simple syllables that could shatter worlds—or build them.

Silence stretched between us. His eyes devoured me, drinking in every flutter of my pulse, every catch in my breath. His hand rose to trap mine against his face, and his thumb painted circles on my skin that felt like ancient runes of protection.

"Atreya..." My name fell from his lips like a blessing, like a curse. "*Atreya...*"

The forest held its breath. His blood-bright eyes searched mine with desperate intensity, hunting for truth or lies or salvation. The muscle in his jaw jumped, a tell I'd learned meant he was fighting himself. "When you're near, my chest caves in. My hands..." He curled them into fists, tendons standing out like steel cables. "They shake with need to protect you, to guard your dreams. But these same hands have painted centuries in crimson. They've—"

I pressed my palm flat against his chest, where a heart had slumbered for three hundred years. "These hands caught me when gravity betrayed me." My fingers splayed across the rough fabric, seeking phantom warmth. "They've shown more gentleness than you give them credit for."

A shudder ripped through him like an earthquake. His hand crushed mine harder against his chest, as if he could force life back into that quiet space through sheer will. His other hand tangled in my hair, cradling my skull like it held all the secrets of the universe. Pine needles and magic danced on the wind, lifting strands of my hair to caress his face like curious spirits.

He moved like a predator—slow, deliberate, giving prey time to flee. But I wasn't prey, not anymore. His gaze dropped to my mouth, a question burning in those immortal eyes.

My chin dipped in the barest nod, heart thundering against my ribs like it was trying to escape. His hand slid from mine to cup my face, grip sure but tender as he mapped the curve of my jaw with his thumb.

Then his mouth found mine, and the world tilted on its axis. The kiss was soft as sin, sweet as salvation. His lips moved against mine with the patience of centuries, drawing responses from my body I didn't know I was capable of. His fingers tightened in my hair, dragging me closer like he could absorb me through touch alone, like he'd waited lifetimes for this moment.

Maybe he had.

His fingers tightened in my hair, the possessive grip drawing me deeper into his kiss. The hand at my face shifted, his thumb ghosting across my lips before his mouth blazed a burning trail down my jaw, my neck, each kiss a brand against my skin that made me shiver.

The familiar fog began creeping in—that dissociative haze that had been my shield for so long. Ronan sensed it immediately, pulling back just enough to catch my gaze. "Stay with me," he pleaded, "*Stay with me.*"

My fingers twisted in his shirt, desperate for an anchor. His scent flooded my senses—pine needles and night air and something darker, something uniquely *him*. He was everywhere, seeping into my blood like a drug, filling every hollow space inside me until there was nothing left but *this*.

"Ronan," I gasped, a promise in his name. I would stay. Here. Now. Present.

He dropped to his knees like a man in worship, pressing reverent kisses through my traveling cloak. His hands snaked up my legs, fingers finding purchase at my waistband. The trail of his mouth burned lower, lower, until he buried his face between my thighs, inhaling deeply like he could breathe in my soul.

"Gods," he growled against my flesh, the word vibrating through me. "You're intoxicating, Atreya." His cold breath sent lightning racing up my spine. His lips—gentle yet demanding—painted paths of liquid fire that left me gasping for air.

My fingers tangled in his hair, guiding him closer as my body arched into his touch. The groan that rumbled from his chest sent shockwaves of pleasure coursing through my veins.

"We can't—" The protest died in my throat as he shook his head, crimson eyes blazing with a hunger that matched the inferno building inside me.

"Here and now, Atreya," he demanded, thick with need. "I need you." The raw desperation in his gaze stripped away my last defenses. I nodded, surrendering to the intensity that crackled between us like storm clouds heavy with lightning.

His hands were everywhere at once, deftly working at the ties of my pants. He followed the fabric's descent with his mouth, leaving wet, teasing kisses that made my knees weak. The smooth plane of his cheek brushed my inner thigh, his icy breath ghosting across my center.

When his mouth found me, the world fractured into a thousand glittering pieces. His tongue traced patterns that set my nerves aflame, the sounds of his pleasure—those primal growls and hungry laps—driving me higher. The noises he pulled from my throat were foreign to my own ears, desperate and wanting.

The flat of his tongue worked against my slick flesh, and tension coiled tighter in my core. My fingers clenched in his braided hair as I ground against his face, chasing the pleasure that threatened to tear me apart. His name fell from my lips like a prayer to a forgotten god.

"Ronan," I moaned as the wave crested, my body trembling in his grip. He held me through it all, my feet leaving the ground as my legs wrapped around his head. His mouth was relentless, drawing out every last shudder until I was boneless and gasping.

He lowered me with a gentleness that belied his strength, his face gleaming with evidence of my pleasure. I traced the sharp angles of his face with trembling fingers, wiping away my essence. He caught my hand, pressing a burning kiss to my palm before lacing our fingers together like a promise.

"You're incredible, Atreya." His voice was gravel and silk, those blood-bright eyes holding me hostage. I saw everything in them—desire, love, a raw need that echoed the storm raging in my own chest.

I yanked him to me, claiming his mouth. The taste of myself on his tongue only stoked the fire burning beneath my skin. My fingers found his hair, threading through the loose strands before giving his braid a sharp tug that pulled a feral sound from his throat.

His body was hard and cold against mine, his arousal evident. I reached down, my hand finding him, wrapping around him. He was larger than I thought, so much so that I hesitated a moment before sliding my hand up to cup him.

He gasped against my lips, his body stiffening at my touch. I stroked him, from base to tip, delighting in the rough sounds he made, the way his body responded to my touch. Thick veins and soft skin. I gathered the slick residue of myself in my hand, running my fingers through it, painting it down his length while he throbbed against my palm like a second heartbeat.

I pulled him down with me, the forest floor cradling my back as I shed my cloak. He lifted my tunic with reverent hands, exposing my skin to the night air. His legs bracketed my hips as he positioned me, his hands mapping the curves of my body like he was committing them to memory.

The sight of him undressing sent lightning through my veins. Moonlight carved shadows in the valleys of his muscles, highlighting the silver trail that led to where my body ached for him. He was devastating—a dark god carved from marble and shadow.

I guided him to me, positioning him at my entrance. He adjusted himself at my there, teasing me with his tip before pushing in slowly. He looked down at me, his eyes questioning, asking for my consent. I nodded, my breath hitching as he pushed all the way in me. There was a moment of discomfort, a stretching that was quickly replaced by a need so intense it left me breathless.

He moved slowly at first, his movements measured and deliberate. But as the pleasure built, his pace quickened. His thrusts were deep, hitting places I never knew existed. His name was a mantra on my lips, my body moving in sync with his.

My hands roamed his body, tracing his muscles, feeling the power beneath his skin. My nails dug into his back as he moved, a silent plea for more. He responded with a groan, his pace quickening, his thrusts deepening. The tension building within me—a coil winding tighter and tighter. His thrusts were relentless, driving me closer and closer to the edge. His lips were on my neck, the graze of his fangs on my jugular. His mouth found mine and I felt the fullness of his tongue exploring mine. I flicked my tongue over his fang, the prick of pain dulling away and tasting my blood, offering it to him.

He hissed against my mouth and rode me harder, driving my back into the ground, a soft curse escaping his lips. He pulled back, his eyes meeting mine, the crimson of my blood staining his teeth. His tongue flicked out and ran along his fang, a stream of his blood dripping down his chin. Without a word, he offered his tongue out to me, a silent invitation.

I hesitated for a moment, my heart pounding in my chest. But then I saw the look in his eyes, a mixture of desire, trust and something deeper. And so, I leaned in, my lips wrapping around his tongue, and sucked.

The effect was immediate. A rush of energy coursed through my veins, a warmth that radiated from my core. I felt his power, his essence seeping into me, binding us in a way no physical act could. He growled, a low, animalistic sound that vibrated through me, intensifying the sensations coursing through my body.

"Ronan," I breathed against his mouth, "I love you."

His rhythm faltered. "Say it again."

"I love you."

"Again, Atreya. I need to hear it," he implored. His fervor intensified, plunging to new depths. The heightened sensations sent me into a dizzying whirl of pleasure. His lips danced over my skin, tracing a path of fire that left me breathless.

His name tumbled from my lips, "Ronan," the words, soft yet clear, hung in the air between us. A new urgency took over his movements, deeper, harder.

"Say it one more time, Atreya," he murmured, straining.

"I love you, Ronan," I managed to whisper.

He pressed his forehead to mine, crimson eyes burning into my soul. "Come on me, Little Light."

And then everything exploded. Pleasure crashed through me in waves, my body convulsing around him as I cried out his name. He followed moments later, his release filling me as his fingers dug furrows in the earth beside my head.

We lay there, spent and panting, the night air cool against my heated skin.

His fingers traced lazy patterns on my back, my cloak thrown over us.

"It will be dawn soon," he murmured. I nodded through the haze of sleep that threatened to swallow me whole.

"Cave?" I asked, my hoarse.

He gently disentangled himself from me, rising to his feet. He pulled on his clothes, then extended a hand to help me up.

After a while, we found a cave, hidden amongst the trees. It wasn't much, but it was shelter, a place we could rest until nightfall again. We made our way inside, the darkness enveloping us.

Ronan settled down first, his back resting against the cool stone wall of the cave. He pulled me down next to him, my head finding a comfortable spot on his chest. His arm wrapped around me, pulling me closer.

"It's not much, but it'll do," he murmured, his breath tickling my ear. I hummed in agreement, my eyes already drooping with exhaustion. His fingers played with the ends of my hair, the rhythmic movement lulling me further into sleep.

And in the midst of dreaming, I heard it.

"I love you too."

CHAPTER 42

Atreya

S unset painted the sky in blood-red hues as we made our way toward
Port Ambrose. The forest gradually thinned, giving way to rolling hills
that would eventually lead us to the coast. My body ached in the most
delicious way, memories of last night sending heat coursing through my
veins.

Ronan hadn't left me alone since we'd emerged from the cave at dusk.
His hand found mine constantly, fingers intertwining with mine like they
belonged there. It was... different. The deadly creature who'd once kept
such careful distance now couldn't seem to stop touching me.

"Your scent has changed," he murmured, pressing his nose against my
neck for what felt like the hundredth time that evening. His lips brushed
my skin, sending shivers down my spine. "It's mixed with mine now."

I tried to keep walking, but his arms snaked around my waist, pulling me
back against his chest. "Ronan, we need to reach Port Ambrose before—"

"Before what?" His laugh rumbled through me as he pressed a kiss
behind my ear. "Before midnight? Before the moon reaches its peak?"

Another kiss, this time at the junction of my neck and shoulder. "I've waited centuries to feel this way, little light. To feel... whole."

The raw honesty in his confession made my chest ache. I turned in his arms, finding his crimson eyes soft with an emotion I was still getting used to seeing there.

"I love you," he said, as if testing the words on his tongue. They came easier now, after that first confession in the cave. He'd whispered them against my skin countless times since then, like he was making up for centuries of silence.

"You're getting better at saying that," I teased, trying to ignore how my heart stuttered every time he did.

His fingers traced my cheekbone, reverent as a prayer. "Practice makes perfect." He dipped his head, capturing my lips in a kiss that made my toes curl. When he pulled back, his eyes were darker. "And I plan to practice very, very often."

"We'll never make it to Port Ambrose at this rate," I mumbled against his mouth, even as my fingers curled into his shirt.

He hummed in agreement, but his kisses only grew more insistent. "Would that be such a terrible thing? Just you and me, lost in these hills forever?"

The thought was tempting—so tempting. But reality had a way of intruding, even on the most perfect moments.

I pulled back with a laugh, pressing my palm against his chest. "Ronan."

He sighed, pressing his forehead to mine. "I know, I know. We need to keep moving." His thumb traced my lower lip. "But know this, Atreya—now that I have you, now that I know what it feels like to love you, to be loved by you... I'm never letting go."

The possessive edge to his promise should have frightened me. Instead, it made me feel... safe. Protected. Wanted.

"Good," I whispered, rising on my tiptoes to press one last kiss to his lips. "Because I'm not letting go either."

His answering smile was brighter than the fading sun. He caught my hand again as we resumed walking, his thumb tracing patterns on my skin that felt like ancient runes of protection.

"Tell me again," he said after a while, gently.

I didn't have to ask what he meant. "I love you."

His grip tightened, and I caught the flash of his smile from the corner of my eye. "Again."

"You're impossible," I laughed, but the words came easily. "I love you, Ronan."

"Impossible?" He tugged me to a stop, spinning me into his arms. "I prefer 'determined.' Or perhaps 'devoted.'" His nose traced along my jaw-line. "After all, I have centuries of loneliness to make up for."

And as his lips found mine again, as his arms wrapped around me like he'd never let go, I thought perhaps Port Ambrose could wait just a little longer.

The salt-laden breeze grew stronger as Port Ambrose finally came into view, its weathered docks stretching out into the inky waters like skeletal fingers. Lanterns swayed in the night air, casting dancing shadows across the worn planks and shabby buildings that lined the harbor.

"There," Ronan murmured, his hand tightening around mine as he nodded toward a small vessel moored at the furthest dock. The boat was modest but sturdy—a fishing vessel with a single mast, its white sails furled tight against the night sky. The name "Morning Star" was painted in fading letters across its hull, the irony not lost on me given our nocturnal nature of travel.

"It looks... cozy," I offered, noting the intimate cabin space visible from where we stood.

Ronan's lips curved into that predatory smile I was growing far too fond of. "Wait here." He pressed a kiss to my temple, his nose lingering against my skin for a moment longer than necessary. "I'll handle the arrange-ments."

I watched as he approached the small crew—three men playing cards by lamplight on deck. Even from this distance, I could see the moment his compulsion took hold. Their faces went slack, eyes glazing over as Ronan's compulsion carried across the gentle lap of waves, too low for me to make out the words.

One by one, they stood, gathering their belongings with mechanical movements. Their expressions remained vacant as they filed past me on the dock, not even registering my presence. It should have disturbed me more, this display of supernatural control, but after everything we'd been through, it seemed a small price for our safety.

"All yours, little light," Ronan called out, already aboard the vessel. He extended his hand to help me across the gap between dock and deck, pulling me close once my feet touched the weathered planks. "The captain was kind enough to decide he needed a few days' rest in port."

"How generous of him," I said dryly, but couldn't help smiling as Ronan's arms wrapped around me from behind.

"Mmm," he hummed against my neck, "I can be very persuasive when properly motivated." His lips traced the shell of my ear. "And keeping you safe is all the motivation I need."

The boat rocked gently beneath us as the tide pulled at its moorings. It was small but well-maintained, with a modest cabin that would shield us from the sun during our journey. The deck was clean, fishing nets and equipment neatly stowed along the rails. It wasn't luxurious by any means, but it would serve our purpose.

"Do you know how to sail?" I asked, watching as Ronan moved to untie the mooring lines with practiced ease.

He shot me a look that managed to be both amused and offended. "I'm eight hundred years old, love. I've captained ships that would make this one look like a child's toy." His hands moved surely over the rigging. "Though I must admit, this will be the first time I've had such... distracting company aboard."

Heat bloomed in my cheeks at his words, but before I could respond, the sails unfurled above us with a snap. The wind caught them immediately, and Port Ambrose began to shrink behind us as we glided into the waiting darkness of the open sea.

The Morning Star had been cutting through the waves for hours when Ronan suddenly stiffened at the helm. His hands tightened on the wooden wheel, knuckles white with tension.

"Here," he said, tight with certainty. "This is where we need to be."

I looked around at the endless expanse of black water, seeing nothing but stars reflected on the rolling waves. "Here? There's nothing—"

"Trust me." He moved with supernatural speed, securing the helm before dropping the anchor. The chain rattled against the hull as it plunged into the depths, the sound eerily loud in the midnight silence.

The boat rocked gently as it settled, and Ronan pulled me against his chest, his nose pressed to my hair. "Watch," he whispered.

At first, nothing happened. Then... a shimmer. Like heat waves rising from summer-baked earth, but here, in the middle of the ocean. The air itself seemed to ripple and fold, reality bending like paper in invisible hands.

"Ronan?" I wavered as the distortion grew larger, spreading across the water like spilled ink.

His arms tightened around me. "Don't look away," he murmured. "You'll want to remember this."

The shimmer intensified, and suddenly—impossibly—buildings began to materialize out of the darkness. First just shadows, then solid forms: gleaming spires that pierced the night sky, streets that seemed to float on water, bridges made of what looked like liquid moonlight.

New Solara.

Eldra's Kingdom.

We were finally here.

My breath caught in my throat as New Solara materialized before us, its impossible architecture both beautiful and terrifying. Each heartbeat felt like thunder in my chest as the reality of what we were about to do crashed over me like the waves against our hull.

Eldra. After all these years.

My fingers gripped the ship's railing until my knuckles went white, memories flooding back with each pulse of ethereal light from the city. The last time I'd seen him, we'd torn the Great Wood apart trying to kill each other.

"You're afraid." Ronan's lips were soft against my ear, his hands settling on my waist.

"I'm not—" The lie died on my lips as another spire emerged from the void, its crystal surface reflecting starlight like a warning. "Yes," I admitted. "I am."

The city continued to unfold before us, each new revelation making my stomach twist tighter. Somewhere in that maze of moonlight and magic, Eldra waited. The man who'd set his soldiers upon the Hyperion Market and took Joslynn from me. My enemy. The only person who might be able to help us now.

Magic simmered beneath my skin. The want to kill him still very much present.

"If there was any other way..." I whispered, more to myself than to Ronan.

"But there isn't." His fingers interlaced with mine. "And you're stronger than you give yourself credit for, little light."

I leaned back against his chest, drawing strength from his solid presence as New Solara continued its impossible emergence. The city seemed to breathe as it materialized, each exhale bringing new wonders: gardens suspended in mid-air, their flowers glowing with internal light; fountains that flowed upward, their waters dissolving into stardust; streets that spiraled through space in defiance of natural law.

"The last time I stood before him," I said, watching a bridge of pure light construct itself from nothing, "I swore I'd tear his heart out."

The person who'd fought Eldra in the Great Wood had been driven by raw hatred and grief. Now... now I had something to lose. Someone to protect.

Vrys. Ember. Ferenz.

"If he so much as looks at you wrong, I'll finish what you started that day."

I let out a bark of laughter, just as the boat hit the shoreline.

Men in gold cloaks swarmed our boat the moment we touched the shoreline, their armor catching the ethereal light of New Solara like captured flames. I tensed, magic crackling beneath my skin, but their movements weren't hostile—more ceremonial than threatening.

"The Lightweaver," one of them announced. The golden helm he wore was crafted to resemble a sun in mid-eclipse, matching the insignia emblazoned on their cloaks. "Lord Eldra's Dawn Guard welcomes you both."

That made me pause.

They were expecting us.

I glanced at Ronan and he went still, a muscle feathering in his jaw.

He kisses me one last time before we get off the boat, his lips pressing against mine deeply, desperately—like he's trying to memorize the feel of this moment. His fingers thread through my hair, cradling my head as if I'm something precious, something that might slip away if he's not careful. When he finally pulls back, those crimson eyes burn with an intensity that makes my breath catch. In this moment, suspended between the familiar darkness of the sea and the otherworldly glow of New Solara, we're just two hearts beating in sync, holding onto each other before stepping into whatever fate awaits us on these impossible shores.

CHAPTER 43

Atreya

R onan shadowed me as we climbed the winding cobblestone streets of New Solara, his presence warm and steady at my back. The gold cloaks of the Solaris soldiers caught the moonlight, and something inside me twisted—memories of the Hyperion Market flooding back like a tide of blood. Magic sparked beneath my skin, dancing at my fingertips like warning flares.

His hand found mine, anchoring me to the present. Safe. Loved.

The city pulsed with life around us—faces so different from the hollow-eyed masses of Ferenz. These people were sun-kissed and soft, their features unmarred by darkness. They drifted past in their bubble of peace, blind to what was coming. Blind to who walked among them.

The castle rose before us like a giant's gravestone. Cold. Grey. Windows staring down like dead eyes. A cluster of figures waited at the top of the steps, and my heart stuttered when I spotted him.

Eldra fucking Solaris.

He wore pure white, playing king—golden crown shaped like sun rays, black hair framing that face I'd seen in a thousand nightmares. His queen stood beside him, her auburn hair a river of fire down her back, her own crown catching moonlight like a blade's edge.

Ronan squeezed my hand once before letting go, a silent promise in the gesture. I climbed those steps and took in Eldra's circus. Four of them. A dark-skinned man with starlight eyes and a pink scar splitting his chin. A blonde man radiating false serenity in purple robes. A green-skinned woman crackling with barely contained fury, black claws gleaming. And finally, a blue-haired beauty with bronze skin, her braids mapping constellations across her scalp.

The blue-haired one broke first—a gasp like she'd been gut-punched. The green one hissed something in a language that slithered through the air. Eldra snapped back, voice like thunder on a killing horizon. His queen stumbled as if struck, color flooding her cheeks.

"My Gods," the queen whispered, words torn from her throat. Her green eyes were dinner plates of shock.

The blonde took a step forward, and I fought the urge to bare my teeth. His blue eyes drilled into me like he was trying to peel back my skin.

"Eldra, what is—" The queen started, but one look from her husband silenced her.

I knew what they saw. A feral thing in blood-stained clothes, dirt under my nails like war paint. Three months of running, fighting, surviving carved into every line of my body. Let them stare.

I squared my shoulders, lifted my chin. Met their gazes head-on.

They flinched like I'd slapped them.

"You're the Furian Slayer?" Blonde man asked.

Now it was my turn to flinch.

Eldra raised his hands like he was soothing a wild animal. "Welcome, Atreya Blackwater. To the Kingdom of New Solara."

Welcome. The word tasted like ash. I searched his face for lies, imagining what it would feel like to rip his heart out through his pristine white suit.

"It's been a long time, Eldra," I said, ice coating every syllable. "You look different when you're not beneath my claws."

Ronan shifted closer, his presence steady at my side. The others bristled like angry cats.

But Eldra? That fucker smirked.

Ronan coughed, quickly moving to my side.

Eldra's smirk stretched wider, moonlight catching on teeth too white, too sharp. Something dark danced in his eyes—amusement mixed with surprise at my audacity, like I was a pet that had learned a clever new trick.

The others weren't sharing his twisted humor. The dark-skinned man retreated a step, those starlight eyes blown wide with shock. A hiss slithered from the green woman's throat as black claws extended like daggers from her fingertips. The blonde's face remained a mask of serenity, but tension rippled through his shoulders, his hands curling into white-knuckled fists beneath those elaborate purple sleeves. And the blue-haired woman... she stared at me like I was a puzzle she couldn't quite solve, curiosity warring with confusion in her eyes.

"It is so good to see you again," Eldra said.

My gaze snapped to his face, then to Ronan—who'd been too quiet, too still since we'd left the boat. His expression was carved from stone, and something cold settled in my gut. "You aren't surprised I'm here," I said slowly, the pieces clicking into place like a death knell. Ronan had sworn he had no connection to Eldra, had insisted we were coming to beg mercy from New Solara's king.

"Of course not." Eldra's voice carried the weight of a closing trap. "I am the one who sent for you."

My mind stumbled over the words. Sent for me? I turned to Ronan, then back to Eldra, the world tilting beneath my feet. "Sent for me?"

Eldra's eyes flicked to Ronan, and then back to me. I knew it then. Ronan had lied to me.

"Why?" The question clawed its way out of my throat, meant for both, meant for neither.

It meant that Ronan had planned with Eldra to take me. It meant that this whole thing was orchestrated by them.

Ronan moved then, climbing the steps to Eldra's side like a puppet pulled by invisible strings. "I've brought her to you. My end is done." His voice was hollow, empty of everything I thought I knew.

Pain splintered through my chest. "Ronan?"

He wouldn't look at me. The braid I'd woven into his hair with loving fingers just hours ago swayed in the night breeze as he held out his palm to Eldra. The king nodded, passed his hand over Ronan's waiting palm. A ring materialized there, shimmering with ancient power. When Ronan's eyes finally met mine, they were dead things, bottomless pools of nothing as his fingers closed over the ring. Gold light wrapped around them both like chains before shattering into a thousand glittering pieces.

"The blood oath is done then?" Eldra's wife asked, arms crossed like she was watching a particularly dull play reach its end.

Thunder cracked overhead, and lightning split the sky. I stared at the two men before me—one I'd loved, one I'd sworn to kill—and felt my rage rise like a tide of fire.

"Eldra!" The snarl ripped from my throat as my fists clenched at my sides, magic crackling beneath my skin.

"Please." He raised his hands like I was some wild thing to be soothed. "I will explain everything. You are a guest here, not a prisoner. I swear it on my honor."

The man with starlight eyes moved between us, hand extended like an offering of peace. "You have friends here. Ones who won't harm you."

I wanted to laugh. Friends. As if I hadn't learned what that word truly meant in the past three months. As if I hadn't just watched the man I loved trade me away like a piece of cattle.

My gaze cut between them—Eldra with his serpent's smile, the others coiled like vipers ready to strike, and Ronan... Ronan, who suddenly found the ground more interesting than the woman whose lips he'd kissed not an hour before.

"No." The word tasted like poison on my tongue. "I'm done trusting anyone."

I spun away from them, my feet already moving. The guards surged forward like a golden tide, as if their pretty armor could stop what I'd become. What they'd made me.

Magic exploded from my fingertips—white-hot and hungry. The stairs behind me erupted into rubble and smoke, and then I was running. My feet pounded against stone, each step a heartbeat of freedom. Lightning arced behind me, keeping the shadows of my pursuers at bay. Run. Run. Run. The command thrummed through my blood like a war drum.

His words chased me through the streets: I love you. I'll never let you go. I'll keep you safe. Each memory a knife in my back, each promise revealed as ash and lies. Lies. Lies. LIES.

The magic inside me roared to life—a caged beast finally unchained. It built beneath my skin like storm clouds gathering, like thunder waiting to break. I didn't fight it. I surrendered. Let it consume me, burn through me, remake me.

And then—oh gods—I was flying. The world blurred into streaks of color and light, buildings and people nothing but shadows in my wake. Wind tore at my hair, stung my eyes, pulled my lips back in a snarl. My heart slammed against my ribs like it wanted to break free, each breath burning in my lungs like liquid fire.

I was lightning incarnate, and New Solara's streets were my storm.

I cut through alleys and around corners, my eyes fixed on the promise of forest beyond the city walls. Those dark trees beckoned with shadows deep enough to swallow me whole. I didn't care about what lurked in those depths—Boarux, Hags, monsters worse than both. Let them come. I was done being the prey. Done being trapped. Done being betrayed.

Vrys.

Three months. Three fucking months wasted chasing a lie. My son was out there somewhere, waiting, while I'd let myself believe in false promises and gentle touches.

I ran faster, harder, my rage feeding the storm inside me. The only thing that mattered now was finding my son. Everything else—everyone else—could burn.

CHAPTER 44

Ronan

"What in heaven's name...?" Gaelin's words hung in the air, his face twisted with confusion.

Eldra's laugh was sharp. "That's what I'd like to know." His eyes found mine, cold as winter steel. "Care to explain?"

The ring burned like hellfire against my palm, a constant reminder of my betrayal. Shit. Here we go.

"You had one job." Eldra's voice dropped low, dangerous. "Tell her who sent you."

I forced a smirk, aiming for casual and probably missing by a mile. "Guess it slipped my mind."

The night split open with shouts and crackling energy. Lightning carved violet scars across the sky, illuminating the forest where she'd disappeared. This wasn't just bad—this was catastrophically fucked.

"Lies," Eldra snapped. "You were supposed to make her feel safe here."

Something inside me snapped. "You think she'd ever feel safe with you pulling the strings?" I snarled, getting in his face. "She's lost everything—her kid, her home, the man she loved. You're the demon in her nightmares, Eldra. The moment I told her you sent me, she would've been gone."

Ameria's voice cut through the tension. "Eldra, why does she—"

"Enough." Eldra's command cracked like a whip. His attention focused back on me. "Though from where I'm standing, you've taken my place as the villain in her story. That look she gave you? Pure hatred. Not exactly what we planned, was it?"

Heat crawled up my neck, and I wanted to deck him. Because he was right. I'd gone and done the one thing I swore I wouldn't—I'd fallen for her. Hard. The Daylight ring felt like a hot coal in my palm, a physical reminder of every lie I'd told. Even with its power to let me walk in the sunlight beside her, I knew she'd never forgive this betrayal.

"I told her the truth about not being tied to you," I bit out, meeting his stare. "The ring was all I wanted."

Eldra invaded my space, power rolling off him in waves. "What. Did. You. Do?"

I planted my feet, defiant. The ring's weight anchored me to this moment, to my choices. To hell with it all. Atreya deserved better than my lies, better than being a pawn in this game. "I've known enough monsters to spot one, Eldra. When you pitched this plan to get the Queen of Ember beyond those walls... I couldn't smell the usual stink of violence on you. Atreya is..." My voice cracked. "If I'd thought you meant her harm, I would've never agreed. The Blood Oath was the only chain." The ring seared my skin like judgment. Without that oath, I would've taken her far from this. But the Blood Oath bound me to bring her to him. I stared at the cursed thing glinting in my palm. No power was worth this price.

I flicked my wrist, sending the ring skittering across stone to rest at Eldra's feet. The sun could rot—she'd been my light in the darkness.

"ELDRA!" Emery's scream shattered the night. "She's running for the forest! The Aranha! The Whisperfangs!"

Eldra spun with a curse, launching himself down the stairs, taking them three at a time. Gaelin and Emery's boots thundered after him. My heart tried to claw its way up my throat. The forest held things that made vampires look tame. I should move, should run, should...

But I stood frozen, feeling like someone had carved out my insides with a dull blade. I'd made my choice. Now I had to bleed for it.

CHAPTER 45

Atreya

The forest of New Solara towered above me like ancient gods, their massive trunks wider than castle walls. Each step sank into moss that pulsed with an inner light, sending ripples of blue-green luminescence spreading outward like liquid starlight. The vegetation itself seemed alive with consciousness, tendrils of plants unfurling and glowing as if greeting me. Creatures like living embers danced through the air, their bodies flashing with internal fire.

Beautiful. Deadly. Like everything else I'd been stupid enough to trust.

I collapsed onto a hill carpeted in velvet moss, letting the massive canopy shield me from the world. Leaves whispered secrets above me, casting ever-shifting shadows that matched the chaos in my chest. I was far from Eldra's reach now.

Far from Ronan.

The name carved fresh wounds into my heart. I bit down hard on my cheek until copper flooded my mouth, welcoming the sting.

What a fucking fool I'd been. Ronan had shown me exactly who he was from the start—the way he'd manipulated others like a puppet master pulling strings, the calculated gleam in his eyes when he got what he wanted. His true nature had been written in blood and shadow. But I'd ignored every warning sign, let myself get drunk on sweet nothings and gentle touches. I'd handed him my heart like an offering, practically gift-wrapped it for him to devour.

And devour he had.

The worst part? How masterfully he'd done it. Those long nights when he'd let me pour out my grief about Servat, about the wasteland my life had become. How he'd held me without speaking, becoming the shelter I desperately needed. The absolute bastard—making himself my safe harbor only to sink my ship.

I couldn't even summon tears. Just this hollow ache, like someone had scraped me clean inside.

My weakness. My fault. I'd let him past my walls, invited the vampire in. Had any of it been real?

A sound sliced through my self-loathing—a whimper, small and frightened, coming from the undergrowth. My pointed ear twitched toward it instinctively. The cry hit something raw inside me, and before I could think better of it, I was on my feet.

I pushed through a curtain of glowing vines and found it—a tangled mass of rope forming a brutal cage. Something shifted beneath, and two terrified eyes caught the ethereal light. The creature let out a musical trill before its body rippled and vanished like smoke. Only the gentle movement of the ropes betrayed its presence.

I knelt beside the trap, studying what I could see. The being was small, maybe the size of a well-fed housecat. Its fur and scales shifted colors like oil on water, reflecting the bioluminescent forest around us. Those eyes—gods, those eyes. Yellow as sunflowers and bigger than any animal's had a right to be, they stared up at me with an intelligence that made my breath catch.

The rope was strange, unlike anything I'd encountered—wire-thin but strong as steel cables. My fingers worked the knots carefully, trying not to spook my little captive. It made anxious chirping sounds but stayed still, watching me with those enormous eyes. Curved fangs longer than my fingers protruded from its top jaw, and bony ridges ran from its elongated snout up its skull. Its ears flopped like a puppy's, completely at odds with its otherworldly appearance.

The thing was beautiful in the way a blade could be beautiful—dangerous and strange and utterly mesmerizing.

When the ropes finally gave way, it didn't bolt immediately. It drew in a shuddering breath that made its iridescent fur ripple like waves catching moonlight.

"Hey, sweetheart," I murmured, offering my fingers. It studied them for a long moment before giving a delicate sniff. The fear in those massive eyes slowly melted into curiosity. Another sniff, then it butted its head against my palm like a demanding house cat.

My fingers sank into fur softer than silk, watching colors dance beneath my touch. "What are you, little one?"

It trilled again—a sound like wind chimes in a storm—and climbed into my lap without invitation. Its paws splayed like tiny hands, complete with wickedly curved claws that flexed against my thighs. A forked tongue flicked out to taste my skin.

I couldn't help but laugh. "You should run while you can." Whatever set this trap would be back to check it soon.

Which meant I needed to move too.

The creature went rigid in my arms, ears snapping upright. A high whine built in its throat as its whole body began to shake. The sound of breaking branches echoed through the trees, and my heart plummeted into my stomach.

"Shh, it's alright," I whispered, but the thing was beyond soothing. Its fur stood on end as it let out frantic, musical cries. Claws dug into my legs as it gazed up at me with pure terror.

My eyes darted around frantically before landing on a thick wall of foliage. Without thinking, I stuffed the creature down the front of my shirt and dove behind the leaves. Just in time.

Three figures emerged from the glowing undergrowth—Eldra, flanked by his green-skinned witch and the blonde warrior.

No Ronan. The hollow in my chest ached.

"Eldra, we have to find her before she gets eaten by a Whisperfang," Blonde man called out, tight with urgency.

"Or worse, the Aranha," Green-skin added, her foot connecting with something that made my blood run cold. A trap. My trap. The one I'd just freed my little friend from.

I held my breath as they examined the scene, the creature in my shirt gone eerily still. Eldra's eyes narrowed as he studied the loosened ropes. "These were untied. The Aranha don't release their prey."

Good to know.

"I know you're here, Atreya." His call carried a carefully measured calm that made my skin crawl. "Let me explain. Come back to the castle. The forest isn't safe."

The creature suddenly let out a blood-curdling screech. I clutched it tighter, feeling its fur bristle against my skin as it gazed past Eldra with pure terror.

That's when I saw them.

Eyes. Hundreds of eyes descend from the canopy like stars falling to earth. Massive shadows moved with liquid grace above Eldra and his companions. My heart stopped.

"Don't. Move." Green-skin's warning came too late as Blonde man reached for his sword.

They were beautiful in the way nightmares are beautiful—eight-legged horrors with bodies that merged human and spider. Their thoraxes gleamed with impossible colors, mandibles clicking a symphony of rage. They carried woven reed bags and weapons that looked carved from bone and stone.

The clicking grew to a crescendo. I didn't need a translator to know we were all monumentally in danger.

"Atreya," Eldra whispered, "Stand up. Slowly. Trust me."

Hot breath ghosted across my neck, and I swallowed a scream. With trembling legs, I rose from my hiding spot. The Aranha parted like a curtain of nightmares, their countless eyes fixed on the precious bundle in my shirt. Each step backward felt like moving through honey, their gazes tracking my every twitch. My heart slammed against my ribs, a desperate dance with the tiny heartbeat pressed against my chest.

When I reached Eldra, his eyes dropped to my shirt. "Give it to them."

"No." The word came out razor-sharp.

"Atreya, they won't hurt you if you surrender their prey," he said with an edge of desperation that made me want to rip his throat out. Like he actually gave a shit what happened to me.

I tightened my grip on the creature, feeling its tremors match my own. "You don't get to tell me what to do, Eldra." Venom dripped from every syllable.

The Aranha's mandibles clicked faster, angrier. One raised a spear tipped with something that looked suspiciously like bone. My breath caught in my throat as Eldra lifted his hands, slow and careful.

"Wait. Please—"

But the spider-thing was already moving, eight legs carrying it faster than anything that size had a right to move. Then Eldra did something that made my brain short-circuit—he threw himself between me and certain death, dropping to his knees with raised hands.

The creature pulled up short, letting out a hiss that vibrated in my bones.

"Give them your sword, Gaelin," Eldra commanded, never taking his eyes off the monster looming over him.

"Have you lost your mind?" Green-skin screeched.

"I'm making a trade with the Aranha. She won't give up the Whisper-fang. It's this or they kill us all."

Steel sang through air. The Aranha stomped their legs in protest until one raised a clawed hand. Gaelin's sword arced like liquid silver, snatched mid-flight by impossibly fast reflexes. The blade disappeared into a reed bag, and suddenly all eyes were on me and my precious cargo again.

"Now, Atreya." Eldra's said gently. Like he was coaxing a wounded animal. "Please."

My heart thundered against my ribs as I weighed my options. I didn't trust him. Didn't trust any of them. But dying in this nightmare forest wasn't on my agenda, and I wouldn't let this innocent creature pay for my stubbornness.

With shaking hands, I pulled the Whisperfang from my shirt. It looked up at me with those huge yellow eyes, still trusting despite everything. I held it out like an offering to angry gods.

"Gy'isak," one of them sang, the sound like wind through crystal. It raised a stone knife, and I jerked back instinctively.

"No!"

The creature cocked its head, braids swaying with the movement.

"They're offering to kill it for you," Eldra translated.

"I don't want it dead!" I clutched the Whisperfang closer, its heart racing against my palms.

"Gy'isak," the creature repeated, softer this time.

I shook my head hard. "No Gy'isak," I clumsily said.

To my shock, the creature retreated, sliding its knife away. It pointed at me with narrowed eyes. "Go'sen."

"I don't understand," I whispered.

The sea of nightmares parted, arms extending outward like a macabre honor guard.

"They're telling us to leave," Eldra explained, reaching for my arm. I yanked away from his touch like it burned.

They were letting us go? Just like that? The Whisperfang trembled against my chest as I glared at our unlikely saviors.

"Come on," Eldra urged. "Before they change their minds."

I ripped my gaze from the nightmare behind us, tucking the Whisperfang deeper into my shirt. Its head poked out, those huge yellow eyes darting between shadows as we moved.

Eldra took point, his lackeys falling into step beside him like well-trained dogs. I followed, every muscle coiled tight as I scanned the trees. The weight of the Aranha's stares pressed against my back until we finally cleared their territory.

"What the fuck just happened?"

Eldra dragged a hand through his hair, messing up that perfect royal styling. "The Aranha are hunters. That creature you're holding? One of their rival species."

"So they were just going to eat it?" My arms tightened around the warm bundle against my chest.

"Be grateful they accepted the trade." He turned those too-sharp eyes on me. "I've built a fragile peace with these beings. The forest is their domain—it demands respect."

"I don't want to go back to your castle," I spat.

He inhaled deeply, eyes closing for a moment. "Where would you rather go?"

"Away from here."

"To where?"

"Does it fucking matter?"

"I— Atreya. Please. Let me explain. I'm not the monster you think I am."

Joslynn would disagree. But then... why had she kept that map leading to him? Why were his emblems scattered through her journal like fallen stars?

Those questions had driven me here as much as anything else.

"Why hasn't Ember been attacked?" I asked finally.

"Ramses still holds the crown of Ferenz. Rumors say he sent you to handle the rebels. After what he did to Tor and Paladin..." He shook his head. "The people are too weak, too scared to fight."

"And you?" The question hung between us like a blade.

He swallowed hard. "I am."

"Then why this elaborate scheme to get me?"

The green woman reached for my hair, murmuring something in that liquid language. Her agitation crackled in the air between us.

Eldra's response back in that language made both her and Gaelin gasp like gutted fish.

"What did you say to them?"

"Please. I swear on my blood that neither you nor your son will come to harm. You have my word."

The Whisperfang had gone soft with sleep against my chest. I stood frozen as three sets of eyes bored into me. The woman's gaze shone with something that looked suspiciously like tears. Gaelin blinked like he was trying to memorize every detail of my face.

"Fine." The word felt like surrender. "We go back to your castle. But I want answers. All of them."

Eldra's breath rushed out like a prayer. "Yes."

CHAPTER 46

Ronan

Ameria led me through winding corridors, her footsteps echoing against stone like war drums. Every few steps I'd pause, fighting the urge to go after Atreya, and each time Ameria would snap that Eldra would handle it. That I needed to stay out of it.

The air around her crackled with barely contained fury. She smelled of cinnamon and woodsmoke and rage—a dangerous combination I'd learned to recognize over the centuries.

What had Atreya done to inspire such wrath? Surely not just the destroyed stairs...

Ameria stopped at a metal door with an intricate locking mechanism that looked older than time itself. She pressed her palm against it, and the door swung inward with a groan of ancient hinges.

Arctic air swept over me, stealing my breath.

The chamber beyond was small, claustrophobic, illuminated by a single guttering candle. Shadows writhed across stone walls like living things, hungry things. In the center, atop a pedestal that seemed to pulse with its own heartbeat, sat an ornate box no bigger than my fist.

Ameria yanked open the lid. Colors exploded outward—a vortex of light and power that set my teeth on edge. The humming that had been barely noticeable before grew into a discordant symphony that made my bones ache. Raw power radiated from the box in waves.

"What in the seven hells is that?"

She turned to me, lips pressed into a knife-thin line. "The Heart of Eldra." The words fell like stones. "This magic maintains our shield. If Eldra dies..." She slammed the lid shut with enough force to make the pedestal shudder. "And now he's out there chasing after that girl."

"You sound jealous," I drawled, leaning against the doorframe with forced casualness.

"Jealous?" She spat the word like poison. "I'm bloody furious. Eldra has responsibilities. He can't just abandon them for—"

"For what?" I pushed, arching an eyebrow.

She swallowed whatever she'd been about to say and stormed past me. The door slammed with enough force to throw me into the opposite wall. I exhaled slowly, following her retreating form. Her anger was a living thing, crackling through the air like wildfire. But underneath that rage, I caught the scent of something else—fear, sharp and acrid as burning metal.

I caught up to her in what must have been the great hall, its ceiling lost in shadows above. A massive wooden table dominated the space, chairs arranged with military precision along its length. Ameria stood at the head, staring down at a map spread across the dark wood. Symbols I didn't recognize were etched into the parchment, marking the surrounding forest.

"I should go after her," I said, more to myself than to her.

"As a woman who knows what it's like to be betrayed by someone you love..." she was oddly gentle. "I'd suggest staying far away until she's ready to see you."

I dragged a hand down my face. "I never asked for any of this. Eldra's the one who brought me here. He wanted me to get her out of Ember."

"Typical man." The words dripped with disdain. "Won't take responsibility for his part in things."

"I've already got one woman I need to explain myself to," I growled. "I don't need another."

CHAPTER 47

Atreya

I had learned the names of Eldra's court companions. Gaelin or Gael, was the blonde man with the blue eyes. The one that had met Ronan in the Tavern all those months ago. Hisen was a dark-skinned man with white eyes and a scar on his jaw. Eldra's wife's name was Ameria. Then the blue-haired woman was his Captain of the Guard, Madsen. And finally, Emery, who's native language was something called Arathi.

Eldra droned on as we walked, his voice rising and falling in a rhythm that made my skin crawl. He spoke of ancient magics tied to his bloodline, of barriers and protection spells woven through generations. But my thoughts kept circling back to Ronan like vultures to carrion. I fought the urge to ask where he'd disappeared to, hating myself for still caring.

Eldra's words followed me up the ruined steps of his castle.

"Watch your step," he said, his attempt at humor falling flat.

I ignored him, stepping around the boulder I'd created on the landing. A stone archway curved above us, its roof adorned with an intricately carved dragon. Gaelin and Emery bowed before disappearing inside.

"Where do you keep your dragons?" The question slipped out before I could stop it. Were they trapped in some dark pit like Ramses kept his? Chained and broken?

"Oh, there are a handful of them," Eldra replied with casual ease. "They mostly reside in the pit."

"The pit?"

"It's not what you're thinking," he assured me. "They have free rein to come and go. There aren't many riders left."

"You're a rider," I said, remembering that night he'd appeared astride a beast of legend.

"I am." Something like pride colored his tone. "I have many Wyverns and just a few dragons. No sense in keeping them cooped up in hiding with me."

His attitude stood in stark contrast to Ramses, who hoarded dragons like a miser hoards gold, keeping them caged and broken.

"Ramses has many dragons," I said carefully, watching his reaction.

Eldra's expression turned thoughtful. "Yes, he would. Ramses never understood that true power comes not from controlling others, but from oneself. He thinks that with enough dragons, he can conquer all. But he will fail. His rule will be short-lived and brutal."

"He won the war of Fallen Skies," I countered. "His rule has been long."

"That he did. But things change." His hand landed on my shoulder, and it took everything in me not to flinch away. "Come, let us enter my home. There is much for you to learn, and little time to waste."

He waited, expectant, until I nodded. As I stepped through the entrance, something rippled across my skin like silk sliding over steel.

"What was that?"

Eldra's eyes glazed over for a moment. "My wards," he said softly. "They were just letting you in. Welcome to my home."

Beyond the entrance, warmth wrapped around me like a forgotten embrace. Honey-colored stone caught the light filtering through towering windows, making the walls glow like bottled sunlight. The air tasted of leather-bound books and something sweeter—like memories of summer.

A grand staircase spiraled up to my left, its banister telling stories in carved wood—dragons soaring through clouds, riders leaning into wind. To the right, a doorway opened into what had to be the greatest library I'd ever seen. Shelves stretched toward heaven, groaning under the weight of countless books. Some wore covers of tooled leather and gold leaf, others wrapped in cloth faded by centuries. A few even bore covers of delicate wood, their surfaces etched with symbols that seemed to shift when I wasn't looking directly at them.

A massive stone fireplace dominated the far wall, flames dancing like they were alive. Sparks chased each other up the chimney, playing tag with shadows. Before it sat a desk drowning in papers and quills, its leather chair pushed back as if its occupant had just stepped away.

I set the Whisperfang down, watching as it padded straight to the fire's warmth, curling up like it had found home.

Eldra's boots echoed against stone as he led me through the library and into a long hallway. Portraits lined the walls—riders and their dragons frozen in eternal flight. Men, women, young, old, their faces carrying the weight of history. Dragons of every hue imaginable, from pristine white to midnight black. One caught my eye, half-hidden behind a tapestry, but Eldra was already moving on.

The hallway opened onto a balcony that made my breath catch. Below us, a pit dropped away for what seemed like forever, its walls smooth as glass. At its center lay a dragon that could have swallowed a house whole. Golden scales gleamed like fresh-minted coins, its massive chest rising and falling in sleep.

"That is Thrane," Eldra's face softened with genuine affection. "My oldest friend. We've seen centuries together. He's one of Seraphix's Hatchlings."

A shadow passed overhead, and another dragon descended like falling starlight. Smaller than Thrane, with scales like liquid silver. It landed beside us with impossible grace, studying me with ancient eyes.

"This is Eira," Eldra touched her neck gently. "Young yet, and curious. You're the first stranger she's seen."

My heart clenched as memories of another silver dragon flooded back. "My son..." I swallowed hard, "He has a dragon that looks just like her."

Eldra stared at me, his face unreadable. But I could see something in his eyes, something that made my heart race. I could see a glimmer of hope, a flicker of joy. And I could see something else, something that made no sense. Sorrow.

My hand trembled as I reached for Eira. Her scales burned warm against my palm, smooth as river stones. Those ancient eyes never left mine as she pressed into my touch like she'd been waiting for it.

"They can just... leave?" The question felt raw in my throat. "Why do they come back?"

"They choose to." A smile ghosted across his face. "No chains, no cages. Just loyalty. Just love. A bond deeper than steel or stone."

The tenderness in the way he spoke sparked something violent in my chest. "How can you stand there so fucking calm? How can you look me in the face after everything you've done? Last time we met, we were trying to kill each other."

His smile shattered. "I never tried to kill you, child." His voice dropped low, urgent. "Never. I wanted to stop you, save you from a war that would've drowned us all in blood. I saw Ramses' poison in your eyes, the way he'd twisted your grace into something feral. You were his weapon, his pawn. I only wanted to disarm you, not destroy you."

"You sent those men to Hyperion Market. They killed the only mother I'd ever known."

Eira chose that moment to dive into the pit, chirping at Thrane like nothing in the world was wrong.

"I never sent men to Hyperion."

"I was there! I fucking saw them!"

"Did you?" he hissed, "Or did you see what Ramses wanted you to see?"

The certainty I'd carried for so long wavered. Could it be true? Had Ramses played me even then, using my grief like puppet strings? But how could I trust any of these men with their honey-sweet lies?

His fingers brushed my arm. "Come. Walk with me. Let me show you the truth of that day."

I nodded, numb, and followed him on the balcony. We walked along the railing, overlooking the pit. Thrane lay below, his golden scales glinting in the moonlight. Eira flitted about his head, her silver scales shimmering.

"I never sent men to Hyperion," Eldra began.

"But the fight..." I trailed off.

"Was staged," Eldra finished for me. "Ramses had planned it, had deliberately set his men against his own men. Dressed in gold cloaks. He sought to make me appear the aggressor, to turn the people against me."

I shook my head, trying to dispel the fog clouding my mind. "I was there..." I protested, but it sounded hollow even to my own ears.

"Think about it, Atreya. When you saw me last, you saw my men in an encampment in the Great Wood. You went with dozens of men and dragons. But my men were illusions. They weren't real. I would never risk my men when I have so little, when I have made a world of peace for them. In the end, the only person that really came was me."

His words struck a chord within me, echoing through my memories. I closed my eyes, forcing myself to relive that night in Hyperion. The clash of steel, the roar of dragons, the scent of smoke and sweat. But as I delved deeper into the heart of the battle, I realized that something had been off. The enemy had been too easily defeated, too quick to fall. They hadn't fought with the ferocity of men defending their lives.

A cold dread began to seep into my bones. Had I been blind? Had I let my panic—my rage and grief cloud my judgement?

"The woman you lost," he asked, "What was her name?"

The world tilted beneath my feet. I gripped the railing like it was the only solid thing left.

"Joslynn," I whispered. The name tasted like ashes. "Joslynn."

Ramses had killed her.

He'd wanted to see how far I would bend before I broke. How much pain it would take to forge me into his perfect weapon.

My knees gave out. Bile burned up my throat as I retched onto the stone floor.

Deep down, I'd known. Gods help me, I'd known Eldra spoke truth. He was beside me in an instant, gathering my hair back with gentle hands.

"Joslynn?" The way he said it made me look up.

"Did you know her?" The question tumbled out. "She had drawings—a map to New Solara. Your emblem was everywhere in her journal. She—" I buried my face in my hands, unable to continue.

Eldra's hands found my waist, gentle despite everything. Like I might shatter if he pressed too hard. "Come with me," he murmured, his breath warm against my ear. "There are truths you need to hear."

I let him guide me, my body moving on autopilot while my mind splintered into a thousand jagged pieces. The hallway stretched endless before us, our footsteps echoing off stone walls that seemed to press closer with each step.

The spiral staircase appeared like a wound in the floor, corkscrewing down into darkness. Eldra's boots struck each step with military precision. The temperature dropped as we descended, cold seeping into my bones, silence wrapped around us like a shroud.

The hall that greeted us at the bottom stole my breath. Portraits lined the walls, but these weren't the proud, pompous paintings I'd expected. These were ghosts captured in paint—faces etched with battle scars and haunted eyes. Their dragons were all ash and smoke, varying shades of grey from morning mist to storm clouds.

"The Hall of the Fallen," Eldra's shoulders slumped with the weight of centuries. "Where we honor those lost in the War of Fallen Skies."

My feet carried me forward without permission, drawn to each face, each story written in oils and pain.

Then I saw her.

My knees hit stone before I registered falling. The portrait captured every detail with cruel precision—those tight braids I'd watched her weave each morning, the determined set of her jaw, those dark eyes that had watched over me for years. She sat astride a snarling green wyvern, wrapped in armor that gleamed like captured sunlight.

"Joslynn," I gasped. She was—but how? *How?*

"Joslynn of Zay'Nath. She was a warrior, a rider of great skill and an even greater heart. She fought for what was right, even when the cost was high. And in the end, she gave her life for this city, for these people. She died during the War of Fallen Skies."

"No! No. She was alive! She died in the market!" I slammed my fists into the ground. "What are you saying Eldra? What are you saying?" I felt like I had been punched in the gut. I couldn't catch my breath, couldn't think. Joslynn, my Joslynn, had been fighting on the same side as Eldra?

Eldra sank down at the largest part of the wall, settling beneath a different portrait. "You have to understand. We all thought they were dead. I had no idea Joslynn also survived for as long as she did."

My tears were falling silently. "How could you think they were dead?"

"Because they were. Zaezar was Joslynn's wyvern. She was torn in two. There were countless bodies, Atreya. We fought for so long. Then Ramses came with this mist that swallowed up all the dead…"

"Joslynn was my nursemaid. She wasn't a rider!" But how did he know she was from Zay'Nath?

"She must've still had milk from her own babe."

"Joslynn had no children!" I shouted.

"She does. She has a daughter."

"You're lying!" I sobbed. He was quiet for a moment.

"Up until a few minutes ago, I didn't know Joslynn had lived beyond the War of Fallen Skies. I imagine what happened to her, must be what happened to Aislinn."

I rocked back on my heels, hands and knees stinging. "Aislinn was alive when I killed her in the arena. She was Ramses' prisoner."

Eldra flinched, his jaw clenching. He had just as much right to hate me for what I had done to her. "She died during the war. I held her in my very arms when there was no breath nor beat left inside of her. She was dead. I watched Ramses' mist swallow her up."

"The war happened decades before I went into the arena with her!" I screamed. There was no way he was telling me this. Telling me that Ramses held that kind of power, to bring people back from the dead? To watch me suffer after Joslynn's death like that when he could have saved her a second time?

He rested his head against the stone, his voice muffled. "It kills me to know that. To know Aislinn had been brought back, and lived through whatever horrors before meeting you in the arena all those years later. To know she would die all over again and I couldn't save her," his voice broke and I turned my head to witness tears streaming down his face. "it kills me to think of it. To know Ramses forced that upon you when you were nothing more than a youngling."

I said nothing and he continued.

"To know that Ramses is capable of such wickedness to use you like that—to hurt *me*. Then to marry you, to continue using you as a pawn against me all this time. To know you endured the life of a Blackwater woman. Oh, Atreya, it fucking *kills* me. I would have done anything to protect you. You have to know—" he cut off and closed his eyes.

I couldn't understand it. Why did he weep like that so openly to the woman who killed his friend? Slowly, my eyes tracked to the portrait above him. A woman sat atop a dragon as black as midnight, its red eyes glinting like stars. The woman was dressed in silver moonbeam, her long black hair streaming behind her in the wind. I knew who this woman was, with her brown eyes searing into me accusingly. It felt like the earth beneath me had tilted.

I had only ever seen her face once before, decapitated and twisted into a grimace near my feet, her black hair curtained over her, blood smeared, obscuring her.

But now that I could see her properly, in all her glory—

I looked at Eldra with new eyes. The silver-blue fire in his gaze. Those black waves framing sharp features. The beauty mark on his left cheek. His power that had consumed my lightning like it belonged to him.

Because it did.

Gods. Eldra—he's—

I looked upon Aislinn again, trying to separate her from the drawing that Joslynn had made of my mother holding me as a babe.

The world came to a standstill and I couldn't breathe, couldn't think, couldn't move.

Eldra was my father—

Aislinn Furian was my mother.

And I had killed her.

CHAPTER 48

Atreya

Eldra let me scream until my voice shattered, until my throat was raw and bleeding. He just sat there while my world imploded, while everything I'd ever known turned to ash in my mouth.

The silence that followed pressed against my skin like a physical weight, broken only by the desperate gasps that clawed their way from my chest. I couldn't look at him. Couldn't bear to see the truth reflected in those eyes that were so much like my own. So I stayed there, cheek pressed against cold stone, letting the tears drain until I was hollow.

"How long have you known?" The words scraped past my lips.

"Since the moment I saw you." His voice was steady, but something trembled beneath the surface. He hadn't moved from his spot against the wall, hadn't tried to comfort me. Why would he? I was just a ghost to him, a fragment of a past he thought he'd buried.

"How?"

"How did I know?"

I waited, silence my only answer.

"You look like her when you're angry," he said softly.

A pang shot through me at his words, a sharp ache that felt like a knife twisting in my gut. It hurt, oh gods, it hurt. Like he'd reached inside me and found the very thread of my being, and was slowly, inexorably pulling it apart.

"And then your magic... It's like mine."

I rolled onto my side, finally meeting his gaze across the space between us. "Did you know about me?" The question burned.

"No. I mean—I knew of you as Atreya. I was told Ramses had married a girl who killed Aislinn Furian. The Furian Slayer."

"Who told you?"

"Hisen. He has a gift for speaking with the dead. We call them whispers."

I wondered what stories the dead told about me. What horrors they whispered in the dark.

"I didn't know," I said quietly. "I was told my parents died in the war. That my father had the gift of foresight. My son has your gift."

"I don't have foresight. Never have."

My head snapped up. "What?"

He shrugged. "I control lightning and light. My father was a Starbringer—his light could rival the sun. But foresight? No. And I don't know anyone on your mother's side who had it."

I pushed myself up. "But Vrys has foresight—and shadowlight magic."

"Perhaps it's in the Blackwater blood? Ramses doesn't have such power?"

"Ramses controls elements. Can steal warmth from a room. He was shocked when Vrys first showed his magic." I shook my head. "Do the others know about me?"

"Not everyone. I imagine it's a shock to them, seeing you here with her face and my eyes. Emery figured it out quickly. Gael's probably filling in Hisen and Madsen now."

"And your wife?"

His shoulders sagged, eyes dropping to the floor. "She has more grace than I deserve."

"It's not every day your husband brings home a woman who happens to be his child," I said, trying to inject some humor into the situation. But it fell flat, ringing hollow even to my own ears.

I still couldn't believe it. This was my father, and he wasn't some evil man that Ramses had painted to me. He loved his people. He loved Aislinn so much that he was willing to risk his own life to see a glimpse of me.

I thought back to Tor. The ruins, the people who lived in poverty and despair. The way Siorsen swooped in and destroyed what little they had. Those were *my* people. My mother's people.

Eldra broke the silence, "Atreya... I know this is a shock. I never expected to see you again, not after all these years. But you must know, you are my daughter, my flesh and blood. And I will do everything in my power to protect you, just as I would for any of my people."

I felt nothing at his words. Just a cold numbness.

"Did Ronan know?"

It was the first time I had mentioned him since finding out he had conspired to bring me.

"No." Eldra's teeth ground together. "He was supposed to tell you I requested to see you. That I orchestrated this."

"Well, he fucking didn't."

"He believed you wouldn't have come if you'd known."

A laugh ripped from my throat, bitter as poison. "He was right. I would've rather died than come here willingly. Instead, your lapdog fed me some bullshit about saving Ember." My fingers curled into fists. "I thought I was making my own choices. What a joke."

Eldra flinched. I didn't give a damn. My entire world had shattered into pieces, each shard cutting deeper than the last. Ramses. Ronan. Every truth I'd built my life on was nothing but smoke and mirrors.

"Why?" I whirled on Eldra. "Why send your pet snake instead of coming yourself?"

He raked a hand through his hair, sighing. "I didn't know if you'd even look at me, Atreya. After everything... I couldn't find the words to make you understand."

"Did you order him to fuck me too? Was that part of your grand plan?"

Eldra exploded to his feet, a snarl ripping from his chest. "He what?"

Tears burned behind my eyes, but I wouldn't let them fall. Not here. Not for this. "Why did Ronan really agree to this? Just another man wanting to bed the famous Furian Slayer?"

Lightning crackled around Eldra's form, his rage a physical thing. "That's a question you can ask him yourself. Right after I rip his throat out." He stormed toward the winding staircase, each step crackling with barely contained power.

"Wait!" I lunged for his arm, but he shook me off like I was nothing.

"Eldra!" I called after him, but he was already gone, taking the stairs two at a time.

I chased him, following his thunderous path through twisting corridors. What choice did I have? When had I ever had a choice at all?

CHAPTER 49

Ronan

Ameria's invitation to stay felt like a lifeline thrown into churning waters. She'd stopped me from chasing after Eldra—from running after Atreya like the desperate fool I was. My muscles screamed with the effort of holding myself back.

The court was a disaster. Hushed sobs and muttered curses filled the air like poison.

"Am I missing something?" I asked Emery and Gaelin, their hushed whispers by the fireplace grating on my nerves. Madsen slumped in her chair, hands buried in her hair, while Hisen stood beside her, his gaze blank and unfocused.

Ameria swiped at a tear on her cheek. Fuck. This was bad.

"RONAN!" Eldra's roar shattered the silence, bouncing off stone walls until I couldn't tell which direction it came from. My neck prickled, animal instinct screaming danger.

"What did you do?" Ameria's question was soft. Deadly.

"I didn't do anything," I denied, though I couldn't meet her eyes. It was a lie, one I had been telling for weeks now.

Another thunderous bellow echoed through the castle, closer now. My fists clenched, body coiling for the fight I knew was coming. I'd fucked up. Gods, I'd fucked up so badly. Fear crawled across my skin, but not of Eldra—of her. Her scent was getting stronger, mixed with the tang of her anger and the salt of her tears.

What would happen when she knew everything? Would I lose the only person who'd ever... No. I couldn't think about that. Not now.

First, Eldra. My gut twisted, but I shoved the feeling down deep. I'd made my choices. Time to face the bloody consequences. Footsteps crashed down the hallway, each one a hammer blow counting down to my execution. The doors exploded inward, and there they were—Eldra, crackling with power, and Atreya clinging to his arm. Her eyes found mine, confusion warring with the first bitter taste of betrayal.

I'd put that look there. Me.

"Eldra, stop!" Atreya's demand cracked like a whip, but her words might as well have been whispers in a hurricane. Lightning danced over Eldra's skin, his face twisted into something ancient and terrible. I planted my feet, shoulders back, spine straight. I'd faced death before. I'd face it again.

"You played me for a fucking fool." The words dripped from Eldra's lips like venom.

My jaw clenched. "I did exactly what you asked."

"No!" Thunder crashed outside. "You were my desperate gamble." His laugh was bitter poison. "Trust a snake like you to twist a Blood Oath."

"Blood Oath?" Atreya's question sliced through the tension. Neither of us answered. "Ronan?"

Fuck. Fuck. FUCK.

This was his fault. All of it.

"It was a mistake."

Eldra's eyes flashed murderous, and he stalked forward. "A mistake?" Each syllable was a death threat.

"I need to talk to Atreya. Alone." I tried to shoulder past him, but it was like pushing against a mountain.

Atreya moved like lightning, inserting herself between us. Her hands pressed against Eldra's chest, and something in my gut twisted at the sight.

"You promised me truth," she spat. "I'll have it. Every fucking piece. Let me decide what to do with it."

Eldra's glare could have melted steel, but he stepped back. "Ameria. Love. Come." His stance softened for her. "It grows late." Ameria rose like smoke from her chair, gliding to his side. Her eyes cut between me and Atreya, sharp as razors. The courtiers followed like good little sheep, leaving me alone with my beautiful disaster.

She leaned against the table, arms crossed like battle armor over her chest. Christ, how many times had I bent her over that same table? Tasted heaven between her thighs? The memory hit like a physical blow—I might never touch her again. Never taste the storm on her skin or drink the starlight from her lips.

What kind of hell had I walked into?

Blood beaded on her lip where she worried it between her teeth. Those eyes—usually brighter than any star in the fucking universe—had gone dull, glazed with tears she was too proud to let fall. She looked everywhere but at me, and each second of avoidance was another knife in my gut.

"Atreya—"

"You." The word was barely a breath, but it cut deeper than any blade.

She was biting her lip, so hard a bead of blood welled up. Her eyes, usually bright as the stars, were dull and glossy with unshed tears. She looked anywhere but at me—at the walls, the floor, the shadows dancing in the corners—and each second of avoidance was another nail in my coffin.

"Atreya—"

"You." One word. Three letters. Enough venom to kill a man where he stood.

"I—"

"YOU!" The scream tore from her throat like it was ripped from her soul. Her finger slammed into my chest hard enough to bruise, and her face flushed with a rage so pure it was almost beautiful. Almost. "This is all you!" The words echoed off the stone walls like a death sentence. Then she was on me like a storm, all wild energy and destruction, her fists pounding against my chest.

"Please. Atreya, please." I tried to catch her wrists, but she was lightning in Fae form, impossible to contain.

"You lied to me!" she screamed again, tears finally spilling down her cheeks. "You lied, and you lied, and you lied! You fucking liar!"

"Yes." The admission burned. "Yes, I am."

"You lied to me!"

"I did," I admitted, feeling a stinging sensation in my eyes. "I did."

"You betrayed me!" she spat, her face twisted in anguish.

"I did." My own tears fell, hot and foreign on my face.

When was the last time anyone had made me cry? Had anyone ever?

"You told me you loved me!" she threw at me, cracking on the last words.

I drew in a shaky breath. "I *do*."

Her laugh was a broken thing, all sharp edges and pain. "Bullshit. You used me, Ronan. Like a fucking toy. Like a game piece on your board."

Each word was another knife between my ribs, and I deserved every single one. I deserved her fury, her disgust, her hatred. I'd earned it all.

"I'm sorry." The words were worthless, but they were all I had left to give.

"I loved you."

Loved.

Past tense.

My soul hemorrhages. Screams. Bleeds. But outwardly, I'm stone. That's what centuries of existing does to you—teaches you to wear masks like second skins.

She's waiting. The silence between us stretches thin as a blade.

"Say something," she demanded, "For once in your life, just tell me the truth. Tell me why you would join in a Blood Oath with Eldra? I thought you had no prior connection with him."

I ran a hand down the length of my face.

"Gaelin met me in a tavern outside of Ember. I was with Xaneth. Xaneth had a big mouth and was telling the world we had been invited by royal decree of the king. Gael—well... Gael approached me and I thought it was just for *fun*."

One perfect eyebrow arches. She always could cut me to ribbons with just a look. I didn't need to elaborate.

"When we went up to the inn keep rooms he opened a portal and I landed here, in New Solara." I started pacing.

"And what was I to do? I was surrounded by all of them. Eldra gave me an offer, and I couldn't refuse."

"What did he offer you?" Dead voice. Dead eyes. She's already buried me in her mind.

"A Daylight ring. Said I could walk in the sun if I got you outside the wall. Wanted me to keep his name out of it. After Servat..."

Her eye twitches. It's the only tell that she's not completely carved from ice.

"So you got your sun?" Still won't look at me. It's killing me, this careful distance. This calculated coldness.

"No."

"But the ring—"

"I threw it away."

"Why?"

"Because, I had the sun for three months. And I hurt her."

I've never been this naked with anyone, never bled my heart out like this. But for her? I'd tear myself open. Paint sonnets on her skin with my blood. Dance in holy fire if it meant hearing 'I love you' one more time.

Her face goes blank. Impenetrable. Part of me wants her to scream, to rage, to tear me apart with those lightning-kissed hands. Anything but this silence that flays me alive.

"I didn't mean to hurt you." Pathetic. Worthless. True.

Her laugh is all razor blades. "But you did. You played me like a fucking fiddle. You and everyone else—liars, betrayers, users." She pushes away from the table, all lethal grace. "I need time."

"Time?" The word comes out desperate. Broken.

"To decide if you're worth forgiving." Her eyes catch the lamplight, turn to molten gold. "He's my father. Did you know that?" Her smile is a cruel, beautiful thing.

"What?" I managed to stammer.

Atreya's smile was a cold, cruel thing. "Eldra Solaris. He's my father." The words hung in the air between us, heavy with implications. "And Aislinn Furian was my mother," she added, her demeanor cracking. Tears pricked at the corners of her eyes, and lightning licked over her skin.

"What?" I repeated, unable to process what she was telling me.

Atreya's laughter echoed through the room again, a wild, hysterical sound. "Ramses, he has some kind of power to make the dead come back to life. Aislinn was killed during the war, while pregnant with me. I don't know what I am. A monster maybe," she said, her eyes welling up with tears.

"You're not—" I step forward, reaching for her. "I *know* monsters."

She stops me with one raised hand. "Will you stay?" A whisper. A plea. My turn to break. "Can I?"

That smile—gods, that smile could bring empires to their knees. "I'll talk to Eldra." She moves toward the door. "But right now? I need to be alone."

Lightning dances over her skin like a lover's caress. Beautiful. Deadly. Everything about her that's turned me inside out since the moment I saw her. A spark jumps from her finger to the table, leaving its mark.

Just like she's left hers on me.

CHAPTER 50

Atreya

Seven days felt like seven centuries, each sunrise dragging across my skin like barbed wire. They all watched me like I was made of glass—fragile, breakable, moments away from shattering into a thousand useless pieces. Only Ronan dared to stay close, a shadow in my peripheral vision, silent and waiting. Waiting for what? For me to break? To run? To tell him to leave?

The room Eldra gave me was a prison dressed in silk and gold leaf. Sure, the bed could fit an army, and the marble bathroom probably cost more than most people see in a lifetime. But a cage is still a cage, even when it comes with a balcony view that makes your heart ache. My closet was stuffed with dresses that whispered against my skin—some of them Joslynn's work, her stitches holding together more than just fabric. But I moved through it all like a ghost, touching nothing, feeling nothing.

Every day, like clockwork, Eldra appeared. His knock echoed through my self-imposed exile, followed by that too-bright voice asking, "Have you eaten?" He'd waltz in with plates piled high with food I couldn't stomach, his smile stretched so wide it looked painful. Each time he beamed at me, something in my chest twisted like a knife. I hadn't stepped foot outside this room in a week. Couldn't. Wouldn't.

The nightmares were worse now.

Blood painted my dreams in violent strokes. My mother's head rolling across sand. Servat's body, charred beyond recognition. Vrys' white hair like an accusation. Sleep became my enemy—I'd rather face exhaustion than see those images again.

The knock came right on schedule.

"May I come in?" Eldra asked with that same forced cheer through the wood. I stared at the door, too drained to even answer. It creaked open anyway, and there he was, brandishing another tray like a shield.

"Brought you lunch," he announced to my silence. I watched him settle on my bed's edge, wondering how long he'd keep up this charade of normalcy.

"You need to eat," he pressed, false brightness coating every word. "Keep your strength up."

Strength? What strength? I hadn't felt strong since... since when?

His fingers wrapped around my wrist, warm and gentle. I felt nothing. Not even a spark of connection.

"Ronan needs to go," he finally said, the words dropping like stones. "He's not good for you."

Something inside me snapped. "Don't you dare tell me what's good for me." The words tore from my throat, raw and honest. "Ronan is the only thing keeping me sane. I'd tear the sky apart for him."

"He doesn't love you," Eldra countered, each word precise and cutting. "Vampires don't love—they own. They possess. What you think is love is just twisted desire. You're his property, nothing more."

"You don't know him!" The scream ripped from somewhere deep inside me. But doubt, that poisonous little whisper, had already taken root. Was Eldra right? Had I been fooling myself all this time?

Ronan. Gods, Ronan.

I wanted to run to him. To scream and cry and hold him until we both broke. He stayed for me. It had to be for me.

Right?

"Atreya." Eldra sighed, his fingers running through his hair as disgust flickered across his face.

"You don't even know me," I spat.

He flinched like I'd slapped him.

"No," he admitted, really looking at me for the first time. Sadness and regret painted his features. "I don't. And I'm sorry for that, Atreya."

"Why?" The word came out barely above a whisper. "Why are you sorry?"

His chest rose and fell with a heavy breath. "For more than you know." His hand found mine, warm against my cold skin.

"There's someone you need to meet," he said, uncertainty dancing in his eyes. It was the first real emotion I'd seen from him in days.

"Who?"

His smile grew, genuine excitement replacing the forced cheer. "Someone interesting," was all he'd say. Such a simple word. Interesting.

"Come to the pit with me," he urged, practically vibrating with anticipation. "Trust me—this will help." Then he was gone, leaving me alone with my thoughts. But for the first time in days, grief wasn't my only companion. A tiny spark of curiosity had taken root, and despite everything, I wanted to know more.

* * *

The dragon pit wasn't just a hole in the ground—it was a wound carved into the castle's heart, black stone walls stretching up like ribs around us. The stench of sulfur and smoke burned my nostrils. Workers scurried around like ants, their movements careful and practiced as they cleaned and filled water troughs.

"Dragons hunt for themselves," Eldra said, gesturing to the organized chaos below. His words echoed off the obsidian walls. "We just maintain their space."

Massive tunnels branched out like veins from the main chamber. Silver scales glinted from one—Eira, probably. My stomach twisted.

"Why am I here?" The words tasted like ash in my mouth. Eldra's perpetual smile cracked, just for a second.

"There's someone you need to meet." He pointed to a shadowed cave. "Emreth!"

The dragon that emerged made my heart stop. She moved like liquid metal, scales shifting between gold and bronze and blood-red in the dim light. Her eyes found me—twin infernos that stripped me bare. Every muscle in her serpentine body rippled with barely contained power. Those wings could block out the sun, all delicate membrane and deadly grace, folded against her sides like deadly fans.

When Emreth stepped fully into the light, my blood turned to ice. That crown of horns, that distinctive shape—

"Siorsen," I choked, stumbling backward.

"His mother," Eldra confirmed.

Emreth's inspection was thorough, her snout lowering to my level. Each breath she took could have swallowed me whole.

"Unlike her son, she's never tasted blood in battle," Eldra added softly. "She chose peace when others chose war."

Ramses would've put her down for that weakness. The thought made me sick.

"She's magnificent," I whispered, because she was.

"She is. And she has gifts—she feels what others feel. Takes away their pain."

"Heals?" The word caught in my throat.

"Among other things. She's only ever accepted one rider."

I wanted to run. To hide. To burrow so deep in my bed that the world forgot I existed. "That's it, then?"

Eldra's pause felt heavy as stone. "No," he admitted. "There's someone else."

The darkness itself seemed to move.

My heart stopped.

The dragon that emerged was night given form, scales so black they devoured light. Its eyes blazed like dying stars, ancient and terrible. Twice Emreth's size, its very presence made the air heavy with power. When it roared, the sound shook my bones.

"Seraphix." The name fell from my lips like a prayer. The legend. The nightmare. The dragon I'd freed from Ramses's chains.

My mother's other half.

"He knows you. Remembers her."

Seraphix's gaze pierced my soul. Grief hit me like a physical blow. Then—

Images flooded my mind. Blood and fire. My mother's sword catching sunlight. Ramses's hatred.

I remember you, little one. At the gates... Not yet, I said...

The voice in my head felt like thunder. I gasped, reality snapping back into focus.

"They can speak?"

Eldra's smile turned genuine. "When they choose to."

Seraphix moved closer, his massive form blocking out the world. Fear warred with something else—something that felt like coming home. A piece of my mother, breathing and real.

When his head lowered, my hand reached out on instinct.

The moment I touched his scales, the universe exploded.

Joy. Pain. Love. Loss. My mother's laugh. Her tears. Her triumph. Her terror. Every memory Seraphix had hoarded like treasure crashed through me. I saw her young and fierce, saw her broken and dying. Felt Seraphix's helpless rage as Ramses destroyed her. Felt his grief mirror my own.

I ripped away, shaking apart.

"I'm so sorry," I broke.

She knew, little one. At the end, she knew. And she forgave.

Something shattered inside me—something that had been broken so long I'd forgotten it was there. I hit my knees, sobs tearing free.

Eldra caught me. Seraphix and Emreth curled around us like living walls, their heat seeping into my frozen bones. For the first time since everything went wrong, I felt safe.

"Tell me," I begged into Eldra's shirt. "Tell me everything about her."

His mask finally cracked completely. The raw grief in his eyes matched my own.

And there, surrounded by dragons and truth, he began to speak.

CHAPTER 51

Ronan

An axe zoomed by my head and landed in the wooden beam next to my head. I let out a heavy sigh.

"Good evening to you too, Madsen."

I was just leaving my less-than-comfortable accommodations that Eldra provided—something akin to a broom closet with a bed and a few other things—to go to the kitchens where Ameria arranged for me to bleed a goat.

Yes. A goat.

"See you're still here, bastard," Madsen snarled, hulking forward to dig her axe out of the beam, and then maybe stabbing me in the back with it.

"So long as she wants me here. I was just about to grab dinner." I flashed her my longer fangs at her. "Care to join me for a bite?"

"You will never have peace, so long as I am around."

I rolled my eyes. "Yeah. I've gathered as much."

She yanked the axe free with enough force to send splinters flying. "You think you're so clever, don't you? Worming your way into Eldra's good graces, playing the tame little pet."

"Actually, I think I'm quite dull. Just a simple man trying to enjoy his simple goat blood in peace." I started walking toward the kitchens, keeping my peripheral vision locked on her weapon. "Though I have to ask—what's your preferred method of stress relief? Because throwing axes at house guests seems a touch extreme. Have you considered knitting?"

"One of these days, Eldra won't be around to protect you," Madsen said, falling into step behind me. Just close enough to be threatening, just far enough that I couldn't easily disarm her. "And when that day comes—"

"Yes, yes, you'll separate my head from my shoulders, feed my remains to wild dogs, dance on my ashes, et cetera." I waved a dismissive hand. "You know, for someone who hates me so much, you spend an awful lot of time thinking about me."

The whistle of the axe cutting through air was my only warning. I ducked, and the blade embedded itself in the wall ahead of me.

"Your aim's getting better," I said cheerfully. "That one almost hit me."

"Keep talking, bloodsucker. See what happens."

"You know what your problem is?" I asked, pausing to examine the new hole in the wall. "You're too predictable. Axe throw, death threat, axe throw, death threat. It's like watching a very angry pendulum."

I could practically hear her teeth grinding. The sound of her boots on the stone floor told me she was closing the distance between us—probably reaching for her backup weapon. She always had at least three on her person. I'd counted.

"Tell me, what did vampires do to earn such special hatred? Kill your family? Destroy your village? Turn your beloved into a thrall?" I glanced over my shoulder. "Or is this just good old-fashioned prejudice?"

"You really want to know?" Her voice had dropped dangerously low. Never a good sign.

I should have kept walking. Should have made my way to that waiting goat and left well enough alone. But curiosity had always been my fatal flaw—well, that and the whole blood-drinking thing.

"Actually, yes." I turned to face her fully, noting the dagger she'd drawn from her boot. "I would like to know. Because if I'm going to have axes hurled at my head every time I leave my room, I'd at least like to understand why."

For a moment, something flickered across Madsen's face—something raw and haunted that made me regret asking. Then her expression hardened into its usual mask of contempt.

"You want to understand?" She took another step forward, blade catching the torchlight. "Then maybe I should show you exactly what your kind did to—"

"There you are!" Ameria's voice cut through the tension like a warm knife through butter. She appeared at the end of the hall, wiping her hands on her apron. "Your dinner's getting cold. Well, room temperature. You know what I mean."

I'd never been so glad to hear about lukewarm goat blood in my life.

"Coming!" I called back, offering Madsen a slight bow. "We'll have to continue this delightful chat another time. Perhaps over tea? Or would you prefer something stronger? Blood of your enemies, perhaps?"

The dagger embedded itself in the wall where my head had been, but I was already walking away. Some might call it running. I preferred to think of it as a tactical retreat.

I wasn't expecting to see Gael at my dinner table. He was leaning against it, nose curling at the large bowl of goat's blood that had been set out for me. I preferred a wine glass or goblet, but whatever.

"Funny seeing you here," I said, dropping down into the wooden chair.

"Wanted to see how you were fairing."

I closed my eyes and sighed. "Must we do this? You and I—we had our almost-fun—now you see that I am happily taken and you're wondering about what could-have-been."

He chuckled at that. "No hard feelings I hope?"

"Gael, I didn't even get a chance to feel anything hard before you kidnapped me and turned my life upside down." I took a sip thoughtfully. "Though, I suppose I do have you to thank for my meeting Atreya."

Gael frowned. "So it's true then? You and Atreya are an item?"

"Who's asking?"

"Just curious," Gael said, but his posture stiffened ever so slightly. "Word travels fast in these circles. I may not have the Fae senses you all have, but I have ears."

I took another long drink, letting the blood coat my tongue. It wasn't fresh from the vein, but Ameria had at least had the decency to warm it to just below body temperature. "Mm. And which circles would those be, exactly?"

"You know how it is." He waved a hand vaguely. "Eldra announced to the Court that Atreya is his heir. That she is the daughter of Aislinn. You know that means by law she is the rightful heir to Tor." He paused, and then added, more quietly, "If you two married it would make you the first vampire king in history."

I choked on the goat blood.

"Excuse me?" I spluttered, dabbing at my chin with a sleeve. The goat blood had left an unfortunate stain. "I think you've gotten quite ahead of yourself there. And by 'quite ahead,' I mean several leagues, possibly continents."

Gael's lips twitched. "So you hadn't considered it?"

"Considered it? I'm still trying to survive Madsen's daily attempts at turning me into a pincushion." I pushed the bowl away, suddenly less hungry. "Besides, Atreya hasn't mentioned anything about—"

"You are courting a princess and the thought never occurred to you to marry her?"

I held up a finger—the middle one. "One. She is technically already a queen. Two she *is* married. I am an adulterous whore."

"She brings Blackwater, Solara, and Furian together. That is significant."

I pinched the bridge of my nose. "When you put it that way, it sounds so dramatic."

"It is dramatic. You're courting the most politically significant person in the realm, and you're sitting here drinking goat blood from a bowl like a common—"

"If you say 'leech,' I will throw this bowl at you," I warned. "I am already getting enough of the 'what-are-your-intentions-with-my-daughter' from Eldra."

"Your intentions are the least of anyone's concerns right now," Gael said, his expression growing serious. "The Court is... unsettled. Whispers of a vampire with potential claim to the throne?"

"Whispering what? 'Oh no, the bloodsucker might actually have to attend our tedious garden parties?'" I reached for my bowl again, if only to have something to do with my hands. "I have no interest in playing political games."

"You never told us what Xaneth wanted from Atreya. When Ramses invited you both to Ember."

I shrugged. "I assume Ramses wanted to use Xaneth's gift on Atreya. He is a Siphoner on a capacity of which I have never seen before. He never said anything to me about it."

"That's exactly the problem." Gael leaned forward, "You're not playing the game, but you're on the board whether you like it or not. And there are pieces moving against you."

"Is this why Madsen's been extra stabby lately?" I asked, though I already suspected the answer. "Here I thought she just really needed a hobby."

"Madsen is the least of your worries. She's just the visible blade." He glanced toward the kitchen door, where Ameria was humming as she worked. "There are those who would see Atreya's claim invalidated because Eldra and Aislinn were never married. Or see that by her association with you, she is tainted in some way—let along her having been married to Ramses. Others who would use your relationship to push for reforms they've wanted for centuries. And some..." He trailed off. "I don't believe everyone will adjust well to her being heir."

"Shocking. Though I have to ask—why are you telling me this? Last I checked, you weren't exactly president of my fan club."

Gael's mouth twisted into something that wasn't quite a smile. "Let's just say I prefer my realm-shattering political upheavals to be intentional rather than accidental. Besides," he added, standing up straight, "watching you fumble through Court politics might actually be entertaining."

"Glad I can provide amusement," I muttered. "Any other cheerful news you'd like to share? Perhaps a prophecy about my doom? A curse? A strongly worded letter from the Vampire Hunter's Guild?"

"Just..." Gael hesitated at the doorway. "Watch your back. And maybe consider upgrading from goat blood. If you're going to be a target, you might as well be at full strength."

I stared into my now-cold bowl of blood, appetite completely gone. "Wonderful. As if dating wasn't complicated enough without adding political assassination to the mix..."

The worst part was, he wasn't wrong. I'd been so focused on surviving day to day, on navigating my relationship with Atreya and avoiding Madsen's axes, that I hadn't stopped to consider the bigger picture. A vampire and a queen? It sounded like the beginning of a bad joke, or maybe a tragic ballad.

A shadow fell across the table, and I looked up to find Emery standing there, her expression unreadable as usual. She gestured at the bowl of blood, then at me, managing to convey both curiosity and mild disgust with just a tilt of her head.

"*Sanga?*" she asked in Arathi, one of the few words we'd managed to establish meant 'blood' in our limited communications.

"Yes, *sanga*," I replied, probably butchering the pronunciation. "Goat *sanga*. Not exactly fine dining, but it keeps me alive."

She nodded slowly, then said something rapid-fire in Arathi that I had absolutely no hope of understanding. I caught maybe one word in ten, and even those I wasn't sure about. From her tone and the way she kept glancing at the door, I gathered she was trying to warn me about something.

"Slow down?" I tried, making a decreasing motion with my hand. "I'm still learning your language, remember? I'm about as fluent in Arathi as Madsen is in showing mercy."

Emery frowned, then pointed at Gael's recently vacated seat. "*Danra*," she said firmly, which I knew meant 'danger' - that had been one of the first words we'd needed to establish, given our circumstances.

"Danger from Gael?" I asked, pointing at the chair. When she shook her head, I tried again. "Danger from what he said?"

She nodded vigorously at that, then made a sweeping gesture that encompassed the whole castle. "*Danra k'thor*," she added, her expression grave.

"Danger everywhere," I translated, rubbing my temples. "Yes, I got that impression from our friend Gael. Though I appreciate you trying to warn me too."

She stood there for a moment longer, clearly frustrated by our inability to communicate more complex thoughts. Finally, she reached out and tapped the bowl of blood, then shook her head.

"What, you're saying I shouldn't drink it?" I asked, suddenly suspicious. "Is it poisoned?"

But she was already walking away, leaving me to stare at my potentially contaminated dinner. Perfect. Now I had to worry about assassination attempts in my food as well as axes to the head.

"Next time," I called after her, "maybe we could try charades?"

She didn't turn around, but I swore I heard something that might have been a snort of amusement. Or possibly contempt. With Emery, it was always hard to tell.

Atreya's room is a fucking trap.

Seventeen windows. I count them again, just to be sure. Seventeen ways for sunlight to turn me into ash, and that's not even counting the pretentious as hell skylight Eldra had installed. Real subtle.

My fingers work methodically, yanking down curtain after curtain. The heavy fabric whispers against the stone floor, and each window I cover feels like a small victory. But there are so damn many of them.

Clever bastard, Eldra. Give your daughter the sunniest room in the castle. Make it impossible for any vampire to sneak in without getting third-degree burns. Daddy of the fucking year.

A stray beam of light catches my hand as I reach for the next curtain. Pain sears across my skin, and I bite back a curse. Not enough to do real damage, but enough to remind me that I'm not welcome here. Not by the architecture. Not by the inhabitants. Definitely not by Eldra.

The room slowly dims with each curtain I draw, transforming from a death trap into something almost welcoming. Almost. That damn skylight still bathes the center of the room in amber light, but I can work with that. Just have to stick to the shadows, like always.

After my window-blocking crusade, I notice a stack of books piled on Atreya's bedside table. Curiosity gets the better of me—it usually does—and I edge around the shaft of skylight-sunshine to investigate. There's a mix of historical texts, political treatises, and what appears to be some very spicy romance novels. I grab the whole stack and sprawl across her bed, careful to stay in the shadows.

The top book is some dusty tome about the Great Accords between the Fae Courts. Riveting stuff, really. But Gael's words keep echoing in my head, drowning out the dry political prose. *First vampire king in history.*

I twist a strand of hair between my fingers—a nervous habit I thought I'd kicked centuries ago—and try to imagine it. Me, wearing a crown. Me, at Court functions, trying not to drink the guests. Me, making decisions that affect entire kingdoms when I can barely decide what to have for breakfast (goat or... goat).

"This is ridiculous," I mutter to the empty room, letting the book fall onto my chest. The idea of marrying Atreya isn't the ridiculous part—that part makes my dead heart do strange things I'm not ready to examine. It's everything else: the politics, the plots, the probability of getting assassinated before I can say "I do."

I pick up one of the romance novels instead. At least if I'm going to torture myself with impossible fantasies, they might as well involve heaving bosoms rather than heaving responsibilities.

CHAPTER 52

Atreya

"You were gone all day," Ronan said from behind his book. He lay comfortably in my bed, as if he'd been invited. His presence irritated me, but I said nothing.

"What are you doing here?" I asked, stripping off my corset and dress. I could see him watching with rapt enthusiasm from the floor-length mirror. Suddenly, I felt self-conscious about the baby pooch I never lost after Vrys was born. But Ronan had seen me naked before. This was supposed to be his punishment.

Look, but don't touch.

I fumbled in a drawer, found a nightdress, and headed to my large bathroom. I reeked of dragon and smoke. I needed to clean myself.

Ronan followed me, rising quickly from the bed. "You seem in a better mood," he said.

I turned, glaring at him. "Wrong choice of words."

He smirked, undeterred.

I stepped into the giant tub, sinking into the already heated water. "I met my mother's dragon today."

He arched a brow. "Oh?"

"I mean...I've met it before. Kind of. When I first tried leaving the gates, he sent a vision to me and told me to wait." I dipped under the water, wetting my hair. "Then I accidentally let him and a few other dragons out weeks later."

"Sounds like you," he snorted.

I smiled to myself. Maybe this day wasn't a total loss.

"You don't have to stay here anymore, you know," I said dismissively.

He was quiet for a bit. I had my back to him, busying myself with the soap.

I didn't hear him slip into the water behind me.

His arms circled my waist, pulling me against his chest. I gasped, surprised. He was cold to the touch, and he smelled of leather and ink. I tried to push him away, but he held tight.

"You smell of smoke," he murmured, nuzzling my hair. "I like it."

I rolled my eyes, even though he couldn't see. "You're ridiculous."

"Maybe," he said, his breath tickling my ear. "But you smell good."

I sighed, but I didn't try to push him away again. It was nice, having him hold me. I missed it, even though I was furious at him.

He did give up the Daylight ring—his whole reason for taking me in the first place.

He plucked the soap from my hand, running the bar up the front of me, lathering over my breasts

I gasped at his touch. But he didn't push further, just kept washing me with slow, gentle strokes. My heart raced, but I didn't stop him. It was confusing, my body responding to him even though I was angry.

"You smell of smoke," he said again, his voice low. "But you always smell *so* good."

I didn't answer. I didn't know what to say. I was still mad at him, but a part of me was glad he was touching me again.

"I'm sorry," he said after a bit, his voice quiet. "I know I messed up." He moved the bar lower, across my stomach. My body flushed at his touch. His lips were on my neck, trailing wet kisses down my shoulder. "You have to know how sorry I am."

He brought the bar of soap down beneath the surface of the water. I heard the dull thump of it hitting the bottom of the pool. His fingers curled into my folds, slowly moving back and forth, stroking me.

I gasped, my head falling back against his shoulder. His touch sent a jolt of pleasure through me, making my toes curl. I should have been angry, should have pushed him away. But I didn't. I let him keep touching me, let him keep kissing my neck.

"I'm so sorry, Atreya," he whispered, his fingers moving faster. "I know I hurt you. I know I shouldn't have given up the ring. I was just so scared of losing you."

I didn't answer. I couldn't. My breath was coming in short gasps, my heart racing. His touch felt so good, felt like it had been years since he last touched me like this.

Suddenly, he slid a finger inside me. I moaned, my hips bucking against him. He groaned, nipping at my ear. "You feel so good," he whispered. "I missed you so much."

I didn't answer. I couldn't. I could only moan and whimper as he kept touching me, kept kissing me.

He slid another finger inside me, moving them in and out at a slow, torturous pace. I moaned, my head thrashing against his shoulder. I was so close, so close to falling apart.

"Ronan," I moaned, my voice shaking. "I'm so close."

"I know," he whispered, full of need. "Let go, Atreya. Let go."

And with his words, I did. I fell apart, pleasure washing over me in a wave. I moaned, my body shaking. It felt so good, felt like I was melting into the water. His fingers slowed but never left me. He slowly turned me, backing up to the pool's edge. he lifted me by the waist seating me out of the water.

"I have to taste you," he said, a desperate plea.

He dropped to his knees, pulling my legs apart. I was still reeling from my orgasm, barely able to process what was happening. He leaned in, his mouth closing over me. I gasped, my hips bucking against his face. His tongue flicked out, stroking me. I moaned, my fingers tangling in his silver hair.

He groaned, his mouth moving harder against me. His fingers dug into my thighs, holding me in place. I was at his mercy, unable to do anything but feel. He sucked on my clit, sending a jolt of pleasure through me. I moaned, my head falling back.

"Ronan," I moaned, shaking. "Oh god."

He hummed, his mouth vibrating against me. He slid two fingers inside me, moving them in and out.

I gasped, my hips moving with his touch. I was so close, could feel myself building toward another orgasm.

He lifted his head, looking up at me, mouth glistening. His red eyes were dark, full of need. "Let go," he whispered. "I want to taste you come."

I nodded, barely able to speak. He dropped his head again, his mouth closing over me. He sucked hard, his fingers moving faster.

I was so close, could feel myself on the edge.

And then I fell apart. Pleasure washed over me, making my body shake. I moaned, my fingers tangling in his hair. He groaned, his mouth moving harder against me. He drank me in, not letting a drop escape. I was vaguely aware of him standing up, his hips centered between mine.

His body draped over mine, his silver hair falling over us like a curtain. "Tell me to stop and I will. Tell me to leave and I will."

"Don't stop," I rasped out.

His low chuckle vibrated through me.

I felt him shift, the head of his cock notching at my entrance.

I tensed, feeling a stretching sensation as he slowly slid inside me. I gasped, my head falling back against the tile. He filled me completely, his thick length hitting deep inside me. He groaned, his mouth moving back to my neck. His hips drew back, his cock almost leaving me before he slid forward again. I cried out, my hips rising to meet his thrust.

He set a slow, torturous pace, his cock dragging along my walls and sending sparks of pleasure through me. I writhed under him, my nails digging into his back.

He grunted, his hips moving faster. His mouth moved back to my ear. "Does that feel good, love?"

"Yes," I hissed. And then I was biting him, drawing blood from his shoulder.

He groaned, his hips moving frantically, the water sloshing about us. I pulled off of his mouth and he slammed his lips against mine, shoving his tongue in my mouth. I could taste myself on his lips, mixed with his blood.

He brought his arm under the crook of my leg and lifted, my knee almost touching the side of my head.

He groaned, his hips moving harder, his cock hitting a new spot inside me. I moaned, my mouth falling open. He took advantage, his tongue stroking against mine. I could feel myself building again, could feel pleasure coiling in my belly.

And then I fell apart screaming his name. He kept moving, kept slamming into me even as I came.

I could feel myself milking him, could feel him swelling inside me. He groaned, his hips stuttering.

He groaned, his body tensing. He slammed into me once, twice, and then he stilled. His cock pulsed inside me, sending a warmth flooding through me.

He collapsed against me, his silver hair tickling my face.

We lay there for a bit, the only sound our heavy breathing. I could feel his unusually slow heartbeat against my chest, could feel him still inside me. I was sated, could feel myself drifting towards sleep. His arms came around me, holding me close. I didn't push him away, just let him hold me.

He held me for a bit longer, and then he slowly slid out of me. He sat me up, turning me to face him. His red eyes were dark, full of need even still. He cupped my cheek, his thumb stroking my skin. "I love you, Atreya," he rasped. "I know I messed up, but I'll do anything to make it right. Just please...please give me another chance."

He could have left. He had the Daylight ring in his possession. He let it go to prove that it didn't matter to him anymore. Not if it meant losing me.

He was sincere, I could see it in his eyes. He was sorry, really sorry.

"You have to earn back my trust, Ronan. That's going to take time."

He leaned in, his lips pressing against mine. "Lucky for you, I have nothing but time."

I would try, would try to move past what he did. I would try to trust him again, try to love him again. Because I knew that was what I wanted, knew that was what would make me happy.

So I would try. For him, for us, I would try.

CHAPTER 53

Ronan

I was hiding from Death.

Literally. Beams of sunlight cut through the library's high windows like divine execution orders, but I'd found my dark corner, settled in with a dusty tome about the War of the Gods. The candlelight flickered over the pages, casting dancing shadows that felt more like home than anywhere else in this gilded prison.

Then Eldra's shouting shattered my peace.

"Ronan!"

For fuck's sake.

His footsteps thundered between the shelves like war drums, and I barely had time to roll my eyes before he appeared, all righteous fury and protective rage. The book didn't stand a chance—he ripped it from my hands like I was holding his precious daughter instead of ancient history.

His face got right up in mine, close enough I could count the gold flecks in his iris. "You will leave," he snarled, breath hot against my skin. "You will leave these lands and never return."

I arched an eyebrow. "Why?"

"You know damn well why. Your job is done. Get out."

"No," I answered quietly, controlled, even though everything inside me wanted to tear this library apart. His accusations burned, but worse was the way he looked at me—like I was nothing but a monster who'd corrupted his perfect princess. If the fool only knew I'd been trying to protect her too, in my own fucked-up way.

His fangs flashed. "Tell me why. Was she just another conquest for your collection?"

I didn't miss how his nostrils flared, catching her scent all over me. Good. That's exactly why I hadn't bathed—let him smell the truth he didn't want to face.

"No!" The word exploded out of me, my careful control snapping like a bowstring. "I love her, you absolute fucking idiot!"

He sneered. "I've heard the stories about you, Ronan. Your games. Your toys."

"Not. With. Her."

"What then? Revenge against me?"

I couldn't help it—I laughed. "Maybe at first. But has it occurred to your thick skull that your daughter is impossible not to love? She's like a disease, but the kind you want to catch."

His hands found my throat faster than I could blink, lifting me off the ground like I weighed nothing. His grip was iron, and if I needed air to live, I'd be seriously screwed. My vision started going dark around the edges as I clawed at his wrists.

"She is not your plaything," he growled.

When he dropped me, I hit the floor hard, wheezing more from habit than necessity. I glared up at him, rubbing my throat. "You really suck at this, you know that?"

"At what?"

I waved a hand at his whole threatening stance. "This whole 'touch my daughter and die' routine. It's amateur hour." Gods only knew, it was not my first time pissing some girl's father off. This was just more annoying than anything else.

His eyes narrowed to slits. "Stay away from her, Ronan. I won't tell you again."

I surged to my feet, getting right in his face. "Fuck. That. If she tells me to go, I'm gone. But you?" I bared my own fangs. "You don't get to decide this."

A growl rumbled through his chest. "You'll regret crossing me."

I brushed off my clothes, lips twisting. "Already do."

"What was that?"

I flashed him my sweetest smile. "Nothing at all."

"Ronan—"

I held up my hands. "Not a thing."

"Get out."

I gave him a mock bow. "As you command. But just from the library."

I turned and walked away, leaving him to stew in his rage. The future was a mess of shadows and uncertainty, but one thing was crystal clear—I wasn't giving up. Not on her. Not ever.

Even if her father wanted to rip my heart out through my throat.

CHAPTER 54

Atreya

The training yard rang with the clash of steel against steel. I rolled my shoulders, watching Madsen run through her warm-up sequences. From their perch on the wooden benches, Gael and Hisen observed with matching expressions of careful neutrality, though I caught Hisen's slight lean forward when Madsen executed a particularly complex maneuver.

Emery stood beside me, silent as always, but I could feel her assessment of each move, each stance. She might not speak much, but her eyes missed nothing.

Madsen finished her sequence with a flourish that would have decapitated any opponent foolish enough to stand in her way. When she turned to me, there was a gleam in her eye that I recognized all too well.

"Care to dance, Your Majesty?" She twirled her practice sword with deceptive casualness. "Unless you're too busy with your... houseguest."

The slight pause before 'houseguest' carried enough venom to drop a horse. I pretended not to notice.

"Trying to goad me into a fight, Madsen?" I stepped into the practice ring, selecting a blade from the weapon rack. The familiar weight settled in my palm like an old friend. "You could just ask nicely."

"Where's the fun in that?" She settled into a fighting stance, and I noticed she'd positioned herself so the setting sun cast her shadow directly into my eyes. Clever. "Besides, thought you might need the practice. Can't imagine your vampire's much use for sparring."

I mirrored her stance, adjusting my grip. "You'd be surprised what vampires are good at."

Her first strike came fast and hard—no warm-up, no warning. Just the way I liked it. I parried, letting her momentum carry her past me, then pivoted for a counter-strike that she barely blocked.

"Careful," she grunted, already moving into her next attack. "People might start to think you're fond of him."

"People," I said, ducking under her blade, "might want to mind their own business."

The next few exchanges were wordless, just the sharp song of steel and the dance of footwork we both knew by heart. Madsen fought like she did everything else—direct, brutal, efficient. No flourishes, no wasted movement. Just pure, focused intent.

I caught Gael leaning forward from the corner of my eye, probably analyzing every move for political implications. Even here, in the training yard covered in dust and sweat, I couldn't escape the weight of the crown I hadn't even claimed yet.

Madsen's blade whistled past my ear, closer than comfort. "Getting distracted?" she taunted. "Or just rusty?"

I answered with a combination that forced her back three steps, her boots scraping against the packed earth. "Just warming up."

"Warming up?" Madsen spat, recovering her footing with practiced ease. "Like how your bloodsucker warms up his meals?"

The jab was meant to throw me off, but I channeled the flash of anger into my next strike. Our blades met with enough force to send vibrations up my arm. "You know, this obsession with my personal life is starting to seem less like duty and more like jealousy."

That hit its mark. Madsen's next series of attacks came faster, harder, her blade singing through the air with deadly precision. "Jealousy?" She laughed, but there was no humor in it. "Of what? Your pet monster?"

I parried her strikes, recognizing the pattern she used when emotion started overriding technique. "He has a name."

"A name?" Madsen's blade arced in a vicious overhead strike. "Names don't make monsters into men."

I caught her blade with mine, steel screaming against steel. Our faces were inches apart, both of us straining against the deadlock. "And prejudice doesn't make you right."

She broke away with a snarl, but I was ready for her next attack. The clash of our blades echoed across the yard, drawing a small crowd of onlookers. Guards, servants, courtiers—all pretending they weren't watching.

"Prejudice?" Madsen's next strike nearly took my knee. "I've seen what they do. What they are. You're being blind—"

"And you're being predictable." I caught her blade in a bind, twisted, and sent her weapon flying. It clattered against the packed earth, but Madsen was already moving.

She came in low, shoulder-first, catching me in the midsection. We both went down hard, practice swords forgotten as the fight devolved into something more primal. My back hit the ground, driving the air from my lungs, but muscle memory took over. I tucked my chin, brought my knee up, and rolled with the impact.

Dust clouded around us as we grappled. Madsen had size and raw strength on her side, but I'd learned long ago how to fight larger opponents. I snaked an arm around her neck, locked my ankles, and used her own weight as leverage.

"Enough!" Gael's voice cut through the haze of combat, but neither of us stopped. Madsen's elbow caught my ribs, and I responded by tightening my hold.

"ENOUGH!" Eldra's voice joined Gael's, a different kind of force.

The crack of magic split the air like thunder, forcing us apart. I rolled to my feet, tasting blood where I'd bit my lip. Madsen crouched a few yards away, chest heaving, murder in her eyes.

Eldra stood at the edge of the practice ring, power crackling around him like static before a storm. The crowd of onlookers suddenly found other places to be, scattering like leaves in a strong wind.

"If you two are quite finished acting like children," he said, his voice carrying that particular tone of disappointment that made me feel about five years old, "perhaps we could discuss this like civilized people?"

"Nothing to discuss," Madsen muttered, wiping blood from her split lip. She shot me a look that promised this wasn't over.

I straightened my tunic, trying to maintain some dignity despite being covered in dust and sporting what would definitely become an impressive collection of bruises. "Just a friendly sparring match."

"Friendly?" Eldra's eyebrow arched so high it nearly disappeared into his hairline. "Is that what we're calling attempted murder these days?"

Gael cleared his throat. "If I may, Your Grace—"

"You may not," Eldra cut him off, then turned to Madsen. "You are dismissed. And if I hear of any more 'accidents' involving axes and our guest, we will have a much less pleasant conversation."

Madsen's jaw clenched, but she gave a stiff bow and stalked off, pausing only to retrieve her practice sword. The way she gripped it made me glad it wasn't the real thing.

"As for you," Eldra continued, fixing me with that penetrating stare that seemed to see right through to my bones, "walk with me."

It wasn't a request. I fell into step beside him, feeling every one of Madsen's hits now that the adrenaline was wearing off. We walked in silence until we reached the castle's eastern ramparts, where the setting sun painted the stones in shades of gold and crimson.

"You know why she hates him so much," I said finally. It wasn't a question.

Eldra's hands rested on the stone battlements, his rings catching the dying light. "I do."

"And you're not going to tell me."

"It's not my story to tell." He turned to face me, and for a moment I saw the weight of centuries in his eyes. "But I will tell you this: her hatred isn't without cause. Just as your... affection for him isn't without merit."

I leaned against the wall, watching shadows lengthen across the courtyard below. "You don't approve."

"My approval stopped mattering the moment you became heir," he said, though his slight smile softened the words. "But since you mention it—no, I don't approve. Not because he's a vampire, though that certainly complicates matters."

"Then why?"

"Because loving him will make your path harder than it already is." Eldra's voice grew distant, as if speaking from memory. "Because choosing him means choosing sides in a conflict that's been brewing since before you were born. Because being queen means sometimes sacrificing what we want for what our people need."

"And what do our people need?" I asked, though I dreaded the answer.

"Unity. Stability." He gestured toward the castle below, where lights were beginning to flicker to life in windows. "Not a ruler who divides them further by taking a vampire as consort."

The word 'consort' hit me like one of Madsen's punches. "I haven't—we're not—"

"Not yet," Eldra agreed. "But you're on that path, whether you admit it or not. And others see it too. Why do you think Madsen's so desperate to drive him away? Why do you think Gael's suddenly so interested in your affairs?"

"Politics," I said bitterly. "It's always politics." I couldn't escape the Court, even after escaping Ramses.

"It's always politics," Eldra echoed. "Welcome to the crown, daughter."

CHAPTER 55

Ronan

Night came over New Solara in a blanket of silver light and the stars. The moon was a half-moon and bright enough to illuminate the whole night sky. I wanted to go out, to explore, even if just for a bit. But Eldra was literally everywhere. Every corner I turned, he or his friends were there, arms crossed.

With the freedom of the outdoors denied me, I turned my attention elsewhere. If I wasn't burried in Atreya, I was bored.

Call me petty, but I did enjoy the look on Eldra's face whenever I walked by him and he could smell her essence on me.

I chose to wander the castle halls. I strode through long expanses of hallways, memorizing every nook and cranny of the place. There was a long hallway that went from the throne room to a large balcony that overlooked a dragon pit. I was fairly certain this is where Atreya said she had found out about her mother.

I approached the balcony railing, peering into the depths below.

There was a single dragon in the pit, a magnificent creature with scales that shimmered like gold in the moonlight. Its body was long and muscular, its tail a powerful whip that thrummed against the stone floor. Its wingspan stretched the width of the pit, wings folded against its back like a cape of molten metal. It looked up as I appeared, its eyes locking onto me. For a moment, we just stared at each other, the only sound its low, rumbling breathing.

And then it snorted at me dismissively.

Had to be Eldra's dragon with an attitude like *that*.

Then, another dragon appeared, crawling up the side of the pit. I stepped back as it arched its neck up and over the balcony. It was massive, bigger than Siorsen even. Scales as black as night adorned it, each one etched with a faint, crimson glow like embers. Its eyes glowed a red just as deep as mine, piercing as it examined me. It lowered its head to the balcony and opened its mouth, rows of curved fangs gleaming like obsidian in the moonlight. Its hot breath washed over me, smelling of smoke and fire.

I had never been this close to a dragon. Never looked one in the eyes. It examined me, and I it.

I could feel its ancient power, its raw magic coursing through the air between us.

"Seraphix," I said.

The dragon careened his head closer. Sniffing me. His lips curled back into a snarl and he sneezed.

Oh right. I smell like Atreya. I should really rethink the whole not bathing after sex.

Seraphix snorted again, his hot breath ruffling my hair.

And then, he reached out with a clawed hand. His fingers brushed against my cheek, a surprisingly gentle touch. He sniffed at me again, his expression thoughtful. After a moment, he nodded to himself and turned away.

I watched as he padded back down into the pit, his massive body disappearing into the shadows. I let out a breath I hadn't realized I was holding.

I turned to leave, only to find Eldra standing behind me. His arms were crossed, a scowl on his face. "Well, well, well," he said, "Look at you, making friends."

I rolled my eyes. "Jealous?" I asked, sauntering past him.

"Be glad Seraphix didn't decide to kill you," he said.

"I don't think he was interested in killing me, Eldra," I said.

"That makes one of us," he muttered.

I sighed. "Is there a reason you've come to harrass me this time?"

"There's a problem in Ember," he said, his expression darkening. "Perhaps you can grace with your presence in the war room."

I raised an eyebrow at him. "A problem, you say? How ever did the people of Ember manage without me to solve their problems for them?" I said sarcastically.

Eldra just glowered at me, unamused. "This isn't a laughing matter. There's been...an incident. We need to discuss what to do about it."

I sighed, rolling my eyes. "Fine. Lead the way, oh fearless leader."

He gave me a look, but turned and strode away. I followed him, my mind already turning over what kind of 'incident' could have Eldra in such a mood that didn't have to do with me and his daughter.

We finally reached the war room, the large wooden table in the center covered in maps and papers. The rest of Eldra's council was already there, looking grim. There was a large, charred hole in the middle of the table, as if something had exploded. Or been burnt.

"Ah, good of you to finally join us," Madsen said dryly.

"Didn't realize my presence was required," I snapped dropping into the empty seat beside her. "So, what's this I hear about an incident?"

Eldra crossed his arms, his jaw clenched. "Eldra's hosting an arena event."

"What else is new?" I scoffed, rolling my eyes. I glanced around the table, meeting the gaze of each of the court members. Emery, Ameria, Madsen, Gael, and Hisen were all there in their prospective seats, their faces a mask of worry and anger. But Atreya wasn't.

"Why isn't she hear?" I asked, my brow furrowing. Ameria shifted uncomfortably, her fingers fiddling with the edge of the table. She had that scent to her again - the acrid tang of deception.

"We don't want to upset her more," Ameria replied.

Lying.

"What's happened?" I pressed, leaning forward.

Hisen spoke up then, "We have intel that Ramses is hosting a grand battle in the arena. He is calling it the Battle of The Bastards."

"What in the fresh hell does that mean?"

"It is no secret Ramses has many bastards. He is apparently putting them all against each other in the Arena. Against Vryseris. Vryseris is meant to eliminate all of them," Eldra said.

A chill ran down my spine as understanding dawned. Ramses, with his endless supply of illegitimate children, was using them as pawns in his twisted game. This was all meant to bring Atreya out of hiding—putting their son in an arena the same way he had done to her.

It was as if he were saying "Look at this well of offspring I have. May the best one win."

And it was ultimately my fault. Had I brought the boy along with us, he wouldn't be in this position in the first place. And Atreya would see it that way, and blame me too.

Any hope I had of obtaining her forgiveness was slipping through my fingers like sand in an hourglass.

"When?" I breathed.

"Tomorrow morning," Eldra answered, "We have to decide how to proceed."

She would never forgive me if anything happened to the boy. We couldn't wait until then. It took me three months on foot just to get Atreya here—with all the obstacles and towns on high alert. We had taken a detour through Dragons Teeth and went down the east coast.

It could probably take hours for Eldra to breach any barricades if he went through the Gulf of Ambrose.

"Well?" Eldra barked, slamming his hand on the table. "Do you have anything useful to add, or are you just going to sit there looking like a fish?"

I blinked, focusing back on the war room. Eldra was glaring at me, his face red with anger. The rest of the council was staring at me, waiting for me to say something. Anything.

"I..." I started, then trailed off. What was I supposed to say? I had no idea how to get Vryseris out of this. I had no idea how to fix this mess I had made. I had no idea how to make things right with Atreya now. All I could see was her face in my mind, her eyes when she found out what I had done. And I knew I couldn't blame her. I had ruined everything.

If they all left, it would leave New Solara vulnerable. If they told Atreya what was happening, she would be insistent on leaving and going to her son. Which is exactly what he would want.

There was only a few hours until morning. I had no way of combating the sun. How was I to get the boy out?

"I need some time to think," I finally said, rising from my chair. I had to get out of there, had to get away from their judging eyes. "I'll be back."

Eldra's face turned purple with rage. "You can't just walk out!" he roared. "This concerns you as much as the rest of us!"

But I was already walking away, the door slamming shut behind me.

"Coward!" I heard him yell.

Running away kept me alive over the centuries. And I was running, running right to the balcony overseeing the dragon pit. This had to be the craziest idea I could come up with.

"Seraphix!" I shouted into the darkness below.

In the pit of blackness, two red eyes opened slowly.

CHAPTER 56

Atreya

A crash resounded from outside, followed by the unmistakable roar of an enraged dragon. My heart skipped a beat as I feared the worst: Siorsen had finally come to wreak havoc upon us.

Then Emery and Madsen came barreling into my room. Krix was at their heels, nipping angrily at them. Emery named the Whisperfang for me. Apparently the name meant *crazy* in her tongue.

"You're still here," Madsen said dumbly.

I arched a brow. "Where else would I be?"

The pair exchanged a weighted glance. "Then who—" Emery began.

"She's the one riding Seraphix," Eldra panted, entering the room. He skidded to a halt at the sight of me standing there, very much present and accounted for.

"Who is riding Seraphix?" I asked, my mouth agape. Someone was riding my mother's dragon? They were either crazy or incredibly stupid.

Eldra straightened, shooing Krix away with a wave of his hand.

"Where's Ronan?" Madsen asked suddenly.

"I haven't seen him yet tonight," I blushed, avoiding Eldra's eyes.

"Eldra, you don't think—" Madsen started.

"Damn. Damn him to the Hells of Tespar," Eldra snarled.

"What's going on? Where is Ronan?"

Emery said something in her language and pointed behind me to the large window overlooking the city. I followed her gaze and saw the shadow of a dragon flying against the dark sky. It was Seraphix.

And on his back, a glint of silver.

Ronan.

CHAPTER 57

Ronan

I wonder if the height would kill me from up here. This had to be the dumbest thing I have ever done. And I have done many stupid things.

I could have transformed, used my own wings, but each time I did, I lost a piece of myself to the beast within. The transformations were taking their toll on my mind, leaving gaps in my memory, moments where the monster took control. Besides, even with wings of my own, I wasn't nearly as fast as a dragon. And speed was what I needed now.

Seraphix banked sharply to the left, and I had to fight to keep from being thrown off. He rose higher and higher into the night sky, where the world was awash with starlight and mists of clouds. I could see the world below me as I had never seen it before, a world of dark shadows and slow-moving clouds where the world twinkled with faelight and fire.

Seraphix was less than agreeable when I had called down to the pits. In fact, he ignored me. I had to jump, there was no other way. My stomach was in my mouth as I launched myself off the balcony, time seeming to slow as I sailed through the air. I landed with a thud on his back, the wind being knocked from my lungs. He fought me, crashing against the walls of the pits. I clung to him, my fingers digging into his scales as I prayed I wouldn't fall off.

"Vryseris is in trouble! I need to get there! To Ember!" I screamed into the wind. I don't know if the beast understood me, maybe he had, because he took to the sky then, not waiting for me to get a good grip on him. I had to wrap myself around him, my arms and legs clinging to him as he rose higher and higher.

The wind whipped through my hair, threatening to rip me from his back. I dug my fingers into his scaly hide, praying I didn't slip. The dragon leveled out, flying straight and true for Ember. I could see the glint of water in the distance, a river that wound its way through the heart of the mountains. In the distance I could see the sky slowly giving way to reds and orange, slowly brightening and eating away the darkness. My heart sank, I didn't have much time.

I was racing against death. I knew that. I was fighting the sun. It was hard not to look at—the world was waking up. It was like a God's eye was opening. The light crept up, searing into my eye. I had to squint, forcing myself to look at the rising sun. I could feel the heat of it on my skin, making my skin prickle with pain.

"Move your scaly ass, Seraphix!" I lean forward, practically plastered against him. The dragon roared, beating his wings harder. Seraphix banked again, and my stomach lurched. He was flying practically sideways, keeping the light from encasing me entirely.

"We aren't going to make it!" I screamed again.

At least Atreya would know that I tried. I had to push that thought aside. There was no time for that now. I had to keep going, no matter what. I had to save Vryseris.

"*We will make it*," came a thunderous voice that cracked from the back of my head, making me jump in surprise.

"Did you just talk?" I asked in disbelief.

"*Shut up and hang on!*" Seraphix's mental voice is pure steel, and I don't get time to process the fact that I'm having a conversation with a fucking dragon.

He drops. Just like that—nose down, straight toward the earth like a stone. My stomach relocates somewhere near my throat, and I'm clinging to those obsidian scales like they're the only thing between me and meeting my ancestors. Which, let's be honest, they are.

"We aren't in Ember!" I scream as mountain peaks rush up to greet us like stone daggers. This is it—this is how I die. Not by sun, not by blade, but by becoming a vampire pancake on some godforsaken mountain.

"*Dragons.*" He rumbles through my mind again. "*They can sense other dragons. This is as far as I go.*"

We punch through a layer of clouds, and suddenly there it is—Ember, spread out below us like a child's toy set. The castle walls rise up, the town cowering within them. Hope flutters in my chest like a caged bird.

"*Jump!*" The command booms through my head.

I stare at the river below, a silver ribbon cutting through the land. "Are you out of your fucking mind?"

We're high enough that hitting water will feel about the same as hitting concrete. I've survived a lot of shit, but this? This is new territory.

"*Now!*" Seraphix roars.

"Fuck no!"

The bastard doesn't wait for further argument. He barrel rolls, and suddenly I'm free-falling through empty air, the river rushing up to meet me. Time stretches like taffy, giving me just enough space to think *well, this is going to hurt* before I slam into the water. Breathing in water had always burned my lungs. I was underwater, the pressure making my ears ache. I kicked, forcing myself to the surface. I broke through, gasping for air.

I looked around, getting my bearings. I was in a river, the water cold and fast-moving. I could see Ember rising up from the bank, the castle walls looming above. I kicked, forcing myself to the shore. I dragged myself out of the water, collapsing onto the grass. I lay there for a moment. Light slowly crept over the land. I had to move quickly.

I forced myself up to the wall, tentatively touching it with my hands. There were no new wards put in place. I dug my claws into the sides and climbed to the nearest archway, before swinging my legs over and landing on the other side. I knelt low, using some bushes as camouflage as I listened. I tilted my head. I could hear four heart beats nearest to me. I'd have to do this quick.

An Ember soldier—part of the Brotherhood, marched by me, stopping at the wall and turning back, pacing in the same pattern. When he came back the next time I pounced, my claws out. I landed on his back, wrapping my arms around his throat. He let out a shocked cry as I dug my claws into his skin. He tried to fight me off, but I held tight, my grip like a vice. He fell to the ground, me on top of him. I squeezed, my claws digging deeper. He tried to scream, but I had cut off his air. He flailed under me, but I held fast. He slowly went limp under me, and I let him drop, panting. I lowered my mouth over his spurting blood and drank as much as I could.

This one was a regular Fae. No affinity to any particular magic. Damn, how unlucky.

I had to move fast. I had to get to Vryseris before the sun rose. I could feel it getting closer, the light creeping over the land. I could see the shadows slowly getting shorter. I'd need to navigate to the arena. There are underground tunnels from the courtyard that lead right to the arena. I stripped the soldier of his gear, pulling on the armor clumsily.

I didn't have time to make sure it was properly fastened.

I pulled on his helm, the visor obscuring my face. I had to hope it would be enough.

I kept low, staying close to the walls as I moved. I could hear the sound of voices, growing louder. I peered around a corner, my heart pounding the new blood in my chest. The courtyard was filled with soldiers, all of them in the Brotherhood's colors. I could see the entrance to the tunnels, but there was no way I could get there without being seen. I was trapped. Either I go through as is, or I don't go through at all.

"Shit," I muttered under my breath.

I stood straight, shoulders back. I walked through the throng of soldiers as if I belonged there, mimicking their movements. I had to blend in, just for a minute. I kept my gaze down, fixed on the cobblestones beneath my feet. I could hear the sound of metal singing, the shouts of commanders as they barked orders.

The tunnels were just ahead, a dark mouth in the side of a hill. I could see soldiers marching down into the darkness, their torches flickering like fireflies as they descended.

Suddenly, a hand clamped down on my shoulder, spinning me around. I found myself staring up at a towering figure, a Fae with skin and hair as white as snow. He was a commander, I could tell by the insignia on his shoulder. His eyes narrowed, boring into mine.

"You," he growled, "What is your name and rank?" I froze, my mind going blank. I didn't have a name, didn't have a rank. "Well?" he asked impatiently. I lifted the visor revealing my eyes.

"I am here to see Vryseris before he goes into the arena. You will grant me access." I felt the magic behind my eyes to compel him. His violet eyes glazed over.

The commander's face went slack, his mouth falling open. "Of course," he muttered, releasing my shoulder. "You may pass."

"Thank you," I said, turning to make my way to the tunnels.

I could hear his confused mutterings behind me, but I didn't look back.

I strode down into the darkness—the tunnels were narrow and winding, lit only by flickering torches. Once, long ago, Atreya had been dragged through these very tunnels naked and screaming.

The tunnels finally spat me out into a larger area. There were redheads of all ages lined against the wall. From man to boy. Ramses' bastard children. There were other soldiers standing on either side of the door.

There was no sign of Vryseris.

Twins, no older than Vryseris himself, were cowering in the corner. They were shaking, their eyes wide with fear as they gawked at me.

I turned to one of the soldiers standing guard. "Where is the Prince?" I demanded.

He looked me up and down before answering. "He will be coming down the eastern tunnels," he said.

I nodded, turning to make my way to the eastern tunnels. I could hear the sound of footsteps echoing down the corridor, growing louder with each passing moment.

Suddenly, Vryseris appeared at the end of the corridor. He was flanked by three soldiers, their hands resting on the hilts of their swords. Vryseris himself looked unharmed, but there was a look of defiance in his eyes.

I focused on one of the soldiers. "You are not in charge of escorting the prisoner to the arena," I compelled.

The soldier looked confused, his brow furrowing. He looked at his companions before back at me. "But...I was told I was in charge of the escort," he said.

I just stared at him, my magic swirling in my eyes. "You are not in charge of escorting the prisoner to the arena," I repeated.

He looked at his companions before back at me. "I am not in charge of escorting the prisoner to the arena," he agreed. The other two stiffened but said nothing, turning to leave.

I nodded, turning to Vryseris. "Let's go," I said.

Vryseris' gaze locked onto mine, confusion etched into his features. Once the soldiers were out of sight, I lifted my helm, revealing my face.

His golden eyes flashed with recognition, lips curling into a snarl. "You!" he spat, lunging at me. Dark shadows swirled around him, like living tendrils of his rage.

"Yeah, me," I replied, sidestepping his attack. "We can do without the dramatics, kid. We have to go. Now."

His face twisted. "What did you do with my mother?" he seethed, the words dripping with venom. I could feel the press of his shadows, like a thousand knives pricking at my skin.

"She's safe," I assured him. "I'm here to bring you to her."

Vryseris took a step closer, his hands curling into fists at his sides. His shadows swirled around him, taking on a life of their own. "Prove it," he spat. "Prove my mother is safe."

"There's no time for this," I snapped, trying to cut through his anger. "Ramses is intent on making you suffer to bring her out of hiding. Don't you understand? We have to go!"

"You're the vampire father said took her," he accused, shaking his head in disgust.

"Listen to me," I urged. "Ramses is trying to use you. If you step into that arena, you will be changed forever."

"Father said it was to be the Battle of the Bastards," he said firmly. "That there are people outside of Ember who would question my rightful place as heir. I have to go out there."

"You will go out there and kill your brothers and sisters for a title?" I asked, incredulous. "Has your mother taught you nothing?"

"I won't kill them," he said, conviction in his voice. "I'll refuse. Just as my mother would have done." The shadows around him receded as he spoke, his rage giving way to determination.

"Don't you have the gift of foresight?" I pressed. "Don't you know how this ends?"

"I don't just see things on a whim!" he shot back, his anger returning.

I leaned down close to him, meeting his gaze. "If you go out there in that arena, you will be forced to kill," I warned. "Do not think otherwise. We have to leave, Vrys."

"I can reason with my father," he said, full of a naive belief. And with that, he shoved by me and started towards the arena.

I grabbed his arm, spinning him back to face me. "I will kill them for you," I offered, desperation creeping into my words. "So you don't have to. If it comes to that."

"You will do no such thing!" he growled, yanking his arm from my grasp.

"I can," I said, "And I will, if it comes to that. I won't let you be forced into that. Not if I have anything to say about it."

He was quiet, contemplative, his gaze searching mine. And for a moment, I saw something there, a glimmer of trust. But then it was gone, replaced by stubborn pride.

"I won't let them question my right to the throne," he hissed. "I will go out there, and I will show them all what I am without hurting them."

My heart sank, a cold dread spreading through my chest. I had failed. I had failed, and now Vryseris would be forced to fight for his life. With a surge of desperation, I slammed him up against the wall, hoping to compel him. "You will leave this place with me and you won't put up a fight."

But my magic didn't work on him. He just glowered back at me, his golden eyes burning with defiance. He was too strong, his will too fierce. My compulsion slid off him like water.

He shoved me off him, his chest heaving with ragged breaths. "I won't be swayed," he growled. "I will do what is right."

Suddenly, Seraphix echoed in my head. *"You didn't fail,"* Seraphix rumbled. *"He needs to see this through. But you can't stay here. It isn't safe."*

I looked around, realizing he was right. I was still in the tunnels beneath the arena. If I was discovered now, everything could be lost. But if I didn't go back with Vrys, all would be lost anyway.

I really fucking hate how empathetic I'd become.

So I followed after him, knowing full well the sun was now out.

CHAPTER 58

Atreya

I had dreamt of Vryseris in the middle of a sea of red. Red-haired people were everywhere, holding knives and swords. I remember that dream clear as day.

Eldra's gaze flickered from the gaping hole in the ceiling to me, a mixture of surprise and wariness etched into his features.

My hand closed around the hilt of the silver knife I'd snatched from the tray of food he'd brought me earlier. The blade glinted in the dim light as I aimed for his head. He caught it deftly, his fingers wrapping around my wrist in a vice-like grip. In the same fluid movement, he brought his other hand up to block my fist as it came sailing for his face, my knuckles barely missing his nose.

Madsen and Emery closed in from either side, but Eldra pulled them back with a glare.

"Leave us," he said.

"But—" Madsen started.

"Now."

Emery's green skin shimmered with a cold, hard light. She said something to him in Arathi and he dipped his head. She nodded at the door and Madsen backed away. Once they were both out of sight he turned back to me.

"Really, Atreya, that was unnecessary," he chided, his tone laced with a hint of exasperation.

"When were you planning on telling me that my son was to be sent into that hell hole?" I snarled, my chest heaving with barely restrained fury. My fist still hovered an inch from his nose, trembling with the urge to connect.

"Right now. I swear it," he promised, his eyes locked on mine, filled with a sincerity I didn't believe for a second.

"You told Ronan before telling me—" My words cracked, a painful laugh bubbling up my throat.

"And the bastard ran off like the coward he is," Eldra snapped back, his mask slipping for a moment. I sent a jolt of lightning through his body and he sighed, his shoulders sagging in exasperation.

Oh, right. I can't hurt him with his own magic. That little tidbit I'd forgotten in my rage.

So instead I took my knee and brought it up between his thighs. My knee met with metal and I stumbled back, a pained cry tearing from my lips. "Son of a—"

"That's Madsen's favorite trick," he said. "I've learned my lesson fighting with women."

"Why didn't you offer Vrys the same invitation? Why would you send for me and not him?" I demanded, my hands shaking with barely restrained violence.

He stiffened, his gaze darting away from mine. I watched his throat's apple bob up and down as he swallowed hard.

"I was worried you didn't see things my way," he finally admitted, barely above a whisper.

"What the hell does that mean!" I exploded, my patience snapping like a brittle twig.

"I share no love for Ramses. That is no secret, Atreya, and I won't pretend so," he said, so quietly.

"What does that have to do with Vryseris?" I pressed, my heart pounding in my chest.

He looked away from me, his jaw clenched tight. "I thought it best you come without him. That you would be persuaded to our cause with the right words. With the promise to protect your son should I invade. To secure his future."

I gaped at him, my mind reeling. "This was before I found out he was my grandson."

"You said you thought I was your daughter that night in the Great Wood! You must have thought Vryseris was your grandson!" I accused, my pitch rising to a shout.

I watched his face harden, his features etching into a mask of guilt and regret. "You knew then. And you still left Vrys behind," I hissed, my vision blurring with tears. "Knowing there could be outsiders that would kill him for being Ramses' son!"

He shook his head, his eyes pleading for understanding. "Vryseris is the heir to the Blackwater name. I was wrong for leaving him behind, but you have to know that I never would have—"

"My son is good and kind and everything that Ramses is not," I cut in, "He has never drawn blood from another person. And I cleaved your love's head from her body and you welcome me with open arms." I got to the floor, crawling toward him, feeling this overwhelming, feral need to rip him apart. "It's different," Eldra said, barely audible.

I cocked my head at him, a harsh laugh tearing from my lips. "Ramses has a well of children he sired. Should anything happen to Vrys, he would name a new heir—reluctantly so, but he would. You think Ramses cares for his children? He cares for power."

I reached out, grabbing his wrist in a vice-like grip. My fingers dug into his skin and he winced but I didn't care. "I spent my whole life wondering what you would be like. Wondering If you had been a good man. Wondering if you would be disappointed in me for all the things I had done and for all the things I will eventually do... To come to this moment and be so utterly fucking disappointed in you." I shook my head, tears streaming down my face. "Atreya—"

"No. Listen," I cut in, "Ramses brought Aislinn back with me in her womb. He imprisoned her, and raised me up, to have me kill her again, and then made me his *wife*. To bear his children. And in all that time I defied him where I could. He made me hate you. He took everything from me. Took everything I had to give, because of you. Did you think we were going to be a happy family after this? Did you think I would call you father and weep with joy? Even still, Ramses punishes me because of you."

I let go of his hand and stood, my legs trembling beneath me. "I was afraid," he admitted softly. "Afraid you would choose him over me."

I let out a laugh, the sound bitter and harsh. "Choose Ramses? You think I would ever choose that monster?" I spat, my lip curling up in a snarl.

"I know I was wrong," he said, pushing himself to his feet. "I will do whatever it takes to make it right."

I shook my head, tears streaming down my face. "You can't fix this. You can't fix *us*."

"Atreya—" he started, his hand outstretched.

"No! I don't want to hear it. I don't want your empty promises or your lies."

Eldra took a step towards me, but I held up a hand, stopping him. "You lost the right to call me daughter when you chose to deceive me." As soon as Vrys and I were together again, I was getting far the fuck away from him and his city. "Now, Why did Ronan take Seraphix?"

Eldra's whole demeanor changed. He was distant and closed off, his mask firmly back in place. "When we told him what happened with Vrys, he ran off. He's gone, to save his own hide. Vampires are nothing more than self-serving."

"Sounds familiar," I said quietly, my heart heavy in my chest.

Ronan left. he left me. He left me when I needed him the most. I felt a pang of betrayal and anger. "He left?" I repeated, "He left me?"

Eldra nodded, his gaze locked on mine. "Yes, Atreya. He's gone. He won't be coming back."

I couldn't believe it. I couldn't believe that he would do this to me. I couldn't believe that he would leave me to deal with all of this on my own.

I looked out the window, to the sun rising above the sea. The Battle of the Bastards would be beginning soon. I was too late. My heart felt heavy in my chest, a sense of dread washing over me. I was alone. Truly alone for the first time in my life. And I had no idea how to keep my son and myself alive.

CHAPTER 59

Atreya

The sun taunted me from its perch in the sky, a blazing orb that wanted to drain the hope from my veins. I'd never reach Ember in time, not without a miracle—and Eldra and his court were adamant that Ramses was orchestrating this to flush me from the shadows. The Arena, that crucible of fire and blood that had once forged me into a warrior, would now be the stage for the ultimate horror: witnessing my son's demise, either by the sword or the merciless fate of forcing him to fight for survival.

Memories flooded my mind, making my heart ache. I was a trapped mouse again, waiting anxiously in my room in Ember for Vrys to return from his first outing on dragonback. Then, as now, I felt powerless. Not even the damned mirror worked to show me what was happening.

The door creaked open, and Ameria entered. She wore a plain night-gown, her eyes fixed on the hole in the ceiling I had made in my rage. "We can have that fixed for you," she said softly.

"I don't care if you do," I muttered, not looking at her.

A silence stretched between us, heavy with unspoken thoughts, before she perched on the bed's edge. Her hands were clasped tightly in her lap, knuckles white with tension. "Vryseris will be okay," she said, trying to sound confident.

"You don't know that," I snapped, my fear boiling over.

"Hisen says Ronan is there," she replied.

My head whipped to her. "What?" I demanded, my heart pounding.

"The whispers... Now that the shield is down, the whispers are much louder. He is in the dining room meditating right now," she explained.

I grabbed her by the arm, my grip tight. "Show me. Bring me to him." Ameria nodded, though fear flickered in her eyes. I took a moment to look her over.

Ameria possessed a gentle sort of beauty, the kind that crept up on you. Her skin was dotted with a constellation of freckles across the bridge of her nose. Green eyes and auburn hair. Not the fiery red of a Blackwater, but enough to trigger me. She was tall, well-fed, not thin or willowy like many of my kind.

She moved away from my grasp and waved her hand toward the door. "This way."

We found the dining room vast and empty, the long wooden table gleaming in the soft light. At its head, Hisen sat cross-legged on the floor, his eyes closed. Dozens of candles flickered about him, casting eerie shadows. The whispers seemed to emanate from him, a pulsing cloud of sound that made my skin prickle.

I approached him slowly, not wanting to break his concentration. But as I drew near, his eyes snapped open. "Where is he?" I demanded.

"Who?" he asked, sounding serene.

"My son. Ronan. Where are they?"

Hisen cocked his head at me, the whites of his eyes flashing.

"Ronan is there. Vryseris is in the arena. That is all I know," he replied.

"Ask them! Ask the dead or whatever it is you do!" I exclaimed, desperation clawing at me.

"It is not that simple. Believe me, I am trying," he said with a quiet urgency.

"Please. Please," I begged, my throat tight.

The candle flames went out in a wave. Hisen inhaled sharply.

"What? What is it?" I cried.

Hisen slowly craned his neck up to look at me. "The Battle of the Bastards has begun."

CHAPTER 60

Ronan

Vryseris was already called out into the arena. I was left behind in the chamber, looking over everyone. Dozens of red-haired bastards lined the stone walls, their gazes a heavy weight upon me. The air was thick with the tang of sweat, rust, and something sharper—fear. Even the two soldiers guarding the room stare, their faces a mask of expectation. For a moment, my heart raced—had my ruse been discovered? But then one of the soldiers spoke with a gruff bark.

"Pick the first one to send out to the Prince."

I glanced at them, my mouth gone dry. "Why me?"

The soldiers exchanged a look, a flicker of uncertainty. "Were you not in charge of overseeing the Prince's arrival? Then you should pick the first."

A cold dread spread through my veins. The oldest of the redheads looked like a battle-hardened warrior—tall, with a fiery beard and calloused hands bearing the scars of countless battles. His black robes clung to him, stained with sweat and smoke, the acrid scent of hot metal hanging over him like a dark cloud. A blacksmith, I realized with a jolt. He likely forged the very weapons the soldiers now grasped. Atreya would have my head if I sent a grown man in to fight her child.

"I'll go," a small voice piped up. I turned to see one of the twins I'd noticed earlier, huddled in the corner. They couldn't have been more than a year or two older than Vrys.

"What's your name, boy?"

"Chansie," he replied, his narrow chest puffing out with bravado. "This is my brother, Veren." He stepped aside, revealing Veren cowering behind him, reeking of fear and fresh urine.

"Why do you want to go first?" I pressed, though a sinking feeling had already taken hold in my gut. He glanced at the Blacksmith and then at his brother.

"The Prince is my friend," he shrugged. "We could never hurt each other."

A wave of nausea washed over me, the stone beneath me growing slick with sweat. Because in a moment, I would be sending this innocent child into the arena, clinging to the desperate hope that his words were true. I nodded my head to him, then to the door. "You're up."

Veren jumped from his corner. "Chansie, don't!"

Chansie shrugged him off. "It's better for all of us that I go. I have the king's favor, and Vrys is my best friend." He pulled out a long obsidian knife from his trouser pocket. "See? The king gave me this Veren. He is proud of me as well."

The older redhead – the blacksmith – scoffed. "I've been given many knives like that one boy. Don't fool yourself into thinking that you are special."

Chansie's face fell, but he recovered quickly. "I still have Vrys' favor. And I have Veren. You have no one." He raised his chin, a fierce light burning in his eyes. "I will make sure Vrys knows how you spoke to me."

"And when you do, let him know that Baron the Blacksmith sends his regards, little brother," the Blacksmith added.

I gestured to the soldiers and back to Chansie. "Take him."

The soldiers moved swiftly, their hands closing around Chansie's thin arms as they dragged him towards the door. His brother let out a strangled cry, but Chansie himself was silent, his eyes fixed on mine until he vanished through the doors. Light spilled in and I pushed myself against the wall, avoiding its harsh glare.

I turned back to the remaining redheads. The blacksmith was watching me, a calculating glint in his eye.

"You should have sent me," Baron said gruffly. "You just sent a boy to his death."

Yes, I thought, my stomach churning with the weight of my choice. May Naris forgive me.

I turned to one of the soldiers, willing him to meet my gaze. I needed to exert my influence without alerting his companion. "We should check the tunnel again," I suggested, "Ensure it's secure."

The soldier blinked and nodded slowly. His comrade remained unconcerned and focused elsewhere. "Make it quick," he called after us. The King wants all positions manned."

I led the soldier back down the tunnel, past empty prison cells. Once we were isolated, I spun on him, shoving him into a cell before sinking my teeth into his throat. I swallowed the gushing blood quickly, acutely aware that every drop strengthened me against the sun's lethal touch.

When I was finished I placed his drained body at the furthest part of the wall and buried it with hay. I slipped back out into the corridor, blood now coursing warmly through my veins. I wiped my mouth with the back of my hand.

But then a swing of red hair stopped me. Perched on the opposite wall was a female, her arms crossed over her chest as she watched me.

I bared my teeth at her, recognizing her as the one they called Corina.

"Ronan," she greeted me with a nod. She was wearing the same armor and leather as the guards. "It seems we both had the same idea."

"And what was that?"

"Breaking Vrys out of this mess and getting the hell out of Ember."

I looked her over. "Is that what this outfit is about?"

She snorted. "You're one to talk. Have you ever fitted yourself into armor before? Looks sloppy."

I narrowed my eyes at her. "And how were you planning on getting him out of here?"

"I haven't thought that far ahead yet," she admitted. "You?"

"I was going to let Vrys try to appeal with his father first."

"Gods, you have no plan do you? How did you even get here?"

"Dragonback."

"What dragon?"

"Seraphix."

Her mouth opened slightly. She shook her head. "She isn't here is she?"

"By she, I assume you mean Atreya? She isn't here."

Corina moved off the wall and grabbed my hand, I almost pulled away before she put something in my hand. It was a small, gold pin of a dragon. "You tell her never come back to this place. No matter what. No matter what she hears, she has to stay away."

I held up the pin in my hand. "What is this?"

"Tell her I know about Aislinn. Tell her I'm sorry. Just—keep them safe. Please. Just keep them away from here." She was pulling away now.

"Come with us and tell her yourself," I said, trying to hand the pin back to her. She shook her head.

"I only meant to bring Vrys beyond the wall. I have to stay. Please. Trust me. Please. I have to stay here."

"But—"

Trumpets blared.

"You have to go Ronan. Now. Remember what I said." Then she turned away and was gone. I looked down at the pin in my hand. I placed it in my pocket and made my way back to the open space where the others were.

The soldier eyed me when I came back out into the main space. "Where's Pan?"

"Who?"

"The one you were with."

"Oh. He needed to relieve himself." I gestured down the corridor. "Told him to go ahead."

He groaned. "I told him I had to go over an hour ago. He was the one saying I had to wait."

"If you want to go too, I can stay."

The soldier hesitated, clearly torn. "I shouldn't leave my post."

I shrugged. "Suit yourself. But if you end up pissing yourself in front of the King, don't say I didn't warn you."

He muttered under his breath, but eventually stomped off down the tunnel. I watched him go. This was it—my one chance to get the others out of here.

I spun back to the remaining redheads. "Baron, come here."

The blacksmith raised an eyebrow, but he obeyed, his movements stiff. I jerked my head towards the tunnel. "I need you to take care of the soldier."

"What?"

"I heard what you said. You're right. You want to stop this? Then you need to help me help them." I jerked my chin toward the cowering redheads. "You have a choice."

Baron stared at me, his face unreadable. For a moment, I thought I'd misjudged him entirely. But then he gave a curt nod. "I'll take care of him."

"Remember, you have a choice," I repeated. He nodded again, his jaw clenched. I watched as he disappeared down the corridor, his broad form fading into the shadows.

Poor fucker will be dead if they find out.

Trumpets flared and the Master of Ceremonies made his announcements. I placed my hand on the latch of the door, peering through the cracks of the wood to look out onto the arena.

Vryseris was standing next to Chancie, holding his hand, shoulders thrown back. In the viewing box was Ramses, looking down upon their joined hands with distaste.

The King's called out, "Let the first trial begin! Prince Vryseris, choose your weapon."

I peered through the crack in the door, blood pounding in my ears. Vrys stood tall, his small hand still clasped around Chansie's. He looked up at the King, his face set in a determination.

"I don't need a weapon," he called back, ringing out across the silent arena. "We will not fight."

A murmur ran through the crowd, a ripple of surprise and amusement. The King's face turned red with rage.

"Foolish boy," he spat. "You think you can defy me. You will fight."

Vrys' chin quivered, but he forced his shoulders back. "I won't fight Chansie," he declared.

The King's face reddened. "Guards, bring him a sword!"

Two hulking men stomped into the arena, a small sword clutched between them. Vrys glared down at the glinting blade, then lifted defiant eyes to the King.

"I won't use it," he spat.

His gaze flicked to Chansie, then back to the King. "I won't fight my friend," he repeated, "And I won't use a sword."

The crowd erupted into cheers and jeers, a cacophony of noise filling the arena. The King's gold eyes narrowed, and his hands clenched into fists at his sides.

"Enough of this," he snarled. He turned his venomous gaze on Chansie. "You, boy, you will fight."

Chansie shrank under the King's glare, his eyes darting pleadingly to Vrys. But Vrys just shook his head, his jaw set in a determined line. "I won't fight you, Chansie," he said. "We're friends."

Ramses stood up then, his black cape billowing in the wind. "I am Ramses Blackwater, King of Ember. On this day I have gathered those I have sired. Only the strong survive. You will fight, or I will have soldiers come in and fight you."

Vrys remained silent, his lip curling up in a scornful sneer.

Ramses snarled, "Have it your way." A few well-seasoned guards spilled into the arena, larger than ones I had seen.

The guards moved swiftly, their weapons glinting in the sunlight. Vrys and Chansie stood frozen.

"Father. Stop this," Vryseris pleaded.

The first guard lunged at Vrys, his sword flashing towards the boy's chest. But Vrys was quick, dodging to the side just in time. The sword struck the ground with a loud clang, sending sparks flying.

Chansie took advantage of the guard's momentary stumble. He darted forward, his obsidian knife glinting in his hand. He struck at the guard's leg, the blade sinking into the man's thigh with a sickening squelch.

The guard howled in pain, clutching at his leg. Vrys took advantage of the distraction, picking up the sword the guard had dropped. He held it awkwardly, his smaller hand trembling on the hilt. I could tell the boy had never drawn blood from another person before.

The second guard charged at Chansie, his sword raised high. But Chansie was ready. He ducked under the guard's blow, then struck upwards with his knife. The blade sank into the guard's stomach, and the man fell to the ground with a groan, his hands clutching at his belly.

Vrys and Chansie stood panting, their weapons still clutched in their hands. They looked at each other, then back at the fallen guards.

The crowd was on its feet, cheering and chanting their names. Ramses sat in stunned silence, his face twisted with rage and disappointment.

But the battle was far from over. More guards poured into the arena, their weapons at the ready. Vrys and Chansie stood back-to-back, their eyes scanning the approaching horde.

They knew they couldn't hold out for much longer. They were tired and outnumbered, and the guards were getting angrier by the minute.

"Stop!" Ramses bellowed, slamming his fist on the armrest of his throne. The crowd went silent, and Vrys and Chansie froze, their chests heaving with exertion.

"Bring me out the other one," Ramses snarled, his eyes fixed on the doorway. "The twin. Veren."

"No!" Chansie shouted, his eyes wide with horror. "You can't make him fight!"

Fuck.

Then the guards were making their way back towards my door. I looked over at Veren, cowering in the corner, tears streaming down his face.

"I don't want to go," he whispered, pleading with me.

"I know. I know."

Then Baron was beside me. "This won't end well."

I nodded. "Get the others out of here. If you can manage. Leave Ember."

The door exploded open, its loud bang echoing through the chamber. Blinding light poured in, forcing me to shield my eyes. Veren's strangled cry cut through the air as the guards stormed in, their heavy boots clomping against the stone floor. They descended upon him, their calloused hands closing around his thin arms like vices. Veren kicked and screamed, his small body thrashing wildly as they dragged him towards the door.

Vryseris was crying now.

"Men don't cry," Ramses sneered. "Take pride in what must be done."

I was paralyzed with horror, unable to tear my gaze away from the scene unfolding before me. Vrys and Chansie stood frozen in the arena, their eyes fixed on the doorway as Veren was thrown into the sunlight. Chansie took a step forward, his face contorted with anguish. "Veren, no!" he screamed, but Vrys caught his arm, holding him back.

Then Vrys' eyes met mine. In an instant, they transformed, the bright blue deepening to a murky indigo. Tendrils of shadow crept out from the irises, spreading like dark veins across the whites. A jolt of fear ran through me as Vrys began to shift, his limbs elongating and morphing. His skin itched and rippled, fur bursting forth from his pores. The arena fell silent, all eyes fixed on the monstrous creature Vrys was becoming.

His face stretched into a snout, his teeth sharpening into razor-sharp fangs. His arms transformed into powerful forelegs, ending in curved claws. A black mane erupted from his neck, cascading down his back like a river of obsidian. Vrys let out a deafening roar, the sound vibrating through the air. I gaped at him, my mind struggling to comprehend what I was seeing.

Vrys was a lion.

Like Aislinn Furian had been.

Vrys lunged at the guards, his claws swiping through the air.

The guards froze in terror, their weapons trembling in their hands. Vrys tore through them like paper, his claws ripping through armor and flesh with ease. The arena erupted into chaos, the crowd screaming and scattering in all directions. Ramses leapt from his throne.

"Stop him!" he bellowed, pointing a shaking finger at Vrys.

He tore through their ranks, his jaws snapping shut around a guard's throat. The man let out a strangled gurgle before collapsing to the ground, his body twitching feebly. Vrys turned his attention to the next guard, his claws swiping across the man's chest. The guard stumbled back, his armor dented and bloody, before falling to his knees.

The arena fell silent, the only sound the heavy panting of the lion. Vrys stood in the center of the arena, his chest heaving with exertion. His eyes scanned the crowd, his gaze lingering on Ramses before moving on.

"Chansie, fight!" Ramses bellowed, "Or I'll have the guards kill your brother!"

Chansie's gaze darted to Veren, huddled in the corner. Veren's eyes were wide with terror, his breath coming in short gasps. Chansie's hand trembled as he raised his obsidian knife. With a burst of desperation, he launched himself at Vrys. Vrys' eyes went wide, and he leapt to the side, barely avoiding Chansie's slashing blade.

"Vrys, no!" Chansie screamed, tears streaming down his face. "I've had Veren my whole life. He is my brother!" He charged at Vrys again, his knife raised high.

Vrys lunged back, his jaws snapping shut just inches from Chansie's face. Chansie ducked to the side, then struck out with his knife. The blade sank into Vrys' shoulder, and the lion let out a pained roar.

Vrys spun around, his claws swiping wildly. Chansie dodged and weaved, avoiding the blows by mere inches. But then Veren was there, trying to intervene. "Stop! Please, stop!" he cried, throwing himself between Chansie and Vrys.

But it was too late. Vrys' claws swiped across Veren's face, and the boy let out a strangled cry. He fell to the ground, clutching at his mauled face. Chansie's eyes widened in horror, and then a wave of rage washed over him.

His magic surged to the surface, icy cold and burning with fury. The arena began to chill, the air growing frosty and bitter. Ice crept along the sands, spreading like a dark stain. Vrys stumbled back, his eyes fixed on Chansie in shock.

Chansie's gaze met his, and for a moment, they just stared at each other. Then Chansie was moving, his knife flashing in the sunlight.

Vrys morphed back into his fae body, his claws retracting.

"Wait!" he cried, but Chansie ignored him. He struck out with the knife, and Vrys staggered back, a line of red forming on his chest.

Veren had gone quiet.

I needed to get out there—sunlight be damned.

I darted out of the arena, the sun blazing its heat on my exposed skin. "Vrys!" I shouted.

Chansie jumped on him. They were wrestling for the knife.

"Ronan!" I heard my name. Heard my master's voice and almost halted. I felt his proximity, his call working over me to bring me to his side.

No no no no no. I have to get to Vrys. Please. Let me get to—

The smell of blood filled my nose, and I stumbled, falling on my knees.

"Ronan! Come!" Xaneth called, and I looked up to see him in his ghastly yellow robes, black eyes boring into me. My skin began to smoke and burn. I couldn't move, couldn't even feel my limbs as Xaneth's call took over me.

Chansie was on top of Vrys, his body going limp. Vrys rolled him off, holding the bloody knife in his hand, his face a mask of shock and horror. Chansie was dead.

"Vrys!" I screamed, reaching for him with the only strength I had left.

"Chansie?" Veren whimpered, clutching his mutilated face. "Chans?"

Veren limped his way to his fallen brother, just as Vrys got to his feet. "I didn't mean to!"

Veren knelt over Chansie's body, his fingers brushing over his nose, his cheek, then to the blooming red of his tunic. "Chansie? Chansie?

Chansie!" He screamed and then the sands around us exploded. The sands swirled and lifted in the air, whipping about us. The air became unbearably hot, and I knew I was dying.

The sands melted into shards of glass and formed a tornado, twisting and writhing like a living thing. I tried to scramble back, but my skin was burning too badly. I was paralyzed with pain, unable to move or escape the inferno. The glass tornado howled and screeched, the sound piercing my eardrums. I felt myself being lifted off the ground, sucked into the heart of the storm. The world around me dissolved into a chaotic whirl of heat and glass and sand. I was consumed by agony, my body feeling like it was being flayed alive and melted at the same time. I tried to scream, but the cacophony of the tornado drowned out all sound.

The glass shards cut into my skin, tearing me apart from the inside out. I felt my bones melting, my muscles liquefying. I was being erased, bit by bit.

And then, like a beacon in the darkness, light burst forth. It was blindingly bright, a radiance that cut through the tornado like a knife. I saw Vrys, his form glowing with an ethereal intensity, his hand reaching out towards me like a lifeline. Xaneth and Vrys were both reaching for me on opposite ends.

"Ronan!" they shouted in unison.

Vrys' hand closed around my ankle, his grip like a vice. In an instant, the world went white. The pain, the fear, the desperate scrabble for survival—all of it was ripped away, replaced by a void of perfect silence and stillness. I was adrift in a sea of light, my sense of self unraveling thread by thread.

I'm dead, I thought, the realization washing over me like a wave. Gods, I'm dead. And in that moment, all I could think of was Atreya, her face etched into my mind.

CHAPTER 61

Atreya

H isen couldn't tell us anything more. I paced back and forth, my mind racing with memories I'd rather forget. Krix gnawed on a bone on the floor, curled up in a protective ball. Vrys had always wanted a pet... I had feared Ramses would traumatize him the way he had me. Maybe feed his pet to him the way he had fed Snow to me.

Regret burned a bitter path up my throat. I should have done so many things differently.

Eldra said that the best course of action was none. None of the dragons were currently in the pit. I couldn't fly off the way Ronan had.

The coward.

Scorch marks marred my once pristine bedroom. Every time I saw them, I could smell the acrid tang of smoke, hear the roar of flames. I would think back to Siorsen and how he had overtaken Tor.

How the only full-grown Dragons in the pits were Thrane, Emreth, and Seraphix—and Emreth refuses to fight.

Eldra was right. We were no match for Ramses. Not with his magic. Not with his dragons or army.

The ground shook violently, and my head snapped back. A massive explosion rocked the castle. I spun around, my pulse pounding in my ears. "Eldra!" I screamed back, dashing out of the room. Krix yelped, scurrying after me.

The castle was in chaos. Servants ran wildly, some shrieking, others pale and silent. I nearly collided with a guard, his sword drawn, his eyes wide with fear.

"Where's Eldra?" I demanded, grabbing his arm.

He pointed down the hall, his hand shaking. "T-the throne room, Princess."

I ignored the Princess part. Seems like everyone knew who I was now.

I sprinted down the hall, my heart heavy with dread. What had happened?

I burst through the doors to the throne room. Ameria was on her knees, her hands covering her mouth. Ronan lay on the floor, his body twisted at an unnatural angle.

But then my heart came to a shuddering stop.

In the doorway stood my flawless boy, Vryseris, his face a gruesome mixture of blood and dirt, laced with cuts and bruises. His bloodshot eyes gleamed with unshed tears, and his swollen lips were parted in a pained whisper. Gripping a knife no bigger than my palm, the sunlight danced along the obsidian blade—he was like a radiant star. I had never seen him wield such magic before, only his tendrils of shadowlight.

His hair had turned white.

Ronan lay at his feet, suffering and whimpering as his skin charred and turned to ash under Vryseris' unbearable light.

"Vrys! Vrys!" I attempted to rush to him but found myself yanked back by my hair in a strong grip.

"He's about to erupt," Eldra hissed. Ameria scrambled away from Vryseris, her hands covering her mouth.

Then, Eldra pushed me behind him, his arm crossed over my chest for protection. "Boy," he said firmly. Vryseris' eyes locked on Eldra, his nostrils flaring in agitation. The sight sent alarm bells ringing in my head; he resembled Ramses right then. I couldn't help but realize that whatever events had transpired had been enough to break him.

"How did you get here?" Eldra asked. I shook off my fear, positioning myself in front of Eldra and extending my hand.

"Sweetheart... Ronan is injured. He needs us," I expressed, trying to keep my heart steady.

Vryseris gazed down at Ronan's disintegrating skin as it turned into ash before our eyes. In a deep gravelly voice, he confessed: "He tried helping me. He tried to stop me. He said he would kill him for me so I didn't have to."

Confusion washed over me—Ronan tried to kill Ramses? Then I asked, "How did you get here?"

"I-It came to me in dreams. I never knew it was real. In the final moment... the place where I'd feel safe emerged in my mind and we ended up here. I never intended to hurt him, I swear!" As tears streamed down his face, he snarled in frustration, swiping them away with his claws and inadvertently slashing his own cheek.

"Vryseris, please, I want to help you," I pleaded.

"Father always told me I needed to be a man, that I had to be strong. He said a man makes tough choices and sees them through. But was I really strong enough for this?"

"What did he ask you to do?" I whispered.

Vryseris's body tensed up, his grip on the knife grew firmer, and his eyes narrowed. He lifted the knife to his face. "I got my prize."

The knife—Chansie's very own.

"Vrys... What have you done?" I asked hesitantly. He shook his head, and his gaze was icy cold.

"Father put me in the arena. I thought I'd show him I wouldn't fight. I was ready—eager even. I wanted so much to prove myself. I thought it would be easy to stand up to him. You had done it so many times before..." He hiccuped on a cry and bit his bottom lip. "I cried so much. Father wasn't pleased. He said men don't cry and that I should take pride in doing what had to be done. But I didn't want to; he forced me. Said that I had to choose between a title, or my best friend. My *brother*. Do you think Chansie was proud of me? Can he ever forgive me for stabbing him in the heart? There were so many. So many heads of red. I was meant to kill them all. Veren screamed while I killed Chansie. He screamed so loud." A chilling mechanical laugh escaped his lips. "Father always said that my compassion was a weakness. That I got it from you. That it's a plague."

The knife fell to the ground as he grew silent, his eyes fixed on the ground. I wanted to say something to console him, to reach for him and pull him away from the dark memories that haunted him, that Ramses had put there.

"Men don't cry. Men don't cry," he kept repeating as he stared into the distance, his harsh breathing filling the air. The light from him grew and took over the room, blinding us.

"This boy is about to break," Eldra warned, and it dawned on me that the light was also a weapon. It was a weapon of death to Ronan—and to anyone within a blast radius.

With teary eyes, Ronan looked my way and took a shaky breath. "Atreya." He closed his eyes, bracing himself for whatever came next.

"Grab Ronan!" I screamed at Eldra, dashing toward Vryseris. His eyes had turned a ghostly white while his mouth gaped in a scream. The room quaked under the sheer power of his roar, causing the walls around us to fracture and the floor to tremble beneath our feet. The light's intensity swelled relentlessly.

"Eldra! Ronan!" I begged desperately, but Eldra had already vanished, with no trace of Ronan in sight.

It was just Vryseris and me.

"Vryseris, please! Find your calm. I'm here now, with you!" The room quaked so ferociously that I lost my footing. I tumbled to the floor, landing on my hands and knees.

"What about before?" he bellowed at me. "Where were you when Father sent me into that arena? Where were you when I desperately needed you?"

A wave of agony washed over me, followed by crushing remorse. I had let him down. For all these years, I had endured Ramses' torment and degradation so Vryseris wouldn't have to bear it – but now, it was all coming back to haunt me with a vengeance.

I had fallen prey to the false sense of security woven around me for so many years, foolishly believing that Ramses would never expose our own son to such horrors.

Yet he did just that, forcing our child to slaughter his own sibling in cold blood—a mere pawn used to illustrate his twisted point—favoring one illegitimate son above the rest of his brood.

No one was secure, and Ramses would consistently overpower me. He always did. He saw the vulnerability of my heart as I allowed the servants to escape, and ruthlessly manipulated it. He sent me out to shatter those unsuspecting families, to devastate their lives. Ramses knew I couldn't leave Vryseris; that I'd submit to his merciless commands—yet even that wasn't enough.

A sob caught in my throat. "Vrys, my love. I'm so terribly sorry. I should've taken you far away from his evil grasp. I should've done more than merely shield you from my torments. I should've safeguarded you from all this horror. I know the monster he is, but I wasn't strong enough to stand up to him. Please...please..." Overwhelmed, I collapsed back onto my knees, arms outstretched towards him, begging for forgiveness.

"Men don't cry! Men don't cry! I'm a man! I'm a man!" he yelled, frantically attempting to hide his face with his hands. His body trembled violently as darkness swirled around him, drowning out the blinding brilliance surrounding him.

"May Kamani fill your life with peace and joy. May the memory of your beloved brother never fade. May Inamak strengthen your heart, enabling it to withstand the cruel nature of this world. May Naris guide you on the path to forgiveness. May Elenaria leave a space in your heart for all the splendor that surrounds us..." I fervently prayed. "May Shaza bestow upon you wisdom and a deep insight into the world's intricacies. May Matriak provide the fortitude needed to confront the inevitable challenges that are to come your way. May Desrat shield you as you seek retribution."

There remained one Goddess—one whom I had become acquainted with but never dared to pray to. The Goddess of Darkness, the Underworld, and the Night, the overseer of grim creatures like Ronan: she who ruled over death itself.

In my mind's eye, I could see Priestess Andes arrayed in her sacred robes, her auburn hair cascading down her back, her eyes wide with astonishment and worry as she warned me: "Lady Atreya, this is a path you must not tread."

She wasn't someone I would typically turn to for my son's sake—but for Ronan, I had no choice. I couldn't see him or know if he was still among the living. If he were gone, then his soul was at the mercy of Nexus. The thought of it was too much to bear. I realized silently that Ronan would never be so foolish as to believe he could kill Ramses by himself.

"He tried helping me. He tried to stop me. He said he would kill him for me so I didn't have to." Vryseris had said it. Ronan was going to kill *Chansie*

for him, so that way he wouldn't be forced to do it himself. Ronan had been willing to sacrifice himself so that he could spare my son from being tormented by a choice.

My heart clenched. I needed Ronan to be alive. I needed him to stay with me. I needed him to be with me.

So I prayed silently to Nexus, begging for her to intercede on my behalf. I prayed to her to not let Ronan die. I prayed that I would get the chance to see him again. And though I didn't say my prayers out loud, I hoped she would hear me.

"Men do not cry!" Vryseris furiously yelled at me, his body quivering uncontrollably. The floor trembled beneath us as cracks spider-webbed across walls and shattered them. Paintings plummeted from their perches and the ceiling collapsed in on itself, raining debris down upon us. Vryseris clenched his fists, the air around him shimmering with intense heat. The ground continued to splinter and smolder beneath his feet as he struggled to regain control. His powers were like a wildfire, unpredictable and fierce—a force that threatened to consume everything in its path.

"Vryseris," I whispered softly, "the best of men shed tears. And you—you are just a boy." I inched forward, circling my arms around his shaking body. It burned like fire to hold him, my eyes closed in pain.

But just as soon as I said those words, the wailing erupted from him and he sagged against me, his hands gripping my shoulders. His tear-streaked face buried itself into my chest as he wept uncontrollably. I held him tighter, caressing his hair and whispering soothing words into his ear while his light slowly ebbed away. I buried my nose into his hair, inhaling his scent, where Chansie's blood and sweat still lingered. The pounding of my heart echoed in my ears, and I rubbed my face fervently against his to rid him of that smell. He felt so small in my arms.

"I'm sorry," Vryseris choked out between sobs, muffled against the fabric of my dress. "I'm so sorry, I didn't mean for any of this to happen."

"I know," I whispered back, holding back my tears. "I know you didn't."

We stayed like that for what felt like hours, his body wracked with sobs, my heart aching with an overwhelming surge of emotions. I felt his pain, his fear, his guilt, and they were as much mine as they were his.

His tears eventually subsided, replaced with the soft rhythm of his breath. I could feel his heartbeat against mine, erratic and fast.

"Vryseris," I said softly, pulling back slightly to look at him. His eyes were red-rimmed and swollen. "We'll get through this," I told him, "You're not alone."

With a final sniffle, Vryseris relaxed into my embrace, his body heavy with exhaustion. I held him closer, gently swaying from side to side in a soothing motion. His breathing slowly evened out, deepening into the steady rhythm of sleep. I sat there on the ruined floor, surrounded by the destruction his loss of control had wrought, and held my son as he finally found some measure of peace.

As I sat there, I couldn't help but think of all the times I had failed him. The weight of my guilt was crushing, threatening to consume me whole. I had let Ramses turn our son into a weapon, all in the name of preserving a fragile sense of peace.

But that peace had been an illusion, a thin veneer masking the rot of Ramses' cruelty. And now, that cruelty had blossomed into something monstrous, forcing Vryseris to confront horrors no child should ever have to endure.

I held him closer, burying my face in his hair as a sob finally tore free of my throat. I wept for my failures, for the pain I had allowed him to suffer. I wept for the boy he used to be, the boy he might have been if only I had been stronger.

A hand rested on my shoulder. I raised my head, looking up to see Eldra, his mouth set in a firm line.

"He didn't mean to," I whispered.

"Has he done that before?"

I shook my head. "I've never seen him harness light like this. It was always shadows."

"I can take him and put him to bed."

I hesitated letting Vrys go as Eldra knelt to scoop him in his arms. "He didn't mean to," I repeated.

Eldra looked at me softly, sighing heavily. "I know... he will be alright. He's home now."

I inhaled sharply at that. *Home.* Eldra had said the word. Had invited us to stay without ever asking. Opened up his arms and welcomed us in, despite all the grief I had given him. Despite everything. I closed my eyes.

Could this really be home?

CHAPTER 62

Atreya

I remained steadfast by Vrys' side, watching like a hawk as the healers worked tirelessly to stabilize him. Every so often, a jagged crack would splinter across his skin, and brilliant light would spill out, forcing me to shield my eyes against its blinding intensity.

Eldra said it was his magic. That it was volatile. That Vrys was a *Star-bringer*.

I reached out, gently brushing a strand of Vrys' snowy hair out of his face.

Ronan had brought my son back to me, having bridged the chasm that once separated us. If there was ever a time to truly forgive him and let go of past resentments, it was now.

"Ronan is still asleep," Eldra said as if he had reached into my very thoughts.

"He is okay?" I asked, swallowing. I had been too afraid to ask before. Seeing the way his skin had been damaged, how his face had begun to peel away from bone.

"He is healing," Eldra reassured me. "I have given him the Daylight Ring. Its power will mend his wounds."

My head snapped to him. "You what?"

He shrugged. "He did do his part in bringing you home. Both of you."

Ronan could walk in the sunlight now. I smiled.

"The boy's hair is white," Eldra said carefully.

I nodded, running my fingers through it. "I supposed there is no denying that. It was black, like mine."

"When he passed the threshold of the castle, whatever illusions you had on him would be stripped away," he explained.

I swallowed.

"The question is... why? Why was he illusioned to begin with?"

I could finally say it out loud, without any repercussions, without worry. The truth.

"Because he is not Ramses' son," I confessed, the words tumbling out of me in a rush. I kissed my son's forehead, my tears falling onto his skin. "I was in love with Ramses' half-brother, Servat. He is Vrys' father."

Eldra inhaled sharply.

"Joslynn had changed his hair when he was born, to match mine. Ramses is not his father, but his uncle."

I could visibly see his shoulders sag, as if a weight had been lifted from him momentarily.

I know what he was thinking. He was relieved he wasn't the grandfather to Ramses' child.

"I didn't know that," he said quietly.

"How could you? No one knew, No one accept Joslynn, me, and Servat. And two of them are dead. Ronan figured it out, though. Rather quickly," I chuckled

He winced at that.

"Seraphix is back in the dragon pit. Perhaps you could bring Vrys down to meet him properly when he's awake."

I nodded, smiling through my tears. "I would like that."

He gave me a soft smile before turning to leave.

"Wait," I called out, halting him.

He turned back.

"Thank you," I said, "For saving Ronan."

Eldra looked at me, his expression unreadable. But he gave me a single nod before disappearing through the doorway. The soft click of the door closing behind him echoed in the silence.

My gaze drifted over to Ronan, who was still fast asleep. I could see the faint glow of the Daylight Ring peeking out from beneath the covers. Eldra had said it would heal him, and I trusted in its power. Still, I couldn't help but feel a pang of worry as I took in the sight of his pale skin. His face was relaxed in sleep, the lines of pain and exhaustion smoothed away.

I reached out a trembling hand, hesitating for a moment before gently brushing a strand of silver hair back from his forehead. His skin was cool to the touch, but not alarmingly so. I took a deep breath, trying to calm the racing of my heart. He was going to be okay. The Ring was working, even if the progress was slower than I had hoped for.

"I don't know if you can hear me. I don't know if you can listen—and I promise to tell you all of this again when you are awake..."

I leaned in closer to him. "Thank you for saving my son. Thank you for saving me countless of times, even when I wasn't aware of it. Thank you for seeing me in my worst moments and still choosing to stay. For allowing me to discover things about myself without judgment. For healing me in ways I didn't know I needed to be healed."

"I love you. I love you with every fiber of my being. I will be yours, and you, mine, for all the life that is left to me. I would choose you in every life."

I swiped at a tear that had fallen from my eye. The words stumbled out of me in a rush. I felt like I was drowning in emotion. I couldn't bear the thought of losing him, of having to spend the rest of my life without him.

With trembling fingers, I reached out and took a strand of my dark hair, then carefully lifted a piece of his silvery locks. My hands moved with practiced precision despite my shaking, weaving the strands together in a delicate braid—black and silver intertwining like night and starlight. The knife I kept in my boot was nothing special, just plain steel with a wooden handle I had stolen from the kitchens, but it served its purpose. The blade made a soft whisper as I carefully severed the braided strands close to our scalps. I wonder if he would notice right away. Did Vampire hair even grow back?

The small token felt precious in my palm, a physical manifestation of our connection. A piece of us, bound together.

Forever.

I had never felt this way before, this depth of love and fear and desperation all tangled together. It was overwhelming, but it was also the most real thing I had ever experienced.

CHAPTER 63

Atreya

A soft groan ripped through the silence, and my heart damn near stopped. Vrys stirred on the bed, those dark lashes fluttering against his too-pale cheeks like broken butterfly wings. His eyes cracked open—unfocused at first, like he was swimming up from the depths of some dark ocean—before they finally locked onto my face.

"Mother?" The word scraped out of his throat, rough as gravel, barely more than a whisper.

"Right here, baby." I squeezed his hand so hard it probably hurt, forcing my lips into what I hoped passed for a smile while my eyes burned with unshed tears. "How were you holding up?"

He tried to push himself up and immediately winced, pain flashing across his face like lightning. My hands shook as I helped him with the pillows, and that's when the morning light streaming through the windows caught his hair—fucking hell, his *hair*. It was white as fresh snow now, gleaming like scattered starlight, and my stomach twisted into knots because I knew what was coming.

His fingers found a strand, confusion darkening those golden eyes. "My hair... something's wrong with it."

The truth I'd carried for so long sat in my chest like a lead weight, pressing against my ribs until I could barely breathe. Time was up. No more running from this shit.

"Vrys." I perched on the edge of his bed, still gripping his hand like it was the only thing keeping me anchored to this world. "There's something I should've told you a long time ago."

Those eyes of his—so trusting, so goddamn innocent—stared up at me, and my throat closed up like I was being strangled.

"The magic in the castle... it stripped away an illusion that was placed on you when you were born." I squeezed his hand tighter. "Your hair was always meant to be white, like your father's."

Vrys went very still. "But Father's hair is red... mine has always been black, like yours."

"Ramses..." I swallowed hard. "Ramses isn't your father. Your true father was his half-brother, Servat."

The silence that followed felt endless. I watched as understanding dawned in his eyes, followed by confusion, hurt, and something else – relief?

Tears welled in his eyes, sliding silently down his cheeks. "Is that why..." he paused, his voice breaking. "Is that why I never felt like I belonged? Why I was so different?"

I gathered him into my arms, my own tears falling freely now. "You belong exactly where you are, my beautiful boy. You are loved. So deeply loved. I'm so sorry I kept this from you for so long. I was trying to protect you, but perhaps I only caused you more pain."

He cried quietly against my shoulder, his tears soaking into my dress. But his arms wrapped around me tightly, holding on as if I might disappear.

"Did he... did my real father love me? Did he know that I was his?" The question was so soft I almost missed it.

"Oh, Vrys." I pulled back just enough to cup his face in my hands. "Servat loved you more than life itself. He died protecting us, making sure we would be safe. He died in the arena to get us out." I needed to believe that. That Servat knew what he was doing and had his reasons for what he did.

Something in his expression shifted, a weight lifting that I hadn't even realized he'd been carrying. "That's why my magic is different, isn't it? Why I can do things the others can't?"

I nodded, brushing away his tears with my thumbs. "You're a Star-bringer. Not because of Servat..."

I paused, my hands trembling against Vrys' cheeks. There was more—so much more he needed to know. The weight of another secret pressed against my heart, demanding to be freed.

"Not because of Servat," I continued, "but because of *my* father. Your grandfather." The words felt strange on my tongue, forbidden after so many years of silence.

Vrys' eyes widened, his grip on my arms tightening. "Your father? But I thought—"

"King Eldra Solaris." The name rang through the room like a bell, clear and undeniable. "The Rebel King himself."

My son went completely still, his breath catching in his throat. The morning light seemed to intensify around him, as if his very blood had recognized the truth I'd spoken.

"That's... that's not possible," he whispered, but I could see in his eyes that he was already connecting the pieces—

The silence between us hummed with the weight of generations, of power and sacrifice, of loves lost and found. My son—my beautiful, powerful son—carried the blood of kings and warriors, of stars and shadows.

"How long have you known this?"

"I only just found out recently."

"But Eldra Solaris is a traitor King. A False King. He can't be your father," he whispered.

I grasped his hand tightly in mine. "Forget everything you think you know about Eldra Solaris. Forget everything you were taught and read about the War of Fallen Skies. Forget the stories your father told you of the Kings. Forget everything. Because it was all lies."

"But he was never actually my father was he... I am a bastard born."

"Do not call yourself that—"

"It's true," he said bitterly. "I thought I would inherit a kingdom, but instead I'm the son of a bastard and a traitor."

He was quiet for a long moment, processing everything. Then, unexpectedly, he gave me a small, watery smile. "I always felt... wrong, trying to be like fath—Ramses. Like I was failing at being his son. Now I know why."

My heart broke and mended all at once. "You could never fail me, Vrys. You are exactly who you were meant to be."

He leaned into my embrace again, his breathing steadying. "Thank you for telling me the truth, Mother."

I flinched, unable to meet his eyes.

Vrys groaned. "Nooo, there's more?"

My fingers twisted in the fabric of my dress. The final truth burned in my throat. After holding so many secrets for so long, it felt like standing at the edge of a cliff, knowing I had to jump.

"Your grandmother..." I forced myself to look at him. "My mother was Aislinn Furian. The Rebel Queen."

Vrys leaped from the bed as if it had burned him, his white hair wild around his face. His eyes were huge, mouth opening and closing like a startled fish. "WHAT?!"

"The woman I killed in the arena. Your grandmother."

Vrys stumbled backward until he hit the wall, sliding down to sit on the floor. His chest heaved with rapid breaths, and I could see his magic flickering around him like starlight, responding to his distress.

"You... killed her." His voice cracked. "The Furian Slayer. That's what they called you. I remember the stories, but I never..." He pressed his hands to his temples. "This is too much. This is—"

"I know," I whispered, staying where I was, giving him space. "When Ramses forced me into that arena, I thought I was fighting a beast. She had been transformed, trapped in the form of a lioness. I didn't know it was her until after, when the magic faded and I saw her true form."

The morning light caught in Vrys' white hair, so like Servat's, and I saw him trembling. "Did you know? When you killed her, did you know what she meant to you?"

"No." I wrapped my arms around myself, feeling the phantom pain of that day. "I didn't learn about my true parentage until coming here. Ramses kept so many secrets from me, used me as his weapon without my knowledge at times. The day I killed Aislinn Furian was the day he claimed me as his future queen."

I didn't know then. I couldn't have known.

"And my father—Servat—he knew?" Vrys asked, sounding small.

"I'm not sure how much he knew," I admitted bitterly.

"So I'm not just any bastard. I'm the grandson of the Rebel King and the Rebel Queen, born to their daughter and a royal guard." He laughed, but it was hollow. "I'm a *royal* bastard."

I moved then, crossing the room to kneel beside my son. "You are so much more than your bloodline, Vrys. You are—"

A crack of magic exploded in the room as Vrys stood, his white hair blazing with power.

"I don't know what I am," he interrupted, meeting my eyes. "But I am tired of everyone telling me what I am, or who I am supposed to be."

A sharp knock interrupted us. Before we could respond, the door swung open, revealing Eldra.

His presence filled the doorway like a storm cloud, dark and charged with potential energy. Our eyes met – the same storm-gray-blue – and in that moment, three generations of secrets and power hung in the balance, waiting to either destroy us or set us free.

Vrys scrambled to his feet, pressing himself against the wall. His magic crackled visibly now, little sparks of starlight dancing around his fingers. I rose slowly, positioning myself between them.

"Father," I said, the word still foreign on my tongue.

Eldra's eyes, the same storm-gray-blue as mine, moved from me to Vrys, softening as they took in his grandson's changed appearance. "I felt the surge of power," he said quietly. "I should have known you'd tell him everything."

The silence stretched between us like a drawn bow. Vrys's magic continued to spark and flutter, casting strange shadows on the walls. His eyes darted between Eldra and me, as if trying to find traces of himself in our features.

"So you're him." He trembled. "The man they called the False King. The Mad King. The King Beyond the Wall."

Eldra's face remained impassive, but I saw the slight tightening around his eyes. "Is that what they taught you, boy?"

Vrys nodded.

"Then perhaps it's time for the whole truth." Eldra moved into the room with the fluid grace of a predator, his dark robes whispering against the stone floor. "Look at me, grandson. Look closely. Do you see madness in these eyes?"

Vrys straightened, his chin lifting in a gesture so familiar it made my heart ache. Despite his fear, he met Eldra's gaze steadily. "I see someone who started a war that tore the kingdom apart."

A bitter laugh escaped Eldra's throat. "Is that what the history books say? That I started the war?" He shook his head, silver streaks in his dark hair catching the light—not from age, but power. "The war began long before I drew my sword, child. It began with whispers in dark corners, with children disappearing from their beds, with magic being twisted into something it was never meant to be."

"What do you mean?" Vrys asked, his magic calming slightly as curiosity overtook fear.

Eldra's eyes met mine. "Your mother knows. She's seen it firsthand, hasn't she? The way Ramses uses magic like a weapon, bending it to his will without regard for its true nature." He turned back to Vrys. "The Starbringers were never meant to be warriors or kings. We were guardians of the balance, keepers of the old ways. But I, like my father before me, fell into a crown that was too big for us to wear. We are all casualties of someone else's war, son."

"But you killed people," Vrys pressed, though with less certainty now. "You burned cities."

"Did I?" Eldra's lips curved in a sad smile. "Or did Ramses's armies burn them in my name? History is written by the victors, grandson. And Ramses... he has always been skilled at crafting narratives that suit his purposes."

"But the Starbringers..." Vrys trailed off as he stared at his own hands, still sparking with residual magic. "If we weren't meant to be warriors, then what were we supposed to be?"

Eldra moved closer, his movements careful, as if approaching a spooked horse. "We were healers once," he said softly. "Bridges between the stars and the earth. The magic you feel coursing through your veins? It's not meant for destruction. It's meant for creation, for restoration." He gestured to the window, where the morning light still streamed in. "The stars don't wage war, child. They simply are. Ramses forced my hand to fight. We lived in peace when there were four kingdoms. When we shared the land. When we, the leaders, gave magic back to the world."

Vrys took a hesitant step forward, his white hair catching the sunlight. "But if we were meant to be healers, why do I feel so much... power? It doesn't feel gentle. It feels like it could tear the sky apart."

Eldra's eyes flickered to mine and I shook my head slightly. I couldn't bring myself to tell Vrys that I was born of whatever dark magic that brought my mother back from the dead while I was still in her womb.

"Power and gentleness are not opposites," Eldra said, taking on a teacher's patient tone. "The same force that can tear mountains apart also makes flowers bloom in spring." He held out his hand, palm up, and a small sphere of light materialized above it, pulsing like a heartbeat.

"Watch," he whispered.

The light expanded, filling the room with a soft, silvery glow. Tiny motes of starlight danced through the air, and where they touched the stone walls, delicate crystals began to form, spreading like frost across the surface. The air hummed with energy, but it wasn't the violent crackle of battle magic—it was more like a lullaby, sung in a language too ancient for words.

Vrys gasped as one of the light motes brushed his cheek. I saw his eyes widen as the contact sent a visible shiver through him, his own magic responding like a musical instrument finding its harmony.

"That's... that's what it's supposed to feel like?" he breathed.

"Yes." Eldra's eyes were kind now, the hardened warrior melting away to reveal something older, something wiser. "The magic in your blood isn't meant to destroy—it's meant to understand. To connect. To heal."

"But I've never..." Vrys swallowed hard, looking down at his hands. "Everything I was taught was about control. About containing it."

"Because that's what Ramses fears most," I said softly, watching the interplay of light between my father and my son. "Magic that can't be controlled. Magic that flows freely, that connects people instead of dividing them."

Eldra nodded, closing his hand and letting the lightshow fade. "The old stories say that before there were kingdoms, before there were wars, the Starbringers were bridges—not just between stars and earth, but between all peoples. We helped maintain the balance of Fae and human." His expression darkened. "But balance doesn't build empires."

Vrys took another step forward, almost unconsciously. "Is that why the war really started? Because someone wanted to control the magic?"

"It is how all wars start. There was a great war centuries before The War of Fallen Skies. It is why there were four kingdoms. Someone wanted to control everything," Eldra corrected gently. "The magic, the people, the very land itself. And when they couldn't control the Starbringers..."

"They tried to destroy them," I finished.

"And why those who survived learned to hide what they truly were. My Blood is extremely diluted... I've never seen such power in someone so young," Eldra added, his gaze heavy with memory. "Your grandmother—" he paused, glancing at me apologetically, "—Aislinn, she held an old power as well... she was one of the *last* shifters left."

Vrys shook his head. "I did. In the arena," he said slowly, his fingers curling into fists. "I... changed. Just for a moment. I had fur, black as night." He looked up at Eldra, desperate hope in his eyes. "Was that—did I—?"

"The gift wasn't lost," Eldra whispered, wonder spreading across his weathered features. "After all this time, the bloodline still carries it. In *you*."

"But shifting is *forbidden* magic," Vrys whispered, taking a step back. "The laws—"

"Were written by those who feared what they couldn't control. Ramses did that." Eldra finished. His storm-gray eyes flickered with an ancient anger. "Just as they feared the Starbringers, they feared the shifters. Both were too powerful to be contained by their laws and borders."

"What about my shadow magics? Where did that come from?" Vrys asked.

"I wish I knew. Perhaps your true father's mother's side had that magic. I wish I could tell you." Eldra turned to me. "Do you know of Servat's mother?"

"She was a lowborn who worked as a—" I cleared my throat pointedly.

"A whore," Vrys deadpanned.

"Vryseris!" I gasped.

He shrugged his shoulders. "I've seen plenty of them." I felt myself blush as he added, "A lot of them."

"And you spent time with them because...?" I asked carefully, dreading his answer.

"Father brought them to my tent when I went beyond the wall with him."

I closed my eyes briefly, another wave of anger at Ramses washing over me. Of course he would expose my son to such things, trying to corrupt him early.

"That's enough of that topic," Eldra cut in smoothly. "What matters now is understanding who you are, Vrys, and what you can become."

Vrys's shoulders slumped slightly. "And what exactly am I supposed to become? A healer? A shifter? A shadow wielder? I have no titles. I have no dragon. I have nothing now. I killed my best friend. I killed my *brother*. Because I was trying to be someone you could be proud of and be someone that my father—my *uncle*—Gods!" He threw his hands up in the air in frustration.

"Stop." Eldra cut through Vrys's spiral, firm but not unkind. He crossed the space between them in three long strides, grasping Vrys's shoulders. "Look at me, boy."

Vrys tried to pull away, but Eldra held firm. "Everything you've done, everything you've been through—it wasn't for nothing. The pain you carry, the guilt that eats at you... I know it well. Too well," he said roughly. "But you're wrong about having nothing."

"He's right," I said softly, moving to stand beside them. "You have something far more valuable than titles or dragons."

Vrys let out a bitter laugh. "What? The blood of traitors and rebels?"

"Freedom," Eldra and I said in unison.

The word hung in the air between us, heavy with promise. Vrys stilled, his magic settling like dust after a storm.

"Freedom from Ramses's lies," Eldra continued. "Freedom from trying to be something you're not. The truth may feel like a burden now, but it's also a gift." He released Vrys's shoulders, taking a step back. "You're no longer bound by false expectations or manufactured destiny."

"But Chansie... He died because I was trying to prove myself worthy of a legacy that was never mine."

I reached for his hand, and this time he didn't pull away. "He died because of Ramses's machinations, not because of you. He's been playing all of us like pieces on a board, even his own son."

"And now?" Vrys asked, looking between us. "What am I supposed to do with all of... this?" He gestured vaguely at himself, at the magic still shimming faintly around him.

Eldra's eyes softened, and for a moment, I saw the father he might have been if circumstances had been different. "Now, grandson, you learn who you truly are. Not what others want you to be, but who you choose to become."

"And if I choose wrong?"

"Have faith in yourself," Eldra said quietly.

Vrys closed his eyes, taking a deep breath. When he opened them again, something had shifted in their depths. The lost boy was still there, but something else too—something stronger, more determined.

"Then teach me," he said to Eldra. "Show me what this magic is really meant for. Show me how to be more than just another weapon in someone else's war."

A smile spread across Eldra's face, transforming his stern features. "First lesson, then: hold out your hands."

Vrys complied, and Eldra placed his larger palms beneath them. "Now, forget everything you know about controlling magic. Instead, feel it. Let it flow through you like starlight through glass."

I watched in wonder as tiny points of light began to dance between their hands, weaving patterns that seemed to whisper of ancient secrets and forgotten songs. And in that moment, I saw what we could become—not rulers or warriors, but bridges between what was and what could be.

The magic built between them, grandfather and grandson, past and future, until the room was filled with a soft, silvery glow that felt like hope.

Hope.

CHAPTER 64

Ronan

Her scent hit me first—sweet and familiar, wrapping around my senses like a forgotten melody.

"Atreya?"

I clawed my way to consciousness, bracing for the kind of pain that makes you wish for oblivion. But there was nothing. Not even a whisper of the agony I'd expected. What greeted me instead was worse—sunlight, streaming through the window like nature's personal vendetta against my vampiric existence.

I hissed, recoiling, but... wait. No burning. No smell of scorched flesh.

The glint of metal caught my eye—the Daylight ring, wrapped around my finger like it had never left. But that was impossible. I'd thrown the cursed thing away, watched it disappear into darkness. Yet here it sat, mocking me with its presence.

"Welcome back to the land of the living." Eldra's voice grated across my nerves like broken glass.

I tried to sit up, fighting against what felt like every blanket in the kingdom. Gone was my cold, bare-bones cell. Instead, I was drowning in luxury—polished wood floors worth a king's ransom, grey stone walls that whispered of old money, and a window big enough to make any vampire's survival instincts scream in protest. No bed though—just this ridiculous nest of blankets that seemed determined to swallow me whole.

"Where—" My voice came out sounding like crushed gravel. I swallowed hard. "Where in heaven's name am I?"

Eldra ignored me, his joints cracking like ancient timber as he shifted in his chair. "You helped the boy."

Memory slammed back. Vryseris. The rescue. The fight. "Is he okay?"

A curt nod was my answer. My eyes drifted to the window again, drawn to the ocean beyond. The water sparkled like someone had scattered diamonds across its surface, all turquoise and gold. I hadn't seen anything this beautiful since...

"You could have died," Eldra growled, his face hard as granite.

I couldn't help the laugh that bubbled up. "Newsflash—I'm already dead."

He snorted, but there was something different in his eyes. "When we planned the charge to get the boy, you disappeared. I called you a coward." His jaw clenched. "I was wrong."

The admission hung in the air between us.

I glanced down at myself. Naked. Perfect. My armor was gone, along with everything else. "There was a pin in my pocket. From Corina Blackwater. She had a message for Atreya—tell her never to come back to Ember. No matter what she hears."

"Not going to be a problem," Eldra said, then fell quiet. "You brought Vryseris home. After everything I said about you being weak-minded, about leaving..." He looked like the words physically pained him. "You were right. Ramses played us all."

I had to admit, hearing him admit he was wrong would never get old.

"Is she..." My throat closed up. "Is she happy?"

The smile that twisted his lips was small but real. "Happy doesn't begin to cover it."

Relief flooded through me, and I sank back into my blanket prison. "Good." It came out barely more than a whisper. "That's all I ever wanted."

The silence stretched between us before he broke it. "I'm glad to hear that... because you being here has complicated everything."

I met his gaze, surprised by the conflict I saw there.

"I never thought..." He shook his head. "You two weren't supposed to fall for each other. This thing between you—it's going to break her."

Bitter laughter clawed its way up my throat. "After everything I've done to protect her, to love her, you still want me gone? That's rich."

"No." He scrubbed a hand over his face. "I don't want you gone. But like I said—this is complicated." Another sigh. "I never meant for any of this to happen."

My chest felt tight. "If she wants me to leave, I'm gone," I swore, the words burning like silver. "I won't be the one to break her."

His expression twisted into something that looked almost like pity. "Ronan. There's something you need to know."

CHAPTER 65

Ronan

My bones were ice. Fucking ice, and no amount of internal screaming was going to change that.

The hall loomed around me like a gilded cage, those damn stained-glass windows bleeding their colors all over the marble floor. Red. Gold. A circus of light that should've burned but didn't—not anymore. Not with this cursed ring of Daylight wrapped around my finger like a lover's promise gone wrong. My fingers kept finding it, kept reminding me just how far I'd fallen.

They were coming. Our "guests." The thought hit my gut like acid, and I wanted to rip my own heart out just to stop feeling this shit.

Ameria had played dress-up with me—black robes, silver thread that caught every fucking ray of light like it was mocking me. My hair? A waterfall of silver down one shoulder, woven with gold trinkets that whispered of a life I'd lost. A life I'd be crawling back to soon enough, tail between my legs.

Eldra broke the silence first. His footsteps echoed like fire shots, that crown of his flashing like a warning. He stopped dead when he saw me, and I watched pity flood his eyes before he could hide it behind that carefully crafted mask of indifference.

The pause stretched like a rubber band about to snap. Then the Court poured in, their laughter sharp as broken glass, their eyes gleaming with the kind of hunger that made my skin crawl. Had they known? Had they all known, watching me stumble around in the dark like some pathetic puppet?

Atreya floated in next, because of course she did. Beautiful. Deadly. Her dark hair braided tight, face painted in silver and gold like some ethereal creature I had no right to touch. That black dress dipped low, showing skin that used to be mine to kiss.

Vryseris was right there with her, their fingers tangled together like they'd never known anything else. Both wearing smiles that cut like knives. He ran those fingers through his white hair, and I wanted to break something.

I should've run. Should've disappeared into the shadows where I belonged. But I stayed rooted to the spot like an idiot, needing to see it all burn down with my own eyes.

They whispered. They laughed. Their eyes found me and their smiles grew sharper.

Vryseris approached first, hand out like we were old friends. "Thanks for saving me. Sorry about... you know." Those golden eyes—Ramses's eyes—stared back at me, and I wanted to laugh at the Gods' sick sense of humor. I shook his hand once, quick, like touching fire.

"Whatever," I managed, and then Atreya was there, wrapping around me like she still had the right.

"Eldra told me about the ring," she whispered against my skin.

I nodded, drinking her in like the poison she was. The sparkle in her eyes, those curved lips, the way she looked at me like I was her whole world. Her fingers traced my face, and I fell into her kiss like the desperate fool I was, trying to brand myself into her memory.

Vryseris made a gagging sound. Atreya pulled back laughing, and something in my chest cracked.

Her fingers laced with mine, holding on like she meant it. The world spun, and there was only her. Her lips formed those words—'I love you'—and they destroyed me completely.

I said nothing. Couldn't. The walls I needed were crumbling faster than I could rebuild them.

Then the doors opened one last time.

The gasp that tore through the room was a death knell. I watched her face change, watched her smile shatter like glass hitting stone. Her hand went slack in mine, then pulled away completely. Tears filled her eyes, and I knew. Gods, I knew.

"Servat," she breathed, and my world ended.

I turned, because what else could I do?

There he stood, this man who'd cheated death, looking at her like she hung the fucking stars. His smile was soft, his eyes burning with the kind of love I could never give her. The father of her child. Her sun. Her everything.

Because that's what she was—pure light, pure warmth. And me? I was nothing but shadows, ring or no ring. This was my destiny, my curse. Alone in the dark where I belonged, where I should've stayed.

His smile deepened. "Hello, love," he said, and those two words gutted me completely.

About the author

Genesis spends much of her time writing and with her family in Upstate New York. Her favorite things are books and pens. Cracked-spined books are a huge no for her.

More works by Genesis:

Night Lore

The Stars of Ember

Tales of Arcadea: Secrets Of Hellharth

Works under G.B Knight:

Gilded Cage- Spoken Word Poems

Save Me A Seat

Stay tuned for the next installment of the Night Lore Series:

Shadow's Dawn

Stay up-to-date with the latest news, behind-the-scenes insights, and exclusive content by following Genesis Batista on social media:

Instagram: Gigixbites

Facebook: Gigibytes

Twitter: Gigixbites

Bluesky: Gigixbytes

Tiktok: Gigixbytes

Subscribe to Gigiwrites.org

Scan QR Code to leave reviews!

Shadow's Dawn

In the next installment of the Night Lore Series...

Ronan

The air grew thick with an ancient magic that made my teeth ache. Through the dense trees ahead, something moved—not with the natural sway of branches in wind, but with purpose.

I froze.

"What is that?" Atreya whispered, her hand finding my sleeve.

I pulled her behind me, every instinct screaming danger. Through the mist, a structure emerged that defied all logic. A hut, if you could call it that, perched atop two massive chicken legs that flexed and shifted like living flesh. The legs alone stood taller than most village homes, ending in scaled feet with razor-sharp talons that dug deep furrows in the earth.

The hut loomed before us, a twisted mockery of shelter that screamed; come closer and die. Its weathered planks writhed like living things, defying nature as they curved and spiraled in ways that hurt my eyes to follow. The walls seemed to breathe—actually breathe—expanding and contracting with slow, deliberate movements.

Dark liquid oozed from the thatched roof, viscous drops falling with dull, wet sounds that echoed in the unnatural silence. Bones of creatures I couldn't—didn't want to—identify had been woven into the structure's flesh like grotesque ribbons, creating patterns that shifted when viewed too long. Wind chimes made of teeth—gods, actual teeth—clinked together in a breeze I couldn't feel, their hollow song raising gooseflesh along my arms.

But the windows...They peered into my soul. Sickly yellow light pulsed behind warped glass, like fever-bright eyes watching us. As we stood frozen, those eyes blinked—the hut wasn't just alive. It was aware. And it was hungry.

"A Grandmother Hut," I breathed, pushing Atreya further behind me. "One of the old ones. The kind that knows neither law nor boundary. The kind that devours flesh and spirit alike." The kind you don't fuck with.

The hut shifted on its massive legs, turning to face us fully. A door creaked open like a yawning mouth, revealing nothing but darkness within. The smell that wafted out was a nauseating mix of herbs, decay, and something sickeningly sweet—like summer blooms in a graveyard.

Death.

"We need to leave. Now." I started backing away slowly, keeping myself between Atreya and the hut. "These places belong to creatures older than time, witches who've forgotten how to be human—or fae—or whatever it is they started out as. They collect souls like trinkets and grind bones to bake their bread."

"Are you trying to scare me?"

"Do you want to find out?"

The hut takes a step that shakes the earth, and something inside laughs—the sound of old lungs drawing breath for the first time in decades.

"Run."

www.ingramcontent.com/pod-product-compliance
Lightning Source LLC
Chambersburg PA
CBHW070832260626
47170CB00007B/2346